# God's

Benedict Kiely is one of the most celebrated living writers of novels and short stories. His published collections of stories include *A Journey to the Seven Streams* and *A Letter to Peachtree*; his novels include *There was an Ancient House*, *Proxopera*, *The Cards of the Gambler* and *Nothing Happens in Carmincross*; his non-fiction works include *Counties of Contention*, *Poor Scholar: A Life of William Carleton* and *Modern Irish Fiction*. Benedict Kiely is also well known as a broadcaster. He lives in Dublin.

*Also by Benedict Kiely*
*and available from Minerva*

**Drink to the Bird**

# BENEDICT KIELY

## God's Own Country

Selected Stories 1963 – 1993

Minerva

**A Minerva Paperback**
GOD'S OWN COUNTRY

First published in Great Britain 1993
as a Minerva Original
by Mandarin Paperbacks
an imprint of Reed Consumer Books Ltd
Michelin House, 81 Fulham Road, London SW3 6RB
and Auckland, Melbourne, Singapore and Toronto

'The white wild bronco'; 'The heroes in the dark house';
'A view from the treetop'; 'The house in Jail Square';
'Homes on the mountain'; 'The dogs in the great glen';
'A journey to the seven streams' originally published
in *A Journey to the Seven Streams* (Methuen, 1963)

'A great God's angel standing'; 'The little wrens and robins';
'A room in Linden'; 'God's own country'; 'A ball of malt and
Madame Butterfly'; 'Down then by Derry' originally published in
*A Ball of Malt and Madame Butterfly* (Gollancz, 1973)

'There are meadows in Lanark'; 'Bluebell meadow'; 'The night
we rode with Sarsfield'; 'The fairy women of Lisbellaw'
originally published in *A Cow in the House* (Gollancz, 1978)

'Your left foot is crazy'; 'A walk in the wheat';
'The python'; 'A letter to Peachtree' originally published
in *A Letter to Peachtree* (Gollancz 1987)

This collection copyright © Benedict Kiely 1993
The author has asserted his moral rights

A CIP catalogue record for this title
is available from the British Library

ISBN 0 7493 9708 X

Printed and bound in Great Britain
by Cox and Wyman, Reading, Berks

*For* Stephen McKenna
*in Omagh Town*

# Contents

# Introduction

Henry James, to whom we all must sometimes listen, said that the art of fiction was in telling not what happened but what should have happened. My father who, as a member of an Order now extinct but then known as the Leinster Regiment, had found himself in many strange places and could tell strange stories of the places he had been and seen, put it more simply. He said: 'Never spoil a good story for the sake of the truth.'

Antoninus Pius (and my father in the course of all his wanderings never did encounter him) said: 'Whatever happens is as common and well known as a rose in the Spring or an apple in Autumn. Everywhere up and down, through ages and histories, towns and families are full of the same stories.'

I now find that looking back, or walking or stumbling back over more than fifty or so years of living and trying to tell stories, can be a disturbing experience. What happened? What should have happened? What was the good story? What exactly was the truth? Who were the real people? Did you transform or disfigure them? Would they speak in a friendly way to you if you ever encountered them again, in this world or the next? If, that is, there is a next?

For instance: there was in my home town a man who was so well read in the literature of what we used to call the Wild West, from Fenimore Cooper to Zane Grey and even W.C. Tuttle, that at times he half-imagined he had been there. He simply wished intensely that he had, and the wish fathered thoughts and dreams and words. It was harmless dreaming. He never fired a shot; and he entertained himself and many others with his stories. He belonged to an imaginative and literary family: his brother was a notable authority on, and performer of, traditional music.

So remembering him some years after he had gone to God, or Manitou, I wrote a story inspired, if that's the word, by that man. A schoolfriend who had actually seen the carter stun the white animal ('The White Wild Bronco') was embarrassed. By that time, although he was still my friend, that schoolfriend had become an eminent banker, and with the caution of his profession he could not approve of coming too close to the truth in a work of fiction. My idea was that the story-teller stumbled over an idea; somebody told you something and it stayed in your head, or you saw something and remembered it. After all, the man who thought, or pretended he thought, that he had been in the Wild West had only been telling short stories.

But a nephew of that imaginative man said something to me that made me feel a lot less guilty. He was a liberal and pleasant man that nephew, a famous boxer and amateur actor. He said: 'Who, anyway, would remember Uncle Jamie if you had not written that story?'

Then there is haunting me still that business about the heroes and/or the old man in the dark house. Back in the 1940s I wrote a book about the novelist William Carleton (1794–1869). I was back celebrating in my native town of Omagh, County Tyrone, when I got a message from a man called Robert Bratton in the neighbouring village of Seskinore, he would have been what was then in the north-east of Ireland called a Liberal Unionist: that is, a Unionist of the type that went back to before the Carsonite and High Tory agitation against Home Rule for Ireland destroyed Gladstone's great movement. Bratton had also known that Andrews, the man who built the Titanic and sank with it. He (Bratton) told me that he would be in Omagh if I were on holiday, and I met him in a restaurant, where he told me that he had also written a book about William Carleton. I took the typescript of his book away with me and tried hard to find a publisher for it, to no avail. Nobody at that time was much interested, and if it weren't for the help of two friends, Robert Farren, the poet, and Francis MacManus, novelist, my own book would never have seen the light of day, or whatever.

Then that fine man, Robert Bratton, told me a sad story.

He had been carrying another book, a collection of folk-tales that he had heard from old country-people, around with him for some time. Then someone told him (this was in the war years in the 1940s) that there was in Belfast City a Major McCutcheon, US Army Cultural Relations, who might be interested. So he brought the book up to the Major who looked at it and was delighted. But that night in Seskinore Robert Bratton was awakened by the thunder of trucks on the road and in the morning the US Army was gone. It was D-Day and the book of folk-tales was never published. So I tried to build a story around that. I changed the locale and placed it down south, near Campile in the County Wexford, a place I knew well and liked at that time. I put another man in the place of Robert Bratton. The ancient folk-heroes, breaking rocks and climbing mountains and all that, seemed to belong.

Then there was a tall, stern, puritanical, and most admirable clergyman to whom some lady had once, in Scotland, presented a copy of that poem in which William Morris speaks of a 'Great God's Angel Standing'. He, the clergyman, passed the poem on as a gift to me. I tried to write about him and myself, all together, but it would not work. Then in the town of New Ross, in Wexford, I met a rake of a fellow who was notorious for being a menace to all the maidens of the countryside. A little later in Dublin City I heard stories about a similar type of fine young man.

I rolled the two of them into one and made that one

man the friend of the tall priest; and that gave the story the springboard that I felt it needed.

The place of the original giving of the book I moved from Scotland to the Peaks of Otter and the Blue Ridge Mountains of Virginia, USA. I had recently been around that way and I felt it necessary to mention that wonderful land.

So, you see, that's how stories get made.

Then there was a man, a friend of mine, who when he was a young fellow used to climb up to the top of the great tree on the green of Duleek village in County Louth. He could spend half a day up there quite happily, viewing the world from his tree-top. On the green under that tree Father Theobald Mathew, the nineteenth-century Franciscan and advocate of temperance (keep the Irish sober), had preached and Johnny Patterson, the great circus-clown had performed. The river Boyne was down there below, and the place where William and James had disputed the Crown of England.

At the time when my friend was up that tree the village schoolmaster was a man by the name of Brennan. I had the honour of knowing him and walking with him along the battle field of the Boyne. Then away to the west in Aughrim, County Galway, there was another schoolmaster. His name was Joyce. He was a sound historian and even kept a schoolhouse museum containing relics of the fatal Williamite-Jacobite Battle of Aughrim. With him I walked the fatal field. And it was true that some of his pupils stole relics of the battle out of the school museum.

So for the sake of a story I rolled those two gentlemen, and those two battlefields, into one. May all the ghosts forgive me.

Where then does the stealing, or borrowing, from life end and where does invention begin? It differs from story to story, and from story-teller to story-teller. There are some elect spirits who live completely in their own imaginations and are quite proud of that. And, often rightly so.

Yet, re-reading my own stories, I find that faces peep out,

voices are heard. Are they, or are they not, frowning faces, accusing voices?

But you, my reader, need have no such worries. Perhaps the story-teller is, in the end, only searching to find himself or herself: a face and/or a spirit in the crowd. He, or she, may even be trying to laugh at himself, or herself, and frequently succeeding.

*Benedict Kiely*

# The white wild bronco

At the age of five, when asked what he wanted to be when he grew up, Isaac said he wanted to be a German. He was then blond and chubby and not at all pugnacious. Because he stuttered, he pronounced the word, German, with three, sometimes with six, initial consonants. He had heard it by his father's bedside where, propped most of the day on high pillows, the old fusilier remembered Givenchy and Messines Ridge in the hearing of his friends: Doherty the undertaker; Mickey Fish, who sold fish on Fridays from a flat dray and from door to door, and who stopped young women – even under the courthouse clock – to ask them the time of evening; Pat Moses Gavigan who fished pike and cut the world's best blackthorns; and the Cowboy Carson, the only man in our town who lived completely in the imagination. Occasionally the old fusilier read aloud out of one or other of the learned anthropological tomes dealing with the adventures of Tarzan the ape man, but mostly the talk was about Germans. Isaac, quiet on his creepie stool, liked the sound of the word.

Bella, the loving wife of the old fusilier, had received her husband home from the war, we were told, in a glass case, the loser by a stomach shot away when – all his superior officers dead – he, the corporal, gallantly led an action to success, carried the kopje or whatever it was they carried in Flanders, and stopped just short of advancing, like the gallant Dublins, into the fire of his own artillery. Back home, stomachless in his glass case, he cheated the War Office on the delicate question of expectation of life, collected a fine pension and lived at ease until the world was good and ready for another war. No crippled veteran, left to beg at the town's end, was the old fusilier. Secure in his bed, in his lattice-windowed room in his white cottage that was snug in the middle of a terrace of seven white cottages, he talked, read about Tarzan, told how fields were won and, on big British Legion days, condescended to receive homage from visiting celebrities, including, once, Lady Haig herself. On the creepie stool, chubby Isaac absorbed the wonder of half-comprehended words, pondered the girth of the undertaker, the lean, loveless face of the fish merchant who thought that only beauty could tell him the time on a June evening, watched the hands of Moses as they cut a thorn or measured the monstrousness of an escaped pike, studied the cowboy's eyes that squinted, by way of twopenny paper-covered books, back to the Texas Panhandle and the Old Chisholm Trail.

The undertaker, or the pike fisherman, or the fish merchant, or the Cowboy would say, 'Isaac, what do you want to be when you grow up?'

Isaac would say, 'I want to be a German.'

Then the four visitors would laugh. His father, pale on his pillows, would laugh – forgetting Germans once seen in the sulphurous haze as he charged roaring through shot and shell to become a hero. His father would read the next instalment:

'When Tarzan of the Apes realised that he was in the grip of the great jaws of a crocodile he did not, as an ordinary man might have done, give up all hope and resign himself to his fate. . . .

'His body trailed out beside the slimy carcass of his captor, and into the tough armour the apeman attempted to plunge his stone knife as he was borne to the creature's horrid den. . . .

'Staggering to his feet the apeman groped about the reeking, oozy den. . . .'

In the moonlight the Cowboy walked home, pulling imaginary guns and talking in admonitory tones to Wyatt Earp, 'Stand there, Earp. You may be a big man, but I'll cut you down. Do I have to push you into slapping leather?'

Alone in the moonlight on the hill that went down to the red-and-white creamery, the brook, the Cowboy's hut, the fields beyond, he pulled and whirled and fired three times. With satisfaction he listened to the echoes dying away at the town's last fringe of shabby, sleeping terraces, over the tarred iron roofs of Tansey the carter's stableyard, over the railway-engine shed and the turntable. On green-and-white moorland beyond the Dublin railway a mystic, white bronco galloped in circles as, noiselessly, the Cowboy slipped the smoking Colt back into the holster. He turned then and went on down the hill to Tansey, the carter's, and supper. Every day he worked, carrying bags of meal to clumsy four-wheeled drays, in the warehouse of Dale, the grain-merchant, nicknamed Attention, who was an amateur astronomer and had a telescope installed in a beehive-shaped structure at the back of his store. Every night after the fusilier's reading the Cowboy ate his supper of yellow Indian porridge and buttermilk in the huge coppery kitchen where Tansey the carter was a smiling extrovert Buddha in the middle of six stout sisters who had never shown the least inclination towards matrimony.

'Every day, Cowboy, Attention's back is stiffer and stiffer,' Tansey said.

'He sat on a poker,' said the third sister.

The sisters were all red-faced and brown-haired. The fourth one cooked the porridge.

'I hear he got drunk on wine gums in Devlin's sweetie shop in Bridge Lane,' Tansey joked. 'The sergeant had to wheel his bicycle home for him.'

Seriously resenting the imputation, the Cowboy, thumbs in the armholes of his patched and darned grey vest, drawled, 'The Big Boss is a fast man on the draw. He never touches hard likker.'

'We heard he can stare the sun in the face up in that spinning beehive of his,' said the second sister.

The carter said, 'It takes a good man to stare the sun in the face.'

On a hook behind the broad oak door the first sister considerately hung the Stetson that a rope juggler in a travelling circus had once given to the Cowboy.

'What goes on between the sun and himself is his own business,' said the Cowboy reverently. 'There was a cattleman in Wyoming had as big a spyglass. Could spot an Injun or a stray ten miles off.'

'You and Wyoming,' gently said the sixth sister.

'The Big Boss reaches me my wad. At the door of the bunk-house. Your pay, Michael, he says. Count it. I counted one pound, nineteen and eleven pence. A penny short, boss, says I. One penny deducted, Michael, for a box of matches purchased on credit last Tuesday at eleven ah em. He misses nothing.'

'Your porridge,' said Tansey the carter, 'and give us another bit of the story.'

'The place I was in at that time,' said the Cowboy. 'Down Deep South. There was a river. Alligators. As plentiful as trout in the brook. This day I went for a swim. Just the way you'd go for a swim above the salmon leap by the hospital on the Camowen River.'

'Showing off and strutting before the nurses,' said the third sister. 'For shame, Cowboy.'

'And what should happen when I was out in deep water but an alligator. Silent-like he grabs me by the arm. I could show you the marks still. But cute enough, he doesn't take the arm off. He needed it, you see, to drag me down.'

'In this life you'll always get somebody to drag you down,' said the second sister.

'Down to where?' asked the carter.

'Not down the town to a pub or the pictures, anyway. Down to his cave. They live in caves in that river.'

'No homes to go to,' said the third sister.

'Was he big?' asked the carter. 'Would he be the size now of the last pike Pat Moses Gavigan caught at Blacksessiagh?'

'Size! Ten times the size. A mouth that wide. And the growls of him. Well, there was I. My body beside the slimy carcass of my captor. But I had a knife. A stone knife. Never swam without it. Wouldn't be safe in those parts. And as I was borne to the creature's horrid den I attempted to plunge my knife into the tough armour of the reptile.'

'Cowboy,' said the carter, 'you're the lucky man to be alive and eating porridge there this blessed night.'

'Lucky! Quickness: that's what does it. An ordinary man might have given up all hope and resigned himself to his fate.'

From the stables came a wild volley of hooves on cabbining wood, then a second volley, then a slow thud – thud – thud and one mad, high, equine scream.

'That savage you bought,' said the fifth sister. 'He'll never cart.'

'He'll cart,' said Tansey. 'More India-buck porridge, Cowboy?'

That was the time when Isaac desired – as every child, male or female, sometimes desires – a pony. It was, of course, long before he found his vocation and in a green lane above the engine shed – the town's unroofed gymnasium – learned to become the best fighter our town ever had. Poise and stance, dynamite right and cunning left, footwork, speed, quick eye, cool head and iron muscles, the fusilier's son was a natural champion. And, graduating from the green lane, he brought belts, cups, medals, honour and glory home with him from every part of the country. We were proud of him.

But in the days of his desire for the pony there were no blows struck but one. Where would a boy go who wanted a pony or a stable to house him but to Tansey's yard where the great cart-horses stamped with the assured gravity of savants, where the Taggarts, the horse dealers, displayed the shaggy, sullen-eyed animals they brought in droves from the mountains away to the south-west, even from tinker camps in the province of Connacht. Roosted high on the shaft of an idle dray, Isaac was there the day Tansey bought the wild, white horse. In among the brown, shaggy brutes he was white-limbed Tarzan among the ape people of Akut and, until he felt on his quivering flanks the confining shafts, he concealed horror in docility. Then he reared to the perpendicular, assaulted the heavens, came down again and lashed out backwards, did the rounds of the yard like a Derby winner while old and young, Isaac among them, ran for shelter. With great Tansey swinging from the reins the horse went round and round and round until the cart was in firewood and broken shafts trailed the ground.

'Powerful God,' said Tansey to the Taggarts, 'where did you get this one?'

'In Ballinasloe in the County Galway,' they said.

As if that explained everything.

'Take him back to Ballinasloe,' said Tansey.

'But no, linger now,' he said. 'There's life in him. He'll cart. I'll coax him.'

Dreaming at a safe distance, Isaac saw himself coaxing the savage with gently-proffered lumps of sugar, and all through the white one's novitiate under Tansey, Isaac was in constant, reverent attendance. But no coaxing, no lump sugar, no whispers or magic hands, could reconcile the untamed tinker-spirit of Ballinasloe to the base servility of the shafts of a dray.

'He has good blood in him,' Tansey said. 'I'll try him in a trap.'

Some of the fragments of the trap, they say, were found fifty yards away on the railway line, and the great white creature stood shivering as if, if it were human, it would burst into hysterical sobs. For a whole fortnight, with Isaac perched on high walls or drays or snug on the hay in the hayshed, the wooing went on, and it was one evening in the stable that Isaac said: Give him to me, Mr. Tansey. I'll tame him for you.

For one half second while the carter, distracted, turned and

laughed, the horse lunged and snapped, the razor teeth grazing
the back of Tansey's skull and gashing the lobe of his left ear.
The blood came out like a spout and Tansey dyed his hand in
it. Then, disregarding it, he looked sadly at the animal. With
no sign of temper he went to the back of the stable, picked up a
crowbar from a heap of rusting metal and, with the deliberation
of God, struck the animal between the eyes and stunned it.
When it woke up an hour later it went, almost of its own accord,
to the shafts. Isaac's sugar lumps were never needed.

By the fusilier's bedside that evening the Cowboy was sitting
straddle on a stool, knees in, feet out, hands wide, showing how
he had held the reins and stayed in the saddle when lesser men
had bitten the dust of the rodeo ring. Isaac chewed toffee. He
said, 'Tansey the carter broke a bronc today. I saw him.'

He told his story.

'Tansey's a brute,' said Doherty the undertaker. 'He'd slay
his six sisters before he'd lose two pounds sterling.'

'You'd benefit,' said Pat Moses Gavigan. 'Six coffins.'

'They're six fine big girls,' said Mickey Fish.

'Not a watch between them,' said the fusilier. 'Time doesn't
count in Tansey's.'

The fusilier read: Screaming with terror the Maoris were
dragged from their lofty perches. The beasts, uncontrolled by
Tarzan, who had gone in search of Jane, loosed the full fury of
their savage natures upon the unhappy wretches who fell into
their clutches. . . . Sheeta, in the meanwhile, had felt his great
fangs sink into but a single jugular. . . .

Afterwards when the guests had gone Isaac said, 'The
Cowboy Carson had a ranch once on the Rio Grande. He told
me he had seventy pinto ponies.'

'Son,' said the fusilier, 'I hate to rob you of your fancy. But
better for your father to do it than for the hard world and the
black stranger. The Cowboy Carson was never out of this town
except perhaps to carry Pat Moses Gavigan's bag as far as the
pike-water at Blacksessiagh. It all comes out of the wee books

you see in the paper-shop window: Deadwood Dick and Buffalo
Bill, and Hit the Tuttle Trail with Hashknife and Sleepy.'

'But he was a gun-slinger, da, in Texas.'

'Guns, he never saw guns,' said the fusilier – musing for
a minute and remembering Flanders and the roar of the iron
monsters.

In the dusk the Cowboy walked home, spurs jingling, stiff and
stilted on high heels, bowlegged from the saddle, left to right
and right to left practising the cross-draw and remembering
with affection his deceased friend, Buck Duane, the Lone Star
Ranger. He was light and elated. There was no pressure of
crushing bags of grain on his old, bony shoulders. Melodious
with beeves, a freight train from the West truckled on towards
Belfast. The Cowboy made his customary crooked way to the
kitchen of Tansey the Carter.

'You broke the bronc today, I'm told,' he said to Tansey.

'I broke the bronc, Cowboy, the only way my father taught
me. If I buy a horse to cart he has to cart. Or a woman to
cook.'

'He never bought a woman,' said the third sister, and the six
sisters laughed.

'Your porridge, Cowboy.'

'Did I ever tell you about the time I was in New Zealand?'

'You never did,' said Tansey the carter.

When the Americans came to our town on their way to
meet Hitler somebody told them about the Cowboy and
one of them, meeting him, said, 'Haven't we encountered you
before?'

'Was it in Tucson?' said another.

'More whisky,' said a third, 'it was in Tombstone.'

'Not there,' said the Cowboy. 'I guess and calculate it might
have been in Deadwood.'

'Deadwood it was,' said the three of them. 'Well, we'll be
doggone darned.'

'Tell us about Deadwood, Cowboy,' said the man behind the bar.

'I was riding shotgun at that time,' said the Cowboy. 'Stiff knee, you see. Couldn't mount a bronc.'

For corroborative purposes he displayed his stiff knee. They listened with a little laughter. They weren't cruel. They were, in fact, kind, because the worst thing you could have done was to tell him he was never there.

By that time the old fusilier was dead, and buried by Doherty the undertaker; Attention Dale had been succeeded by a nephew who couldn't face the sun and sold the telescope; Mickey Fish was confined to a mental home for chasing young girls to ask them the time of evening; and arthritis prevented Pat Moses Gavigan from fishing pike or cutting blackthorns. And Isaac the fusilier's son, had realised that he would never be a German. He came like a bird as a paratrooper into Narvik, came out again alive, and possibly helped the three Americans who had listened to the Cowboy to storm the French shore. Until he was killed at the Rhine crossing he remained the best fighter our town ever had.

# The heroes in the dark house

'They were gone in the morning,' the old man said.

His name was Arthur Broderick, and the young folk-tale scholar sat quietly, listening for the story that had been promised him.

'Lock, stock and barrel,' said the old man. 'The whole U.S. garrison, off for the fair fields of France. Jeeps, guns, and gun-carriers. In the dump behind the big camp at Knocknashee Castle the handful of caretakers they left behind slung radio sets and bicycles and ran a gun-carrier with caterpillar wheels over the lot, and as good as made mash of them. Very wasteful. War's all waste. Those bicycles would have kept every young boy in the county spinning for the next five years.'

Like the plain girl that nobody wanted Mr. Broderick's nine-times rejected manuscript-folk-tales set down with such love and care in high-spined script lay between them on an antique drawing-room table. The table's top, solid oak and two inches thick, was shaped like a huge teardrop pearl with the tip abruptly nipped off.

'Oak,' Mr. Broderick said through the smoke. 'Solid oak and two centuries old. In 1798, in the year of the Rising, it was the top of a bellows in a smithy. Look here where the British yeomanry sawed the tip off it so that the rebels could no longer use it for the forging of the pikes. When I was the age of yourself I converted it into a table. Sixty years ago last July.'

Around them in the ancient, musty, tapestried room the wreathing smoke might have come from the fires of 1798.

Birdsong outside, sunshine, wind in the creepers were as far away as Florida. The greedy, nesting jackdaws held the flues as firmly as ever at Thermopylae or the Alamo or Athlone, or a score of other places all around the battered globe, unforgotten heroes had held passes, bridgeheads or gun-burned walls. And unforgotten heroes had marched through the smoke in this room: Strong Shawn, the son of the fisherman of Kinsale, triumphant, with the aid of white magic, crossed the seven-mile strand of steel spikes, the seven-mile-high mountain of flames, the seven miles of treacherous sea, and came gloriously to win his love in a castle courtyard crowded with champions and heroes from the four sides of the world; the valiant son of the King of Antua fought with Macan Mor, son of the King of Soracha, in the way that they made rocks of water and water of rocks, and if the birds came from the lower to the upper world to see wonders it was to see these two they came.

Mr. Broderick went on with his tale. All night long through the village below the old, dark, smoky house that had once been a rectory the lorries had throbbed and thundered on the narrow, twisted street and above, in the upper air, the waves of planes had swept east towards Europe.

'They were gone in the morning,' he said. 'Lock, stock and barrel. There was never a departure like it since the world was made. For quick packing, I heard afterwards, they drove the jeeps up the steep steps of the courthouse below. It reminded me of the poem about the three jolly gentlemen in coats of red who rode their horses up to bed.'

'They were gone,' he said, 'like snow off a ditch.'

It was as much as the young scholar could do to see him for smoke. But with an effort that would have done credit to Macan Mor or Shawn of Kinsale he managed to control his coughing.

In the old dizzy chimney the jackdaws were so solidly entrenched that at times Mr. Broderick had found it hard to see the paper he transcribed the folk-tales on. The smoke no longer made him cough, but at eighty-five his eyes were not as keen as they had been when he was in his prime and from the saddle of a galloping hunter could spot, in passing, a bird's nest in a leafy hedgerow. Lovingly he transcribed the tales in the high, spidery handwriting that – like himself, like his work for Sir Horace Plunkett in the co-operative creameries, his friendship with Thomas Andrews who had built the Titanic and gone bravely with it to Wordsworth's incommunicable sleep – belonged to a past, forgotten time. For years of his life he had followed these tales, the people who told them, the heroes who lived in them, over miles of lonely heather-mountain, up boreens that in rain became rivulets, to crouch in mountain cabins by the red hearth-glow and listen to the meditative voices of people for whom there was only the past.

Peadar Haughey of Creggan Cross had sat on the long, oaken settle with his wife and three daughters and dictated to him the adventures of the son of the king of Antua, as well as the story of the giant of Reibhlean who had abducted from Ireland a married princess. Giants as a rule preferred unmarried princesses. Peadar told the story in Irish and English. His wife and daughters understood only English but together they rocked in unison on the settle and sang macaronic songs in a mixture of both languages. That simple world had its own confusions. At times in his smoky house he found it hard to separate the people in the tales from the people who told them.

Bed-ridden Owen Roe Ward, in a garret in a back-lane in the garrison town ten miles away, had told him the story of the King of Green Island and other stories that were all about journeys to the end of the earth in search of elixirs that could only be won by herculean labours. Hewing trees for hire in a tangled plantation whose wood had once paid for the travels and other activities of D'Orsay and Lady Blessington, Owen had brought down on his hapless spine a ton-weight of timber. Paralysed in his garret he travelled as he talked to find life-giving water in the well at the world's end.

A woman of eighty by the name of Maire John (she still sang with the sweet voice she had at twenty and displayed the fondness for embracing men that, according to tradition, had then characterised her) had told him of the three princesses who sat in the wishing chair. One wished to marry a husband more beautiful than the sun. The second wished to marry a husband more beautiful than the moon. The third stated her honest but eccentric preference for the White Hound of the Mountain. It was a local heather-flavoured version of the marriage of Cupid and Psyche, and Maire John herself was a randy old lady who would, in the days of silver Latin, have delighted Apuleius.

The stories had come like genii, living, wreathing from holes in the wall behind smoky hearths, or from the dusty tops of dressers, or from farmhouse lofts where ancient, yellow manuscripts were stored. By Bloody Bridge on the Camowen River (called so because of no battle, but because of the number of fine trout killed there) he had heard from Pat Moses Gavigan a completely new version of the story of Fionn MacCumhail and the enchanted Salmon of Wisdom.

Plain and mountain and river-valley, the places he knew were sombre with the sense of family, and folk-tales grew as naturally there as grass. Heroes, princesses, enchanters good and bad, he had marshalled them all, called them to order in his own smoky room, numbered them off right to left, made his roll-call, described them in that high-spined handwriting he had studied so laboriously in the old manuscripts. Properly thus caparisoned they would go out into the twentieth century. He made his own of them. He called them his children. He sent them out to the ends of the earth, to magazine editors and publishing houses. They came back rejected to him, as if being his children they could have no life when torn away from him. Then one day in the smoky room under the power of the squabbling enchanters of jackdaws he had the bitterness of discovering that his children had betrayed him. In a Dublin newspaper he read the review of the young scholar's book:

'The scholar who has compiled, translated and edited these folk-tales has a wise head on young shoulders. Careful research and a wide knowledge of comparative folklore have gone into his work. He has gleaned carefully in the mountainous area ten miles north of the town where he was born. He presents his findings with an erudite introduction and in an impeccable style. . . .'

The smoke wreathed around him. The reviewer's weary sentences went on like the repetition of a death-knell:

'His name is worthy to rank with that of such folklorists as Jeremiah Curtin. Particularly notable is his handling of the remarkable quest tale of the King of Green Island. . . .'

Mr. Broderick couldn't blame the three princesses for leaving the wishing chair and making off with a younger man. That scholar, wise head on young shoulders, could be Cupid, more beautiful than the sun and the moon: he might even be that enigmatic character, The White Hound of The Mountain. But Shawn of Kinsale could have been kinder to old age, and so could all those battling heroes or venturesome boys who crossed perilous seas, burning mountains and spiked strands.

He wrote to the young scholar at the publisher's address: 'While I am loath to trade on your time, I have, it would seem, been working or wandering about in the same field and in the same part of the country. We may share the acquaintanceship of some of the living sources of these old tales. We certainly have friends in common in the realms of mythology. Perhaps my own humble gatherings might supplement your store. So far I have failed to find a publisher for them. If you are ever visiting your home town you may care to add a few miles to the journey to call on me. My congratulations on your achievement. It gratifies me to see a young man from this part of the country doing so well.'

A week later he took up his stick one day and walked down the winding, grass-grown avenue. An ancestor was rector here long years ago, he thought, as in the case of William Yeats, the poet, who died in France on the eve of this war and who had an ancestor a rector long years ago in Drumcliffe by the faraway Sligo sea. Mr. Broderick's house had been the rectory. When the church authorities judged it a crumbling, decaying property they had given it to Mr. Broderick for a token sum – a small gesture of regard for all that in an active manhood he had done for the village. Crumbling and decaying it was, but peace, undisturbed, remained around the boles of the trees, the tall gables and old tottering chimneys, the shadowy bird-rustling walks. Now, as he walked, yews gone wild and reckless made a tangled pattern above his head.

Weeks before, from the garrison town in the valley, war had spilled its gathering troops over into this little village. Three deep, burdened with guns and accoutrements, they slouched past Mr. Broderick on the way down the hill to their courthouse billet. Dust rose around them. They sang. They were three to six thousand miles from home, facing an uncertain future, and in reasonably good humour. A dozen or so who knew Mr. Broderick from the tottering house as the old guy who made souvenirs out of blackthorn and bog oak, waved casual, friendly hands. Beyond and behind them as they descended was the blue cone of Knocknashee Hill where the castle was commandeered and where a landlord had once stocked a lake with rainbow trout that like these troops had been carried across the wide Atlantic. The soldiers' dust settling around him in wreaths and rings, Mr. Broderick went down the road to collect his mail at the post-office. There had been no troops in this village since 1798 when the bellows had been mutilated and the soldiers then, according to the history books, had been anything but friendly.

The long red-tiled roofs and white walls of the co-operative creamery, the sheen of glasshouses from the slopes of the model farm were a reminder to Mr. Broderick of the enthusiasms of an active past. People had, in his boyhood, been evicted for poverty in that village. Now every year the co-operative grain store handled one hundred and fifty thousand tons of grain. An energetic young man could take forty tons of tomatoes out of an acre and a quarter of glasshouses, and on a day of strong sunshine the gleam of the glasshouses would blind you. Crops burst over the hedges as nowhere else in that part of the country. It was good, high, dry land that took less harm than most places from wet seasons and flooding, and the cattle were as heavy and content as creamy oxen in French vineyards.

Over the hedge and railings by the parish church the statue of the old Canon, not of Mr. Broderick's persuasion, raised a strong Roman right arm. The pedestal described the Canon as a saintly priest and sterling patriot and to anybody, except Mr. Broderick, that raised right arm might have been minatory. To Arthur Broderick it was a kind memory of hero and co-worker, it was an eternal greeting in stone.

'Arthur,' the statue said, 'yourself and myself built this place. There was a time when you'd have clambered to the top of a telegraph pole if somebody'd told you there was a shilling there would help to make the village live. You did everything but say mass and I did that. You got little out of it yourself. But you saw they were happy and strong. Look around you. Be proud and glad. Enjoy your dreams of lost heroes in the mist. No young man can steal from you what you want to give away.'

High above the dead stone Canon the Angelus bell rang. Before him, down the cobbled footwalk, so steep that at times it eased itself out with a sigh into flat, flagged steps, went a tall soldier and a small young woman. Mr. Broderick knew her. She was one of the eighteen Banty Mullans, nine male, nine female, all strawheaded and five feet high, the males all roughs, and the females, to put it politely, taking in washing for the Irish Fusiliers in the town below. She was ill-dressed, coarse-tongued and vicious. She carried in her left hand a shiny gallon buttermilk-can. Stooping low, the tall warrior eased the handle of the can from the stumpy, stubborn fingers

and, surprised at a gentlemanly gesture that could never have
come from a pre-war fusilier trained in the old Prussian school
and compelled in public to walk like clockwork, she asked with
awe, 'Aren't you feared the sergeant will see you?'

'In this man's army,' he said.

He could be a Texan. It was diverting to study their accents
and guess at States.

'In this man's army, sister, we don't keep sergeants.'

Suddenly happy, Arthur Broderick tripped along behind
them, kicked at a stray pebble, sniffed at the good air until
his way was blocked by the frail, discontented figure of Patrick
who kept the public house beside the post-office and opposite
the courthouse, and who sold the bog oak and blackthorn
souvenirs to thirsty, sentimental soldiers.

'Lord God, Mr. Broderick,' said Patrick. 'Do you see that
for discipline? Carrying a tin can like an errand boy.'

'But Patrick, child, it's idyllic. Deirdre in the hero tale
couldn't have been more nobly treated by the three Ulster
brothers, the sons of Uisneach. Hitler and Hirohito had to
bring the dough-boys over here before one of the Banty Mullans
was handled like a lady.'

'Mr. Bee,' said Patrick, 'we all know you have odd
ideas on what's what. But Mr. Bee, there must be a line
of demarcation. Would you look across the street at that for
soldiering?'

In sunshine that struggled hard, but failed, to brighten
the old granite walls and Ionic columns of the courthouse
the huge, coloured sentry had happily accepted the idea that
for that day and in that village he did not have to deal with
the Wehrmacht. Unlike the courthouse he looked as if he had
been specially made by the sun. He sat relaxed on a chair,
legs crossed, sharing a parcel of sandwiches with a trio of
village children. Behind him on a stone ledge, his weapon
of war was a votive offering at the feet of a bronze statue
of a famous hanging judge who, irritated by the eczema of
the droppings of lawless, irreverent birds, scowled like the

Monster from Thirty Thousand Fathoms. Then clattering down the courthouse steps, came fifty young men, very much at ease. Falling into loose formation they went jauntily down the hilly street to the cookhouse at the bottom of the village. To the rhythm of their feet they played tunes with trays and table utensils.

'Their morale is high,' said Mr. Broderick.

Dark, hollow-cheeked, always complaining, persecuted by a corpulent wife, Patrick resented the young warriors with every bone in his small body. Some local wit had once said that he was a man constitutionally incapable of filling a glass to the brim.

'Those fellows, Mr. Bee, are better fed than yourself or myself.'

'They're young and growing, Patrick. They need it more. Besides, doesn't the best authority tell us an army marches on its belly?'

'They're pampered. Starve the Irish, Lord Kitchener said, and you'll have an army.'

'Ah, but Patrick the times have changed. I had the pleasure of serving under Lord Kitchener. But he never impressed me as a dietician.'

'Soft soles on their boots,' said Patrick, 'and their teeth glued together with chewing gum and all the girls in the country running wild since they came.'

'Life,' said Mr. Broderick, 'we can't suppress. Every woman worth breathing loves a warrior who's facing death.'

'Once upon a time,' Patrick said, 'your old friend, the Canon, made a rake of a fellow kneel at the church gate with a horse collar round his neck to do public penance for his rascalities with the girls.'

'Lothario in a leather frame, Patrick.'

Mr. Broderick laughed until his eyes were moist, at the memory and at the unquenchable misery in the diminutive, unloved, unloving heart of hen-pecked Patrick.

'Today, Patrick, there wouldn't be enough horse collars to

go round. The horse isn't as plentiful as it was. The Canon had his foibles. He objected also to tam o'shanters and women riding bicycles. That was so long ago, Patrick. We'll drink to his memory.'

Everything, he thought as he left the public house and stepped on to the post-office, was so long ago. Patrick could hardly be described as part of the present. His lament was for days when heroes went hungry, when the fusiliers in the town below were forbidden by rule to stand chatting on the public street, were compelled to step rigidly, gloves like this, cane like that under the oxter – like a stick trussing a plucked chicken in a poulterer's shop. Patrick in his cave of a pub was a comic, melancholy, legendary dwarf. His one daring relaxation was to brighten the walls of his cave with coloured calendars of pretty girls caught with arms full of parcels and, by the snapping of some elastic or the betrayal of some hook or button, in mildly embarrassing situations. With startled but nevertheless smiling eyes they appealed to Patrick's customers.

'Your souvenirs sell well, Mr. Bee,' Patrick said. 'The pipes especially. But the sloe-stone rosary beads too. Although it puzzles me to make out what these wild fellows want with rosary beads.'

'They may have mothers at home, Patrick, who like keep-sakes. They're far from home. They're even headed the other way.'

At the post-office the girl behind the brass grille said, 'Two letters, Mr. Broderick.'

He read the first one. The young scholar said that he had read with great interest of Mr. Broderick's interest in and his collection of folk-tales. He realised that folk-tales were often, curiously enough, not popular fare but he still considered that the publishers lacked vision and enterprise. He had only had his own book published because of the fortunate chance of his meeting a publisher who thought that he, the young scholar, might some day write a book that would be a moneymaker. The young scholar would also in the near future be visiting his native place. He thanked Mr. Broderick for his kind invitation and would take the liberty of calling on him.

The second letter came from an old colleague in the city of Belfast. It said: 'Arthur, old friend, yesterday I met a Major Michael F. X. Devaney – it would seem he has Irish ancestry – who has something or other to do with cultural relations between the U.S. troops and ourselves. He's hunting for folk-tales, local lore, to publish in book-form for the army. I thought of you. I took the liberty of arranging an appointment and of loaning him a copy of some of the stories you once loaned me.'

Mr. Broderick went to Belfast a few days later to keep the appointment. From the window of the major's office the vast, smoky bulk of the domed City Hall was visible. He turned from its impressive Victorian gloom to study the major, splendidly caparisoned as any hero who had ever lived in coloured tales told by country hearths.

'Mr. Broderick,' said the major, 'this is real contemporary.'

'Old tales, major, like old soldiers.'

'This spiked strand and burning mountain. I was in the Pacific, Mr. Broderick. This seven miles of treacherous sea. A few pages of glossary, Mr. Broderick. A few explanatory footnotes. How long would that take you?'

'A month, major. Say a month.'

'We'll settle for a month. Then we'll clinch the deal. These tales are exactly what we want, Mr. Broderick. Tell the boys something about the traditions of the place.'

He took the train home from the tense, overcrowded city to the garrison town in the valley. The market-day bus brought him up over the ridge to his own village. All that warm night the lorries on the steep street robbed him of his sparse, aged sleep as the troops moved; and they were gone in the morning, lock, stock and barrel, and on the far French coast the sons

of the Kings of Antua and Soracha grappled until they made
rocks of water and water of rocks, and the waves of the great
metal birds of the air screamed over them.

High in the sky beyond Knocknashee one lone plane droned
like a bee some cruel boy had imprisoned in a bottle to prevent
it from joining the swarm. At his hushed doorway sad Patrick
the publican looked aghast at the newspaper headlines and
more aghast at the cold, empty courthouse that once had
housed such thirsty young men.

'You'd swear to God,' he said, 'they were never here at all.'

Arthur Broderick left him to his confusion. He walked
home under twisted yews, up the grass-grown avenue to his
own smoky house. The heroes had gone, but the heroes would
stay with him for ever. His children would stay with him for
ever, but, in a way, it was a pity that he could never give his
stories to all those fine young men.


'Come in,' Mr. Broderick said to the young scholar, 'you're
welcome. There's nothing I'm prouder of than to see a young
man from these parts doing well. And we know the same
people. We have many friends in common.'

'Shawn of Kinsale,' the young scholar said, 'and the son
of the King of Antua.'

'The three princesses,' said Mr. Broderick, 'and the White
Hound of the Mountain.'

He reached out the hand of welcome to the young scholar.

'Publishing is slow,' the young man stammered. 'They have
little vision. . . .'

'Vision reminds me,' Mr. Broderick said. 'Do you mind
smoke?'

He opened the drawing-room door. Smoke billowed out to
the musty hallway.

'My poor stories,' he said. 'My poor heroes. They went
away to the well at the world's end but they always came
back. Once they came very close to enlisting in the U.S. army.
That's a story I must tell you sometime.'

The manuscript of his tales lay between them on the table that had once been part of the rebel's bellows. Around them in the smoke were the grey shadows of heroic eighteenth-century men who, to fight tyranny, had forged steel pikes. And eastwards the heroes had swept that earth-shaking summer, over the treacherous mined sea, over the seven miles of spiked strand, over the seven and seventy miles of burning mountain.

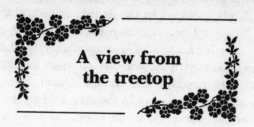

# A view from the treetop

There were two famous trees in the village: the cork tree and the lime tree. The cork tree was a decrepit foreign character who stood guiltily and raggedly, as if he knew he was an intruder, on the unkempt slope below the railway station. Nobody knew who had planted it, but the Old Master had the theory that some mysterious brown man, passing that way, had taken a seed out of his pocket and blown it from the palm of his hand to seek shelter and mercy from our soft earth.

'In Portugal,' the Old Master once read out in the course of a geography lesson, 'the freshly cut trunks of the cork oaks are in July deeply flushed with red.'

It was a long way from Portugal to the scrubby slope below the station where the bark hung loosely, half-on and half-off, our poor, leprous cork-oak. There was no view worth talking of from the top of it and, even if there had been, nobody could climb it in comfort, because you couldn't get a grip on it; the bark came off in your hands. But from the top of the lime tree, on the triangular green in the centre of the village, you could see the world. Nobody knew that better than Paddy Sheehan. Paddy spent a whole August morning in the lime tree. As he told me himself, long afterwards, it was worth being hungry and thirsty, lost and missing for an August morning, just to see what he saw and to realise himself as he did.

'I was never the same after that morning,' he said. 'I knew I was a bit of a god.'

Down the road from his father's large, square, stone house to the double bridge over the river two damson trees from one wild orchard grew out over a straggling hedge. This sunny morning Paddy galloped to the double bridge, plucking, on the way, two damsons, one from each tree, not for himself but for his invisible horse who, unaccountably, liked damsons. Horses you invented need not diet on grass or oats or hay particularly when you did the eating for them. Because there was a white horse in training in the long field by the railway, and because this horse was in his mind, the horse he ate the two damsons for was a racehorse. At the double bridge he unsaddled and unbridled it, smacked its flank and sent it off to graze on the wide field in the loop of the river where his father, a big grazier and the village butcher, said was the best fattening land in Ireland.

The bridge had to be a double bridge because the river, one time in high flood, had changed its course. The older half of the bridge now spanned a muddy sunken ditch lined with reeds and willows, where water had once flowed. In every subsequent flood the water tried unavailingly to return to its ancient channel. That struggle between restless river and solid grazing land was one of the topics the Old Master loved to talk about when he wasn't talking – which he mostly was – about the wonders of the battle-field on the far side of the village.

'On that black plain,' he would say, 'nearly three centuries ago, two kings played at pitch-and-toss for the crown of England.'

The Old Master was as much part of the village as the ancient battlefield was: born and reared there he had come back to take over the school and talk to generations of boys about the history of the place.

Sunlight danced on glittering water. Wagtails darted and dipped over the wide salmon pool above the bridge. Heavy cattle churning in the mud of the old channel sought the shade of the willows and fortified themselves against the day's heat. When Paddy's horse was contentedly grazing he went back homewards, bent on breakfast.

To the left of the road was a high, ivy-grown wall. It was part of the morning game to clamber up a few feet, clutching the ivy, and to peer through a hole in the wall at the mad major who had suffered sunstroke in India. Most mornings he worked in the gardens at the back of his big house. Nobody in the village could afford for shame to wear clothes as tattered and dirty as the major wore. He affected an ancient battle-dress held together by strings and pins, and a wide straw hat and furious red whiskers. Nobody in the world talked so loudly or took such long strides or could shoot snipe better or was more given to fits of high-pitched laughter. It was exciting to peer through a hole in the wall at this wonder of a man talking to himself as he worked, and sometimes talking to the plants and blossoms. The only thing in the village that was at all like him was the rare and alien cork tree.

Before Paddy's eyes then, as he peered through the hole in the wall, the major became the cork tree. It was as real to Paddy as if he had been dreaming. The magic of sunlight on flowers in the old walled garden dazzled him and set him playing a new game: Close my eyes, open them, I see the major; Close them again, open them again, I see the cork tree. To vary the fun he made the cork tree talk with a high foreign voice, and made the battle-dress peel like brown, crumbling bark off the hapless major. That was why, when he looked sideways and saw the Old Master coming towards him from the direction of the bridge, and the station and the cork-tree, he panicked and ran. He couldn't think of the cork tree and the Old Master at one and the same time without sharp feelings of guilt. Because when he thought of the cork tree he had also to think of the seventeen musket balls he had abstracted from the school museum. They were hidden in a tin box in a hole under the roots of the cork tree.

The Old Master, he hoped, was yet too far away to see him. So he dropped from the wall and ran, up the slope and around the corner into the main street of the village and across the triangular green; and, having come so far, it seemed as

natural to run up the great lime tree as to run further along
the ground. There was nobody to be seen except the parish
priest who, fifty yards away and with his back to Paddy,
was reading his breviary. Up and up Paddy went and then
on a broad branch, his back to the trunk, he rested straddle,
soothed by the sound of morning air in the leaves and the
gentle, swaying motion of high timber. He looked down on
his world and began to examine his conscience.

In school the previous day things had come to an embarrassing
point of discovery when the Old Master had been proudly
displaying his museum to the schools inspector with the white
moustache who talked half in Irish and half in English, quoted
poetry most of the time, breathed out whisky all the time, and
was for ever jingling money in the pockets of his trousers. The
Master and the Inspector had known each other since college
days in Dublin. Old friends together, they talked and jingled
round the room. The Inspector was a big man and bulky in
tweeds. The Old Master, small, mild, and stooped, his left
ear wired for hearing, went ahead of him like a tug before a
liner, around the senior schoolroom which, with glass cases
filled with relics of that battle long ago, was a miniature
museum.

'About here where this school stands, James,' the Inspector
bellowed, 'the last shots were fired on that black day three
hundred years ago.'

He intoned in Irish some mournful verse about a lost battle
and a broken cause.

'Boys,' he roared at us, 'you should be able to feel history
and you going to school here. Not Gettysburg nor Mons were
more renowned than this place. That stream across the road
there, that you catch pinkeens in, more than likely ran red
with blood.'

We listened. The stream was in a brown fresh that day after
a cloudburst in the hills and we could hear it rushing down
the slope to join our river below the double bridge. Perhaps

the more imaginative of us could hear above the sound of the falling water the echo of the last salvoes, the agony of the last cries.

'They're strong on history,' said the Old Master.

He was proud of us, God knew why.

'And they were as industrious as beavers, these good pupils of mine going on all fours over the battlefield, searching with fine combs for relics of the battle. The things we found.'

'Turn a sod and start the muse of history,' said the Inspector.

'Take a look at our glass cases.'

'Didn't I read in the papers,' the Inspector roared and jingled, 'about the things you found? Wonderful, James. A credit to you and these good boys. The children of decent parents, I'll be bound.'

They studied a brutal-looking lump of wood so long buried in the black earth that it looked as if it had been turned into stone.

'A digging wedge,' said the Old Master.

'The oldest digging instrument in the world,' said the Inspector. 'The Hottentots used it.'

'And the South Sea islanders.'

They moved from glass case to glass case. They studied a stone with the mark of a fossil on it. Concerning that stone, Paddy told us, he used to have nightmares. He was an imaginative, red-headed, bony-kneed, hard-knuckled boy of thirteen. Every stone in the world, he said, even the stones in the walls around the mad major's house and gardens, might be just waiting to burst open to let monsters, part fish, part bird, part reptile, fly out. The major himself was a fossil cased in stone.

The Old Master and the Inspector studied two muskets, and a blunderbuss it would have taken a giant to raise to shooting level. They studied an old clay pipe with a slender stem and a long bowl, and stamped on the bowl, a heart and a hand and the name of Parnell. They examined brass five-shilling pieces made from the broken, melted metal of old guns.

'Payment in kind,' said the Inspector, 'from greedy kings to needy soldiers.'

He jingled his own coins.

'Do you know, when I set the boys searching the battlefield we dug up musket balls as plentiful as blackberries or those edible nuts the pigs grub for?'

'How many of them,' moralised the Inspector, 'might have accounted for a good man's life.

''Twas a great work to collect all these things, boys,' he said. 'It's a pity that any relic of the past should be lost. Didn't the Lord himself say: Colligite quae superaverunt fragmenta ne pereant.'

We sat in horror in case he might ask us to translate but, gentleman that he was, he did the dirty work himself: 'Gather up the fragments that remain lest they be lost.'

'And furthermore, James, don't you think as a reward we could give them a holiday tomorrow?'

Our cheering rattled the objects in the glass cases. When the tumult had subsided the Old Master said, 'I'll give you one of these musket balls as a keepsake, Matthew. You can rattle it with your ha'pence.'

'My mother always said a rattler would never be a spender. I wish I could say she was right. I'd be a rich man today.'

In Irish too fast and idiomatic for us to follow the two old men talked together, then laughed loudly, until the Old Master choked and the Inspector turned purple.

From the junior room next door, separated from us only by a glass-and-wood partition, the voice of the Young Teacher haranguing his misfortunate pupils rose high in strident envy. He wasn't a very good teacher. If it hadn't been for the Old Master, whose assistant he was, the Inspector would have given him bad reports. He was a most dislikeable man: thin-lipped, ill-tempered, pointy-eyed, with a sideways beak of a nose and oiled, black hair pasted down flat and shining like a polished floor. His only virtue, if it could be counted a virtue, was that he was almost as good a sporting shot – snipe, duck, grouse, or pheasant – as the Mad Major, but it was said of him that, like a Frenchman, he'd shoot the sparrows in the hedges. He envied and elected to despise the Old Master who treated him with the charity of God.

Once peering and eavesdropping at the back window of one of the village pubs, Paddy and myself had caught the Young Teacher in action among the scruff who were his familiars.

'I could instruct him about real guns,' he said. 'Guns that shoot. Like this.'

Imaginary gun to shoulder he pivoted on his left heel, and sighted, followed and pinked an imaginary fowl. His claque applauded – he was paying for their drink.

'Living in the past like a mole in the ground,' he said. 'His guns are stopped up with clay like his deaf ears.'

Now, enraged by our cheers and delight, and by the camaraderie of the two old men, his voice, berating some boy, rose an octave higher.

The Old Master led the Inspector to the last of the glass cases and opened it, then looked long and sadly at the empty corner where the musket balls had been.

'Somebody,' he said quietly, 'seems to have removed them.'

There was a horrified silence. Every boy in the room looked fixedly at the digging wedge as if he expected it to give tongue and name the culprit.

'I suppose we are lucky that all the muskets are still with us,' the Old Master said.

'I'd put up a notice, James,' said the Inspector, 'warning all travellers: Heads down when passing this village. A clever boy could be a David and use those balls as slingshots.'

'When I was young,' said the Old Master, 'I was a dab hand with the sling myself.'

He closed the glass case slowly. He said, 'Boys, you found them once. I'll expect you to find them again.'

That was all, but to Paddy Sheehan it was worse than brutal words and birchings.

He was a sailor high in the swaying crow's nest. Close my eyes, open them again, and all around is the heaving limitless Pacific and, far on the skyline, the dark green palms of a coral island like a thumb-smudge on a painted wall. Close them again, open them again, the tattered mad major is bent over the begonias in his garden, the morning sun still glitters on the salmon pool above the double bridge and the Old Master, as small as a rabbit, is walking along the street towards his house.

On the green at the foot of the tree the story had it that Johnny Patterson, the famous clown, had once pitched his tent and joked and danced and sang. Because of that hallowed memory an old, broken-down clown, performer once at fairs and rural football games and now no longer fit for the road, had parked his caravan there to spend his last days under the shelter of the lime tree. He was unshaven and witless. The village was kind to him. No children mocked him – possibly because the illustrated bible-history used in the school had one vivid, exemplary picture of bears eating up boys who had mocked just such a man. For a few coppers he could paint, with some talent, gaudy landscapes and portraits that came fairly close to the originals, or play the fiddle by holding the bow in his teeth and sawing the instrument backwards and forwards or rattle bone-clappers in each hand and play a whistle with one side of his mouth and sing with the other, and simultaneously dance the Irish Washerwoman. The old horse that had drawn his caravan to haven was, like himself, no longer fit for journeying, so it idled and grazed on the commonage that was part of the battlefield and slept at night, like a dog, by the steps at the caravan door. When the clown emerged for his morning wash in a bucket of water, he roused the horse, gave him a sniff of oats in a basin and, as the Old Master said, day had officially begun in the village.

The clown washed. The Master talked to him and tapped the hide of the horse gently with his blackthorn. Paddy, masthead-high and swaying with the gentle wind, looked down on them and felt like Judas and wondered what the Master would say to the Inspector, his guest for a few days, when he returned from his morning walk and they breakfasted together. Would they talk of the missing musket-balls and of skill with the sling?

Part of the agony was that Paddy was an expert with the sling, and the whole world and half the windows in the parish knew it. His father used to say not without a certain pride, that half the profits of his shop went in putting back the panes Paddy smashed. One evening, when it was his turn to stay behind and tidy the senior room, he had fallen to thievery simply because, in a blinding flash of inspiration, he had realised that, while muskets were out, slings, for the adept, were still in. Then walking home, his trouser-pockets weighed down, his braces creaking with the strain, shame and guilt had overtaken him. How could he have done this to the Old Master? It was far worse than stealing. How could he make restitution? Restore them openly and admit his shame? Restore them as he had taken them: secretly? But suppose he was caught in the act and the effort at restoration mistaken for crime? To gain time he had buried them under the cork tree.

The Mad Major was running around his garden clapping his hands and leaping in the air. Chasing a butterfly?

The clown's old spavined horse tottered off towards the commonage.

The Old Master tapped on up the street and vanished into his house.

Smoke and the smell of cooking came up from the section of discarded rainspout that made a chimney for the caravan. Hunger and guilt in the high tree were miserable companions and, ironically, the blue innocence of the morning heaven seemed only grasping distance away.

Far on the fringe of the commonage the Young Teacher

fired his last morning shot and, Paddy fervently hoped, missed. That year was too mild for early duck although the Bully Cryan, and he was probably telling lies, said that one morning when he was out with the Young Teacher he saw a flight of at least four hundred passing – well out of range. Now, through a framework of leaves, Paddy watched the slow, homeward plodding of the Young Teacher and the Bully Cryan, his stupid, faithful Sancho Panza, one of the few boys in the school who, if civil war had been declared, would have gone with the Young Teacher against the Old Master. He was a surly steam-roller of a boy with close-cropped black hair and porcine features, a terror to the smaller boys because of his weight, but no skilled fighter and unwilling ever to try conclusions with Paddy, a quick mover and a leader of men. The Young Teacher, perhaps sensing the slavish weakness behind the bullying heaviness or, less likely, pitying a boy whose existence seemed so pointless, used him as a body-servant.

Bearing bag and gun he trudged along behind the Young Teacher. He was born to be a gilly. Paddy loftily surveyed their progress: from the open common into the fruit-bearing area where apples from bending branches sank to orchard grass or even plopped into small slow streams; through a maze of lanes and by higgledy-piggledy cottages bowered in laden trees, then round the corner by the church and across the green to halt at the foot of the lime tree.

'Run home now, Cryan,' said the Young Teacher.

'Yes, sir.'

'We had poor luck for duck.'

Paddy was delighted to hear it.

'But we'll do better next time.'

'Yes, sir.'

'Call to my house at twelve-thirty post meridiem.'

'Yes, sir.'

'My wife wants to send across a cooked pheasant to brighten the luncheon table for the Inspector.'

'Yes, sir.'

'Give him for once a taste of good cooking.'

'Yes, sir.'

'He's not likely to get it where he is.'

'No, sir.'

Among the leaves Paddy seethed. But then the thought of the Bully Cryan as an authority on cooking, good or bad, was so comic, and so sad, that his resentment rapidly melted. The Young Teacher went one way. Relieved of bag and gun and very likely without two pennies to clink in his pocket the Bully Cryan descended to the riverside lane where he lived. We could more easily have believed that the Young Teacher was being kind to the Bully and not merely using him if, as a recompense for all the gillying, any coin of the realm had ever changed hands.

The village was alive now.

From the byre behind his house the Soldier Sweeny, the shoe-maker, drove his one cow and two goats out to graze and deprecate on roadside hedges and insufficiently-fortified gardens. Back in the days of World War One, when the soldier had been clinked for drink, a sympathetic fellow-soldier and sentry had funnelled porter to him through the lock-up window and down the barrel of a rifle.

The pimply Badger Smith who worked for Paddy's father and in his spare time taught the village boys to use foul language was taking down the shutters from the butcher's shop.

One old voteen of a woman, dark in widow's weeds, was first into the church for mass, then three girls, the doctor's daughters, in light summer frocks and with coloured handkerchiefs, in obedience to Saint Paul, covering their heads.

At the door of the post-office a postman straddled a bike and pushed off towards the station to meet the train.

Window blinds went up wearily in lazy households. The tall tree swayed with a lulling gentle motion and, now that the first attack of hunger was over, he decided he'd stay aloft a little longer. His mother would assume that he had gone to mass. Besides he was growing fond of tree-living and he knew that once he put his foot back on the grass he would again assume the guilty weight of the cached musket-balls. Nearly three centuries ago they had whizzed through the air and the battlesmoke over the common, bringing death and destruction with them. Ill-luck, he felt, had followed them since.

Molly, the doctor's maid, neat and black-and-white, ran across to the newsagent's, her high heels clicking as clearly as castanets. Thoughtfully, the Badger rested on the block a cleaver he had raised and looked after her.

The mad major was gone from the garden and Paddy knew why. For the train was pulling out of the station and all of a sudden the glorious white racehorse the major owned was in the long, narrow, rising limestone field that went parallel with the railway track for a resounding four hundred yards. Glued by nature to the silver back the major raced and paced the horse against the train and, swaying on the tree, Paddy felt in his blood the thud of every marvellous hoofbeat.

'On the day of the battle,' the Old Master had said, 'legend has it that a chieftain from the Midlands was shot dead off his war-horse. And, riderless, the noble steed, stirrups and reins swinging wild, galloped halfways across Ireland to fall dead with a broken heart at the gate of its master's castle. You see, it knew that the day was lost.'

For ever in Paddy's mind a white horse, proud bitter messenger of defeat, hammered on and on across a darkening land.

His father in his gleaming new Austin pulled up at the shop, issued some instructions to the Badger, then drove away out of the village. There was a cattle-fair in a town twenty miles away.

The worshippers had long gone home from mass. On the gravel outside the church the parish priest was talking to the doctor. By now his mother would be beginning to wonder what was keeping him from his breakfast. But there was euphoric contentment, ease, exaltation in being up so high and swaying so gently as if you moved with the deep breathing of the earth and, although he knew he should descend and go home, his limbs wouldn't obey him.

With an empty potato-sack over his hunched shoulders Grandfather Cryan set off to pick cinders in the dump at the railway station. Ten minutes later the Burglar Cryan, one of the Bully's many uncles, set off with an iron rod in his hand and a wooden box containing a ferret, strapped to his back to catch rabbits. A gaunt, tubercular man, he was notable for three things: his skill in rabbit-catching; his having done time for breaking and entering; and once, at the corner of Brennan's smithy where he spent his spare time seated on an antique mounting-block whittling sticks, for having arisen patiently to knock down his virago of a mother-in-law because she had tavered him even beyond the endurance of a man who had uncomplainingly suffered much.

Ten minutes later the Poacher Cryan, the Bully's father, went by in another direction. He had once, by day, given his expert knowledge to help a group of fishery conservators stock a stretch of the river with fingerlings and then, by night, when the fish were grown, he had removed them illegally to barter them for drink or to feed them to his own brood.

The two small Cryans, one male, one female, each bearing two iron buckets, went from door to door collecting kitchen scraps for pig-swill. Behind them grandly strode the Bully wheeling a wooden handcart into which the buckets were emptied, and making certain, since he only played the servitor to the Young Teacher, that his smaller relatives did all the work. They could be a brother and sister. Or they could be cousins. There were, Paddy knew, scores or hundreds of Cryans. Nobody knew for certain how many because they were never seen all together in public. There were three generations of them living in the one lane in the one row of whitewashed cottages and it was suspected that they even had the great-grandfather, dead but stuffed, in the boarded-up cottage at the end of the lane. It was commonly accepted, too, that there had been so many Cryans in the British Army that, in spite of official histories and the alien names of Foch, Haig and Pershing, it was the Cryans all the time who had won the war. And once when a brother of the Burglar had died it was true that at the funeral one old shawled woman had said to another: God sees, Mary, that's the first of the Cryans ever died.

The Badger downed tools and, wiping big hands in apron, came to the door of the shop to teach the three Cryans a few more bad words, as if they didn't know enough already.

Two loafers emerged from a lane to join the Badger. The Bully moved on rapidly when he saw the Young Teacher's wife, strong in breasts and buttocks, vivid in high-piled, ash-blonde hair, orange sweater, tartan slacks, red shoes, coming with her shopping-basket down the street. She was the first woman in the village ever to wear trousers. She was fast, violent and dominating, and she drank, and it would seem that the Young Teacher had his own troubles: dirty shirts, an occasional black eye, and now and again a claw mark on his jaw that might have meant love but was scarcely the signature of domestic bliss. So as we grew up we learned that there were reasons for the Old Master's protective leanings towards his assistant.

Down the street she sailed, a stately ship of Tarsus bound for the isles of Javan or Gadire, with all her bravery on and tackle trim, sails filled and streamers waving. She addressed a few words to the Badger: admonitory words, Paddy guessed, because not the best beef ever grazed on the fat ground where Paddy had that morning set his dream-horse on grass was good enough to satisfy that woman. The Badger, standing in an obsequious crouch, listened attentively. The two loafers withdrew to a cowardly, diffident distance. But when she had dismissed the Badger and walked off down the street the three of them came together again like vultures over a delectably-decayed corpse, and studied the retreating movement of her swaying rear, radiant in ersatz tartan, and whispered and sniggered.

Paddy, if you can believe him, says that at that moment he saw all life like maggots on bad meat. Below his eyes the Badger and the two loafers swayed backwards and forwards as if they were on strings and, again if you can credit Paddy, an imaginative boy, straddle on a strong branch, his back to the trunk, he fell asleep. He will admit though that if he had really been asleep he could have fallen out of the tree. But if it wasn't true sleep, he says, it was a trance, and the world was all white horses and tartan women, and the acrid smoke of battle rolled over the black commonage and vicious musket-balls chipped the apples off the trees. The remote earth was his easy cradle.

When the trance had passed he looked down and saw the Bully Cryan, covered tray in hands, stepping out of the Young Teacher's doorway. There and then he knew why inexorable destiny had sent him up the tree.

The Young Teacher's wife who, in spite of her faults, was a good cook and very proud of her cooking had gone to great trouble about that particular Phasian bird.

Chestnut brown and cream and black, iridescent with specks of green and purple, its sad gentle face bright red and featherless, its spurs short and blunt, to tell of youth and tender flesh, the bird had given beauty to the woods beyond the battlefield and by the big river to which our river was but a tributary. Then the proud woman had sent forth her husband, the sharp-faced, mean-eyed hunter, and the hunter's gilly had gone like a retrieving hound to gather the soft bleeding body from the crushed grass.

The hanging, plucking, drawing of entrails, the trussing and roasting, could all have been part of a necromantic rite designed to mortify the Old Master and his kind, silver-haired wife, plain people who were content with plain fare. It was known that the Inspector was fond of his stomach.

The Young Teacher's wife didn't stuff the bird with two snipe as Brillat Savarin recommended, but she did ornament the cooked stern with a few tail feathers – a practice disapproved of, possibly on grounds of propriety, by Mrs. Beeton. She made the hollow, where the entrails had been, delicious with molten butter. She tied rashers over the breast before roasting. She prepared the fried breadcrumbs with which to serve it. She laid the savoury brown morsel, now devoid of life, that once had carried colour through the woods, on one of her best willow-pattern platters. She circled it with little rashers, crisp and rolled and pierced by toothpicks and coy as any Gallic escargots. She placed above it her most gleaming dish-cover and her whitest linen cloth. She steadied the tray in the gilly's hands and said, 'Cryan, don't waste one second. Are your hands clean? Go directly across the green. Don't trip or stumble. You clumsy fool.'

'Yes, ma'am.'

Then she went back to her husband and cold with triumph and drawn together by a common malice they drank gin and tonic for half an hour.

The first of Paddy that the Bully saw was his feet in the air as he swung like a pendulum for his leap to the grass. They were aggressive feet. They came so close to the precious tray that the Bully backed a step and almost stumbled. On the caravan steps the Clown was seated swabbing with a crust his midday meal, a greasy mess, from an iron pan.

'Mind your big feet,' said the Bully.

Then he saw Paddy crouching on the grass before him.

'They're looking for you, Sheehan,' he said. 'You'll be killed. Get out of my way.'

There was, as dearly he gripped the tray, the crack of panic in his voice.

'Who's looking for me?'

'Your mother asked me where you were.'

'In Mars,' said Paddy. 'I'm just back. I'm Jack the Giant-Killer. I was up the beanstalk.'

He touched the white linen. He knew his Shakespeare. He said, 'What find I here?'

'You'll be killed for this, Sheehan.'

'Who'll kill me?'

He lifted off the cloth and dish-cover and dropped them on the grass. The brown body, bedecked with feathers, ringed with rashers, was exposed, and the very air under the tree was as good as edible. To look and sniff, the Clown moved closer. Transfixed with horror at the incredible event the Bully was helpless: his hands were bound to the tray.

'The Teacher,' he said, 'will slay you.'

'Sucks to the Teacher.'

'I'll tell him you said sucks.'

'Sucks to you, too. Yum yum.'

The first rasher was gone. He gave the second to the clown.

'Yum yum,' said the Clown.

He rubbed his belly and smacked his lips.

'Eat up,' said Paddy.

To the appreciative Clown he gave the left leg of the pheasant. When the Bully, with tears in his eyes, opened his mouth again to protest Paddy popped a rasher into it and, sizzling hot as it was, it went down in one agonised gulp. With the trembling of the Bully's hands the platter rattled on the tray.

'Careful with the delph,' said Paddy, 'or Daisy Coloured Trousers will smack hims iddle bottom.'

He took four splendid bites of pheasant. He restored the mangled corpse and the dish-cover and the cloth, on which he delicately wiped his fingers.

'Go thy way in peace, B. Cryan Esquire,' he said. 'Sin no more.'

He went back up the tree. It seemed the only place to go. Where did David go after he had eaten the loaves of sacrifice?

And the Bully who hadn't the wit or the courage to turn back went on at a trot to lay the half-burnt offering between the Old Master and the Inspector.

There was hell to pay afterwards of course, because Daisy Coloured Trousers cried to heaven for vengeance and Paddy's

parents had to take punitive measures and the Old Master
had to pretend that he did. But the days of the Bully Cryan
were numbered and Paddy was the hero of the school. He
had discovered, too, that he could really think and size things
up and get control of life by sitting up in the lime tree and
meditating. So a fair share of his boyhood and youth was spent
up that tree. Man, at times he felt, was meant to live in trees;
and one sullen, clouded afternoon when the white horse had
flashed like a star along the narrow field, and when the last
puff of the pacing train had faded away towards the coast, he
heard the Old Master call him from the Green.

'The Lord called to Zaccheus,' said the old man. 'Come
down, Paddy Sheehan, come down. Are you a boy or
a bird?

'By eating a bird, Paddy,' he said, 'it may be that you
became a bird. A condign punishment. According to a maxim
in civil law, Paddy, qui non habet in aere luat in pelle, or
he who can't pay in coin will have the price taken out of his
hide. Come for a walk with me. Be the staff of my old age.'

By lanes twisting around orchards they walked towards
the common. That was a rich year for apples and in the dark
day, under the heavy sky, the fruit glowed like gems. Shuffling
along with short steps – he had the arthritis bad in the feet
– the Old Master leaned on Paddy's shoulder and now and
again gave him a shrewd, sideways look from under the wide
brim of a black hat that he wore in memory of a fashion of
his youth.

'And talking of birds, Paddy, history has it that the men
of this village were once geniuses at the netting of plover.
'Twas said they could even take them out of the air. A feat
only possible, believe me, if the netter is the extreme expert.
Most bird-catchers have to wait until the bird actually lodges
before springing the net. But then we have had many famous
men in this place. Did you ever know that the major swam on
a line under the waters of the Nile and, in spite of an encounter
with a crocodile crossed safely from bank to bank. A travelled,

amazing man. They say he'd have been knighted by the King of England only he'd never use his handkerchief. Perhaps it was in the dust of the lining of his coat-pocket that the seed of the cork tree came home to us.'

High in the lime-branches Paddy could escape from the cork tree and its grisly secret, but down on the ground the leprous monster followed him about: a crooked, accusing, many-armed ghost.

Ahead of them the common-land, once a part of the place of battle and death, was black under rolling seaward clouds.

'There's a fury in the skies and clouds now, Paddy, wasn't in them in my youth. Or perhaps as the years pass you read more meaning into the colours and the motions of the clouds. But, young or old, I always thought that this little stream here made the sweetest of all sounds.'

Bearing with it a few apple-droppings from the orchards that fringed the common the stream went onward placidly to fall down the slope by the schoolhouse. Strong water-cress grew thickly where the water splayed out below a one-arched bridge. Retrieving a few apples, Paddy plucked also for the Master some cress with its metallic burning flavour, and munching apples and cress, they went on together. From somewhere, far away and unseen on the great plain, came the pop-popping of sportsmen's guns: faint echoes of a lost battle.

'I wasn't much older than yourself, Paddy, the day they dug the skeleton of the soldier out of the Black Trench ahead of us there. Clutching his gun just the way he fell two hundred years before. They dug themselves into the trench and fought to the last. There were a lot of old guns and bones, and coins scattered among the bones. Did they plan to spend them when the day was done? Did they rattle them in their pockets the way the Inspector does?'

The Inspector, deprived of the musket-balls, was, like the cork tree, an accusing ghost.

'Some day I'd like to see a stone raised here, Paddy, by the Black Trench and in memory of all the dead.'

'Would the big tree have been there on the day of the battle, Master?'

'It could well have been.'

'If a man was up there could he have seen it all?'

'The cavalry. The foot. The cannon. The camp-followers. The dead and dying.'

'The war-horse that went home alone.'

'Or just glimpses through gaps in the smoke, Paddy. Old-time battles were smoky affairs.'

'If men lived in trees they'd see a lot more, Master, wouldn't they?'

'You're a great lad for the trees, Paddy?'

'I like trees, Master.'

'Climbing up on high, Paddy, a man comes closer to himself. The saints and the sages and the Lord himself proved that. There's that mountain in the West of Ireland where Saint Patrick climbed up to pray. You'll go to it sometime on the pilgrimage. Thousands of people and lots of them fasting and barefooted going up like saints or goats over sharp stones in the early morning. Then the sun comes out and the mist breaks and down below you see the hundreds of islands in Clew Bay, the islands of the blest, and spread out beyond them the whole ocean, infinity, eternity. That's what Saint Patrick was after. People climb up, Paddy, to repent of their sins.'

'Yes, Master.'

'When you were up the tree, Paddy, did you ever find out why you broke the sweeping-brush and the floorboards?'

'Yes, Master,' he said.

It had been an evening of brown fresh in the river, and the trout below at the double bridge gaping their mouths wide for bait-feeding, and Paddy and the Bully Cryan and two others had been detailed as a punishment for lessons missed to stay behind and clean and dust the entire school. Taut with vexation Paddy had suddenly, and only imperfectly knowing

why, started to hammer the floor with his brush until he made
bits of the brush and smashed a hole in the floor-boards.

'It was to frighten Bully Cryan, Master.'

'Did it succeed?'

'A bit, I think. Coming down the tree frightened him more.'

'It would. The violent are seldom really frightened by
violence. But they would be by a blinding light on the road or
by a descent from above. And did you ever discover, Paddy,
why you ate the pheasant?'

'I hate the taste of pheasant, Master. Nobody should ever
eat those lovely birds. And it drives you mad with thirst.'

'Not an act of greed so, or even of hunger. But perhaps an
act of repentance.'

'It was to make up for the musket-balls, Master. The
musket-balls are in a box in a hole under the roots of the
cork tree.'

'That I know, Paddy. Like yourself I'm a great man for
trees. But too old and stiff to go on the branches now, Paddy,
I content myself with poking among the roots.'

'You knew all the time, so.'

'No, Paddy. Only since the morning I saw you running up
the tree. The day of the pheasant.'

'You knew all the time I was up the tree? Even when I
was missing?'

'What goes up must come down, Paddy. I knew you
weren't lost or drowned. I knew you couldn't go far astray
if you were merely closer to heaven than anybody else in the
village: thinking your own thoughts.'

'We'll walk as far as the cork tree, Paddy,' he said, 'and
reclaim that box of musket-balls. Nobody but ourselves need
be any the wiser.'

They walked to the cork tree and back to the schoolhouse
and the museum was complete again.

'And some day, Paddy, when you've a particularly good
speckled trout, make a present of it to the Young Teacher's
wife. I hear she's great on fish sauces. And even if her

husband's a fine shot he still isn't so good with the rod and line. Not patient enough, perhaps.'

'Yes, Master.'

As it happened the next good fish Paddy got was a spring salmon which Daisy Coloured Trousers gratefully accepted and expertly cooked. She sent ample savoury cuts to the Old Master's wife and to Paddy's mother. On his next visit, too, the Inspector got his portion of the musket-balls, one of which, to the day of his death, ornamented his watch-chain.

The white horse went to the Curragh and the Phoenix Park, Baldoyle, Tramore, Galway, Listowel and, in the end, to Newmarket and won all before him. But as the mad major, who increased his fortune, by stake-money and the lavish laying of bets, said, 'It was to be expected. It was on the cards. It was in the stars and in signs in the heavens. Was there ever in history another horse that was trained by a steam-engine?'

# The house in Jail Square

When my mother went to school as a day pupil in the Mercy Convent in the town of Clonelly she lodged in Jail Square in the house of a respectable widow who had two daughters aged between twenty and thirty. Thirty years later when my mother sent me down from the mountains to the Brothers' School in the same town, she lodged me in the House in Jail Square with two stranded, derelict, time-worn, desiccated beldames aged somewhere between fifty and sixty. They were happier people, I soon found out, when my mother knew them, or perhaps in her days they had hope and things seemed different. Or perhaps, as I had reason to think, they just didn't like males. I was twelve years old, a timid biddable boy, at least as far as elderly ladies were concerned, and for two school terms I lived in slavery to Maryanne and Ellen. During the Christmas holidays I was unable even to begin to reveal to my mother the depth of my servitude to those two female dragons. In their cold grey stone mansion I was message-boy, gardener, waiter, scavenger, scullery-maid, chamber-maid, butler, duster, polisher, and something to scold, abuse and lecture. They would have had no life without me and, to give the situation its irony, my mother underwrote their tyranny to the extent of thirty shillings weekly.

'Aloysius, you will run home punctually at lunch hour.'

That was practically my morning greeting.

Sleep still in my eyes, the sour prospect of school before me, I would feebly protest, 'Half-hour. We don't get an hour.'

'Aloysius, don't quibble. At lunch hour you must go for the daily paper and do another message.'

Give me the penny now and I'll get the paper on the way home. That'll save time. I'll be biffed if I'm late for afternoon school.'

'We will give you the penny at the fit and proper moment.'

'What other message?'

'Never mind, Aloysius. Just you do as we say. That's what your dear mother would wish you to do. We still have to decide about the other message.'

So my lunch half-hour went into sprinting. In Clonelly, a hilly town, Jail Square was at the top of one high hill. To get to the Brothers' School you descended and ascended again along Old Castle Street. The school was halfway up that street and the shops of the town were all at the top of it. I found it was easier on the wind and sinews if I pelted up the steep blue pavement of Old Castle Street to the rhythm dreamed up by that Wizard of the North and bore of the schoolroom, Sir Walter Scott. With my lips compressed and breathing through my nose as somebody had told me the supreme athletes did, I repeated in my mind, 'Fleet foot on the corrie, sage counsel in cumber, red hand in the foray, how sound is thy slumber.' It was rubbish, but it helped me to run, swept me ultimately back to school in time, and diminished the aggregate of corporal punishment.

On days when Walter Scott wouldn't work in harness with me I thought, to speed my stride, of the great running horses of that season. As I'll point out shortly, I had good and sufficient reason to know their noble names and, although I should have hated them, I didn't. There was Ramtapa who had hard luck at Newmarket where Flares gave a fine performance; Corofin who was fancied for the Irish Cesarewitch in spite of the claims of Spion Hill, Lady Ellen, Call Him, Silver Salt, Ringwood Sun, Yellowdine, Gorgia, Glen Levin. There was the slinky femme fatale, Serpolette, and Statarella, lovely as a poppy, who was headlined as the best of the fillies; and Speakeasy II, who in spite of the bibulous habits of himself and his sire, got the vote for the chief event in Naas; and Eastern Ford and Foxy and Port Lester. They were all allies in my sprint. It saddens me to think that by now they may all be dead.

Clutched in one hand I would have the penny that Maryanne had given me for the day's paper. Clutched in the other hand I would have the two sixpenny bits – sixpence each way – wrapped in paper, that Ellen had given me for the bookie. The name of the chosen runner was written on the paper. Idling on the steep slope of Old Castle Street my free-and-easy school companions, who had no lunchtime chores to do, would click their tongues or catcall or whistle rhythmically to the beat of my feet. As well as I could, and that wasn't completely, I closed my eyes and ears to their presence.

'Run, Alo, run.'

'You'll never have the bet laid in time.'

'He couldn't run so well up hill if we hadn't put the shoes on him the day he came down from the mountains.'

'Nothing but bare feet up where he comes from.'

'Run, Alo, run rabbit, run, run, run.'

The House in Jail Square looked solid from the outside. It was one of eight grey stone houses in which the higher officials of the prison had lived when there had been a prison high on a hill where the river escaped from the last red metal bridge and curved northwards away from the town. But, in spite of its appearance of dry stone solidity, that house was musty with dry rot and when you moved in it everything rattled or jingled. There were hundreds of things to rattle and jingle. Maryanne and Ellen had accumulated the years around them in whatnots congested with china ornaments, pictures of officers in antique dress-uniforms or noble ladies standing languidly where smooth marble steps descended to smoother artificial water, in useless creaking furniture, clocks that didn't work, stones shaped fantastically by some remote ocean, sea-shells on mantelpieces, family portraits by the score, and coloured glass balls used as floats by trawler fishermen. The most cluttered, clinking room in the house was the museum of a drawing-room where the ritual of choosing the horse of the day was observed with unholy solemnity. On Saturday mornings when I was free from school, and provided I was sufficiently advanced with my housework, I was allowed or compelled to witness it.

'Have you the hatpin, Ellen?'

'I have. The Lord direct us, Maryanne.'

'Pray, Aloysius, pray.'

Maryanne's right hand enclosing Ellen's left and both their hands grasping a hatpin, long and bent like a sabre, they would sneak up on the previous day's evening paper where it lay prostrate and helpless on a couch.

'Sacred Heart guide our hand.'

Plunge and then stab and the broad couch was pierced and the horse or mare impaled. It was a savage rite, and when I watched it I waited to hear the whinnying scream of a noble animal wounded by witchcraft. For I loved horses just because they were horses, and I loved old sporting prints and photographs of horses, and fast-galloping horses in the acrid dust of western films, and the noise of the hooves of carthorses on the old streets of the town, and the sound of a trotting horse pulling a trap on a country road on a June evening. Maryanne and Ellen, you'd know to look at them, may have seen but never loved a horse.

Maryanne – tall, scrawny, brown-skinned, ribbed like the skeleton of a salt sea-herring, as prickly as a blossomless whin bush, with black, brooding eyes and a nose like a beak and a distinct moustache – would inspect the mutilated newspaper and read out the name of the perforated horse, 'It's a nice name today.'

'It could be a lucky name.'

Small, round-faced, with soft, rubicund cheeks that bore no relation to her hard black nut of a heart, Ellen would write the name on a slip of paper, wrap the paper around the two sixpenny bits, never, oh God never, not even once by accident or error, around a single shilling. Times I thought they must be minting their own sixpennies.

'The boy's day-dreaming, Maryanne.'

'Arouse yourself, Aloysius. Thinking long never buttered bread.'

'Here's the money for the message. The name's on the paper.'

'And don't dare to turn back on the way. It's bad luck to turn back. Did you put on your left or your right shoe first this morning?'

'My right.'

'We hope you're truthful. It's bad luck to put on the left shoe before the right.'

'Saint Colmcille was being pursued by enemies,' said Ellen, 'and they caught him because he put on the left shoe first.'

'And the saint put an everlasting curse on anyone after him who would ever put on the left shoe before the right.'

I always left unexpressed my sceptical feeling that Saint Colmcille, like the Franciscans a mile outside the town, would have worn sandals. Yet such is the power of early conditioning that, as God is my judge, to this day I always put the right shoe on before the left.

'And don't waste a second,' said Maryanne, 'even if it is Saturday morning.'

'You have the potatoes to scrub and the hall-floor to polish.'

'Your pocket money will have to go to help to replace the flower-pot you knocked off the pedestal and down the basement stairs last Saturday.'

'Sheer vandalism. Boys are destructive demons.'

'The good flower-pot our mother left us with the Saint Joseph's lily. The lily will never bloom again.'

'And when you come back you can run out again for the morning paper.'

'Couldn't I do the two messages together?'

'Do as we say, Aloysius. You have an idle day from school.'

'The devil and idle hands, you know.'

'Think of Montgomery,' said Maryanne, 'the man who was

hanged for murder in the days of the Old Jail. In the death cell he cursed the idle hours and companions that led him to the scaffold.'

In Maryanne's stygian cosmos both saints and sinners spent a lot of time cursing things and people.

'Run now. Stop to speak to nobody. Idle words never sowed corn.'

It was at least a momentary relief to run from them, steeply up Old Castle Street, shutting my agonised soul to the vision of the freedom other boys enjoyed on Saturday morning. I was fleetfoot on the corrie, whatever that was. I was a horse, I was a jockey, I was a centaur, I was Pegasus, Bucephalus, and Tipperary Tim who won the Grand National at a hundred to one. The town's blue, grain-picking pigeons scattered before my galloping hooves. I was cossacks, I was United States cavalry, I was cowboys and Indians and the Light Brigade. I was Ascot and Aintree and the Curragh of Kildare and the Dublin Horse Show, and the colour and the paddocks, the cheers, the satin sheen of bay mares and black stallions. For a few galloping moments the silence and gloom of the musty old house were as remote as the death-cell with its curses and repentant statements before hanging.

My most satisfactory release from Maryanne and Ellen – they couldn't deny me fresh air – led, in my odd moments of leisure, out of the Square through the arched gateway of the Old Jail. Once through the gateless arch, the echoes of your feet clanking on the flagstone like metal, you were out into complete freedom on a windy escarpment high above the looping river. By constant quarrying for other building the strong walls of the Jail had been reduced to an archaeological pattern, and the seasons had mercifully half-clothed the grey remains in nettles, dock-leaves and parched yellow grass. On the dusty flagstone, where prisoners had once stood to hear bolts barred behind them and to know despair, I stood and sensed liberation and saw far away the blue curves of my own mountains. The best and longest time I ever spent there was the sunny day of the horse-jumping and the military tattoo in the flat holm beyond the river. There went the wonderful horses, curvetting, rising and descending in the most graceful of jumping dances, taking or refusing walls or fences, displaying dressage, melting their own sensitive moods into the skills of the riders. No daft old women in a dark house could prick them with a hatpin. I wanted so badly to be across the river and down on the flat land with the crowds, but that week my pocket money had gone down the drain to compensate for two soup plates that had slipped to destruction when I was washing the dishes; and those two hags made the confiscation of the pocket money my mother sent me appear in the light of a favour.

'Aloysius, when will you learn to be careful?'

'We don't really like making you pay for the damage you do.'

'But we don't want to let your mother know you're so destructive. It would break her heart.'

The day of the horse-jumping, too, was the day I first saw the inscribed stone. A rustle in the weeds, a rat, set me hunting and poking, stick in hand, through the ground-pattern of small, coffin-narrow shapes that had once been cells. Insects scurried away from the stick into mazes of yellow sun-starved stems, and there lay the damp, fallen stone sharply-lettered to do honour to justice: Thomas Henry Montgomery was hanged here for the murder of William Glass. My first chill thought was that it was a bitter thing to hang any man in such a corner of weeds and crawling desolation. But then my imagination couldn't help rebuilding the confining walls, the cell, the scaffold, the trap, the dangling rope. The morning knell tolled. Towards this corner the slow, heavy steps approached. The parson prayed the last prayer. The blind-folded body dropped like lead. The neck cracked. The helpless pinioned feet swinging in a pendulum could have cut the air just where my head and shoulders were.

The relief it was to find that the walls were not really around me, that I could be an Indian on a pony and trot back to the bluff above the river and, hand shading eyes, look down on the pale-faces at their capers in the showgrounds and see the smoke signals of my own people spiralling and puffing up from blue hills that seemed as far away as Montana. Out there in the evening behind those curved hills the old men would be walking to the forge at the crossroads. Old men were my favourite people. They were complete, and alive like bushes; and for three of the old men of our mountains I had a particular veneration.

Old Paddy Horish had made his son a priest and, in the process, spent two hundred pounds. In those days on the mountain, where cautious men had the heart in twopence, that was big money. For ever after he judged the magnitude of any enterprise by whether or not it cost two hundred pounds. At Taggart's smithy, outside in summer, inside in winter by the glowing forge, Paddy, silent and thoughtful, his life's great work accomplished, listened while Chuck Taggart, the smith, and the other men talked of the news of the world. The Germans were to build the biggest airship the world had ever seen.

'Do you think now, Chuck, would it cost two hundred pounds?'

The Yankees were putting up in New York a building would scrape the stars.

'Do you think now, Chuck, would it cost two hundred pounds?'

Next week the British would launch on Belfast Lough a liner a mile long.

'Do you think now, Chuck, would it cost two hundred pounds?'

Nobody ever laughed. Paddy's standard of measurement was no more comic than the twelve inch-rule or old Peter Scott's one and only known way of judging the desirability of a woman. From as high on Broughderg Mountain as human life could exist Peter Scott rode bareback on a white jennet to the smithy to punctuate the fine talk with lament for mischance in marriage: I always thought I would marry a fine, healthy, red-cheeked girl.

The wife the Lord had allowed him was yellow-faced and ailing, a drain on his resources in doctor's bills, a valiant sufferer but no great bearer of sons and no use at all in a heavy harvest or at carrying pots of spuds to the pigs. As the women of the two worlds of Erin were, by the power of the Dagda, the father of the gods, paraded in vision before the eyes of the lovesick Aengus, the sun-god, so, through the mind of old Peter Scott, all the strong girls he had never possessed passed like a procession of buxom, dancing village maidens in a festival in Faust: 'I always thought I would marry a fine, healthy, red-cheeked girl.'

The talk would always touch on a consideration as profound as the nature of the First Cause: When would Big Joe Gormley, who was bedridden, allow his son-in-law to move the five-gallon keg of poteen embedded in the thatch since the day of wrath when the bishop of the diocese made the distilling, and transporting or consuming of illicit whisky a reserved sin. On the bed from which he would never arise, Joe, once the mountain's best distiller and most furious drunkard, had developed religious scruples. It was a sight to see him haul himself to a sitting position with the aid of a rope tied to the foot of the bed and look in love and horrors of remorse at that symbol of past sin, the brown protruding belly of the keg.

'We'll drink it at his wake,' Chuck the smith would say. 'We'll drink the bishop's health.'

And Chuck, who sang bass in the parish choir, would roar out to the rhythm of swinging hammers and flying sparks the words of a randy old Limerick ballad:

> 'And there, by my sowl, were the priests in a bunch
> Round a big roaring fire drinking tumblers of punch,
> Singing Ballinamona, ho ro,
> And the juice of the barley for me.'

'There was a robber in London yesterday,' somebody reading the paper would say, 'stole a jewel as big as your fist from the flat of a film actress.'

'Do you think now, Chuck, would it cost two hundred pounds?'

Those were my mountains and those my beloved old men, and out there was the happy holiday freedom of my home: hedges, laughter, hay-making, strong tea on the windy, sunny, upland bog at the saving of the turf, running on white roads, and the Rooskey river wriggling for ever down its long valley. There was a grey heron always haunted the one pool in the Rooskey river. His day-long meditation, broken only by an odd lightning dart at the sweetness of a speckled trout, was my perfect symbol of content and peace. The world, as he saw it, was water like moving crystal, clean sand and silver gravel. Looking down now, from my height, on the deep soiled river escaping from the town's sprawling limbs my heart made my eyes transfer the heron from the happy mountains to that tired, ravished water and, seeing the heron, I saw home and heard the Rooskey river and the wind in rowan trees and whin bushes, and the contented garrulity of men as old as the Fenians, and the melodeon at a mountainy dance and the laughter of the young – until the shriek of round-faced Ellen, with the voice of barbed wire, recalled me to the shades of the prison house.

'Aloysius. Stop idling, boy. It's time and more than time to prepare for tea.'

Then back through the gateway, where happy men had once passed to freedom, I went to dust and polish, wash dishes, peel potatoes. Times, meditating on my life in Jail Square, I'd think also the fine thing it could be to be hanged decent and have it all over with.

I told them about my discovery of the murder stone.

'To think of it lying there all those years,' said Maryanne, 'as a lasting testimony to the wickedness of man.'

'Like the Ten Commandments graven in stone,' said Ellen.

I was rash enough to ask them who Thomas Henry Montgomery had been.

'He was a policeman,' Maryanne said.

'What would a policeman be doing murdering?'

'Don't contradict, Aloysius. He was a policeman, as we said. A high officer. He was a wicked man and he's damned in hell. He cursed the hour that ever he was born.'

'Idleness and evil companions,' said Ellen.

In bits and scraps of sombre dialogue I heard from them, by way of homily, the story of the famous case. It had been a good old-fashioned Irish murder, direct as dynamite. 'Twas with the sharpened point of a file Montgomery did it, striking Glass in the ear, as he stooped, totting and computing, over his banker's desk.

'Pretending all the while to be his friend,' said Ellen. 'Oh, the rascality of men.'

'Glass was no better,' said Maryanne. 'There was something at the trial that he knew about his sister and Montgomery.'

'Poor woman. Betrayed between two villains.'

'There was that in it too, as well as money. Drink and gambling, debts and evil passion.'

'And there was a coward of a man from your part of the country, Aloysius, a farmer who saw the murder with his own two eyes and was afraid to say a word about it.'

'He feared the police would say he did it.'

'The police would say anything.'

'He drove past the bank standing up in his cart at the very moment Montgomery struck the fatal blow. He could see in through the top half of the bank window.'

'Years afterwards, on his deathbed, he confessed what he saw.'

'And Montgomery rifled the safe and hid the money in a wood.'

'And didn't the flood come and wash the notes down the stream, and a little boy saw them and told his father.'

'The hand of God.'

'Working in mysterious ways.'

'Grinding slowly, but exceedingly small,' said Ellen.

'Drink and gambling.'

'And sin and idleness, Maryanne.'

'Indeed, yes. Let his fate be a warning to all young men.'

My discovery of the stone enabled them for days to dwell happily, all the time pointing morals for my benefit, in the shadow of the murder. If I was dilatory in rising in the morning or in my lunchtime gallop, or slovenly in washing, scrubbing or polishing, or merely happily absent with my own thoughts and the heron in the Rooskey river, I was reminded of the fate of Thomas Henry Montgomery. They quoted, or invented, his death-cell speech of repentance, his bewailing of bad company, his renunciation of the world – which meant, according to Maryanne, all his fellow males. The thought of the accident, the hand of God, that had betrayed him, disturbed even my moments of contemplation above the big river. For every tiny island of foam struggling away from the weir became a pound note, eloquent of robbery and murder, drifting on for ever to find some horrible, eternal sea. Then home from school I came one day to find the stone enthroned on the broken lily's pedestal in the narrow polished hallway. With washing soda and hot water they had scoured it in a big zinc bath. The lettering stood out sharp and harsh as a recrimination. The daily dusting of the stone became part of my duties. It was the mercy of God, I thought, whatever about his vengeful hand, that they demolished the scaffold after the hanging of Montgomery. Dusting and scrubbing a scaffold would be uphill work.

'That there's a historic stone,' Maryanne said. 'He was the last man ever to get the rope in the Old Jail.'

'The very last,' said Ellen.

'Not but that there were many since in this town,' said Maryanne, 'would have benefited from similar treatment.'

'We could name their names,' said Ellen.

* * *

It was Red Cunningham and the new lodger who in their different ways sowed within me the seeds of revolt. Left to myself I'd have been a sheep for ever. Red Cunningham was a mountain ram. He was small, snub-nosed and freckled, with baggy tweed pants that were too long for him, and a blue serge jacket too tight for him and spotted like an archipelago with assorted stains and straining to snapping point at one brown incongruous button. Sharp blue eyes peeped out like the eyes of an animal watching from under a burning bush of red, red hair. There never was hair as red as his. The nailed boots he wore were made for hard usage in rough places. They rattled like castanets on the blue pavement of Old Castle Street. They were too big for him, and the square black toes that would never take a shine turned up like the toes of Dutch clogs. But the first day a town boy made, in his presence, the inevitable joke about the short length of time it was since the barefooted country boys had been shod, Red Cunningham used the dull, ungainly boots to doleful effect. It was against all rules of the ring and fair fighting, but the display was awesome. The offending town boy, tall, athletic, a bit of a boxer, struck time and again at the wild red head but, with all his height, reach and science, he might as well have been playing a tin whistle. Like mechanical hammers, and with merciless precision the boots worked over his shins and knees, and when Red had him howling, and marked so that he limped for a week, Red made his only tight-lipped comment, 'Damme, you'll know more about boots the next time.'

He was the only man I ever knew who said damme, but long afterwards I heard it was common usage in his part of the country.

But, savage as he could be when roused, he was to me, first, a well of sympathy and then a shining example. He never jeered or whistled when I galloped up Old Castle Street. Sharing a desk with me in school he, with cunning kindness – he never looked more like a compassionate ferret than at that moment – drew from me the true story of my life in the house in Jail Square.

'Damme, they say in the town that when that Maryanne one go to a whist-drive she cheats with one hand and has the rosary beads under the table in the other.'

He made me laugh. He knew all the talk of the town about my two dragons.

'Damme, I wouldn't stand for that treatment.'

'What can I do?'

'Tell them.'

I told him about the gullibility of my mother.

'Damme, your mother's a fool. Tell her the truth.'

'She'd never credit it. Nobody would.'

'I do. I'd do something. I'd take the boot to that Maryanne one.'

He made me laugh again.

'Up and tell them you're no skivvy. Tell them, damme, to wash their own spuds.'

Then one momentous evening he came clattering up the flagged garden pathway to the door of the house in Jail Square, to borrow my *Elementa Latina* – he was always mislaying or losing his own books. Visitors were as rare as laughter in that house, very likely because normal human beings were repelled by the claw-like curiosity; the glittering eyes, the drilling, searching questions of Maryanne. She was on fire to know everything about everybody and Cunningham was welcomed like a bird into a trap and, to his mystification, put sitting with a cup of tea in his hand, on a hard chair, in the exact geographical centre of the dungeon of a kitchen. Around him there was, as always, the effluvium of cigarette butts for he and all his many brothers, and possibly his many sisters, had been chain smokers from about the age of four. In hands stained with nicotine up to the wrists, and devoid of any but the merest chewed stumps of finger-nails, he clutched cup, saucer and spoon and a slice of seed-cake no thicker than a tram ticket. The knot on his twisted rope of a necktie was no bigger than a dried pea.

'You're a studious young boy, I'd say,' said Maryanne.

'I do my best, ma'am.'

'Very fond of his Latin,' said Ellen.

She was like somebody saying that the dog liked bones.

'There's worse than Latin,' Cunningham conceded.

'What part of the country would you come from?' said Maryanne.

'Ardstraw, ma'am.'

'Any relation of the Master Cunningham who taught school there?'

'He's my father, ma'am.'

'Goodness, how interesting,' said Ellen. 'That's where the boy gets the love of the learning.'

'How many brothers and sisters have you?'

Unless you knew the red man as well as I did you wouldn't have noticed the twitching of his feet that told his blood was rising.

'Twenty-two of us. All on the baker's list, thank God, and all well fed.'

'Goodness, what a lot of children to have. Your poor mother,' said Ellen.

'She's quite well-off and happy, ma'am, thank you.'

'Are they all as red in the head as you?' said Maryanne.

'Half red and half black.'

'What colour are your parents?'

'My mother's as grey as a badger and my father's as bald as a coot.'

'But the poor woman,' said Ellen. 'All those children.'

'Damme, more than you'll ever have by the look of you,' said Red Cunningham.

The descending body of Montgomery the murderer jerked no more fearfully when the neck snapped than did the bodies of Maryanne and Ellen in response to that statement.

'How dare you,' said Ellen.

'That's no way to speak to ladies,' said Maryanne.

'It's a good way, damme, to teach pokenoses to mind their own business.'

'You're a vile boy,' said Ellen.

'Leave this house,' said Maryanne.

'Observe me dust, ma'am, and thanks for the tea and the cake.'

Although to this day I can hardly believe it, he left the house unscathed and in triumphant possession of the last word. Perhaps the continuing roll and clog-rattle of his boots would have made mockery of any attempt to reduce him by a valedictory reproof. But the storm burst as we heard the door closing.

'Aloysius, you are never again to speak to that boy.'

'If I told your mother the company you keep.'

'But I sit beside him at school.'

'The vile odour of nicotine,' said Maryanne.

'I could have swooned,' said Ellen.

'And his language,' said Maryanne.

'We'll speak to the Brothers. We'll have him put to sit somewhere else.'

'We could have him expelled. We could write letters about him to the parish priest.'

But somehow they never did speak to the Brothers or, if they did, the Brothers paid no heed to them and, if they wrote to the parish priest, he too disregarded their complaints. Red Cunningham and myself went on sailing the same ship and by degrees the seeds of sedition took root in my soul. All that was needed for open revolt was the new lodger in Jail Square.

The new lodger came in the spring at the same time as the frenzy of preparation began for the annual whist-drive in the pillared courthouse – a benefit for the school's athletic club. The tidings of the new arrival were simply, if indirectly, announced to me when in the basement scullery I was scrubbing the mud off the nine potatoes allotted for Saturday's lunch.

'Aloysius,' Maryanne called down the stairs, 'have you scrubbed the nine?'

'Yes, miss. Almost.'

'Then scrub another three.'

The new lodger was a schoolgirl, the child of some rich relation of Maryanne and Ellen.

Red Cunningham said, 'Somebody to share the skivvying with you.'

It didn't turn out that way for, although Red Cunningham knew about boots, cigarette butts, and the tickling of brown trout, he still had a lot to learn about the oddities of women. The new lodger meant more than three more potatoes to scrub, for, since I was the official bootblack, there were also more shoes to polish. She did help at the dish-washing, but even at that her superior airs made her so obnoxious that her aid was an aggravation. She was plump and bespectacled. She was two years older than me. She went to school to the Mercy nuns and Maryanne and Ellen told me time and again, was highly regarded by them. She was a brilliant scholar, they said, she was a paragon of learning and of all the graces, virtues and accomplishments. She carried off prizes and scholarships by the cartload. She played the piano, and she sang, and one of my new duties was to sit and listen.

'Divine,' said Ellen.

She was, in fact, a pampered, overbearing brat, and why I'm not the world's meanest misogynist I'll never know. She also made a fourth for whist in the practice games in which Maryanne and Ellen were engaged as desperately and viciously as they were in the daily stabbing of the horses; for when they went to a whist-drive they went all out to win.

'Whist, I'm sick of whist,' I said to Red Cunningham. 'I loathe the sound of the word.'

He mocked me. He said, 'Up in Freddy the Shoemaker's select boarding house we don't even know what it means. Poker's the game for men.'

'I missed my Latin today and got bashed because I had no time to learn anything. It's as much as they'd do to give you time to go to sleep. They stay awake all night, whispering to each other, planning crooked deals.'

'Leave the place. Come down to Freddy's and join the boys. Damme, go on strike. Be a blood.'

'I wish to God I could.'

'Fourteen of us staying there, as well as a journeyman carpenter with a red face, and two commercial travellers. Food plain, but wholesome and plentiful. Damme, fights, morning, noon and night. The best of fun. It's the only place in the town for a fellow to lodge in.'

'It's easy for you to talk.'

'Freddy has a Lee Enfield rifle he's not supposed to have. Last night he showed us how the self-ejector worked.'

'Better than whist anyway.'

'And the company. Damme, Punjab pedlars with bags full of chemises and silk scarves. And tramps and tinkers and travelling people come into the shop. Damme, Freddy knows the world.'

'Whist,' I said, 'and that fat girl.'

'And one night a few of the senior boys, real hard chaws, sipped methylated spirits. Not to get drunk or anything, but just to see what it tasted like. And the other night Jim Ring put seidlitz powder in the journeyman carpenter's chamber-pot. He thought he was done for when it fizzed.'

Freddy the Shoemaker's sounded like heaven, but it seemed just as far away.

'But cheer up,' said the Red Man. 'I hear the whist-drive's the best of gas. The boys do all the serving at the refreshment interval.'

'A lot of use that'll be. I'll be in the madhouse by then.'

'Cakes and lemonade for all, and all for free.'

'Whist. I haven't even time to look at the mountains or the river. I can see nothing but hearts, clubs, diamonds and spades dancing before my eyes.'

'Last year, Jim Ring, they say, drank twenty-seven pint bottles of sarsaparilla.'

Red Cunningham's prophecy of the delights of the night of the annual whist-drive was no exaggeration. So it came to pass that in the course of the splendid chaos of the catering I found myself, flatulent with lemonade to the point of intoxication, on the second-floor landing of the Courthouse with Red Cunningham and three other kindred spirits. We leaned on the bannisters. We looked down the stairway.

'I couldn't drink another drop,' I said.

In my hand was a pint tumbler, full and sparkling to the brim.

'Pour it over them so,' said Red Cunningham.

Ascending the stairs from the ladies' powder-room came Maryanne and Ellen and between them that pudgy, piano-playing girl. A boy may, I suppose, do in lemonade the sort of thing men might do in hard liquor. Yet if Cunningham, who was a superb mimic, had not just then called to Maryanne in the voice of Ellen, and thus added the intoxication of laughter to the effervescence of the lemonade, I might never have struck my blow for liberty. It was all so simple. Maryanne, startled, looked up. When I was quite sure she saw me leaning over the bannister I gave her in the face, and fled, the contents of my glass. If I couldn't convince my mother that Maryanne and Ellen were mean I'd convince her that I was evil or; at any rate, a walking menace to the peace of two lone, lorn women.

It was the end of term and the end of my imprisonment. There could be no going back to Jail Square and for my last night in the town before the Easter holidays I sought refuge in Red Cunningham's lodgings. Then, without my luggage and with the money for my fare borrowed from Freddy the Shoe-maker, I headed for the mountains and home. The story, in a special letter hand-delivered by the postman, was there before me.

Blessedly my mother was no believer in corporal punishment but she had a weakness for trying to find out the why of things, and all through the holidays the dreary inquisition went on and on.

'Aloysius, whatever came into you?'

'How could you, Aloysius, throw slops over two old ladies?'

'They're not that old. They stole my pocket-money. It was lemonade anyway.'

'They say it was slops.'

'If they do I wish it had been slops. It was good lemonade. They made a skivvy and a message boy out of me.'

'They were only trying to teach you discipline, Aloysius. You had it too easy at home.'

After that I gave up. I sought sweet silence. My mother, as Red Cunningham said, was a fool: a nice fool, but a fool.

'You had such nice lodgings, Aloysius. Now I'll have to send you to a common boarding house.'

I said nothing. To a common boarding house was, after heaven itself, exactly where I wanted to go.

'There's only one other place in the town and the accommodation there is most unsatisfactory.'

I said nothing. My mother would never understand the meaning of that splendid freedom in which brotherly battles were of common occurrence nor could she be expected to appreciate the delights of the company, in Freddy's club for young gentlemen, of tramps, travelling people and Punjab pedlars. For her the inner workings of a Lee Enfield would hold no poetry, nor would she be edified by the sight of senior boys – real hard chaws – sipping experimentally at methylated spirits, or swapping tall tales about the travels and amorous adventures of Paddy the Irishman. But for me, the accommodation would be most satisfactory.

'What will become of you, Aloysius?'

I said nothing. Wonders I knew would become of me. I'd be an outlaw and one of a noble band of outlaws. I'd fight with the fists as well as Red Cunningham fought with the turned-up toes of his boots. I'd be a man among men. I'd be on my way to the admired contentment and completion of old age. With a flick of the wrist and a splash and splatter of lemonade I had proved my manhood. When I went back to school after the holidays I proved it still further by taking my thrashing without even attempting to defend myself. That was generally considered the manly thing to do. Afterwards I was to hope that my silence was a subconscious admission of guilt, an act of reparation to childless ageing women whose way of life was charted in loneliness and shadows. After all, my mother had thought well of them and they had been good to the new lodger. They would never know of my repentance. When, a month later, I went to their house to apologise they refused to open the door. Like pig-tailed girls refusing to come out to play they called to me through the keyhole to go away. But whether they knew or not, the divine balance would be readjusted. What more could a gentleman do?

# Homes on
# the mountain

The year I was twelve my father, my mother, my brother and myself had our Christmas dinner in the house my godmother's husband had built high up on the side of Dooish Mountain, when he and she came home to Ireland from Philadelphia.

That was a great godmother. She had more half-crowns in her patch pockets than there were in the Bank of England and every time she encountered me which, strategically, I saw was pretty often, it rained half-crowns. Those silver showers made my friend Lanty and myself the most popular boy bravados in our town. A curious thing was, though, that while we stood bobby-dazzler caramels, hazelnut chocolate, ice cream, cigarettes and fish and chips by the ton to our sycophants, we ourselves bought nothing but song-books. Neither of us could sing a note.

We had a splendid, patriotic taste in song-books, principally because the nearest newsagent's shop, kept by an old spinster in Devlin Street, had a window occupied by a sleeping tomcat, two empty tin boxes, bundles of pamphlets yellowed by exposure to the light, and all members of a series called Irish Fireside Songs. The collective title appealed by its warm cosiness. The little books were classified into Sentimental, Patriot's Treasury, Humorous and Convivial, and Smiles and Tears. Erin, we knew from Tom Moore and from excruciating music lessons at school, went wandering around with a tear and a smile blended in her eye. Because even to ourselves our singing was painful, we read together, sitting in the sunshine on the steps that led up to my father's house, such gems of the Humorous and Convivial as:

'When I lived in Sweet Ballinacrazy, dear, the girls were all bright as a daisy, dear.' Or turning to the emerald-covered Patriot's Treasury we intoned: 'We've men from the Nore, from the Suir and the Shannon, let the tyrant come forth, we'll bring force against force.'

Perhaps, unknown to ourselves, we were affected with the nostalgia that had brought my godmother and her husband back from the comfort of Philadelphia to the bleak side of Dooish Mountain. It was a move that my mother, who was practical and who had never been far enough from Ireland to feel nostalgia, deplored.

'Returned Americans,' she would say, 'are lost people. They live between two worlds. Their heads are in the clouds. Even the scrawny, black-headed sheep – not comparing the human being and the brute beast – know by now that Dooish is no place to live.'

'And if you must go back to the land,' she said, 'let it be the land, not rocks, heather and grey fields no bigger than pocket handkerchiefs. There's Cantwell's fine place beside the town going up for auction. Seventy acres of land, a palace of a dwelling-house, outhouses would do credit to the royal family, every modern convenience and more besides.'

For reasons that had nothing to do with prudence or sense Lanty and myself thought the Cantwell place an excellent idea. There were crab-apple trees of the most amazing fertility scattered all along the hedgerows on the farm; a clear gravel stream twisted through it; there were flat pastures made for football and, behind the house, an orchard that not even the most daring buccaneer of our generation had ever succeeded in robbing.

But there were other reasons – again nostalgic reasons – why my godmother's husband who was the living image of Will Rogers would build nowhere in Ireland except on the rough, wet side of Dooish, and there, on the site of the old home where he had spent his boyhood, the house went up. There wasn't a building job like it since the building of the Tower of Babel.

'Get a good sensible contractor from the town,' said my
mother, 'not drunken Dan Redmond from the mountain who
couldn't build a dry closet.'

But my godmother's husband had gone to school with Dan
Redmond. They had been barefooted boys together and that
was that, and there was more spent, according to my mother,
on malt whisky to entertain Dan, his tradesmen and labourers,
than would have built half New York. To make matters worse
it was a great season for returned Americans and every one of
them seemed to have known my godmother and her husband in
Philadelphia. They came in their legions to watch the building,
to help pass the bottle and to proffer advice. The acknowledged
queen of this gathering of souls fluttering between two worlds
was my Aunt Brigid, my mother's eldest sister. She was tiny and
neat, precise in her speech, silver-haired, glittering with rimless
spectacles and jet-black beads. In the States she had acquired
a mania for euchre, a passion for slivers of chicken jelled in
grey-green soup, a phonograph with records that included a
set of the favourite songs of Jimmy Walker, and the largest
collection of snapshots ever carried by pack mule or public
transport out of Atlantic City.

Then there was a born American – a rarity in our parts
in those days – a young man and a distant relative. Generous
and jovial, he kissed every woman, young or old, calling them
cousin or aunt; but it was suspected among wise observers
that he never once in the course of his visit was able to see
the Emerald Isle clearly. For the delegation, headed by my
Aunt Brigid, that met him in Dublin set him straight away
on the drink and when he arrived to view the building site
– it was one of the few sunny days of that summer – he did
so sitting on the dickey seat of a jaunting car and waving in
each hand a bottle of whisky. The builder and his men and
the haymakers in June meadows left their work to welcome
him, and Ireland, as the song says, was Ireland through joy
and through tears.

Altogether it was a wet season: the whisky flowed like water, the mist was low over the rocks and heather of Dooish and the moors of Loughfresha and Cornavara, the mountain runnels were roaring torrents. But miraculously the building was done; the returned Americans with the exception of Aunt Brigid, my godmother and her husband, went westwards again in the fall; and against all my mother's advice on the point of health, the couple from Philadelphia settled in for late November. The house-warming was fixed for Christmas Day.

'Dreamers,' my mother said. 'An American apartment on the groundwalls of an old cabin. Living in the past. Up where only a brave man would build a shooting lodge. For all they know or care there could be wolves still on the mountain. Magazines and gewgaws and chairs too low to sit on. With the rheumatism the mountain'll give them, they'll never bend their joints to sit down so low.'

Since the damp air had not yet brought its rheumatism we all sat down together in the house that was the answer to the exile's dream. Lamplight shone on good silver and Belfast linen. My godmother's man was proud to the point of tears.

'Sara Alice,' he said to my mother.

Content, glass in hand, he was more than ever like Will Rogers.

'Sara Alice,' he said. 'My mother, God rest her, would be proud to see this day.'

Practicality momentarily abandoned, my mother, moist-eyed and sipping sherry, agreed.

'Tommy,' he said to my father, 'listen to the sound of the spring outside.'

We could hear the wind, the voices of the runnels, the spring pouring clear and cool from a rainspout driven into a rock-face.

'As far as I recollect that was the first sound my ears ever heard, and I heard it all my boyhood, and I could hear it still in Girard Avenue, Philadelphia. But the voices of children used to be part of the sound of the spring. Seven of us, and me to be the youngest and the last alive. When my mother died and my father took us all to the States we didn't know when we were going away whether to leave the door open or closed. We left it open in case a travelling man might pass, needing shelter. We knocked gaps in the hedges and stone walls so as to give the neighbours' cattle the benefit of commonage and the land the benefit of the cow dung. But we left the basic lines of the walls so that nobody could forget our name or our claim to this part of the mountain.'

'In Gartan, in Donegal,' said my father, 'there's a place called the Flagstone of Loneliness where Saint Colmcille slept the night before he left Ireland under sentence of banishment. The exiles in that part used to lie down there the day before they sailed and pray to the saint to be preserved from the pangs of homesickness.'

My Aunt Brigid piped in a birdlike voice a bit of an exile song that was among her treasured recordings: 'A strange sort of sigh seems to come from us all as the waves hide the last glimpse of old Donegal.'

'Our American wake was held in Aunt Sally O'Neill's across the glen,' said my godmother's husband. 'Red Owen Gormley lilted for the dancers when the fiddlers were tired. He was the best man of his time at the mouth music.'

'He was also,' said my father, 'the first and last man I knew who could make a serviceable knife, blade and haft, out of a single piece of hardwood. I saw him do it, myself and wild Martin Murphy who was with me in the crowd of sappers who chained these mountains for the 1911 Ordnance Survey map. Like most of us, Martin drank every penny and on frosty days he would seal the cracks in his shoes with butter – a trick I never saw another man use. It worked too.'

'Aunt Sally's two sons were there at our American wake,' said my godmother's husband. 'Thady that was never quite right in the head and, you remember, Tommy, couldn't let a woman in the market or a salmon in the stream alone. John,

the elder brother, was there with Bessy from Cornavara that he
wooed for sixty years and never, I'd say, even kissed.'

The old people were silently laughing. My brother, older
than myself, was on the fringe of the joke. As my godmother
came and went I sniffed fine cooking. I listened to the mountain
wind and the noise of the spring and turned the bright pages
of an American gardening magazine. Here were rare blooms
would never grow on Dooish Mountain.

'All dead now I suppose,' my father said to end the
laughing.

'Bessy's dead now,' said my Aunt Brigid. 'Two years ago. As
single as the day she was born. Like many another Irishman
John wasn't overgiven to matrimony. But in the village of
Crooked Bridge below, the postman told me that John and
Thady are still alive in the old house on Loughfresha. Like pigs
in a sty, he said. Pigs in a sty. And eight thousand pounds each,
according to all accounts, in the Munster and Leinster Bank in
the town.

'God help us,' said my mother. 'I recall that house as it was
when Aunt Sally was alive. It was beautiful.'

My father was looking out of the window, down the
lower grey slopes of Dooish and across the deep glen towards
Loughfresha and Cornavara.

'It won't rain again before dark or dinner,' he said. 'I
haven't walked these hills since I carried a chain for His
Majesty's Ordnance Survey. Who'd ever have thought the
King of England would be interested in the extent of Cornavara
or Dooish Mountain.'

'Get up you two boys,' he said, 'and we'll see if you can walk
as well as your father before you.'

The overflow of the spring came with us as we descended the
boreen. Winter rain had already rutted the new gravel laid by
drunken Dan Redmond and his merry men. Below the bare
apple-orchard the spring's overflow met with another runnel
and with yet another where another boreen, overgrown with

hawthorn and bramble, struggled upwards to an abandoned house.

'Some people,' said my father, 'didn't come back to face the mountain. Living in Philadelphia must give a man great courage.'

He walked between us with the regular easy step of an old soldier who, in days of half-forgotten wars had footed it for ever across the African veldt.

'That was all we ever did,' he would say. 'Walk and walk. And the only shot I ever fired that I remember was at a black snake and I never knew whether I hit or missed. That was the Boer war for you.'

Conjoined, innumerable runnels swept under a bridge where the united boreens joined the road, plunged over rock in a ten-foot cataract, went elbowing madly between bare hazels down to the belly of the glen. White cabins, windows already lamp-lighted and candle-lighted for Christmas, showed below the shifting fringe of black grey mist.

'This house I knew well,' he said, 'this was Aunt Sally's. The Aunt was a title of honour and had nothing to do with blood relationship. She was stately, a widow, a great manager and aunt to the whole country. She had only the two sons.'

By the crossroads of the thirteen limekilns we swung right and descended the slope of the glen on what in a dry summer would have been a dust road. Now, wet sand shifted under our feet, loose stones rattled ahead of us, the growing stream growled below us in the bushes. To our left were the disused limekilns, lining the roadway like ancient monstrous idols with gaping toothless mouths, and as we descended the old man remembered the days when he and his comrades, veterans all, had walked and measured those hills; the limekilns in operation and the white dust on the grass and the roadside hedges; the queues of farm carts waiting for the loading. Fertilisers made in factories had ended all that. There was the place (he pointed across a field) where a tree, fallen on a mearing fence, had lain and rotted while the two farmers whose land the fence divided, swept away by the joy of legal conflict, had disputed in the court in the town the ownership of the timber. The case never reached settlement. Mountainy men loved law and had their hearts in twopence. And here was Loughfresha bridge. (The stream was a torrent now.) The gapped, stone parapet hadn't been mended since the days of the survey. And there was the wide pool where Thady O'Neill, always a slave to salmon, had waded in after a big fish imprisoned by low water, taken it with his bare hands after a mad struggle and, it was said, cured himself by shock treatment of premature arthritis.

Once across the bridge our ascent commenced. Black brooding roadside cattle looked at us with hostility. On a diagonal across a distant meadow a black hound dog ran silently, swiftly up towards the mist, running as if with definite purpose – but what, I wondered, could a dog be doing running upwards there alone on a Christmas Day. The thought absorbed me to the exclusion of all else until we came to the falling house of John and Thady O'Neill.

'Good God in heaven,' said my father.

For a full five minutes he stood looking at it, not speaking, before he led his two sons, with difficulty, as far as the door.

Once it must have been a fine, long, two-storeyed, thatched farmhouse, standing at an angle of forty-five degrees to the roadway and built backwards into the slope of the hill. But the roof and the upper storey had sagged and, topped by the growth of years of rank decayed grass, the remnants of the thatched roof looked, in the Christmas dusk, like a rubbish heap a maniacal mass-murderer might pick as a burial mound for his victims.

'They won't be expecting us for our Christmas dinner,' said my brother.

To reach the door we went ankle-deep, almost, through plashy ground and forded in the half-dark a sort of seasonal stream. One small uncurtained window showed faintly the yellow light of an oil-lamp.

Knock, knock, knock went my father on the sagging door.

No dogs barked. No calves or cocks made comforting farmhouse noises. The wind was raucous in the bare dripping hazels that overhung the wreck of a house from the slope behind. An evil wizard might live here.

Knock, knock, knock went my father.

'Is there anybody there said the traveller,' said my brother, who had a turn for poetry.

'John O'Neill and Thady,' called my father. 'I've walked over from the Yankee's new house at Dooish and brought my two sons with me to wish you a happy Christmas.'

He shouted out his own name.

In a low voice he said to us, 'Advance, friends, and be recognised.'

My brother and myself giggled and stopped giggling as chains rattled and slowly, with a thousand creaks of aged iron and timber in bitter pain and in conflict with each other, the door opened. Now, years after that Christmas, I can rely only on a boyhood memory of a brief visit to a badly-lighted cavern. There was a hunched decrepit old man behind the opening door. Without extending his hand he shuffled backwards and away from us. His huge hobnailed boots were unlaced. They flapped around him like the feet of some strange bird or reptile. He was completely bald. His face was pear-shaped, running towards the point at the forehead. His eyes had the brightness and quickness of a rodent's eyes. When my father said, 'Thady, you remember me,' he agreed doubtfully, as if agreement or disagreement were equally futile. He looked sideways furtively at the kitchen table half-hidden in shadows near one damp-streaked yellow wall. For a tablecloth that table had a battered raincoat and when our knock had interrupted him Thady had, it would seem, been heeling over onto the coat a pot of boiled potatoes. He finished the task while we stood uncertainly inside the doorway. Then, as if tucking in a child for sleep, he wrapped the tails of the coat around the pile of steaming tubers. A thunderous hearty voice spoke to us from the corner between the hearth and a huge four-poster bed. It was a rubicund confident voice. It invited us to sit down, and my father sat on a low chair close to the hearth-fire. My brother and myself stood uncomfortably behind him. There was, at any rate, nothing for us to sit on. The smoky oil-lamp burned low but the bracket that held it was on the wall above the owner of the voice. So it haloed with a yellow glow the head of John O'Neill, the dilatory lover of Bessie of Cornavara who had gone unwed to the place where none embrace. It was a broad, red-faced, white-haired head, too large and heavy, it seemed, for the old wasted body.

'It's years since we saw you, Tommy,' said John.

'It's years indeed.'

'And all the wild men that had been in the army.'

'All the wild men.'

'Times are changed, Tommy.'

'Times are changed indeed,' said my father.

He backed his chair a little away from the fire. Something unpleasantly odorous fried and sizzled in an unlidded pot-oven. The flagged floor, like the roof, had sagged. It sloped away from the hearth and into the shadows towards a pyramid of bags of flour and meal and feeding stuffs for cattle.

'But times are good,' said John. 'The land's good, and the crops and cattle.'

'And the money plentiful.'

'The money's plentiful.'

'I'm glad to hear you say it,' said my father.

'The Yankee came back, Tommy.'

'He came back.'

'And built a house, I hear. I don't go abroad much beyond my own land.'

'He built a fine house.'

'They like to come back, the Yankees. But they never settle.'

'It could be that the change proves too much for them,' said my father.

Then after a silence, disturbed only by the restless scratching of Thady's nailed soles on the floor, my father said, 'You never married, John.'

'No, Tommy. Bessy died. What with stock to look after and all, a man doesn't have much time for marrying.'

'Thady was more of a man for the ladies than you ever were,' said my father to John.

Behind us there was a shrill hysterical cackle and from John a roar of red laughter.

'He was that. God, Tommy, the memory you have.'

'Memory,' said my father.

Like a man in a trance he looked, not at John or Thady, but into the red heart of the turf fire.

'There was the day, Thady,' he said, 'when Martin Murphy and myself looked over a whin hedge at yourself and Molly Quigley from Crooked Bridge making love in a field. Between you, you ruined a half-acre of turnips.'

The red laughter and the cackle continued.

'Tommy, you have the memory,' said John. 'Wasn't it great the way you remembered the road up Loughfresha?'

'It was great,' said my father. 'Trust an old soldier to remember a road.'

The odour from the sizzling pot-oven was thickening.

'Well, we'll go now,' said my father. 'We wouldn't have butted in on you the day it is only for old time's sake.'

'You're always welcome, Tommy. Anytime you pass the road.'

'I don't pass this road often, John.'

'Well, when you do you're welcome. Those are your two sons.'

'My two sons.'

'Two fine clean young men,' said John.

He raised a hand to us. He didn't move out of the chair. The door closed slowly behind us and the chains rattled. We forded the seasonal stream, my brother going in over one ankle and filling a shoe with water.

* * *

We didn't talk until we had crossed the loud stream at Loughfresha Bridge. In the darkness I kept listening for the haunted howl of the black hound-dog.

'Isn't it an awful way, Da,' I said, 'for two men to live, particularly if it's true they have money in the bank.'

'If you've money in the bank,' said my brother, who suffered from a sense of irony, 'it's said you can do anything you please.'

With a philosophy too heavy for my years I said, 'It's a big change from the house we're going to.'

'John and Thady,' said my brother, 'didn't have the benefit of forty-five years in Philadelphia.'

My father said nothing.

'What, I wonder,' I said, 'was cooking in the pot-oven?'

'Whatever it was,' said my brother, 'they'll eat it with relish and roll into that four-poster bed and sleep like heroes.'

The black brooding roadside cattle seemed as formidable as wild bison.

'Sixty years,' said my father to himself. 'Coming and going every Sunday, spending the long afternoons and evenings in her father's house, eating and drinking, and nothing in the nature of love transpiring.'

Like heroes I thought, and recalled from the song-books the heroic words: 'Side by side for the cause have our forefathers battled when our hills never echoed the tread of a slave; in many a field where the leaden hail rattled, through the red gap of glory they marched to their grave.'

Slowly, towards a lost lighted fragment of Philadelphia and our Christmas dinner, we ascended the wet boreen.

'Young love,' soliloquised the old man. 'Something happens to it on these hills. Sixty years and he never proposed nothing, good or bad.'

'In Carlow town,' said the song-books to me, 'there lived a maid more sweet than flowers at daybreak; their vows contending lovers paid, but none of marriage dared speak.'

'Sunday after Sunday to her house for sixty years,' said the old man. 'You wouldn't hear the like of it among the Kaffirs. It's the rain and the mist. And the lack of sunshine and wine. Poor Thady, too, was fond of salmon and women.'

'For I haven't a genius for work,' mocked the Humorous and Convivial, 'it was never a gift of the Bradies; but I'd make a most iligant Turk for I'm fond of tobacco and ladies.'

To the easy amusement of my brother and, finally, to the wry laughter of my father I sang that quatrain. Night was over the mountain. The falling water of the spring had the tinny sound of shrill, brittle thunder.

After dinner my godmother's husband said, 'Such a fine house as Aunt Sally O'Neill kept. Tables scrubbed as white as bone. Dances to the melodeon. I always think of corncrakes and the crowds gathered for the mowing of the meadows when I recall that house. And the churning. She had the best butter in the country. Faintly golden. Little beads of moisture showing on it.'

'We'll have a game of euchre,' said my Aunt Brigid.

'Play the phonograph,' said my godmother's husband.

He loathed euchre. So on the gramophone, high up on Dooish, we heard that boys and girls were singing on the sidewalks of New York.

I wondered where the hound-dog could possibly have been running to. In a spooky story I had once read the Black Hound of Kildare turned out to be the devil.

My godmother asked me to sing.

'But I can't sing,' I said.

'Then what do Lanty and yourself do with all the song-books?'

'We read them.'

Laughter.

'Read us a song,' said my brother.

So, because I had my back to the wall and also because once when visiting a convent with my mother I had sung, by request, 'Let Erin Remember,' and received a box of chocolates from the

Reverend Mother, I sang: 'Just a little bit of Heaven fell from out the sky one day, and when the angels saw it sure they said we'll let it stay; and they called it Ireland.'

That spring, following my heralding of the descent from Elysium of the Emerald Isle, there was a steady downpour of half-crowns.

# The dogs in the great glen

The professor had come over from America to search out his origins and I met him in Dublin on the way to Kerry where his grandfather had come from and where he had relations, including a grand-uncle, still living.

'But the trouble is,' he said, 'that I've lost the address my mother gave me. She wrote to tell them I was coming to Europe. That's all they know. All I remember is a name out of my dead father's memories: the great Glen of Kanareen.'

'You could write to your mother.'

'That would take time. She'd be slow to answer. And I feel impelled right away to find the place my grandfather told my father about.

'You wouldn't understand,' he said. 'Your origins are all around you.'

'You can say that again, professor. My origins crop up like the bones of rock in thin sour soil. They come unwanted like the mushroom of merulius lacrimans on the walls of a decaying house.'

'It's no laughing matter,' he said.

'It isn't for me. This island's too small to afford a place in which to hide from one's origins. Or from anything else. During the war a young fellow in Dublin said to me: "Mister, even if I ran away to sea I wouldn't get beyond the three-mile limit".'

He said, 'But it's large enough to lose a valley in. I couldn't find the valley of Kanareen marked on any map or mentioned in any directory.'

'I have a middling knowledge of the Kerry mountains,' I said. 'I could join you in the search.'

'It's not marked on the half-inch ordnance survey map.'

'There are more things in Kerry than were ever dreamt of by the Ordnance Survey. The place could have another official name. At the back of my head I feel that once in the town of Kenmare in Kerry I heard a man mention the name of Kanareen.'

We set off two days later in a battered, rattly Ford Prefect. Haste, he said, would be dangerous because Kanareen might not be there at all, but if we idled from place to place in the lackadaisical Irish summer we might, when the sentries were sleeping and the glen unguarded, slip secretly as thieves into the land whose legends were part of his rearing.

'Until I met you,' the professor said, 'I was afraid the valley might have been a dream world my grandfather imagined to dull the edge of the first nights in a new land. I could see how he might have come to believe in it himself and told my father – and then, of course, my father told me.'

One of his grandfather's relatives had been a Cistercian monk in Mount Melleray, and we went there hoping to see the evidence of a name in a book and to kneel, perhaps, under the high arched roof of the chapel close to where that monk had knelt. But, when we had traversed the corkscrew road over the purple Knockmealdowns and gone up to the mountain monastery through the forest the monks had made in the wilderness, it was late evening and the doors were closed. The birds sang vespers. The great silence affected us with something between awe and a painful, intolerable shyness. We hadn't the heart to ring a doorbell or to promise ourselves to return in the morning. Not speaking to each other we retreated, the rattle of the Ford Prefect as irreverent as dicing on the altar-steps. Half a mile down the road the mute, single-file procession of a group of women exercitants walking back to the female guest-house underlined the holy, unreal, unanswering stillness that had closed us out. It could easily have been that his grandfather never had a relative a monk in Mount Melleray.

A cousin of his mother's mother had, he had been told, been a cooper in Lady Gregory's Gort in the County Galway. But when we crossed the country westwards to Gort, it produced nothing except the information that apart from the big breweries, where they survived like birds or bison in a sanctuary, the coopers had gone, leaving behind them not a hoop or a stave. So we visited the woods of Coole, close to Gort, where Lady Gregory's house had once stood, and on the brimming lake-water among the stones, we saw by a happy poetic accident the number of swans the poet had seen.

Afterwards in Galway City there was, as there always is in Galway City, a night's hard drinking that was like a fit of jovial hysteria, and a giggling ninny of a woman in the bar who kept saying, 'You're the nicest American I ever met. You don't look like an American. You don't even carry a camera. You look like a Kerryman.'

And in the end, we came to Kenmare in Kerry, and in another bar we met a talkative Kerryman who could tell us all about the prowess of the Kerry team, about the heroic feats of John Joe Sheehy or Paddy Bawn Brosnan. He knew so much, that man, yet he couldn't tell us where in the wilderness of mountains we might find the Glen of Kanareen. Nor could anybody else in the bar be of the least help to us, not even the postman who could only say that wherever it was, that is if it was at all, it wasn't in his district.

'It could of course,' he said, 'be east over the mountain.'

Murmuring sympathetically, the entire bar assented. The rest of the world was east over the mountain.

With the resigned air of men washing their hands of a helpless, hopeless case the postman and the football savant directed us to a roadside post office twelve miles away where, in a high-hedged garden before an old grey-stone house with latticed windows and an incongruous, green, official post office sign there was a child, quite naked, playing with a coloured, musical spinning-top as big as itself, and an old half-deaf man sunning himself and swaying in a rocking-chair, a straw hat tilted forwards to shade his eyes. Like Oisin remembering the Fenians, he told us he had known once of a young woman who married a man from a place called Kanareen, but there had been contention about the match and her people had kept up no correspondence with her. But the day she left home with her husband that was the way she went. He pointed. The way went inland and up and up. We followed it.

'That young woman could have been a relation of mine,' the professor said.

On a rock-strewn slope, and silhouetted on a saw-toothed ridge where you'd think only a chamois could get by without broken legs, small black cows, accurate and active as goats, rasped good milk from the grass between the stones. His grandfather had told his father about those athletic, legendary cows and about the proverb that said: Kerry cows know Sunday. For in famine times, a century since, mountain people bled the cows once a week to mix the blood into yellow maize meal and provide a meat dish, a special Sunday dinner.

The road twisted on across moorland that on our left sloped dizzily to the sea, as if the solid ground might easily slip and slide into the depths. Mountain shadows melted like purple dust into a green bay. Across a ravine set quite alone on a long, slanting, brown knife blade of a mountain, was a white house with a red door. The rattle of our pathetic little car affronted the vast stillness. We were free to moralise on the extent of all space in relation to the trivial area that limited our ordinary daily lives.

The two old druids of men resting from work on the leeward side of a turf-bank listened to our enquiry with the same attentive, half-conscious patience they gave to bird-cries or the sound of wind in the heather. Then they waved us ahead towards a narrow cleft in the distant wall of mountains as if they doubted the ability of ourselves and our conveyance to negotiate the Gap and find the Glen. They offered us strong

tea and a drop out of a bottle. They watched us with kind
irony as we drove away. Until the Gap swallowed us and
the hazardous, twisting track absorbed all our attention we
could look back and still see them, motionless, waiting with
indifference for the landslide that would end it all.

By a roadside pool where water-beetles lived their vicious
secretive lives, we sat and rested, with the pass and the cliffs,
overhung with heather, behind us and another ridge ahead.
Brazenly the sheer rocks reflected the sun and semaphored
at us. Below us, in the dry summer, the bed of a stream held
only a trickle of water twisting painfully around piles of round
black stones. Touch a beetle with a stalk of dry grass and the
creature either dived like a shot or, angry at invasion, savagely
grappled with the stalk.

'That silly woman in Galway,' the professor said.

He dropped a stone into the pool and the beetles submerged
to weather the storm.

'That day by the lake at Lady Gregory's Coole. The exact
number of swans Yeats saw when the poem came to him.
Upon the brimming water among the stones are nine and fifty
swans. Since I don't carry a camera nobody will ever believe
me. But you saw them. You counted them.'

'Now that I am so far,' he said, 'I'm half-afraid to finish
the journey. What will they be like? What will they think of
me? Will I go over that ridge there to find my grandfather's
brother living in a cave?'

Poking at and tormenting the beetles on the black mirror
of the pool, I told him, 'Once I went from Dublin to near
Shannon Pot, where the river rises, to help an American woman
find the house where her dead woman friend had been reared.
On her deathbed the friend had written it all out on a sheet
of notepaper: "Cross the river at Battle Bridge. Go straight
through the village with the ruined castle on the right. Go on
a mile to the crossroads and the labourer's cottage with the
lovely snapdragons in the flower garden. Take the road to the

right there, and then the second boreen on the left beyond the schoolhouse. Then stop at the third house on that boreen. You can see the river from the flagstone at the door."

'Apart from the snapdragons it was exactly as she had written it down. The dead woman had walked that boreen as a barefooted schoolgirl. Not able to revisit it herself she entrusted the mission as her dying wish to her dearest friend. We found the house. Her people were long gone from it but the new tenants remembered them. They welcomed us with melodeon and fiddle and all the neighbours came in and collated the long memories of the town-land. They feasted us with cold ham and chicken, porter and whisky, until I had cramps for a week.'

'My only grip on identity,' he said, 'is that a silly woman told me I looked like a Kerryman. My grandfather was a Kerryman. What do Kerrymen look like?'

'Big,' I said.

'And this is the heart of Kerry. And what my grandfather said about the black cows was true. With a camera I could have taken a picture of those climbing cows. And up that hill trail and over that ridge is Kanareen.'

'We hope,' I said.

The tired cooling engine coughed apologetically when we abandoned it and put city-shod feet to the last ascent.

'If that was the mountain my grandfather walked over in the naked dawn coming home from an all-night card-playing then, by God, he was a better man than me,' said the professor.

He folded his arms and looked hard at the razor-cut edges of stone on the side of the mountain.

'Short of too much drink and the danger of mugging,' he said, 'getting home at night in New York is a simpler operation than crawling over that hunk of miniature Mount Everest. Like walking up the side of a house.'

He was as proud as Punch of the climbing prowess of his grandfather.

'My father told me,' he said, 'that one night coming from the card-playing my grandfather slipped down fifteen feet of rock and the only damage done was the ruin of one of two bottles of whisky he had in the tail-pockets of his greatcoat. The second bottle was unharmed.'

The men who surfaced the track we were walking on had been catering for horses and narrow iron-hooped wheels. After five minutes of agonised slipping and sliding, wisdom came to us and we took to the cushioned grass and heather. As we ascended the professor told me what his grandfather had told his father about the market town he used to go to when he was a boy. It was a small town where even on market days the dogs would sit nowhere except exactly in the middle of the street. They were lazy town dogs not active, loyal and intelligent like the dogs the grandfather had known in the great glen. The way the old man had described it, the town's five streets grasped the ground of Ireland as the hand of a strong swimmer might grasp a ledge of rock to hoist himself out of the water. On one side was the sea. On the other side a shoulder of mountain rose so steeply that the Gaelic name of it meant the gable of the house.

When the old man went as a boy to the town on a market day it was his custom to climb that mountain, up through furze and following goat tracks, leaving his shiny boots, that he only put on, anyway, when he entered the town, securely in hiding behind a furze bush. The way he remembered that mountain it would seem that twenty minutes active climbing brought him halfways to heaven. The little town was far below him, and the bay and the islands. The unkempt coastline tumbled and sprawled to left and right, and westwards the ocean went on for ever. The sounds of market-day, voices, carts, dogs barking, musicians on the streets, came up to him as faint, silvery whispers. On the tip of one island two tall aerials marked the place where, he was told, messages went down into the sea to travel all the way to America by cable. That was a great marvel for a boy from the mountains to hear about: the ghostly, shrill, undersea voices; the words of people in every tongue of Europe far down among monstrous fish and shapeless sea-serpents that never saw the light of the sun. He closed his eyes one day and it seemed to him that the sounds of the little town were the voices of Europe setting out on their submarine travels. That was the time he knew that when he was old enough he would leave the Glen of Kanareen and go with the voices westwards to America.

'Or so he said. Or so he told my father,' said the professor.

Another fifty yards and we would be on top of the ridge. We kept our eyes on the ground, fearful of the moment of vision and, for good or ill, revelation. Beyond the ridge there might be nothing but a void to prove that his grandfather had been a dreamer or a liar. Rapidly, nervously, he tried to talk down his fears.

'He would tell stories for ever, my father said, about ghosts and the good people. There was one case of an old woman whose people buried her – when she died, of course – against her will, across the water, which meant on the far side of the lake in the glen. Her dying wish was to be buried in another graveyard, nearer home. And there she was, sitting in her own chair in the corner, waiting for them, when they came home from the funeral. To ease her spirit they replanted her.'

To ease the nervous moment I said, 'There was a poltergeist once in a farmhouse in these mountains, and the police decided to investigate the queer happenings, and didn't an ass's collar come flying across the room to settle around the sergeant's neck. Due to subsequent ridicule the poor man had to be transferred to Dublin.'

Laughing, we looked at the brown infant runnel that went parallel to the path. It flowed with us: we were over the watershed. So we raised our heads slowly and saw the great Glen of Kanareen. It was what Cortez saw, and all the rest of it. It was a discovery. It was a new world. It gathered the sunshine into a gigantic coloured bowl. We accepted it detail by detail.

'It was there all the time,' he said. 'It was no dream. It was no lie.'

The first thing we realised was the lake. The runnel leaped down to join the lake, and we looked down on it through ash trees regularly spaced on a steep, smooth, green slope. Grasping from tree to tree you could descend to the pebbled, lapping edge of the water.

'That was the way,' the professor said, 'the boys in his time climbed down to fish or swim. Black, bull-headed mountain trout. Cannibal trout. There was one place where they could dive off sheer rock into seventy feet of water. Rolling like a gentle sea: that was how he described it. They gathered kindling, too, on the slopes under the ash trees.'

Then, after the lake, we realised the guardian mountain; not rigidly chiselled into ridges of rock like the mountain behind us but soft and gently curving, protective and, above all, noble, a monarch of mountains, an antlered stag holding a proud horned head up to the highest point of the blue sky. Green fields swathed its base. Sharp lines of stone walls, dividing wide areas of moorland sheep-grazing, marked man's grip for a thousand feet or so above sea-level then gave up the struggle and left the mountain alone and untainted. Halfways up one snow-white cloud rested as if it had hooked itself on a snagged rock and there it stayed, motionless, as step by step we went down into the Glen. Below the cloud a long cataract made a thin, white, forked-lightning line, and, in the heart of the glen, the river that the cataract became, sprawled on a brown and green and golden patchwork bed.

'It must be some one of those houses,' he said, pointing ahead and down to the white houses of Kanareen.

'Take a blind pick,' I said. 'I see at least fifty.'

They were scattered over the glen in five or six clusters.

'From what I heard it should be over in that direction,' he said.

Small rich fields were ripe in the sun. This was a glen of plenty, a gold-field in the middle of a desert, a happy laughing mockery of the arid surrounding moors and mountains. Five hundred yards away a dozen people were working at the hay. They didn't look up or give any sign that they had seen two strangers cross the high threshold of their kingdom but, as we went down, stepping like grenadier guards, the black-and-white sheepdogs detached themselves from the haymaking and moved silently across to intercept our path. Five of them I counted. My step faltered.

'This could be it,' I suggested with hollow joviality. 'I feel a little like an early Christian.'

The professor said nothing. We went on down, deserting the comfort of the grass and heather at the side of the track. It seemed to me that our feet on the loose pebbles made a tearing, crackling, grinding noise that shook echoes even out of the imperturbable mountain. The white cloud had not moved. The haymakers had not honoured us with a glance.

'We could,' I said, 'make ourselves known to them in a civil fashion. We could ask the way to your grand-uncle's house. We could have a formal introduction to those slinking beasts.'

'No, let me,' he said. 'Give me my head. Let me try to remember what I was told.'

'The hearts of these highland people, I've heard, are made of pure gold,' I said. 'But they're inclined to be the tiniest bit suspicious of town-dressed strangers. As sure as God made smells and shotguns they think we're inspectors from some government department: weeds, or warble-fly or horror of horrors, rates and taxes. With equanimity they'd see us eaten.'

He laughed. His stride had a new elasticity in it. He was another man. The melancholy of the monastic summer dusk at Mount Melleray was gone. He was somebody else coming home. The white cloud had not moved. The silent dogs came closer. The unheeding people went on with their work.

'The office of rates collector is not sought after in these parts,' I said. 'Shotguns are still used to settle vexed questions of land title. Only a general threat of excommunication can settle a major feud.'

'This was the way he'd come home from the gambling cabin,' the professor said, 'his pockets clinking with winnings. That night he fell he'd won the two bottles of whisky. He was only eighteen when he went away. But he was the tallest man in the glen. So he said. And lucky at cards.'

The dogs were twenty yards away, silent, fanning out like soldiers cautiously circling a point of attack.

'He was an infant prodigy,' I said. 'He was a peerless grandfather for a man to have. He also had one great advantage over us – he knew the names of these taciturn dogs and they knew his smell.'

He took off his white hat and waved at the workers. One man at a haycock raised a pitchfork – in salute or in threat? Nobody else paid the least attention. The dogs were now at our heels, suiting their pace politely to ours. They didn't even sniff. They had impeccable manners.

'This sure is the right glen,' he said. 'The old man was never done talking about the dogs. They were all black-and-white in his day, too.'

He stopped to look at them. They stopped. They didn't look up at us. They didn't snarl. They had broad shaggy backs. Even for their breed they were big dogs. Their long tails were rigid. Fixing my eyes on the white cloud I walked on.

'Let's establish contact,' I said, 'before we're casually eaten. All I ever heard about the dogs in these mountains is that their family tree is as old as the Red Branch knights. That they're the best sheepdogs in Ireland and better than anything in the Highlands of Scotland. They also savage you first and bark afterwards.'

Noses down, they padded along behind us. Their quiet breath was hot on my calves. High up and far away the nesting white cloud had the security of heaven.

'Only strangers who act suspiciously,' the professor said.

'What else are we? I'd say we smell bad to them.'

'Not me,' he said. 'Not me. The old man told a story about a stranger who came to Kanareen when most of the people were away at the market. The house he came to visit was empty except for two dogs. So he sat all day at the door of the house and the dogs lay and watched him and said and did nothing. Only once, he felt thirsty and went into the kitchen of the house and lifted a bowl to go to the well for water. Then there was a low duet of a snarl that froze his blood. So he went thirsty and the dogs lay quiet.'

'Hospitable people.'

'The secret is touch nothing, lay no hand on property and you're safe.'

'So help me God,' I said, 'I wouldn't deprive them of a bone or a blade of grass.'

Twice in my life I had been bitten by dogs. Once, walking to school along a sidestreet on a sunny morning and simultaneously reading in *The Boy's Magazine* about a soccer centre forward, the flower of the flock, called Fiery Cross the Shooting Star – he was redheaded and his surname was Cross – I had stepped on a sleeping Irish terrier. In retaliation, the startled brute had bitten me. Nor could I find it in my heart to blame him, so that, in my subconscious, dogs took on the awful heaven-appointed dignity of avenging angels. The other time – and this was an even more disquieting experience – a mongrel dog had come up softly behind me while I was walking on the fairgreen in the town I was reared in and bitten the calf of my leg so as to draw spurts of blood. I kicked him but not resenting the kick, he had walked away as if it was the most natural, legitimate thing in heaven and earth for a dog to bite me and be kicked in return. Third time, I thought, it will be rabies. So as we walked and the silent watchers of the valley padded at our heels, I enlivened the way with brave and trivial chatter. I recited my story of the four wild brothers of Adrigole.

'Once upon a time,' I said, 'there lived four brothers in a rocky corner of Adrigole in West Cork, under the mountain called Hungry Hill. Daphne du Maurier wrote a book called after the mountain, but divil a word in it about the four brothers of Adrigole. They lived, I heard tell, according to instinct and never laced their boots and came out only once a year to visit the nearest town which was Castletownberehaven on the side of Bantry Bay. They'd stand there, backs to the wall, smoking, saying nothing, contemplating the giddy market-day throng. One day they ran out of tobacco and went into the local branch of the Bank of Ireland to buy it and raised havoc because the teller refused to satisfy their needs. To pacify them the manager and the teller had to disgorge their own supplies. So they went back to Adrigole to live happily without lacing their boots, and ever after they thought that in towns and cities the bank was the place where you bought tobacco.

'That,' said I with a hollow laugh, 'is my moral tale about the four brothers of Adrigole.'

On a level with the stream that came from the lake and went down to join the valley's main river, we walked towards a group of four whitewashed, thatched farmhouses that were shining and scrupulously clean. The track looped to the left. Through a small triangular meadow a short-cut went straight towards the houses. In the heart of the meadow, by the side of the short-cut, there was a spring well of clear water, the stones that lined its sides and the roof cupped over it all white and cleansed with lime. He went down three stone steps and looked at the water. For good luck there was a tiny brown trout imprisoned in the well. He said quietly, 'That was the way my grandfather described it. But it could hardly be the self-same fish.'

He stooped to the clear water. He filled his cupped hands and drank. He stooped again, and again filled his cupped hands and slowly, carefully, not spilling a drop, came up the moist, cool steps. Then, with the air of a priest, scattering hyssop, he sprinkled the five dogs with the spring-water. They backed away from him, thoughtfully. They didn't snarl or show teeth. He had them puzzled. He laughed with warm good nature at

their obvious perplexity. He was making his own of them. He
licked his wet hands. Like good pupils attentively studying a
teacher, the dogs watched him.

'Elixir,' he said. 'He told my father that the sweetest drink
he ever had was out of this well when he was on his way back
from a drag hunt in the next glen. He was a great hunter.'

'He was Nimrod,' I said. 'He was everything. He was the
universal Kerryman.'

'No kidding,' he said. 'Through a thorn hedge six feet thick
and down a precipice and across a stream to make sure of a
wounded bird. Or all night long waist deep in an icy swamp
waiting for the wild geese. And the day of this drag hunt.
What he most remembered about it was the way they sold the
porter to the crowd in the pub at the crossroads. To meet the
huntsmen halfways they moved the bar out to the farmyard.
With hounds and cows and geese and chickens it was like
having a drink in Noah's Ark. The pint tumblers were set
on doors lifted off their hinges and laid flat on hurdles. The
beer was in wooden tubs and all the barmaids had to do was
dip and there was the pint. They didn't bother to rinse the
tumblers. He said it was the quickest-served and the flattest
pint of porter he ever saw or tasted. Bitter and black as bog
water. Completely devoid of the creamy clerical collar that
should grace a good pint. On the way home he spent an hour
here rinsing his mouth and the well-water tasted as sweet, he
said, as silver.'

The white cloud was gone from the mountain.

'Where did it go,' I said. 'Where could it vanish to?'

In all the wide sky there wasn't a speck of cloud. The
mountain was changing colour, deepening to purple with the
approaching evening.

He grasped me by the elbow, urging me forwards. He said,
'Step on it. We're almost home.'

We crossed a crude wooden stile and followed the short-cut
through a walled garden of bright-green heads of cabbage and

black and red currant bushes. Startled, fruit-thieving birds rustled away from us and on a rowan tree a sated, impudent blackbird opened his throat and sang.

'Don't touch a currant,' I said, 'or a head of cabbage. Don't ride your luck too hard.'

He laughed like a boy half hysterical with happiness. He said, 'Luck. Me and these dogs, we know each other. We've been formally introduced.'

'Glad to know you dogs,' he said to them over his shoulder.

They trotted behind us. We crossed a second stile and followed the short-cut through a haggard, and underfoot the ground was velvety with chipped straw. We opened a five-barred iron gate, and to me it seemed that the noise of its creaking hinges must be audible from end to end of the glen. While I paused to rebolt it he and the dogs had gone on, the dogs trotting in the lead. I ran after them. I was the stranger who had once been the guide. We passed three houses as if they didn't exist. They were empty. The people who lived in them were above at the hay. Towards the fourth thatched house of the group we walked along a green boreen, lined with hazels and an occasional mountain ash. The guardian mountain was by now so purple that the sky behind it seemed, by contrast, as silvery as the scales of a fish. From unknown lands behind the lines of hazels two more black-and-white dogs ran, barking with excitement, to join our escort. Where the hazels ended there was a house fronted by a low stone wall and a profusion of fuchsia. An old man sat on the wall and around him clustered the children of the four houses. He was a tall, broad-shouldered old man with copious white hair and dark side whiskers and a clear prominent profile. He was dressed in good grey with long, old-fashioned skirts to his coat – formally dressed as if for some formal event – and his wide-brimmed black hat rested on the wall beside him, and his joined hands rested on the curved handle of a strong ash plant. He stood up as we approached. The stick fell to the ground. He stepped over it and came towards us. He was as tall or, without the slight stoop of age, taller than the professor. He put out his two hands and rested them on the professor's shoulders. It wasn't an embrace. It was an appraisal, a salute, a sign of recognition.

He said, 'Kevin, well and truly we knew you'd come if you were in the neighbourhood at all. I watched you walking down. I knew you from the top of the Glen. You have the same gait my brother had, the heavens be his bed. My brother that was your grandfather.'

'They say a grandson often walks like the grandfather,' said the professor.

His voice was shaken and there were tears on his face. So, a stranger in the place myself, I walked away a bit and looked back up the Glen. The sunlight was slanting now and shadows were lengthening on mountain slopes and across the small fields. From where I stood the lake was invisible, but the ashwood on the slope above it was dark as ink. Through sunlight and shadow the happy haymakers came running down towards us; and barking, playing, frisking over each other, the seven black-and-white dogs, messengers of good news, ran to meet them. The great Glen, all happy echoes, was opening out and singing to welcome its true son.

Under the hazels, as I watched the running haymakers, the children came shyly around me to show me that I also was welcome. Beyond the high ridge, the hard mountain the card-players used to cross to the cabin of the gambling stood up gaunt and arrogant and leaned over towards us as if it were listening.

It was moonlight, I thought, not sunlight, over the great Glen. From house to house, the dogs were barking, not baying the moon, but to welcome home the young men from the card-playing over the mountain. The edges of rock glistened like quartz. The tall young gambler came laughing down the Glen, greatcoat swinging open, waving in his hand the one bottle of whisky that hadn't been broken when he tumbled down the spink. The ghosts of his own dogs laughed and leaped and frolicked at his heels.

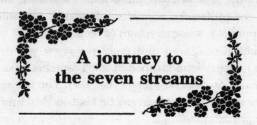

# A journey to
# the seven streams

My father, the heavens be his bed, was a terrible man for
telling you about the places he had been and for bringing you
there if he could and displaying them to you with a mild and
gentle air of proprietorship. He couldn't do the showmanship
so well in the case of Spion Kop where he and the fortunate
ones who hadn't been ordered up the hill in the ignorant
night had spent a sad morning crouching on African earth
and listening to the deadly Boer guns that, high above the
plain, slaughtered their hapless comrades. Nor yet in the case
of Halifax nor the Barbadoes where he had heard words of
Gaelic from coloured girls who were, he claimed, descended
from the Irish transported into slavery in the days of Cromwell.
The great glen of Aherlow, too, which he had helped to chain
for His Majesty's Ordnance Survey was placed inconveniently
far to the South in the mystic land of Tipperary, and Cratloe
Wood where the fourth Earl of Leitrim was assassinated, was
sixty miles away on the winding Donegal fjord called Mulroy
Bay. But townlands like Corraheskin, Drumlish, Cornavara,
Dooish, The Minnieburns and Claramore, and small towns
like Drumquin and Dromore were all within a ten-mile radius
of our town and something of moment or something amusing
had happened in every one of them.

The reiterated music of their names worked on him like a
charm. They would, he said, take faery tunes out of the stone
fiddle of Castle Caldwell; and indeed it was the night he told
us the story of the stone fiddle and the drowned fiddler, and
recited for us the inscription carved on the fiddle in memory

of the fiddler, that he decided to hire a hackney car, a rare and daring thing to do in those days, and bring us out to see in one round trip those most adjacent places of his memories and dreams.

'In the year 1770 it happened,' he said. 'The landlord at the time was Sir James Caldwell, Baronet. He was also called the Count of Milan, why, I never found anybody to tell me. The fiddler's name was Dennis McCabe and by tradition the McCabes were always musicians and jesters to the Caldwells. There was festivity at the Big House by Lough Erne Shore and gentry there from near and far, and out they went to drink and dance on a raft on the lake, and wasn't the poor fiddler so drunk he fiddled himself into the water and drowned.'

'Couldn't somebody have pulled him out, Da?'

'They were all as drunk as he was. The story was that he was still sawing away with the bow when he came up for the third time. The party cheered him until every island in Lough Erne echoed and it was only when they sobered up they realised they had lost the fiddler. So the baronet and Count of Milan had a stone fiddle taller than a man made to stand at the estate gate as a monument to Dennis McCabe and as a warning for ever to fiddlers either to stay sober or to stay on dry land.

'Ye fiddlers beware, ye fiddler's fate,' my father recited. 'Don't attempt the deep lest ye repent too late. Keep to the land when wind and storm blow, but scorn the deep if it with whisky flow. On firm land only exercise your skill; there you may play and safely drink your fill.'

Travelling by train from our town to the seaside you went for miles along the green and glistening Erne shore but the train didn't stop by the stone fiddle nor yet at the Boa island for the cross-roads' dances. Always when my father told us about those dances, his right foot rhythmically tapped and took music out of the polished steel fireside fender that had Home Sweet Home lettered out on an oval central panel. Only the magic motor, bound to no tracks, compelled to no fixed stopping places, could bring us to the fiddle or the crowded cross-roads.

'Next Sunday then,' he said, 'as certain as the sun sets and rises, we'll hire Hookey and Peter and the machine and head for Lough Erne.'

'Will it hold us all,' said my mother. 'Seven of us and Peter's big feet and the length of the driver's legs.'

'That machine,' he said, 'would hold the twelve apostles, the Connaught Rangers and the man who broke the bank at Monte Carlo. It's the size of a hearse.'

'Which is just what it looks like,' said the youngest of my three sisters who had a name for the tartness of her tongue.

She was a thin dark girl.

'Regardless of appearance,' he said, it'll carry us to the stone fiddle and on the way we'll circumnavigate the globe: Clanabogan, and Cavanacaw, Pigeon Top Mountain and Corraduine, where the barefooted priest said Mass at the Rock in the penal days and Corraheskin where the Muldoons live. . . .'

'Them,' said the third sister.

She had had little time for the Muldoons since the day their lack of savoir faire cost her a box of chocolates. A male member, flaxen-haired, pink-cheeked, aged sixteen, of those multitudinous Muldoons had come by horse and cart on a market day from his rural fastnesses to pay us a visit. Pitying his gaucherie, his shy animal-in-a-thicket appearance, his outback ways and gestures, she had grandly reached him a box of chocolates so as to sweeten his bitter lot with one honeyed morsel or two or, at the outside three; but unaccustomed to towny ways and the mores of built-up areas the rural swain had appropriated the whole box.

'He thought,' she said, 'I was a paleface offering gifts to a Commanche.'

'But by their own hearth,' said my father, 'they're simple hospitable people.

'And Cornavara,' he said, 'and Dooish and Carrick Valley

and your uncle Owen, and the two McCannys the pipers, and
Claramore where there are so many Gormleys every family has
to have its own nickname, and Drumquin where I met your
mother, and Dromore where you' (pointing to me) 'were born
and where the mail train was held up by the I.R.A. and where
the three poor lads were murdered by the Specials when you'
(again indicating me) 'were a year old, and the Minnieburns
where the seven streams meet to make the head waters of the
big river. Hookey and Peter and the machine will take us to
all those places.'

'Like a magic carpet,' said my mother – with just a little
dusting of the iron filings of doubt in her voice.

Those were the days, and not so long ago, when cars
were rare and every car, not just every make of car, had
a personality of its own. In our town with its population
of five thousand, not counting the soldiers in the barracks,
there were only three cars for hire and one of them was the
love-child of the pioneer passion of Hookey Baxter for the
machine. He was a long hangle of a young fellow, two-thirds
of him made up of legs, and night and day he was whistling.
He was as forward-looking as Lindberg and he dressed like
Lindberg, for the air, in goggles, leather jacket and helmet;
an appropriate costume, possibly, considering Hookey's own
height and the altitude of the driver's seat in his machine. The
one real love of his young heart was the love of the born
tinkerer, the instinctive mechanic, for that hybrid car: the child
of his frenzy, the fruit of days spent deep in grease giving new
life and shape to a wreck he had bought at a sale in Belfast.
The original manufacturers, whoever they had been, would
have been hard put to it to recognise their altered offspring.

'She's chuman,' Peter Keown would say as he patted the
sensitive quivering bonnet.

Peter meant human. In years to come his sole recorded
comment on the antics of Adolf Hitler was that the man
wasn't chuman.

'She's as nervous,' he would say, 'as a thoroughbred.'

The truth was that Peter, Hookey's stoker, grease-monkey and errand boy, was somewhat in awe of the tall rangy metal animal yet wherever the car went, with the tall goggled pilot at the wheel, there the pilot's diminutive mate was also sure to go. What living Peter earned he earned by digging holes in the street as a labouring man for the town council's official plumber so that, except on Sundays and when he motored with Hookey, nobody in the town ever saw much of him but the top of his cloth cap or his upturned face when he'd look up from the hole in the ground to ask a passer-by the time of day. Regularly once a year he spent a corrective month in Derry Jail, because his opportunities as a municipal employee and his weakness as a kleptomaniac meant that good boards, lengths of piping, coils of electric wire, monkey wrenches, spades, and other movable properties faded too frequently into thin air.

'A wonderful man, poor Peter,' my father would say. 'That cloth cap with the turned-up peak. And the thick-lensed, thin-rimmed spectacles – he's half-blind – and the old tweed jacket too tight for him, and the old Oxford-bag trousers too big for him, and his shrill voice and his waddle of a walk that makes him look always like a duck about to apologise for laying a hen-egg. How he survives is a miracle of God's grace. He can resist the appeal of nothing that's portable.'

'He's a dream,' said the third sister. 'And the feet are the biggest part of him.'

'The last time he went to Derry,' said my brother, 'all the old women from Brook Street and the lanes were at the top of the Courthouse Hill to cheer him as he passed.'

'And why not,' said my mother. 'They're fond of him and they say he's well-liked in the jail. His heart's as big as his feet. Everything he steals he gives away.'

'Robin Hood,' said the third sister. 'Robbing the town council to pay Brook Street.'

'The Council wouldn't sack him,' said my eldest sister, 'if he stole the town.'

'At the ready,' roared my father. 'Prepare to receive cavalry.'

In the street below the house there was a clanking, puffing, grinding tumult.

'God bless us look at Peter,' said my father. 'Aloft with Hookey like a crown prince beside a king. Are we all ready? Annie, Ita, May, George, yourself ma'am, and you the youngest of us all. Have we the sandwiches and the flasks of tea and the lemonade? Forward.'

A lovelier Sunday morning never shone. With the hood down and the high body glistening after its Saturday wash and polish, the radiator gently steaming, the car stood at the foot of the seven steps that led down from our door. The stragglers coming home from early mass, and the devout setting off early for late mass had gathered in groups to witness our embarkation. Led by my father and in single file, we descended the steps and ascended nearly as high again to take our lofty places in the machine.

There was something of the Citroen in the quivering mongrel, in the yellow canvas hood now reclining in voluminous ballooning folds, in the broad back-seat that could hold five fair-sized people. But to judge by the radiator, the absence of gears, and the high fragile-spoked wheels, Citroen blood had been crossed with that of the Model T. After that, any efforts to spot family traits would have brought confusion on the thought of the greatest living authorities. The thick slanting glass windscreen could have been wrenched from a limousine designed to divert bullets from Balkan princelings. The general colour-scheme, considerably chipped and cracked, was canary yellow. And there was Hookey at the wheel, then my brother and father, and Peter on the outside left where he could leap in and out to perform the menial duties of assistant engineer; and in the wide and windy acres of the back seat, my mother, myself and my three sisters.

High above the town the church bell rang. It was the bell

to warn the worshippers still on their way that in ten minutes the vested priest would be on the altar but, as it coincided with our setting out, it could have been a quayside bell ringing farewell to a ship nosing out across the water towards the rim of vision.

Peter leaped to the ground, removed the two stones that, blocked before the front wheels, acted as auxiliaries for the hand brake. Hookey released the brake. The car was gathering speed when Peter scrambled aboard, settled himself and slammed the yellow door behind him. Sparing fuel, we glided down the slope, back-fired twice loudly enough to drown the sound of the church bell, swung left along John Street and cleared the town without incident. Hands waved from watching groups of people but because this was no trivial event there were no laughs, no wanton cheers. The sound of the bell died away behind us. My mother expressed the hope that the priest would remember us at the offertory. Peter assured her that we were all as safe as if we were at home in bed. God's good green Sunday countryside was softly all around us.

Squat to the earth and travelling at seventy you see nothing from cars nowadays, but to go with Hookey was to be above all but the highest walls and hedges, to be among the morning birds.

'Twenty-seven em pee haitch,' said Hookey.

'Four miles covered already,' said Peter.

'The Gortin Mountains over there,' said my father. 'And the two mountains to the north are Bessy Bell and Mary Grey, so named by the Hamiltons of Baronscourt, the Duke of Abercorn's people, after a fancied resemblance to two hills in Stirlingshire, Scotland. The two hills in Stirlingshire are so called after two ladies of the Scottish court who fled the plague and built their hut in the wild wood and thatched it o'er with rushes. They are mentioned by Thomas Carlyle in his book on the French Revolution. The dark green on the hills by Gortin Gap is the new government forestry. And in Gortin village Paddy Ford the contractor hasn't gone to mass since, fifteen years ago, the parish priest gave another man the job of painting the inside of the sacristy.'

'No paint no prayers,' said the third sister.

'They're strange people in Gortin,' my mother said.

'It's proverbial,' said my father, 'that they're to be distinguished anywhere by the bigness of their backsides.'

'Five miles,' said Peter. 'They're spinning past.'

'Running sweet as honey,' said Hookey.

He adjusted his goggles and whistled back to the Sunday birds.

'Jamie Magee's of the Flush,' said my father.

He pointed to a long white house on a hill slope and close to a waterfalling stream.

'Rich as Rockefeller and too damned mean to marry.'

'Who in heaven would have him,' said the third sister.

'Six miles,' said Peter.

Then, with a blast of backfiring that rose my mother a foot in the air, the wobbling yellow conveyance came to a coughing miserable halt. The air was suddenly grey and poisoned with fumes.

'It's her big end Hookey,' said Peter.

'She's from Gortin so,' said the third sister.

The other two sisters, tall and long-haired and normally quiet girls, went off at the deep end into the giggles.

'Isn't it providential,' said my mother, 'that the cowslips are a glory this year. We'll have something to do, Henry, while you're fixing it.'

Hookey had been christened Henry, and my mother would never descend to nicknames. She felt that to make use of a nickname was to remind a deformed person of his deformity. Nor would she say even of the town's chief inebriate that he was ever drunk: he was either under the influence or he had a drop too many taken. She was, my mother, the last great Victorian euphemiser.

'We won't be a jiffy, ma'am,' said Hookey. 'It's nothing so serious as a big end.'

The three sisters were convulsed.

The fields and the roadside margins were bright yellow with blossom.

'Gather ye cowslips while you may,' said my father.

He handed the ladies down from the dizzy heights. Peter had already disembarked. Submitting to an impulse that had gnawed at me since we set sail I dived forwards, my head under Hookey's left elbow, and butted with both fists the black, rubber, punch-ball horn; and out over the fields to startle birds and grazing cattle went the dying groan of a pained diseased ox.

'Mother of God,' said my father, 'that's a noise and no mistake. Here boy, go off and pick flowers.'

He lifted me down to the ground.

'Screw off the radiator cap, Peter,' said Hookey.

'It's scalding hot, Hookey.'

'Take these gauntlet gloves, manalive. And stand clear when you screw it off.'

A geyser of steam and dirty hot water went heavenwards as Peter and my brother, who was always curious about engines, leaped to safety.

'Wonderful,' said my father to my brother, 'the age we live in. They say that over in England they're queued up steaming by the roadsides, like Iceland or the Yellowstone Park.'

'Just a bit overheated,' said Hookey. 'We won't be a jiffy.'

'Does it happen often?' said my father.

Ignoring the question, descending and opening the bonnet to peer and poke and tinker, Hookey said, 'Do you know a funny thing about this car?'

'She's chuman,' said Peter.

'You know the cross-roads at Clanabogan churchyard gate,' Hookey said. 'The story about it.'

'It's haunted,' said my father.

'Only at midnight,' said Peter.

As was his right and custom, my father stepped into the role of raconteur, 'Do you know that no horse ever passed there at midnight that didn't stop – shivering with fear. The fact is well attested. Something comes down that side road out of the heart of the wood.'

Hookey closed over the bonnet, screwed back the radiator cap and climbed again to the throne. He wiped his hands on a bunch of grass pulled for him and handed to him by Peter. Slowly he drew on again his gauntlet gloves. Bedecked with cowslips and dragging me along with them the ladies rejoined the gentlemen.

'Well, would you credit this now,' Hookey said. 'Peter and myself were coming from Dromore one wet night last week.'

'Pouring rain from the heavens,' said Peter, 'and the hood was leaking.'

'A temporary defect,' said Hookey. 'I mended it. Jack up the back axle, Peter, and give her a swing. And would you credit it, exactly at twelve o'clock midnight she stopped dead at the gate of Clanabogan churchyard?'

With an irony that was lost on Hookey my mother said, 'I could well believe it.'

'She's chuman,' said Peter.

'One good push now and we're away,' said Hookey. 'The slight gradient is in our favour.'

'Maybe,' he said to my father and brother, 'you'd lend Peter a hand.'

Twenty yards ahead he waited for the dusty pushers to climb aboard, the engine chug-chugging, little puffs of steam escaping like baby genii from the right-hand side of the bonnet. My father was thoughtful. He could have been considering the responsibilities of the machine age particularly because when it came to team pushing Peter was more of a cheer leader, an exhorter, a counter of one two three, than an actual motive force.

'Contact,' said Hookey.

'Dawn patrol away,' said Peter. 'Squadron Leader Baxter at the joystick.'

He mimicked what he supposed to be the noises of an

aeroplane engine and, with every evidence of jubilation, we were once again under way; and a day it was, made by the good God for jubilation. The fields, all the colours of all the crops, danced towards us and away from us and around us; and the lambs on the green hills, my father sang, were gazing at me and many a strawberry grows by the salt sea, and many a ship sails the ocean. The roadside trees bowed down and then gracefully swung their arms up and made music over our heads and there were more birds and white cottages and fuchsia hedges in the world than you would readily imagine.

'The bride and bride's party,' sang my father, 'to church they did go. The bride she goes foremost, she bears the best show. . . .'

'They're having sports today at Tattysallagh,' said Hookey.

'But I followed after my heart full of woe, for to see my love wed to another.'

We swept by a cross-roads where people and horses and traps were congregated after the last mass. In a field beside the road a few tall ash plants bore fluttering pennants in token of the sports to be.

'Proceed to Banteer,' sang my father, 'to the athletic sporting and hand in your name to the club comm-i-ttee.

'That was a favourite song of Pat O'Leeary the Corkman,' he said, 'who was killed at Spion Kop.'

Small country boys in big boots, knickerbockers, stiff celluloid collars that could be cleaned for Sunday by a rub of a wet cloth, and close-cropped heads with fringes like scalping locks above the foreheads, scattered before us to the hedges and the grass margins, then closed again like water divided and rejoining, and pursued us, cheering, for a hundred yards. One of them, frantic with enthusiasm, sent sailing after us a half-grown turnip, which bounced along the road for a bit, then sought rest in a roadside drain. Looking backwards I pulled my best or worst faces at the rustic throng of runners.

'In Tattysallagh,' said my father, 'they were always an uncivilised crowd of gulpins.'

He had three terms of contempt: Gulpin, Yob and, when things became very bad he became Swiftian, and described all offenders as Yahoos.

'Cavanacaw,' he said, 'and that lovely trout stream, the Creevan Burn. It joins the big river at Blacksessiagh. That there's the road up to Pigeon Top Mountain and the mass rock at Corraduine, but we'll come back that way when we've circumnavigated Dooish and Cornavara.'

We came to Clanabogan.

'Clanabogan planting,' he said.

The tall trees came around us and sunlight and shadow flickered so that you could feel them across eyes and hands and face.

'Martin Murphy the postman,' he said, 'who was in the survey with me in Virginia, County Cavan, by Lough Ramor, and in the Glen of Aherlow, worked for a while at the building of Clanabogan Church. One day the vicar said to him: "What height do you think the steeple should be?" "The height of nonsense like your sermons," said Martin, and got the sack for his wit. In frosty weather he used to seal the cracks in his boots with butter and although he was an abrupt man he seldom used an impolite word. Once when he was aggravated by the bad play of his wife who was partnering him at whist he said: "Maria, dearly as I love you there are yet moments when you'd incline a man to kick his own posterior".'

'There's the church,' my father said, 'and the churchyard and the haunted gate and the cross-roads.'

We held our breath but, with honeyed summer all around us and bees in the tender limes, it was no day for ghosts, and in glory we sailed by.

'She didn't hesitate,' said Peter.

'Wonderful,' said the third sister.

It was more wonderful that she imagined for, as the

Lord would have it, the haunted gate and cross-roads of Clanabogan was one of the few places that day that Hookey's motor machine did not honour with at least some brief delay.

'I'd love to drive,' said my brother. 'How did you learn to drive, Hookey?'

'I never did. I just sat in and drove. I learned the basic principles on the county council steamroller in Watson's quarries. Forward and reverse.'

'You have to have the natural knack,' Peter explained.

'What's the cut potato for, Hookey?' asked my brother.

'For the rainy day. Rub it on the windscreen and the water runs off the glass.'

'It's oily you see,' said Peter.

'Like a duck's back,' said the third sister.

'Where,' said my father – sniffing, 'do you keep the petrol?'

'Reserve in the tins clipped on the running board. Current supply, six gallons. You're sitting on it. In a tank under the front seat.'

'Twenty miles to the gallon,' said Peter. 'We're good for more than a hundred miles.'

'Godalmighty,' said my father. 'Provided it isn't a hundred miles straight up. 'Twould be sad to survive a war that was the end of better men and to be blown up between Clanabogan and Cornavara. On a quiet Sunday morning.'

'Never worry,' said Hookey. 'It's outside the bounds of possibility.'

'You reassure me,' said my father. 'Twenty miles to the gallon in any direction. What care we? At least we'll all go up together. No survivors to mourn in misery.'

'And turn right here,' he said, 'for Cornavara. You'll soon see the hills and the high waterfalls.'

We left the tarred road. White dust rose around us like smoke. We advanced half a mile on the flat, attempted the first steep hill and gently, wearily, without angry fumes or backfiring protests, the tremulous chuman car, lying down like a tired child, came to rest.

'We'll hold what we have,' said Hookey. 'Peter . . . pronto. Get the stones behind the back wheels.'

'Think of a new pastime,' said the third sister. 'We have enough cowslips to decorate the town for a procession.'

With the sweet face of girlish simplicity she asked, 'Do you buy the stones with the car?'

'We'd be worse off without them,' Hookey muttered.

Disguised as he was in helmet and goggles it was impossible to tell exactly if his creative soul was or was not wounded by her hint of mockery, but my mother must have considered that his voice betrayed pain for she looked reprovingly at the third sister and at the other two who were again impaled by giggles, and withdrew them out of sight down a boreen towards the sound of a small stream, to — as she put it — freshen up.

'Without these stones,' Peter panted, 'we could be as badly off as John MacKenna and look what happened to him.'

'They're necessary precautions,' said Hookey. 'Poor John would never use stones. He said the brakes on his car would hold a Zeppelin.'

The bonnet was open again and the radiator cap unscrewed but there was no steam and no geyser, only a cold sad silence, and Hookey bending and peering and probing with pincers.

'She's a bit exhausted,' Peter said.

'It's simple,' Hookey said. 'She'll be right as rain in a jiffy. Going at the hill with a full load overstrained her.'

'We should walk the bad hills,' Peter explained.

'Poor John MacKenna,' Hookey said, 'was making four fortunes drawing crowds to the Passionist monastery at Enniskillen to see the monk that cures the people. But he would never use the stones, and the only parking place at the monastery is on a sharp slope. And one evening when they were all at devotions doesn't she run backways and ruin all the flower-beds in the place and knock down a statue of Our Lord.'

'One of the monks attacked him,' said Peter, 'as a heathen that would knock the Lord down.'

'Ruined the trade for all,' said Hookey. 'The monks now won't let a car within a mile of the place.'

'Can't say as I blame them,' said my father.

'Poor John took it bad,' said Hookey. 'The lecture he got and all. He was always a religious man. They say he raises his hat now every time he passes any statue: even the Boer War one in front of the courthouse.'

'So well he might,' said my father.

Suddenly, mysteriously responding to Hookey's probing pincers, the very soul of the machine was again chug-chugging. But with or without cargo she could not or, being weary and chuman, would not assault even the first bastion of Cornavara.

'She won't take off,' said Hookey. 'That run to Belfast and back took the wind out of her.'

'You never made Belfast,' said my father, 'in this.'

'We did Tommy,' said Peter apologetically.

'Seventy miles there and seventy back,' said my father incredulously.

'Bringing a greyhound bitch to running trials for Tommy Mullan the postman,' said Hookey.

'The man who fishes for pearls in the Drumragh river,' said Peter.

They were talking hard to cover their humiliation.

'If she won't go at the hills,' my father said, 'go back to the main road and we'll go on and picnic at the seven streams at the Minnieburns. It's mostly on the flat.'

So we reversed slowly the dusty half-mile to the main road.

'One night in John Street,' Peter said, 'she started going backways and wouldn't go forwards.'

'A simple defect,' Hookey said. 'I remedied it.'

'Did you turn the other way?' asked the third sister.

Artlessly, Peter confessed, 'She stopped when she knocked down the schoolchildren-crossing sign at the bottom of Church

Hill. Nipped it off an inch from the ground, as neat as you ever saw. We hid it up a laneway and it was gone in the morning.'

My father looked doubtfully at Peter. He said, 'One of those nice shiny enamelled pictures of two children crossing the road would go well as an overmantel. And the wood of the post would always make firewood.'

Peter agreed, 'You can trust nobody.'

Hurriedly trying to cut in on Peter's eloquence, Hookey said, 'In fact the name of Tommy Mullan's bitch was Drumragh Pearl. Not that that did her any good at the trials.'

'She came a bad last,' burst out the irrepressible Peter.

'And to make it worse we lost her on the way back from Belfast.'

'You what?' said my father.

'Lost her in the dark where the road twists around Ballymacilroy Mountain.'

My mother was awed, 'You lost the man's greyhound. You're a right pair of boys to send on an errand.'

''Twas the way we stepped out of the car to take the air,' said Hookey.

By the husky note in his voice you could guess how his soul suffered at Peter's shameless confessions.

'And Peter looked at the animal, ma'am, and said maybe she'd like a turn in the air too. So we took her out and tied her lead to the left front wheel. And while we were standing there talking didn't the biggest brute of a hare you ever saw sit out as cool as sixpence in the light of the car. Off like a shot with the bitch.'

'If the lead hadn't snapped,' Peter said, 'she'd have taken the wheel off the car or the car off the road.'

'That would have been no great exertion,' said my father. 'We should have brought a greyhound along with us to pull.'

'We whistled and called for hours but all in vain,' said Peter.

'The hare ate her,' said the third sister.

'Left up the slope there,' said my father, 'is the belt of trees I planted in my spare time to act as a wind-breaker for Drumlish schoolhouse. Paddy Hamish, the labouring man, gave me a hand. He died last year in Canada.'

'You'd have pitied the children on a winter's day,' my mother said, 'standing in the playground at lunchtime taking the fresh air in a hilltop wind that would sift and clean corn. Eating soda bread and washing it down with buttermilk. On a rough day the wind from Lough Erne would break the panes of the windows.'

'As a matter of curiosity,' my father said, 'what did Tommy Mullan say?'

'At two in the morning in Bridge Lane,' said Peter, 'he was waiting for us. We weren't too happy about it. But when we told him she was last in the trials he said the bloody bitch could stay in Ballymacilroy.'

'Hasn't he always the pearls in the river,' my mother said.

So we came to have tea and sandwiches and lemonade in a meadow by the cross-roads in the exact centre of the wide saucer of land where seven streams from the surrounding hills came down to meet. The grass was polished with sunshine. The perfume of the meadowsweet is with me still. That plain seemed to me then as vast as the prairies, or Siberia. White cottages far away on the lower slopes of Dooish could have been in another country. The chief stream came for a long way through soft deep meadowland. It was slow, quiet, unobtrusive, perturbed only by the movements of water fowl or trout. Two streams met, wonder of wonders, under the arch of a bridge and you could go out under the bridge along a sandy promontory to paddle in clear water on a bottom as smooth as Bundoran strand. Three streams came together in a magic hazel wood where the tiny green unripe nuts were already clustered on the branches. Then the seven made into one, went away from us with a shout and a song towards Shaneragh, Blacksessiagh, Drumragh and Crevenagh, under the humpy crooked King's Bridge where James Stuart had passed on his way from Derry to the fatal brackish Boyne, and on through the town we came from.

'All the things we could see,' said my father, 'if this spavined brute of a so-called automobile could only be persuaded to climb the high hills. The deep lakes of Claramore. The far view of Mount Errigal, the Cock of the North, by the Donegal sea. If you were up on the top of Errigal you could damn' near see, on a clear day, the skyscrapers of New York.'

In his poetic imagination the towers of Atlantis rose glimmering from the deep.

'What matter,' said my mother. 'The peace of heaven is here.'

For that day that was the last peace we were to experience. The energy the machine didn't have or wouldn't use to climb hills or to keep in motion for more than two miles at a stretch, she expended in thunderous staccato bursts of backfiring. In slanting evening sunlight people at the doors of distant farmhouses shaded their eyes to look towards the travelling commotion, or ran up whinny hills for a better view, and horses and cattle raced madly around pastures, and my mother said the country would never be the same again, that the shock of the noise would turn the milk in the udders of the cows. When we came again to the crossroads of Tattysallagh the majority of the spectators, standing on the road to look over the hedge and thus save the admission fee, lost all interest in the sports, such as they were, and came around us. To oblige them the right rear tyre went flat.

'Peter,' said Hookey, 'jack it up and change it on.'

We mingled unobtrusively with the gulpins.

'A neat round hole,' said Peter.

'Paste a patch on it.'

The patch was deftly pasted on.

'Take the foot pump and blow her up,' said Hookey.

There was a long silence while Peter, lines of worry on his little puckered face, inspected the tube. Then he said, 'I can't find the valve.'

'Show it to me,' said Hookey.

He ungoggled himself, descended and surveyed the ailing member.

'Peter,' he said, 'you're a prize. The valve's gone and you put a patch on the hole it left behind it.'

The crowd around us was increasing and highly appreciative.

'Borrow a bicycle Peter,' said Hookey, 'cycle to the town and ask John MacKenna for the loan of a tube.'

'To pass the time,' said my mother, 'we'll look at the sports.'

So we left Hookey to mind his car and, being practically gentry as compared with the rustic throng around us, we walked to the gateway that led into the sportsfield where my mother civilly enquired of two men, who stood behind a wooden table, the price of admission.

'Five shillings a skull missus, barring the cub,' said the younger of the two. 'And half a crown for the cub.'

'For the what?' said my mother.

'For the little boy ma'am,' said the elder of the two.

'It seems expensive,' said my mother.

'I'd see them all in hell first – let alone in Tattysallagh,' my father said. 'One pound, twelve shillings and six pence to look at six sally rods stuck in a field and four yahoos running round in rings in their sock soles.'

We took our places on the roadside with the few who, faithful to athletics and undistracted by the novelty of the machine, were still looking over the hedge. Four lean youths and one stout one in Sunday shirts and long trousers with the ends tucked into their socks were pushing high framed bicycles round and round the field. My father recalled the occasion in Virginia, County Cavan, when Martin Murphy was to run at sports and his wife Maria stiffened his shirt so much with starch it wouldn't go inside his trousers, and when he protested she said, 'Martin, leave it outside and you will be able to fly.'

We saw two bicycle races and a tug-of-war.

'Hallions and clifts,' he said.

Those were two words he seldom used.

'Yobs and sons of yobs,' he said.

He led us back to the car. Peter soaked in perspiration had the new tube on and the wheel ready.

'Leave the jack in and swing her,' Hookey said. 'She's cold by now.'

There was a series of explosions that sent gulpins, yobs and yahoos reeling backwards in alarm. Peter screwed out the jack. We scrambled aboard, a few of the braver among the decent people, rushing into the line of fire to lend a hand to the ladies. Exploding, we departed, and when we were a safe distance away the watchers raised a dubious cheer.

'In God's name, Henry,' said my father, 'get close to the town before you blow us all up. I wouldn't want our neighbours to have to travel as far as Tattysallagh to pick up the bits. And the yobs and yahoos here don't know us well enough to be able to piece us together.'

Three miles further on Peter blushingly confessed that in the frantic haste of embarkation he had left the jack on the road.

'I'll buy you a new one, Henry,' my father said. 'Or perhaps Peter here could procure one on the side. By now at any rate, they're shoeing jackasses with it in Tattysallagh.

'A pity in a way,' he said, 'we didn't make as far as the stone fiddle. We might have heard good music. It's a curious thing that in the townlands around that place the people have always been famed for music and singing. The Tunneys of Castle Caldwell now are noted. It could be that the magic of the stone fiddle has something to do with it.

'Some day,' he said, 'we'll head for Donegal. When the cars, Henry, are a bit improved.'

He told us about the long windings of Mulroy Bay. He explained exactly how and why and in what year the fourth Earl of Leitrim had been assassinated in Cratloe Wood. He spoke as rapidly and distinctly as he could in the lulls of the backfiring.

Then our town was below us in the hollow and the Gortin mountains, deep purple with evening, away behind it.

'Here we'll part company, Henry boy,' said my father. ''Tisn't that I doubt the ability of Peter and yourself to navigate the iron horse down the hill. But I won't have the town blaming me and my family for having hand, act or part in the waking of the dead in Drumragh graveyard.'

Sedately we walked down the slope into the town and talked with the neighbours we met and asked them had they heard Hookey and Peter passing and told them of the sports and of the heavenly day it had been out at the seven streams.

My father died in a seaside town in the County Donegal – forty miles from the town I was reared in. The road his funeral followed back to the home places led along the Erne shore by the stone fiddle and the glistening water, across the Boa Island where there are no longer crossroads dances. Every roadside house has a television aerial. It led by the meadowland saucer of the Minnieburns where the river still springs from seven magic sources. That brooding place is still much as it was but no longer did it seem to me to be as vast as Siberia. To the left was the low sullen outline of Cornavara and Pigeon Top, the hurdle that our Bucephalus refused to take. To the right was Drumlish. The old schoolhouse was gone and in its place a white building, ten times as large, with drying rooms for wet coats, fine warm lunches for children and even a gymnasium. But the belt of trees that he and Paddy Hamish planted to break the wind and shelter the children is still there.

Somebody tells me, too, that the engine of Hookey Baxter's car is still with us, turning a circular saw for a farmer in the vicinity of Clanabogan.

As the Irish proverb says: It's a little thing doesn't last longer than a man.

# A great God's angel standing

Pascal Stakelum, the notorious rural rake, and Father Paul, the ageing Catholic curate of Lislap, met the two soldiers from Devon by the bridge over the Camowen River and right beside the lunatic asylum. It was a day of splitting sunshine in the year of the Battle of Dunkirk. Pascal and the priest were going to visit the lunatic asylum, Father Paul to hear confessions, Pascal to bear him company and to sit at a sealed distance while the inmates cudgelled what wits they had and told their sins. The two soldiers, in battledress and with heavy packs on their backs, were on their way home from Dunkirk, not home to Devon exactly but to Sixmilecross, to the house of two sisters they had married in a hurry before they set off for France. It was, as you may have guessed, six miles from our garrison town of Lislap to the crossroads village where the two sisters lived, and it was a very warm day. So every one of the four, two in thick khaki, two in dull black, was glad to stop and stand at ease and look at the smooth gliding of the cool Camowen.

The bridge they rested on was of a brownish grey stone, three full sweeping arches and, to the sides, two tiny niggardly arches. In a blue sky a few white clouds idled before a light wind, and beyond a wood at an upstream bend of the river a two-horse mowing-machine ripped and rattled in meadow grass. The stone of the bridge was cut from the same quarry as the stone in the high long wall that circled the lunatic asylum and went for a good half-mile parallel with the right bank of the river.

— In France it was hot, said the first soldier.

— He means the weather was hot, said the second soldier.

The four men, priest and rake and soldiers two, laughed at that: not, Pascal says, much of a laugh, not sincere, no heartiness in it.

— Hot as hell, said the second soldier. Even the rivers was hot.

— Boiling, said the first soldier. That canal at Lille was as hot as a hot bath.

— Ruddy mix-up, said the second soldier. The Guards, they fired at the Fusiliers, and the Fusiliers, they fired at the Guards. Nobody knew who was what. Ruddy mix-up.

They took the cigarettes Pascal offered.

— Boiling hot and thirsty, said the second soldier. Never knew such thirst.

Father Paul said: You could have done with some Devon cider.

— Zider, said the first soldier. There were zomething.

— Zomerzet you are, said the second soldier.

They all laughed again. This time it was a real laugh.

The Camowen water where it widened over gravel to go under the five stone arches was clear and cool as a mountain rockspring. Upstream, trout rings came as regularly as the ticks of a clock.

The two soldiers accepted two more cigarettes. They tucked them into the breast-pockets of their battledress. They hitched their packs, shook hands several times and knelt on the motorless roadway for Father Paul's blessing. They were not themselves Arcees, they said, but in camp in Aldershot in England they had been matey with an Arcee padre, and they knew the drill. Blessed after battle, they stood up, dusted their knees as carefully as if they'd never heard of mud or blood and, turning often to wave back, walked on towards the two sisters of Sixmilecross.

— Virginia, Father Paul said, was the best place I ever saw for cider.

Just to annoy him, Pascal said: Virginia, County Cavan, Ireland.

They were walking together on a narrow footwalk in the shadow of the asylum wall.

— Virginia, U.S.A., Paul said. The Old Dominion. Very well you know what Virginia I mean. They had great apple orchards there, and fine cider presses, around a little town called Fincastle under the shadow of the Blue Ridge Mountains. That was great country, and pleasant people and fine horses, when I was a young man on the American mission.

It was a period out of his lost youth that Paul frequently talked about.

In those days of his strange friendship with Pascal he was thin and long-faced and stoop-shouldered with the straining indignant stoop that is forced on tall people when the years challenge the power to hold the head so high. That day the sun had sucked a little moisture out of his pale cheeks. He had taken off his heavy black hat to give the light breeze a chance to ruffle and cool his thin grey hair, but the red line the hat rim had made was still to be seen and, above the red line, a sullen concentration of drops of sweat. He was though, as Pascal so often said, the remains of a mighty handsome man and with such dignity, too, and stern faith and such an eloquent way in the pulpit that it was a mystery to all of us what the bishop of the diocese had against him that he had never given him the honour, glory and profit of a parish of his own.

— In the mood those two boyos are in, Pascal said, it will take them no time at all walking to the sisters at Sixmilecross.

That was the way Pascal, in accordance with his animal nature, thought; and Sixmilecross was a village in which, as in every other village in our parts, Pascal had had some of the rural adventures that got him his dubious reputation, and that made us all marvel when we'd see a character like him walking in the company of a priest. In Burma, I once heard an old sweat say, adulterers kill a pig to atone for their crime, so it was only apt and proper, and even meet and just, that Pascal should be a pork butcher. When he went a-wooing in country places he'd never walk too far from his rattly old Morris Cowley without bringing with him a tyre lever or starting handle, for country girls were hell for having truculent brothers and if they didn't have brothers they had worse and far and away worse, male cousins, and neither brothers nor male cousins, least of all the male cousins, had any fancy for Pascal rooting and snorting about on the fringes of the family. That's Pascal, for you. But at the moment, Paul is speaking.

— A man hungers to get home, he said. The men from Devon won't count the time or the number of paces. Time, what's time? They've come a long walk from the dreadful gates of eternity. Once I told you, Pascal boy, you were such a rake and run-the-roads you'd have to live to be ninety, to expiate here on this earth and so dodge the devil.

Complacently Pascal said: The good die young.

— Ninety's a long time, Father Paul said. But what's time? Here in this part of my parish . . .

They were walking in at the wide gateway. He waved his black wide-brimmed hat in a circle comprehending the whole place, as big almost as the garrison town itself, for all the crazy people of two counties, or those of them that had been detected and diagnosed, were housed there.

— This part of my parish, he said. As much happiness or unhappiness as in any other part of the parish. But one thing that doesn't matter here is time. As far as most of them know, time and eternity are the same thing.

They walked along a serpentine avenue, up sloping lawns to the main door. The stone in the walls of the high building was cut from the same quarry as the stone that bridged the river, as the stone in the encircling wall. The stone floor in the long cool corridor rang under their feet. They followed a porter along that corridor to a wide bright hospital ward. Unshaven men in grey shirts sat up in bed and looked at them with quick bright questioning eyes. The shining nervous curiosity of the ones who sat up disturbed Pascal. He preferred to look at the others who lay quietly in bed and stared steadily at points on the ceiling or on the opposite wall, stared steadily but seemed to see neither the ceiling nor the opposite wall, and sometimes mumbled to nobody words that had no meaning. A few men in grey suits moved aimlessly about the floor or sat to talk with some of the bright curious men in the beds. Beside the doorway a keeper in blue uniform dotted with brass buttons sat and smoked and read a newspaper, raised his head and nodded to the priest, then returned to his pipe and his newspaper.

Father Paul moved from bed to bed, his purple stole about his neck. The murmur of his voice, particularly when he was at the Latin, was distinctly audible. His raised hand sawed the air in absolution and blessing. Once in a while he said something in English in a louder voice and then the man he was with would laugh, and the priest would laugh, and the man in the next bed, if he was a bright-eyed man, would laugh, and another bright-eyed man several beds away would start laughing and be unable to stop, and a ripple of laughter would run around the room touching everybody except the staring mumbling men and the keeper who sat by the door.

Pascal sat beside an empty bed and read a paperbacked book about a doctor in Germany who was, or said he thought he was, two men, and had murdered his wife, who had been a showgirl, by bathing her beautiful body in nitric acid. That sinful crazy waste of good material swamped Pascal in an absorbing melancholy so that he didn't for a few moments even notice the thin hand gripping his thigh. There, kneeling at his feet, was a man in grey clothes, misled into thinking Pascal was a priest because Pascal wore, as did the bright young men of that place and period, a black suit with, though, extremely wide and unclerical trousers. Pascal studied, with recognition, the inmate's grey jacket, the scarce grey hair, the spotted dirty scalp. The kneeling man said: Bless me, father, for I have sinned.

— Get up to hell Jock Sharkey, Pascal said. I'm no priest. You're crazy.

He was, he says, crimson in the face with embarrassment. The keeper was peeking over his newspaper, laughing, saying Jock sure was crazy and that, in fact, was why he was where he was. The keeper also blew smoke-rings from thick laughing lips, an irritating fellow. He said: Fire away, Pascal. It'll keep him quiet. I hear him two or three times a week.

— It wouldn't be right, Pascal said.

He had theological scruples, the only kind he could afford.

Only once in my life, he was to say afterwards, did a man ever ask me to listen to him confessing his sins and, fair enough, the place should be a lunatic asylum and the man, poor Jock Sharkey, that was put away for chasing women, not that he ever overtook them or did anybody any harm. They walked quick, he walked quick. They walked slow, he walked slow. He was just simply fascinated, the poor gormless bastard, by the sound of their feet, the hobbled trot, the high heels, you know, clickety-click, thigh brushing thigh. Poor Jock.

— What he'll tell you, said the keeper, is neither right nor wrong. Who'd anyway be better judge than yourself, Pascal? Even Father Paul doesn't know one half of what you know. You, now, would know about things Paul never heard tell of.

The man on his knees said: I suppose you'll put me out of the confession box, father. I'm a terrible sinner. I wasn't at mass or meeting since the last mission.

— Why was that? said Pascal the priest.

— The place I'm working in, they won't let me go to mass.

— Then it's not your fault, said Pascal. No sin. Grievous matter, perfect knowledge, full consent.

He did, he said afterwards, remember from his schooldays that impressive fragment of the penny catechism of Christian doctrine: the stud-book, the form-book, the rules for the big race from here to eternity.

— But when I go to confession, father, I've a bad memory for my sins. Will you curse me, father, if I forget some of them?

— By no means, Jock. Just recite what you remember.

The keeper, more offensive as his enjoyment increased, said that Pascal wouldn't know how to curse, that he didn't know the language. The head of the kneeling man nodded backwards and forwards while he mumbled the rhythmical words of some prayer or prayers of his childhood. Now and again the names of saints came clearly out of the confused unintelligible mumble, like bubbles rising from a marshy bottom to the surface of a slow stream. Then he repeated carefully, like a child reciting, these words from an old rebel song: I cursed three times since last Easter Day. At mass-time once I went to play.

Pascal was seldom given to visions except in one particular direction, yet he says that at that moment he did see, from his memory of school historical pageants, the rebel Irish boy, kneeling in all innocence or ignorance at the feet of the brutal red-coated captain whose red coat was, for the occasion, covered by the soutane of the murdered rebel priest.

The keeper said: You should sing that, Jock.

— I passed the churchyard one day in haste, Jock said, and forgot to pray for my mother's rest.

— You're sure of heaven, said the keeper, if that's the sum total of your sins. The Reverend Stakelum himself, or even Father Paul, won't get off so easy.

The penitent looked up at Pascal and Pascal looked down at stubbly chin, hollow jaws, sorrowful brown eyes. Poor Jock, Pascal thought, they put you away just for doing what I spend all my spare time, and more besides, at: to wit, chasing the girls. Only you never even seemed to want to catch up with them.

For poor Jock was never more than what we called a sort of a mystery man, terrifying the girls, or so they claimed, by his nightly wanderings along dark roads, his sudden sprints that ended as sharply and pointlessly as they began, his shouted meaningless words provoked perhaps by a whiff of perfume in his nostrils or by that provocative tap-tippity-tap of high hard heels on the metalled surface of the road. A child might awaken in the night and cry that there was a man's face at the window. A girl might run home breathless and say that Jock had followed her for half a mile, suiting his pace to hers, like a ghost or a madman. He couldn't be a ghost, although he was as thin and as harmless as any ghost. So we put him away for a madman.

He stared long and hard at Pascal. His thin right hand tightly grasped Pascal's knee.

— David Stakelum's son, he said. I'd know you anywhere on your father. Thank God to see you in the black clothes. Your father was a decent man and you'll give me the blessing of a decent man's son.

He bowed his head and joined his hands. Behind the newspaper the keeper was gurgling. Pascal said afterwards that his father wouldn't be too pleased to think that his hell's own special hell-raker of a son bore him such a resemblance that even a crazy man could see it. But if his blessing would help to make Jock content then Jock was welcome to it. So he cut the sign of the cross over the old crazy dirty head. He touched with the tips of the fingers of both hands the bald patch on the dome. He held out those fingers to be kissed. The most fervent young priest fresh from the holy oil couldn't have done a better job. Pascal had so often studied the simple style of Father Paul. The keeper was so impressed that he folded the newspaper and sat serious and quiet.

Father Paul walked slowly towards them, along the narrow passage between the two rows of beds. Walking with him came a fat red-faced grey-headed inmate. The fat inmate talked solemnly, gestured stiffly with his right hand. The priest listened, or pretended to listen, turning his head sideways, stretching his neck, emphasising the stoop in his shoulders. He said: Mr. Simon, you haven't met my young friend, Pascal.

The fat man smiled benevolently at Pascal but went on talking to the priest. As you know, sir, I am not of the Roman Catholic persuasion, yet I have always been intrigued by the theory and practice of auricular confession. The soul of man, being walled around and shut in as it is, demands some outlet for the thoughts and desires that accumulate therein.

He had, Pascal says, a fruity pansy voice.

— The child, he said, runs to its mother with its little tale of sorrow. Friend seeks out friend. In silence and secrecy souls are interchanged.

It was exactly, Pascal was to say, as if the sentences had been written on the air in the loops and lines of copper-plate. You could not only hear but see the man's talk: A Wesleyan I was born, sir, and so remain. But always have I envied you Roman Catholics the benefits of the confessional, the ease that open confession brings to the soul. What is the Latin phrase, sir?

Paul said: Ad quietam conscientiam.

— Ad quietam conscientiam, Simon repeated. There is peace in every single syllable. There is much wisdom in your creed, sir. Wesley knew that. You have observed the spiritual similarity between Wesley and Ignatius of Loyola.

The keeper said: Simon, Doctor Murdy's looking for you. Where in hell were you?

— He asks me where I have been, sir. Where in hell.

Father Paul said: He means no harm, Simon. Just his manner of speaking.

Simon was still smiling. From elbow to bent wrist and dangling hand, his right arm was up like a question mark. He said to Father Paul: Surveillance, sir, is a stupid thing. It can accomplish nothing, discover nothing. If I were to tell this fellow where I had been, how could he understand? On this earth I have been, and beyond this earth.

He shook hands with the priest but not with Pascal nor

the keeper nor Jock Sharkey. He walked with dignity past the keeper and back down the ward.

— There goes a travelled man, Pascal said.

Father Paul was folding his purple stole. He said: There are times when religion can be a straitjacket.

— It's not Simon's time yet for the straitjacket, the keeper said. When the fit takes him he'll brain the nearest neighbour with the first handy weapon.

At the far end of the ward where Simon had paused for a moment, there was a sudden noise and a scuffling. The keeper said: Too much learning is the divil.

He thumped down the passage between the beds.

— Now for the ladies, Father Paul said. You'll be at home there, Pascal, They say all over the town that no man living has an easier way with the ladies.

Pascal was to report to myself and a few others that if Paul had wanted to preach him a sermon to make his blood run cold and to put him off the women for the rest of his life, he couldn't have gone about it in a better way.

Is it true that, as the poet said, you never knew a holy man but had a wicked man for his comrade and heart's darling? Was it part of Paul's plan to pick Pascal as his escort and so to make an honest boy out of him or, at least, to cut in on the time that he would otherwise spend rummaging and ruining the girls of town and country? The thing about Pascal was that, away from the companionship of Paul, he thought of nothing but women when, of course, he wasn't butchering pork, and perhaps he thought of women even then. Like many another who is that way afflicted he wasn't big, violent, handsome, red-faced or blustering. No, he went about his business in a quiet way. His hair was sparse, of a nondescript colour, flatly combed and showing specks of dandruff. He wore horn-rimmed spectacles. He was one of those white-faced fellows who would, softly and secretly and saying nothing about it to their best friends, take advantage of their own grandmothers. The women were mad

about him. They must have been. He kept himself in fettle
and trim for his chosen vocation. When the two soldiers and
Paul were, in the sunshine on the Camowen Bridge, talking
of Devon cider, Pascal was thinking, he says, of sherry and
raw eggs, and oysters, porter and paprika pepper.

On the day of Paul's funeral he said to me: A decent
man and I liked him. But, my God, he had a deplorable set
against the women or anybody that fancied the women.

— Except myself, he said. For some reason or other he put
up with me.

— That day at the female ward, he said, at the geriatrics
you call 'em, I cheated him, right under his nose, God forgive
me. And may Paul himself forgive me, since he knows it
all now.

Pascal stood at the threshold of this female ward while
Father Paul, purple stole again around his neck, moved,
listening and forgiving with God's forgiveness, from bed to
bed. Pascal wasn't much of a theologian, yet looking at the
females in that female ward he reckoned that it was God, not
the females, who needed forgiveness. They were all old females,
very old females, and as such didn't interest Pascal. He had
nothing, though, against old age as long as it left him alone.
His father's mother was an attractive, chubby, silver-haired
female, sweet as an apple forgotten and left behind on a rack in a
pantry, wrinkled, going dry, yet still sweet beyond description.
But these sad old females, a whole wardful of them, were also
mad and misshapen, some babbling like raucous birds, some
silently slavering.

He couldn't make up his mind whether to enter the ward
and sit down or to walk up and down the cool echoing corridor.
He always felt a fool when walking up and down like a sentry,
but then he also felt a fool when standing or sitting still. He
was just a little afraid of those caricatures of women. This was
the first time he had ever been afraid of women, and afraid to
admit to himself that these creatures were made in exactly the
same way as women he had known. He was afraid that if he

went into the ward and sat down he would see them in even greater detail than he now did from the threshold. He was young. Outside the sun was shining, the Camowen sparkling under the sun, the meadow grass falling like green silk to make beds for country lovers. But here all flesh was grass and favour was deceitful and beauty was vain. It was bad enough looking at the men. To think what the mind could do to the body. But it was hell upon earth looking at the women. Jock Sharkey, like a million lovers and a thousand poets, had gone mad for beauty. This, in the ward before him, was what could happen to beauty.

He stepped, shuddering, back into the corridor and collided with a tall nurse. He apologised. He smelled freshly-ironed, starched linen and disinfectant, a provoking smell. A quick flurried glance showed him a strong handsome face, rather boyish, brick-red hair bursting out over the forehead where the nurse's veil had failed to restrain it. He apologised. He was still rattled by his vision in the ward. Contrary to his opportunist instinct he was even about to step out of the way. But the nurse didn't pass. She said: It is you, Pascal Stakelum, isn't it? Did they lock you up at last? A hundred thousand welcomes.

He had to do some rapid thinking before he remembered. There were so many faces in his memory and he was still confused, still a little frightened, by those faces in the ward. She didn't try to help. She stood, feet apart and solidly planted, and grinned at him, too boyish for a young woman but still fetching. She was, if anything, taller than he was. Her brother, then he remembered, had gone to school with us, a big fellow, as dark as she was red, very clever but capricious, making a mockery of things that he alone, perhaps, of all of us could understand and, in the end, throwing the whole thing up and running away and joining the Royal Air Force. So the first thing Pascal said, to show that he knew who she was, was to ask about the brother, and when would he be coming home. She said: He won't be coming home.

— Why for not?

She said he had been killed at Dunkirk.

Coming right after the prospect of the mad old women, that was a bit of a blow in the face, but at least, he told himself, clean death in battle was not madness, deformity, decay; and the moment gave Pascal the chance to sympathise, to get closer to her. He held her hands. He said he was sorry. He said he had always liked her brother. He had, too. They had, indeed, been quite friendly.

She said: It's war. He would always do things his own way.

She seemed proud of her brother, or just proud of having a brother dead at Dunkirk.

— This is no place to talk, Pascal said. And I'm with Father Paul. Meet me this evening at the Crevenagh Bridge.

That was the old humpy seventeenth-century bridge on the way to a leafy network of lovers' lanes and deep secret bushy ditches.

— Not this evening, she said. I'm on duty. But tomorrow.

— Eight o'clock on the dot, said Pascal.

That was his usual time during the summer months and the long warm evenings. And he was very punctual.

She walked away from him and towards Father Paul. He looked after her, no longer seeing the rest of the ward. She was a tall strong girl, stepping with decision and a great swing. Jock Sharkey would have followed her to the moon.

Father Paul, the shriving done, was again folding his stole. He joked with a group of old ladies. He told one of them that on his next visit he would bring her a skipping rope. He told another one he would bring her a powderpuff. He distributed handfuls of caramels to the whole crew. They cackled with merriment. They loved him. That was one bond between Pascal and himself. The women loved them both.

— But if he meant to preach to me that time, Pascal said to us, by bringing me to that chamber of horrors, I had the laugh on him.

*  *  *

In the sunshine on the lawn outside, the superintending doctor stood with his wife and his dogs, three Irish setters, one male, two female. The doctor and his wife stood, that is, and the setters ran round and round in erratic widening circles.

Those smart-stepping Devon men were by now approaching Sixmilecross, and the two sisters, and rest after battle and port after stormy seas.

The doctor was a handsome cheery fellow, even if he was bald. He wore bright yellow, hand-made shoes, Harris tweed trousers and a high-necked Aran sweater. The wife was small and dainty and crisp as a nut, and a new wife; and the two of them, not to speak of the three setters, were as happy as children. They talked – the doctor, the woman, Paul and Pascal – about the war, and about the two soldiers from Devon and their two women in Sixmilecross. Then Father Paul wished the doctor and his wife many happy days, and he and Pascal stepped off towards the town. At the gateway they met a group of thirty or forty uniformed inmates returning, under supervision, from a country walk. One of them was gnawing a raw turnip with which, ceasing to gnaw, he took aim at Pascal and let fly. Pascal fielded the missile expertly – in his schooldays he had been a sound midfield man – and restored it to the inmate who was still chewing and looking quite amazed at his own deed. All this, to the great amusement of the whole party, inmates and three keepers. But, oddly enough, Paul didn't join in the merriment. He stood, silent and abstracted, on the grass at the side of the driveway. He looked at the sky. His lips moved as though he were praying, or talking to himself.

Pascal gave away what cigarettes he had left to the hiking party and he and the priest walked on, Paul very silent, over the Camowen. When they were halfways to the town, Paul said: Some men can't live long without a woman.

Pascal said nothing. He remembered that there was a story that Paul had once beaten a loving couple out of the hedge with a blackthorn stick. He remembered that Paul came from a stern mountainy part of the country where there had been a priest in every generation in every family for three hundred years. He thought of the red nurse and the hedge ahead of her. So he said nothing.

— That new wife of his, Paul said, was American. Did you notice?

— She dressed American, Pascal said. But she had no accent.

— She comes from a part of the States and from a class in society where they don't much have an accent, Paul said. At least not what you in your ignorance would call an American accent.

Pascal said: The Old Dominion.

— You're learning fast, Paul said.

The town was before them.

— Three wives he had, Paul said. One dead. Irish. One divorced. English. And now a brand new one from Virginia. Some men can't go without.

Pascal made no comment. He contented himself with envying the bald doctor his international experience. He resolved to travel.

— Most men, said Paul, aren't happy unless they're tangled up with a woman. The impure touch. But the French are the worst. Their blood boiling with wine. From childhood. How could they keep pure?

Pascal hadn't the remotest idea. So he made no comment. He didn't know much about the French but he reckoned that just at that moment in history they had enough and to spare on their plates without also having to worry about purity.

— But pleasures are like poppies spread, Paul said.

He was a great man always to quote the more moralising portions of Robert Burns. Pascal heard him out: You seize the flower, its bloom is shed. Or like the snow falls in the river – a moment white, then melts forever. Or like the borealis race, that flit ere you can point their place.

Or like the rainbow's lovely form, evanishing amid the storm.

— Burns, said Father Paul, well knew what he was talking about. Those, Pascal, are the words of wisdom gained through sad and sordid experience.

Pascal agreed. He was remembering the nurse's dead brother who had been a genius at poetry. He could write parodies on anything that any poet had ever written.

When Pascal met the nurse at the Crevenagh Bridge on the following evening she was, of course, in mourning. But the black cloth went very well with that brilliant red hair. Or like the rainbow's lovely form. There was something about it, too, that was odd and exciting, like being out, he said, with a young nun. Yet, apart from the colour of her clothes, she was no nun. Although, come to think of it, who except God knows what nuns are really like?

Pascal, as we know, was also in black but he had no reason to be in mourning. It had rained, just enough to wet the pitch. Otherwise the evening went according to Operation Pascal. When he had first attacked with the knee for the warming-up process he then withdrew the knee and substituted the hand, lowering it through the band of her skirt, allowing it to linger for a playful moment at the bunker of the belly button. Thereafter he seemed to be hours, like fishermen hauling a net, pulling a silky slip out of the way before the rummaging hand, now living a life of its own, could negotiate the passage into her warm drawers. Pascal didn't know why he hadn't made the easier and more orthodox approach by laying the girl low to begin with and then raising skirt and slip, except it was that they were standing up at the time, leaning against a sycamore tree. The rain had passed but the ground was wet, and to begin his wooing by spreading his trenchcoat (Many's the fine rump, he boasted, that trenchcoat had kept dry, even when the snow was on the ground.) on the grass, seemed much too formal.

Pascal Stakelum's days, or evenings or nights, were complex with such problems.

Later came the formal ceremonious spreading of the trenchcoat on a protective mattress of old newspapers, and the assuming by both parties, of the horizontal. By that time the big red girl was so lively that he swore she'd have shaken Gordon Richards, the King of them All, out of the saddle. She kept laughing and talking, too, so as to be audible, he reckoned, thirty yards away but fortunately he had chosen for the grand manoeuvre a secluded corner of the network of lanes and ditches. He had a veteran's knowledge of the terrain and he was nothing if not discreet.

He was not unmindful of the brother dead in faraway France. But then the brother had been such an odd fellow that even in Pascal's tusselling with his strong red sister he might have found matter for amusement and mockery. As Pascal bounced on top of her, gradually subduing her wildness to the rhythmic control of bridle and straddle and, in the end, to the britchen of his hands under her buttocks, he could hear her brother's voice beginning the schoolboy mockery of Shelley's soaring skylark: Hell to thee, blithe spirit. Pascal and the splendid panting red girl moved together to the poet's metre.

That was one brother Pascal did not have to guard against with starting handle or tyre lever. Working like a galley slave under the dripping sycamore he was in no fear of ambush.

Paul got his parish in the end, the reward of a well-spent life, he said wryly. He died suddenly in it before he was there for six months. That parish was sixty miles away from Lislap, in sleepy grass-meadow country where the slow River Bann drifts northwards out of the great lake. Pascal missed Paul's constant companionship more than he or anybody else would have believed possible and began, particularly after Paul's sudden death, to drink more than he had ever done before, and went less with the girls, which puzzled him as much as it did us. It worried him, too: for in the house of parliament or public house that we specially favoured, he asked me one day was he growing old before his time because he was growing fonder of drink and could now pass a strange woman on the street without wondering who and what she was.

— You're better off, Pascal, I said. What were you ever doing anyway but breaking them in for other men? You never stayed long enough with any one woman to be able in the long run to tell her apart from any other woman.

He was more hurt than I had imagined he would be. But he sadly agreed with me, and said that some day he hoped to find one real true woman with whom he could settle down.

— Like with poor Paul that's gone, he said. Some one woman that a man could remember to the last moment of his life.

— No, I'm not crazy, he said. Two days before his death I was with Paul in his parish, as you know. We went walking this evening after rain, by the banks of a small river in that heavy-grass country. That was the last walk we had together. The boreen we were on went parallel with the river bank. We met an old man, an old bewhiskered codger, hobbling on a stick. So Paul introduced us and said to Methusaleh: What now do you think of my young friend from the big garrison town of Lislap?

— The old fellow, said Pascal, looked me up and looked me down. Real cunning country eyes. Daresay he could see through me as if I was a sheet of thin cellophane. But he lied. He said: Your reverence, he looks to me like a fine clean young man.

— That was an accurate description of me, Pascal Stakelum, known far and wide.

Pascal brooded. He said: A fine clean young man.

— Then that evening, he said, we sat for ages after dinner, before we knelt down to say the holy rosary with those two dry sticks of female cousins that did the housekeeping for him. One quick look at either of them would put you off

women for time and eternity. There's an unnerving silence
in the houses that priests live in: the little altar on the
landing, you know, where they keep the sacrament for sick
calls at night. Imagine, if you can, the likes of me on my
bended knees before it, wondering would I ever remember
the words when it came my turn to lead the prayers. But I
staggered it. Closed my eyes, you might say, and took a run
and jump at it, and landed on the other side word perfect. It
would have been embarrassing for Paul if I hadn't been able
to remember the words of the Paterandave in the presence of
those two stern cousins. One evening one of them sat down
opposite me in a low armchair and crossed her legs, poor
thing, and before I could look elsewhere I had a view of
a pair of long bloomers, passion-killers, that were a holy
fright. You wouldn't see the equal of them in the chamber
of horrors. Six feet long and coloured grey and elastic below
the knee. But when the two cousins were off to bed, and good
luck to them, we sat and talked until all hours, and out came
the bottle of Jameson, and Paul's tongue loosened. It could
be that he said more than he meant to say: oh, mostly about
Virginia and the Blue Ridge Mountains and the lovely people
who always asked the departing stranger to come back again.
Cider presses near Fincastle. Apple orchards. Dogwood trees
in blossom. He went on like that for a long time. Then he got
up, rooted among his books, came back with this one book
covered in a sort of soft brown velvet with gold lettering and
designs on the cover and, inside, coloured pictures and the
fanciest printing you ever saw, in red and in black. He said
to me: Here's a book, Pascal, you might keep as a memory
of me when I'm gone.

— So I laughed at him, making light of his gloomy face,
trying to jolly him up, you know. I said: Where, now, would
you be thinking of going?

— Where all men go sooner or later, he said.

— That was the end of my laughing. That's no way for a
man to talk, even if he has a premonition.

— Keep the book as a token, Paul said to me. You were never much for the poetry, I know. But your wife when you find her might be, or, perhaps, some of your children. You've a long road ahead of you yet, Pascal, all the way to ninety, and poetry can lighten the burden. That book was given to me long ago by the dearest friend I ever had. Until I met yourself, he said. Long ago in a distant country and the wench is dead.

— Those were the last words I ever heard Paul speak, excepting the Latin of the mass next morning, for my bus passed the church gate before the mass was rightly over, and I had to run for it. But bloody odd words they were to come from Paul.

— Common enough words, I said. Anybody could have said them.

— But you didn't see the book, Pascal said. I'll show it to you.

He did, too, a week later. It was an exquisite little edition, lost on Pascal, I thought with some jealousy, both as to the perfection of the bookmaker's art and as to the text, which was William Morris telling us, there in a public house in Lislap, how Queen Guenevere had defended herself against the lies of Sir Gauwaine, and a charge of unchastity. Fondling the book, I was not above thinking how much more suitable than Pascal I would have been as a companion for old Paul. So that I felt more than a little ashamed when Pascal displayed to me with what care he had read the poem, underlining here and there in red ink to match the rubric of the capitals and the running titles on the tops of the pages. It was, almost certainly, the only poem to which he had ever paid any particular attention, with the possible exception of that bouncing parody on Shelley's skylark.

— It's like a miniature mass book, he said. Red and black. Only it was by no means intended for using at the mass. See here.

He read and pointed with his finger as he read: She threw

her wet hair backward from her brow, her hand close to her
mouth touching her cheek.

— Coming from the swimming-pool, Pascal said, when the
dogwoods were in blossom. You never knew that Paul was
a champion swimmer in his youth. Swimming's like tennis.
Brings out the woman in a woman. Arms wide, flung-out,
breasts up. Oh, there were a lot of aspects to Paul. And listen
to this: Yet felt her cheek burned so, she must a little touch
it. Like one lame she walked away from Gauwaine.

— Time and again, Pascal said, he had heard it said that
lame women had the name for being hot. Once he had seen
on the quays of Dublin a one-legged prostitute. The thought
had ever afterwards filled him with curiosity, although at
the time he wouldn't have risked touching her for all the
diamonds in Kimberley.

— And her great eyes began again to fill, he read, though
still she stood right up.

That red nurse, he remembered, had had great blue eyes,
looking up at him like headlamps seen through mist.

— But the queen in this poem, he said, was a queen
and no mistake. And in the summer it says that she grew
white with flame, white like the dogwood blossoms and all
for this Launcelot fellow, lucky Launcelot, and such a pansy
name. One day, she says, she was half-mad with beauty and
went without her ladies all alone in a quiet garden walled
round every way, just like the looney bin where I met that
nurse. And both their mouths, it says, went wandering in
one way and, aching sorely, met among the leaves. Warm,
boy, warm. Then there's odd stuff here about a great God's
angel standing at the foot of the bed, his wings dyed with
colours not known on earth, and asking the guy or girl in
the bed, the angel has two cloths, you see, one blue, one red,
asking them, or him or her, to guess which cloth is heaven
and which is hell. The blue one turns out to be hell. That
puzzles me.

It puzzled both of us.

— But you must admit, said Pascal, that it was a rare book for a young one to be giving a young priest, and writing on it, look here, for Paul with a heart's love, by the Peaks of Otter in Virginia, on a day of sunshine never to be forgotten, from Elsie Cameron. Usually the women give breviaries to the priests, or chalices, or amices, or albs, or black pullovers. She must have been a rare one, Elsie Cameron. Would you say now that she might have had a slight limp? It's a Scottish name. Paul was forever talking about what he called the Scots Irish in Virginia and the fine people they were. All I know is that Scottish women are reputed to be very hot. They're all Protestants and don't have to go to confession.

Pascal had known a man who worked in Edinburgh who said that all you had to do to set a Scotswoman off was to show her the Forth Bridge, the wide open legs of it. That man had said that the Forth Bridge had never failed him.

When I said to Pascal that all this about Paul could have been as innocent as a rose, he said he was well aware of that: he wasn't claiming that Paul had done the dirty on the girl and left her to mourn out her life by the banks of the James River. But that it may all have been innocent for Paul and Elsie only made it the more mournful for Pascal. Fond memories and memories, and all about something that never happened.

— Any day henceforth, Pascal said, I'll go on a journey just to see for myself those Blue Ridge Mountains. Were they ever as blue as Paul thought they were? Cider's the same lousy drink the world over. What better could the orchards or women have been in Virginia than in Armagh? You see he was an imaginative man was old Paul, a touch of the poet, and soft as putty and sentimental away behind that granite mountainy face. Things hurt him, too. He told me once that one day walking he met that mad Maguire one from Cranny, the one with the seven children and no husband, and tried to talk reason to her, and she used language to him the like of which he had never heard, and he turned away with tears in his eyes. He said he saw all women degraded and the Mother of God sorrowful in Nancy Maguire who was as bad as she was mad. An odd thought. He should have taken the stick to her the way I once heard he did to a loving couple he found under the hedge.

But pleasures are like poppies spread, as Paul would say, walking the roads with Pascal ad quietam conscientiam, looking at mad Nancy and listening to her oaths, seeing Elsie Cameron under the apple trees under the Blue Mountains in faraway Virginia. Once I wrote a story about him and it was printed in a small little-known and now defunct magazine. That story was all about the nobility of him and the way he used to chant the words of Burns; and then about how he died.

He came home to his parochial house that morning after reading the mass and sat down, one of the cousins said, at the breakfast table, and sat there for a long time silent, looking straight ahead. That wasn't like him. She asked him was he well. He didn't answer. She left the room to consult her sister who was fussing about in the kitchen. When she came back he had rested his head down on the table and was dead.

Looking straight ahead to Fincastle, Virginia, and seeing a woman white with flame when the dogwood blossomed, seeing the tall angel whose wings were the rainbow and who held heaven, a red cloth, in one hand, and hell, a blue cloth, in the other.

There was no place in that story of mine for Pascal Stakelum, the rural rake.

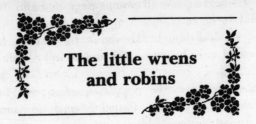

# The little wrens and robins

Cousin Ellen wrote poetry for the local papers and was the greatest nonstop talker you, or anybody else, ever listened to. The poetry was of three varieties: religious poetry, love poetry and nature poetry that went like this, the nature poetry, I mean:

> Farewell to the dreary Winter,
> Welcome to the days of Spring
> When the trees put on their coats of green,
> And the birds with joy will sing.
> The daffodils put on their gowns,
> How proudly they stand up,
> To shake their dewy golden coats
> On the smiling buttercups.

After reading the poem of which that was the opening stanza, I was ever afterwards somewhat in awe of Cousin Ellen: her daring in rhyming only one little up with all those buttercups, her vision of the daffodils as tall fashion models swaying and pirouetting in extravagant golden gowns, of the smirking of those sly little gnomes and peeping-toms, the buttercups, who were so delighted that the stately ladies should shake the dew of their coats to be caught in and savoured from the yellow cups. No one could deny that Cousin Ellen had a poetic mind and a special vision, except my father who loved quietude, and long calm silent days, and a garden growing, and who was driven out of all patience by Ellen's ceaseless clickety-clack when, once a month, she travelled twenty-five miles by train from Hazelhatch to visit us.

— And Uncle Tommy, did you hear that Peter McQuade of Lettergesh sold that bay mare he had at an unimaginable high price, I don't know what the exact sum was, but it was, I hear, absolutely over the moon and out of sight, he ran her at the Maze Races and won all before her and he brought her south to the Curragh of Kildare, and some rich American saw her and bought her on the spot and flew off with her to Hialeah in Florida, that was a travelled mare, they say Florida's lovely, America that's where the money is, not that money's everything if you haven't happiness, get out there to America, Ben boy, before it's too late, as I left it too late and this, Aunt Sara, is an American fashion magazine I brought for you to look over, the styles will absolutely blind you, you should have been at Hazelhatch last Sunday when the Reverend Dr. Derwent preached the most divine sermon about the Sacred Heart, I wrote a poem in my head on the way home from church and sent him an autographed copy, you see he clips every one of my poems out of the papers and pastes them into one big book, he says that he'll be the first person ever to possess my collected works, he's just divinely handsome, too handsome for a priest as they say although personally I see no harm at all in a priest being handsome, Our Divine Lord himself was the handsomest person that ever lived and exactly six feet in height, and very much the favourite man of the bishop at the present moment, he's leading the diocesan pilgrimage to Lourdes, Fatima, Rome and home by Lisieux this year, an all-rounder, and I have every intention of going, I never saw Lisieux and I have always adored Saint Thérèse, they may call her a little flower but she was in her own quiet way a warrior, as Dr. Derwent says, and she wrote the divinest book, solid as a rock just like Mamma who's in the best of health, nothing shakes her, all plans to make the business prosper, we're expecting such a passing rush of tourists this year on the way to West Donegal, they all stop to stock up with food and drink at Hazelhatch Inn, that old picturesque thatch and the diamond-paned latticed windows, particularly those high cosy dormers, catch the eye, you'd be amazed the number of people who stop to take pictures and then come in and buy, beauty and business mixed . . .

Like Molly Bloom she was no great believer in punctuation which is really only a pausing for breath, and Cousin Ellen's breath always seemed as if it would last for hours. My father said that after half-an-hour or less of her monologue, in which she needed no assistance except seemingly attentive faces, he always felt that he was drowning in a warm slow stream, drifting slowly, sinking slowly, brain and body numb, faraway bells in his ears, comfortable, but teetotally helpless. That talk, he claimed, threatened the manhood in a man, which was why all men had escaped, while there was still time, from Cousin Ellen, except Dr. Derwent who was sworn celibate and thus safe, and except for one other wretch whom she talked into matrimony and who lasted for a year and then vanished mysteriously: dead by asphyxiation, my father said, and buried secretly under the apple trees at the back of the old house at Hazelhatch.

Those were lovely apple trees.

Drowning in what deep waters of constant talk was I, the Saturday I walked her through the marketing crowds in from the country, from brown mountains and green river valleys, to our town? We went along John Street and High Street and Market Street, by the Catholic church with the high limping spires that could be seen for miles, by the eighteenth-century courthouse with Doric columns that was once admired by no less a person than Tyrone Guthrie who said that if you tilted the long sweep of High Street and Market Street the other way, the courthouse steps would be the perfect stage on which to produce a Passion Play. Church and courthouse were our architectural prides. Cousin Ellen, as far as I can remember from my drowning swoon, talked about love. Being all of eighteen I was still interested.

— Your sister, Dymphna, in Dublin, she said, is very happy, Edward and myself called to see her two months ago, not rich

but happy and happiness is all, I said to her if only Edward
and myself can be as happy as yourself and your husband, you
know, Ben, Edward and myself are to be wedded shortly and
I do hope everything turns out for the best, and I hope that
suitcase isn't too heavy, but oh you're so young and strong
and athletic, and they really shouldn't allow these fruit-stalls
on the open street any more, not with modern traffic and all
that, although you have to admit that they're most colourful
and picturesque but they really belong to the Middle Ages,
and see me safely now on to the bus for Dromore, the crowd
here is just fearful, and oh this letter I forgot, do drop it
in the post office for me, it's for Edward, love is all, just a
perfect understanding between people and when human love
fails there is always the love of the Sacred Heart which I wrote
in a poem that Dr. Derwent read out from the pulpit, there is
nothing on earth we may cling to, all things are fleeting here,
the pleasures we so oft have hunted, the friends we've loved so
dear . . .

Then off she went not, as it happened, to Dromore where
she had wanted to visit some other relatives, but to Drumquin,
because in the confusion into which she had talked me, I
deposited herself and her suitcase on the wrong bus. To the
casual observer there isn't much difference between Drumquin
and Dromore, but one is twenty miles from the other, and it's
a bind to be in one when you want to be in the other. But
Cousin Ellen found some obliging commercial traveller who
drove her to Dromore, and God help him if he had to listen
to her for the time it took to drive twenty miles. She wrote me
a most amusing letter about it all. She was easier to read than
to listen to. The accident about the buses had really tickled
her, she said, for life was just like that: you headed off for
somewhere and ended up somewhere else. She bore no grudge
and we would be better friends than ever, wouldn't we? We
were, too.

About that time I headed off for Dublin to go through
the motions of a university education, and didn't see Cousin

Ellen again, although we constantly exchanged letters, until the husband had come and gone, and she herself was in hospital close to Hazelhatch with some rare ailment that was to stop her talk forever, and her poetry.

The letter to Edward that that day she gave me to post I found two weeks later when, pike-fishing on the Drumragh River, I had a little leisure and used it to clear out my pockets. Since it then seemed too late to send it to where it should have gone I tore it up into tiny pieces and cast it on the running water. My mother always said that you should never burn letters from friends or, indeed, anything that had to do with friendship. Fire destroyed. Water did not. So she was constantly making confetti out of letters and flushing them down the john.

The deep pike-water of the Drumragh, still patterned with froth from the falls at Porter's Bridge, bore away northwards the words of love that Ellen had meant for Edward. Life, she might have said had she then known, was also like that. Our friendship, at any rate, remained unaltered. After all, she was the only other writer in the family.

> Ah, yes! And the tiny little lambs,
> They, too, will play and skip
> In the fields just decorated
> With the daisy and cowslip.
> The blackbird and the thrushes
> They are glad to see you here,
> The little wrens and robins
> To all you bring good cheer.

She was, as you may remember, addressing the Spring. Her favourite picture hung on a wall of the old oak-timbered country kitchen at Hazelhatch. It was called: Springtime on an Ayrshire hillside, or, the Muse of Poetry descends to Robert Burns while at the plough.

But those words were a paltry effort to describe that picture and, out of respect for the memories of Burns and Cousin Ellen and, of course, of the Muse, I will try to do better.

The poet in the picture wears the height of style: a blue tailed-coat, knee-breeches a little off-white, strong woollen stockings and stout buckled shoes. He has taken one hand, the right, from the plough and is using that hand to raise with a sweep a tall hat of a type that in nobler times may have been general issue for ploughmen, or poets. His profile is noble, his head held high to escape extinction in an ample cravat. He salutes a plump girl in a white revealing nightgown sort of costume of the period, perhaps, of the French Directorate, and who is standing on a cloud about two feet above the backs of two patient and unnoticing horses. The girl on the cloud carries a wreath and it is clearly her intention to put the wreath where the tall hat has been. In the bottom left-hand corner a fieldmouse is playing the part of a wee sleekit cowering timorous beastie yet is clearly, to judge from the glint in her eyes, an intent observer of the coronation ceremony and, in the words of another poet, is confidently aware that a mouse is miracle enough to stagger sextillions of infidels. In the background, for it is spring in Ayrshire and a little late for ploughing the birds are plentiful on the branches and in a pale blue sky.

That picture, I feel, had its influence on Ellen:

> The man whose work is in the field
> From you his joy can't hide,
> As he treads along at break of day
> With two horses by his side.
> He whistles all along his way
> And merrily will sing.
> This is a birthday once again,
> Each morning of the Spring.

That picture, too, is always very much present to me. When the Empress of Hazelhatch, as my youngest sister called Ellen's mother, our grass-widowed aunt by marriage, died, and Hazelhatch passed into the hands of strangers, she left me the picture. Ellen and myself, she said, had liked it, and each other. Was the old lady remembering, too, one sad lulled day of sunshine when we sat in the kitchen at Hazelhatch and looked at the picture and she told me what I had already partly guessed that morning, that Ellen would die in hospital?

All around us in the old kitchen were cases of brown stout just freshly bottled in a careful and religious ritual at which I had been allowed to assist, along with a new girl who was there, from the County Mayo, to work in the bar and grocery and learn the trade. A long procession of girls had come and gone and benefited, perhaps, from the strict wisdom of the Empress, even if they had most certainly sighed and writhed and groaned under her discipline. She still decanted her own port, a good Graham, black as your boot – and solid, but that decanting she did on her own, no assistants, no encouragement even to spectators. Certain things were just too sacred.

That port was famous.

— It fixed her marriage, my father said, good and proper. Your good mother's brother could think of nothing but port and running horses. Never left the bar except to go to Punchestown or the Maze or Strathroy Holm or Galway or Gowran Park or Tramore or Bellewstown Hill or the Curragh itself, or the horsefairs of Ballinasloe or Cahirmee. When he ran away to the States and never came back he was both bow-legged and purple in the face.

— He couldn't come back, said my mother.

She felt very sore about the whole story. He had been her favourite brother. She explained: He went to Canada, not the States, and then jumped the line at Buffalo and could never again get his papers in order. He got in but couldn't get out. There were hundreds like him.

— I often wondered why he ran away, said that youngest

sister with the thin face and the dark hair and the whiplash of a tongue. Then I met the Empress of Hazelhatch with her long black gown and her hair mounted high on a Spanish comb, and dyed horse-chestnut as sure as God, and her pince-nez, sitting behind the bar all night to speak to the better sort of people, but never demeaning herself by serving a customer, and I knew then why he would run to Alberta, or farther if he could get without beginning to come home again round the world.

Because that sister was herself an embryo empress she was never happy at Hazelhatch. For myself, as easy-going as my father or a wag-by-the-wall clock, I loved my visits to the place, the picture of the poet, the strong drone of the old lady's voice, the odour of good groceries and booze, the glow of old oak, the high bedroom with slanted ceiling and dormer window and an angled criss-crossed vision of the road west to Mount Errigal and the Rosses and the ocean, the apples in the orchard, the procession of young, discontented and frequently sportive girls. Memories of those visits stay with me, stilled, separated from all else, not frayed by time. That particular day the Empress said to me: How did Ellen look when you saw her this morning?

Nobody except her mother could have considered or enquired how Ellen looked. She talked so much you didn't see. So, to answer, I had to think back painstakingly. That was all the more difficult to do because we had left the kitchen and gone, rather sadly, out to the orchard where it seemed unkind and even sinful to think how somebody looked who was going to die, and who had loved that orchard.

> Oft times I sit and think,
> And wonder if God sends
> This season, Spring, so beautiful
> To all his city friends.
> Ah no! there are no green fields
> There are no little lambs to play . . .

For one thing, that morning Ellen had not been in the least like the Muse of Poetry descending to salute Robert Burns at the plough. She had always dressed modestly, mostly in browns or mother-of-god blues with the breast-bone well covered in white frills and lace and such; and there had never been a pick on her bones. Never before had I noticed that she was so freckled, scores of tiny dark-brown freckles around her eyes and down the slopes of her nose. The paleness of her ailing face, perhaps, made them more than ever noticeable. Freckled people are always great talkers and even illness could not stop her tongue: only death or the last gaspings that preceded it.

— It must be heavenly for you, she said, to feel that you are really and truly walking the paths of learning, and in a city that has been ennobled by the footsteps of so many great scholars and poets, how I envy you, I always so wanted to get to the university, but when I'm up and about again and out of this bed I promise you a visit in Dublin and you must show me all the sights and famous places, promise, you'll find my mother very quiet and brooding these days, I can't think what's wrong with her, but sometimes she gets like that, it may be that the new girl and herself do not get on so well, a strange girl from the County Mayo, a great singer, she came to see me several times, and sometimes I think she resembles me, she wants to sing just as I write poems, a lovely voice, too, but it's so sad, such clean regular features and an exquisite head of dark hair, but that purple discolouration on one side of her face, God help her, she would have to sing always with one side of her face away from the audience . . .

Because there was winter and the end of things in the room, even if it was high summer outside the window, I told her about the letter forgotten, then torn into fragments and sent sailing on the Drumragh. I told her about my mother and her opinions on fire and water. She said that, perhaps, it would have been better for both of them, meaning the vanished husband and herself, if it had ended the way the letter did: gone peacefully on the easy water. She said my mother had always been kind. She stepped

out of bed and walked with me as far as the door of the room.
She wore a heavy blue dressing-gown. She kissed me. We never
met again.

> Ah no! there are no green fields,
> There are no little lambs to play,
> But walk out in the country
> On any fine spring day . . .

So I in the orchard, all alone and sad, am fixing a
puncture in the back wheel of the lofty ancient bicycle on
which the Empress of Hazelhatch is wont to cruise forth in
deep-green drowsy summers, her skirts high above the dust,
her head high above the hedges, surveying the labour of the
fields, occasionally saluting the workers. To me, and softly
singing to herself for she is proud of her voice and the
old lady flatters her about it, comes the Mayo girl with
the face, flawless and faultless in shape but discoloured on
the left cheek. She stands beside me, at my left hand. Our
hands touch as we run the bicycle tube through a basin of
water so as to raise a bubble and locate the puncture. The
birds in the orchard trees are silent because it is the sultry
month of least song. But the girl for a while sings in a sort
of sweet whisper about, of all things, moonlight in Mayo.
Then she says: It isn't my day off, and I want to get to
Strabane.

— Why?

— What do you think? A fella.

— Ask her for the evening off.

— She's hell on fellas. You ask her. She'd grant you
anything.

— I'm a fella.

— You're the white-headed boy around here. Say you want
to take me to the pictures.

— What picture?

— Any picture. No picture.

> But walk out in the country
> On any fine spring day.
> And there you'll find what art can't paint
> Nature's gifts so fair:
> The trees, the flowers, the streamlets
> And the many birds so rare.

The road is dusty and the hedges high. Had Ellen never written a poem about summer? The girl sings as she walks. It is four miles to the village of Lifford, old houses shaggy with flowering creepers, then across the great bridge where the Mourne River, containing the water of the Drumragh, from Tyrone, meets the Finn River from Donegal to form, between them, the spreading Foyle; then half a mile across level water-meadows to the town of Strabane. She sings about the bird in the gilded cage. But walking through Lifford, curious faces looking out over half-doors, she stops singing and says: Mrs. Lagan is dying, isn't she?

Ellen's married name takes me by surprise. She says: You needn't talk about it if you don't want to. It's just that I like her.

— So do I.

— She's very clever. She's a great poet.

— Not exactly great.

— She gets printed.

— In local papers.

— Nevertheless.

We lean on the bridge and watch the mingling of the Mourne and the Finn, and the wagtails darting and diving over a shining triangle of sand and gravel. She says: The old lady is kindly but very strict. Mrs. Lagan is generous but very sad. They say there never was a man, but one, who could listen to her or talk her down. She should have lived in a world where men talked more.

— Like where?

— New York or Dublin or London or Milan. Big singing

cities. Her soul's mate was a flowery preaching priest. They should have been allowed to marry, the old lady says. They'd have made a perfect couple. She'd have made a perfect minister's wife. Did you ever look at a minister's wife? They're all like that. All poetry and bazaars.

— She could have preached better than anyone.

We follow the level road across the water-meadows. There is a raised footwalk designed to keep pedestrians dry-shod in time of flood. The clock has stopped forever on that still day in Strabane. She says: She likes me to sing when I go to see her.

She sings: Ah, sweet mystery of life at last I've found you. When she has finished singing I declaim:

> You may have your city pleasures
> And its praises you may sing,
> But there's naught on earth that can compare
> With the country's dales in spring.

— What's that?

— The voice of Cousin Ellen.

— I could sing that.

She sings it to a slow sweet tune I never heard before or since. Under the apple trees had Ellen's poetic soul taken possession of the girl?

We sit on the quiet river bank to pass the time until my train departs for Dublin or until her fella arrives. She sits at my left hand. When I hold her chin and try to turn her lips towards me she stiffens her neck, then looks away towards the town. So, when I hear the train whistle, I leave her unkissed there by the Mourne River, waiting for the fella. Often afterwards in Dublin I wonder what song she sings for him, what side of her face does she turn towards him.

# A room in Linden

One day in the dark maze of the yew-hedges Sister Lua, who has arthritis, looks up at him from her wheelchair which he's pushing, and says: Tell me the truth. Don't be modest about it. Are you Nanky Poo?

Since he is a bookish young man it is an exciting thing for him to have history living along the corridor. The Poet he's reading just before he leaves his room writes that there's a wind blowing, cold through the corridor, a death-wind, the flapping of defeated wings from meadows damned to eternal April. The poet has never seen it, but he could have been writing about this corridor. On its dull green walls, a mockery of the grass and green leaves of life, the sun never shines. All day and all night the big windows at the ends of the corridor, one at the east wing of the house and one at the west, are wide open, and from whichever airt the wind does blow it always blows cold. The rooms on the north side of the corridor are, as one might expect, colder and darker than the rooms on the south side, or would be if their light and heat depended totally on the sun.

Before the nuns got here and turned the place into a convalescent home it was lived in by a family famous for generations for a special brand of pipe tobacco. The old soldier who is reluctantly, vociferously fading away in a room on the north side of the corridor, says: This house was built on smoke. Just think of that. Smoke.

The old soldier himself belongs to some branch of the family that emigrated to South Africa and made even more money out of burgundy than the people who stayed at home made out of smoke, and there was always as much soldiering as smoke in the family; and big-game hunting, too, to judge by the fearful snarling mounted heads left behind and surviving, undisturbed by nuns or convalescents, in the entrance hall.

— You'll be nice to the old man, won't you, Mother Polycarp had said to him. He'll bore you to death. But he needs somebody to listen to him. He hasn't much longer to talk, in this world at any rate.

So he talks to the old soldier in the evenings and, in the afternoons, to the old priest and historian, dying as methodically and academically as he has lived, checking references, adding footnotes, in a room on the south side of the corridor. At other times he reads in his own room, or has visitors, or wheels Sister Lua's wheelchair in the ample bosky grounds, or leaves the grounds on his own and goes through quiet suburban roads to walk slowly, tapping his stick, in the public park that overlooks, across two walls and a railway, the flat sand and the bay. It is not an exciting life, but it's not meant to be.

He wheels Sister Lua round and round the dark cloisters of the yew-hedge maze from the corner where Jesus is condemned to death to the central circle where he is laid in the tomb. He tells her that he is not Nanky Poo.

— Well, I heard you had poems in that magazine. And I didn't see your name. And there is this poet called Nanky Poo. And he's very good. About the missions.

— Not me, alas, sister. I was never on the missions.

— Know you weren't. A university student.

Although she is always sitting down and being wheeled she is also always breathless and never quite begins or finishes a sentence, and it is necessary to fill in her words and meanings as she goes along. Bird-like, he knows, isn't much of a description, but she is bird-like, little hands like claws because of the arthritis, of course, a little nose like a beak peeking out from under the nun's pucog. To the left corner of her pale unvarnished little mouth, so often twisted with patience in pain, there's a mole with two hairs. She loves the dark green maze that grew up, like the house, out of smoke and was used by the nuns as a setting for a via dolorosa with life-size figures; and backgrounds of good stone columns and arches robbed from the wreckage of some eighteenth-century mansion. His first faux pas with the old historian had to do with those stations of the cross. One dull evening when the talk wasn't going so well he had, just to make chat, said: Don't they have a big day here once a year? People coming in hundreds to do the stations of the cross. What day does that happen on?

The old man pulls the rug more tightly around his long legs. His feet are always cold. In large bodies, Edmund Burke held, circulation is slower at the extremities, but the coldness of the old man's feet is just the beginning of death. He snuffs black snuff expertly from the hollow between thumb and forefinger, he sneezes, he says with crushing deliberation: Good Friday, my good young man. Even the younger generation should be aware that the Lord was crucified on Good Friday.

He's a carnaptious old bastard and even for the sake of Mother Polycarp, the kindly reverend mother, who is always thanking God for everything, it's sort of hard to suffer him at times. But he has both made and written history, and poems, too, of a learned sort, and collected folksong, and the best people have written about him and discovered an old-world courtesy and all the rest of that rot behind his rude exterior: the old-world courtesy of a Scandinavian sea-rover putting the full of a monastery of shaven-pated monks to the gory hatchet. By comparison the old soldier who has actually killed his man in far-away wars, is a gentleman. But then the old soldier is simply fading away, all battles fought and won, all comrades gone before him, all trumpets sounding from the other side. The old priest, still trying to work, has his last days aggravated by a mind that remembers everything and by the pain of a stomach cancer.

He leaves Sister Lua in the charge of a big red-headed nurse and walks down the main avenue towards suburbia and the park by the sea. The old white-haired vaudeville entertainer who has some sort of shaking paralysis, which he says is an occupational disease, waves to him from his seat by the grotto under the obelisk and gives him three letters to post at the postbox outside the gate. They are, he notices, all addressed to well-known celebrities of screen, stage and television: one in Dublin, one in London, one in New York. Out there is the world of healthy living people.

Life and playing children are, of course, all around him in the park by the sea but it isn't quite the same thing. There isn't enough of life there to help him to stop thinking of old men dying. He is very much on his own either because of his sullenness, or because he thinks that while he may be of interest to himself he couldn't possibly be of interest to anybody else. Nothing humble about that, though. In that park he's really a visitor from a special sort of world, from a cold green corridor damned to eternal December: sort of exclusive, though, a rich old soldier, a famous old historian, the artist who is still in touch with the best people; and only the best die in that corridor.

One old man who sits on a green wooden seat, close to the play-hall where the children run when it rains, talks to him as if he would gladly talk longer. He discourages that old man with abrupt sentences for he has, at the moment, enough of old men. He walks on beyond him and along by the tennis courts. A stout bespectacled girl with strong tanned legs plays awkwardly with a tall blond handsome fellow who wins every set and enjoys his superiority, while she seems to enjoy being beaten. A stranger from a strange land, he enjoys, as he passes or rests for a while on a seat and watches, the leaping of her legs. So everybody is happy and the park is beautiful. The blond boy isn't even good at the game and he, the stranger, knows that if it wasn't for the stiff hip, still slowly recovering, he could challenge him and beat him easily. But then the stout girl, legs excepted, isn't really interesting.

He himself is blond and doesn't take too well to the sun. So his favourite seat is in a shady corner under dark horse-chestnuts whose white candles are fading. He likes the place also because nobody else sits there. Strollers seem to accelerate as they walk past. Once in a while children run shouting, hooting through the dark tunnel, from one shire of sunshine into another. Through a fence of mournful laurels and copper beeches he sees the glitter of the sun on the lake. Out of the corner of his left eye he sees a well-built girl in white shorts flat on her back on the sunny grass. Sometimes she reads. Sometimes she raises her legs and, furiously with flashing thighs, pedals an invisible bicycle, faster and faster until it seems as if she has seven or seventeen legs, until the flash of her thighs takes the shape of a white circle. Her belly muscles must be jingling like springs. The joints in her hips, unlike his own, must be in perfect lubricated condition. She is at the moment one of the five women in his life: Polycarp thanking God for the rain and the sunshine, for the hail and the snow; Lua, twisted in her chair; she who, nameless, cycles on her back on the grass; the strong-legged tennis player whose name, he has heard the blond fellow shout, is Phyllis; and A. N. Other.

To the rear of his shady corner there is a privet hedge and a high wooden fence and a gate with a notice that says no admission except on business. That's exactly the way he feels. Adam in Eden must have had just such a corner where he kept his tools and experimented with slips and seeds. But then before Adam and Eve made a pig's ass out of a good arrangement the garden must have looked after itself and needed none of that sweat-of-the-brow stuff. What would old Thor the thunderer, brooding in his room, biting on his cancer, think of that?

Belloc, says the old priest, was a big man who looked as if all his life he had eaten too much and drunk too much. The best way to learn French is to read cowboy and injun stories. They hold the interest better than Racine.

Aware of his own inanity, he says: translations.

Before that face, oblong, seemingly about twelve feet long, like a head cut out of the side of some crazy American mountain, he is perpetually nonplussed into saying stupidities.

— Cowboys and injuns, my good young man, are not indigenous to the soil of France.

— There's a city called Macon in Georgia, U.S.A.

— There's a city called everything somewhere in the States. Naturally they mispronounce the names.

So it goes on. You can't win with the old bastard.

— Darlington, he says, used to call on Hopkins to take him out for walks. Hopkins was for ever and always complaining of headaches. What else can you expect, Darlington would say to him, immured up there in your room writing rubbish. I'm not so sure that Darlington wasn't right.

He is at that time just entering his Hopkins phase and if he wasn't afraid of that granite face, eyes sunken and black and burning, jawbones out rigid like a forked bush struck by lightning, he would defend the poet, quoting his sonnet about the windhover which, with some difficulty, he has just memorised. Yet it still is something to hear those names tossed about by a man who knew the men, and was a name himself. He feels grateful to Mother Polycarp who, as a friend of his family, has invited him to this place for a while, after his year in orthopaedic, so that he can read his books and learn to walk at his ease. In all that green cold corridor, which is really a place for old men, he is the only person who is going to live. He searches for something neutral to say: Wasn't Hopkins always very scrupulous about marking students' papers?

— He was a neurotic Englishman, my good fellow. They never could make up their minds between imperialism and humanitarianism. That's what has them the way they are. Darlington was English, too, of course, the other sort, the complacent Englishman, thinking that only what is good can happen to him, and that all his works are good. Then a young upstart called Joyce put him in a book. That should have been a lesson to Darlington, if they have books in heaven or wherever he went to.

He should, as Mother Polycarp says, be taking notes, thank God, except he feels that if he did so, secretly even in his room, the old lion might read his mind and take offence. The old man laughs seldom, but he's laughing now, perhaps at some memory of two English Jesuits marooned in Ireland, or at some other memory surfacing for a second in the dark crowded pool behind his square forehead. He has kept his hair, a dirty grey, standing up and out as if it had never encountered a comb. The long bony hands tighten the rug about his knees. The cold is creeping upwards.

In the green corridor he kneels for a while at the prie-dieu before the shrine, not praying, just thinking about age and death, and looking up at the bearded face of St. Joseph, pure and gentle, guardian of the saviour child. With a lily in his hand. Another old man and, by all accounts, very patient about it. What in hell is St. Joseph, like Oscar Wilde or somebody, always doing with a lily in his hand? An awkward class of a thing for a carpenter to be carrying.

Before his hip betrayed him he has had a half-notion of being a priest, but a year in orthopaedic, bright nurses hopping all around him, has cured him by showing him that there are things that priests, in the ordinary course of duty, are not supposed to have.

— You're too young, the old soldier says, to be in this boneyard.

He's a small man with a red boozy face, a red dressing-gown, a whiskey bottle and a glass always to his right hand. The whiskey keeps him alive, thank God, Mother Polycarp says. He is, like St. Joseph, gentle but not so pure, rambling on about dirty doings in far-away places, Mombasa and Delhi are much mentioned, about Kaffir women, and about blokes who got knocked off in the most comical fashion. He laughs a lot. He doesn't need a considered answer or a balanced conversation, just a word now and then to show he's not alone. He shares the whiskey generously. He has bags of money and, when he dies, he'll leave the perishing lot to the nuns.

— They do good, you know. Keep perky about it, too. Who else would look after the likes of me? Ruddy boneyard, though. Elephants' graveyard. Get out of here and get a woman. Make sons. Before it's too late. Would get out myself only nobody would have me any more, and I couldn't have them. Only whiskey left. But I had my day. When I was your age I laid them as quick as my batman could pull them out from under me. Three women shot under me at the battle of Balaclava and all that. Fit only for the boneyard now and the nuns. They don't want it and I can't give it. But there's always whiskey, thank God, as the mother says. A field behind the barracks where old wind-broken cavalry mounts went on grass with the shoes off until they died. At least we didn't eat them like the bloody Belgians. Smell of slow death around this place.

He sniffs the whiskey and laughs and then coughs. By night the coughing is constant. Lying awake and listening, the young man has a nightmarish feeling that they are all in prison cells, all dying, which is true, all the living are dying, and after one night the sun will never rise again on the park, and every time the cycling girl spins her legs she's another circle nearer to the grave. His own healthy youth has already collapsed in illness. Life is one collapse after another. The coughing goes on and on. To be a brave soldier and to end up coughing in a lonely room. Let me outa here. Ho, Sister Lua, I am not Nanky Poo.


— But every day that passes, Mother Polycarp tells him, brings you a day nearer to getting back to your studies, thank God. You made a great recovery in orthopaedic.

She is a tall woman with a long flat-footed step and more rattlings of keys and rosary beads than seem natural even in a nun. When he tells her that, she laughs and says, of course, that she has the keys of the kingdom, thank God. She has a good-humoured wrinkled mannish face, and she is famous everywhere for her kindness and her ability to gather money and build hospitals.

Does she say to the old men: Every day that passes brings you a day nearer heaven, thank God?

She naturally wouldn't mention death as the gate of heaven.

He has a feeling that none of them want to go any farther forward, they look backward to see heaven: on the day a new book was published or a new woman mounted or a new show went well. Heaven, like most things, doesn't last, or could only be an endless repetition of remembered happiness, and would in the end be, like dying, a bloody bore.

In her chair as he wheels her, Sister Lua, chirping like the little robin that she is, prays a bit and chats a bit and, because of her breathlessness and the way she beheads her sentences and docks the tails off them, he has to listen carefully to know whether she is chatting or praying. The life-size figures in the maze of dark yews – fourteen Christs in various postures, with attendant characters from jesting Pilate to the soldiers by the tomb – have acquired a sombre existence of their own. Do they relax at night, yawn, stretch stiff limbs, mutter a curse, light a cigarette, say to hell with show business? He must try that one out on the vaudeville man, shaking his way to the grave, on the seat by the grotto under the obelisk.

— Weep not for me, Sister Lua prays, but for yourselves and for your children.

The lord is talking to the weeping women of Jerusalem and not doing a lot to cheer them up. Some anti-semitical Irish parish priest must have written the prayers that Lua reels off. He didn't think much either of the kind of recruitment that got into the Roman army: these barbarians fastened him with nails and then, securing the cross, allowed him to die in anguish on this ignominious gibbet.

From the prayer book she has learned, by heart, not only

the prayers but the instructions that go with them. She says, as the book instructs: Pause a while.

He pauses. The yew-hedges are a dark wall to either hand. Twenty paces ahead, the lord, in an arbour, is being lowered from the cross. The dying has been done.

— Nanky Poo. Nanky Poo.

— Sister, I am not Nanky Poo.

— But I call you Nanky Poo. Such a lovely name.

— So is Pooh Ba.

— Pooh Ba is horrible. Somebody making mean faces. Nanky Poo, you must write a poem for Mother Polycarp's feast-day. So easy for you. Just a parody. Round Linden when the sun was low, Mother Polycarp the Good did go.

— There's a future in that style.

— You'll do it, Nanky Poo?

— At my ease, sister. Whatever Nanky Poo can do, I can do better.

By the laying of the lord in the tomb they encounter A. N. Other. She tries to escape by hiding behind the eighteenth-century cut-stone robbed from the old house, but Sister Lua's bird's-eye is too quick and too sharp for her.

— Nurse Donovan, Nurse Donovan, the French texts have arrived.

— Yes, Sister Lua.

— When can you begin, Nanky Poo?

— Any time, sister.

— So useful to you, Nurse Donovan, French, when you're a secretary.

She is a small well-rounded brunette who has nursed in the orthopaedic hospital until something happened to her health. He is in love with her, has been for some time. Nothing is to come of it. He is never to see her again after he leaves the convalescent home. The trouble is that Sister Lua has decided that the girl must be a secretary and that Nanky Poo must teach her French, and it is quite clear from the subdued light in the girl's downcast dark eyes that she doesn't give a fiddler's fart about learning anything, even French, out of a book. Worse still: on the few occasions on which he has been able to corner the girl on her own he hasn't been able to think of a damn thing to talk about except books. How can he ever get through to her that pedagogy is the last thing in his mind?

She wheels Sister Lua away from him to the part of the house where the nuns live. Between the girl and himself Sister Lua has thrown a barbed-wire entanglement of irregular verbs. No great love has ever been so ludicrously frustrated.

A white blossom that he cannot identify grows copiously in this suburb. Thanks be to God for the thunder and lightning, thanks be to God for all things that grow.

No, Sister Lua, I am not Nanky Poo, am a disembodied spirit, homeless in suburbia, watching with envy a young couple coming, white and dancing, out of a house and driving away to play tennis, am a lost soul blown on the blast between a green cold corridor of age and death, and the children running and squealing by the lake in the park.

Beyond the two walls and the railway line the sea is flat and purple all the way to Liverpool. He envies the young footballers in the playing fields close to where the cycling girl lies flat on her back and rides to the moon on her imaginary bicycle. He envies particularly a red-headed boy with a superb left foot, who centres the ball, repeating the movement again and again, a conscious artist, as careless as God of what happens to the ball next, just so that he drops it in the goalmouth where he feels it should go. The footballer is on talking terms with the cycling girl. He jokes and laughs with her when the ball bounces that way. She stops her cycling to answer him. From his shadowy corner under the chestnuts Nanky Poo watches and thinks about his latest talk with the vaudeville man on his seat by the grotto under the obelisk.

The obelisk has also been built on smoke to celebrate the

twenty-first birthday of a son of the house who would have been the great-grand-uncle of the old soldier.

— Vanished somewhere in India, the poor fellow. There was a rumour to the effect that he was eaten by wild beasts. A damn hard thing to prove unless you see it happen. Anyway he did for a good few of them before they got him. Half of the heads in the hallway below are his.

The obelisk stands up on a base of a flowering rockery, and into the cave or grotto underneath the rockery the nuns have, naturally, inserted a miniature Lourdes: the virgin with arms extended and enhaloed by burning candles, Bernadette kneeling by a fountain of holy water that is blessed by the chaplain at its source in a copper tank.

— The candles, says the vaudeville man, keep my back warm. He wears a faded brown overcoat with a velvet collar. His white hair is high and bushy and possibly not as well trimmed as it used to be. The skin of his shrunken face and bony Roman nose has little purple blotches and, to conceal the shake in his hands, he grips the knob of his bamboo walking-cane very tightly. When he walks his feet rise jerkily from the ground as if they did so of their own accord and might easily decide never to settle down again. The handwriting on the envelopes is thin and wavery as if the pen now and again took off on its own.

— You know all the best people.

— I used to.

He is never gloomy, yet never hilarious. Somewhere in between he has settled for an irony that is never quite bitter.

— You still write to them.

— Begging letters, you know. Reminders of the good old days. They almost always work with show people. I never quite made it, you know, not even when I had the health. But I was popular with my own kind. This one now.

He points to a notable name on one envelope.

— We met one night in a boozer in London when I

wasn't working. He stood me a large Jameson straight away,
then another, then another. He asked me to dine with him.
We talked about this and that. When we parted I found a
tenner in the inside breast pocket of my overcoat. While we
were dining he had slipped into the cloakroom. No note, no
message, just a simple tenner to speak for itself. He wasn't
rich then, mark you, although as the world knows he did
well afterwards. But he remembers me. He promises to come
to see me. Do you know, now that I think of it, this was the
very overcoat.

The cycling girl has stopped cycling and is talking to the
red-headed footballer. He stands above her, casually bouncing
the ball on that accurate left foot. Whatever he's saying the
girl laughs so loudly that Nanky Poo can hear her where he
sits in gloom and broods on beggary. She has a good human
throaty sort of a laugh.

The night there is no coughing, but only one loud single
cry, from the next room, he knows that the old soldier has
awakened for a moment to die. He rises, puts on slippers
and dressing-gown, and heads down the corridor to find the
night nurse. But Mother Polycarp is there already, coming
stoop-shouldered, beads and keys rattling, out of the old
man's room.

— Thank God, she says, he died peacefully and he had the
blessed sacrament yesterday morning. He wandered a lot in
his time but he came home in the end.

He walks down the stairway to the shadowy main hall.
Do the animals in the half darkness grin with satisfaction at
the death of a man whose relative was eaten by one or more
of their relatives? The front door is open for the coming of
the doctor and the priest. Above the dark maze of yew-hedge
the obelisk is silhouetted against the lights of the suburb. The
place is so quiet that he can hear even the slight noise of the
sea over the flat sand. This is the first time he has been out
of doors at night since he went to orthopaedic. Enjoying the

freedom, the quiet, the coolness, he walks round and round in the maze until his eyes grow used to the blackness and he is able to pick out the men and women who stand along the via dolorosa. They are just as motionless as they are during the day. When he comes back Mother Polycarp is waiting for him in the hallway.

— Now you're bold, she says. You could catch a chill. But every day that passes brings you nearer to freedom, thank God, and you can walk very well now.

She crosses herself as she passes the shrine in the corridor. She says: One thing that you could do now that you are up, is talk to himself. Or listen to him. He's awake and out of bed and lonely for somebody to talk to.

He is out of bed but not fully dressed; and, in a red dressing-gown that must have been presented to him by Mother Polycarp, he doesn't seem half as formidable as in his black religious habit. There is an open book on the rug that, as usual, covers and beats down the creeping cold from his thighs and knees. He is not reading. His spectacles are in their case on the table to his right hand. Above the light from the shaded reading-lamp his head and shoulders are in shadow. For once, since he is red and not black and half invisible, Nanky Poo feels almost at ease with him.

From the shadows his voice says: Credit where credit is due, young man. The first Chichester to come to Ireland was certainly one of the most capable and successful robbers who ever lived. He stole most of the north of Ireland not only from its owners but even from the robbers who stole it from its owners. Twice he robbed his royal master, James Stuart, the fourth of Scotland and the first of England. The man who did that had to rise early in the morning. For although King James was a fool about most things he was no fool about robbery: it was he who got the Scots the name for parsimony. Chichester stole the entire fisheries of Lough Neagh, the largest lake in the British Isles, and nobody found out about it until after he died. *Age quod agis*, as the maxim says. Do what you do. At his own craft he was a master. I dealt with him in a book.

— I read it.

— Did you indeed? A mark in your favour, young man.

— As a matter of fact, sir, the copy of it I read had your name on the flyleaf. Father Charles from your monastery loaned it to me when I was in orthopaedic.

As soon as the words are out he knows he has dropped the biggest brick of his career, and prays to Jesus that he may live long and die happy and never drop a bigger one. He has never known silence to last so long and be so deafening. Even the bulb in the reading-lamp makes a sound like a big wind far away. Blood in the ears?

— They're not expecting me back, so.

— What do you mean, sir?

— You know damned well what I mean. In a monastery when they know you're dead and not coming back they empty your room. There's another man in it now. They were kind and never told me. That room was all I had, and my books. They have sent me to the death-house as they so elegantly say in the United States. This here is the death-house. What do you do here, young man?

He is asking himself that question. So far no easy answer has offered itself.

— Books you build around you, more than a house and wife and family for a layman, part of yourself, flesh of your flesh, more than furniture for a monk's cell, a shell for his soul, the only thing in spite of the rule of poverty I couldn't strip myself of, and my talents allowed me a way around the rule, but man goeth forth naked as he came, stripped of everything, death bursts among them like a shell and strews them over half the town, and yet there are men who can leave their books as memorials to great libraries . . .

Sacred Heart of Jesus, he thinks, up there in the shadows there may be tears on that granite face.

— I'm sorry, sir.

— You didn't know, young man. How could you know?

— You will be remembered, sir.

— Thank you. The old must be grateful. Go to bed now. You have reason to rest. You have a life to live.

In his room he reads for what's left of the night. He has a life to live.

Through a drowsy weary morning he feels he wants to leave the place right away. Never again will he see the old soldier. Never again can he face the old scholar.

— Nanky Poo, Nanky Poo, you won't see your old friend again.

— No, sister. He died last night.

— Not him. Your old friend on the seat by the grotto.

Flying from French, A. N. Other cuts across their path through the maze. But she's moving so fast that not even Lua can hail her. Somewhere in the maze and as quietly as a cat she is stealing away from him for ever. Dulled with lack of sleep his brain is less than usually able to keep up with the chirpings of Lua.

— Is he dead too?

Let them all die. Let me outa here. I am not Nanky Poo.

— A stroke, not fatal yet, but, alas, the final one.

— I'll go to see him.

But Mother Polycarp tells him there's no point in that: all connection between brain and tongue and eyes is gone.

— He wouldn't know whether you were there or not.

— Couldn't he see me?

— We don't know. The doctor says, God bless us, that he's a vegetable.

— I wondered had he any letters to send out. I used to post them for him.

— He can't write any more.

A silence. So he can't even beg.

— It's a blow to you, she says. You were his friend. He used to enjoy his talks with you. But it'll soon be over, thank God.

Pray for him that he may pray for us. For some of us death isn't the worst thing and, as far as we can tell, he's content.

A vegetable has little choice. Refusing to lie down and rest in that green place of death he walks dumbly through the suburb. The white blossoms blind him. When he leaves this place he will do so with the sense of escape he might have if he was running on a smooth hillside on a sunny windy day. But later he knows that the place will be with him for ever: the cry in the night, the begging letters sent to the stars, the pitiful anger of an old man finding another man living in his room. Crucified god, there's life for you, and there's a lot more of it that he hasn't yet encountered. He expects little, but he will sit no longer expecting it alone in any dark corner.

He would like to be able to tell the cycling girl a really good lie about how he injured his hip. The scrum fell on me on the line in a rather dirty game, just as I was sneaking away and over: that's how it happens, you know.

Or: An accident on a rockface in Snowdonia, a bit of bad judgment, my own fault actually.

Or: You've heard of the parachute club that ex-air force chap has started out near Celbridge.

He would prefer if he had crutches, or even one crutch, instead of a stick which he doesn't even need. A crutch could win a girl's confidence for no harm could come to her from a fellow hopping on a crutch unless he could move as fast as, and throw the crutch with the accuracy of, Long John Silver.

There he goes, thinking about books again. He'd better watch that.

The red-headed footballer is far-away and absorbed in the virtues of his own left foot. For the first time Nanky Poo notices the colour of her hair, mousy, and the colour of her sweater, which today is mauve, because when she lay flat on the grass and he watched from a distance, she was mostly white shorts and bare circling thighs.

He sits down, stiffly, on the grass beside her. She seems not

in the least surprised. She has a freckled face and spectacles.
That surprises him.

He says: I envy the way your hips work.

If he doesn't say something wild like that he'll begin talking
about books and his cause is lost.

— Why so?

— I was laid up for a year with a tubercular hip. I'm in
the convalescent over there.

— Oh I know who you are. Sister Lua told me. You're
Nanky Poo. You write poetry.

He is cold all over.

You know Sister Lua?

— She's my aunt. I write poetry too. Nobody has ever
printed it though. Yet. Sister Lua said that some day she'd
ask you to read some of it.

— I'd be delighted to.

— I watched you sitting over there for a long time. But I
didn't like to approach you. Sister Lua said you were stand-
offish and intellectual.

She walks back with him as far as the obelisk and the
grotto. They will meet again on the following day and take a
bus into a teashop in the city. They may even go to a show if
Mother Polycarp allows him – as she will – to stay out late.

He suspects that all this will come to nothing except to the
reading of her poetry which as likely as not will be diabolical.
He wonders if some day she will, like her aunt, be arthritic,
for arthritis, they say, like a stick leg, runs in the blood. But
with one of his three friends dead, one estranged and one a
vegetable, it is something to have somebody to talk to as you
stumble through suburbia. He has a life to live. Every day
that passes brings him a day nearer to somewhere else.

So thanks be to God for the rain and the sunshine, thanks
be to God for the hail and the snow, thanks be to God for
the thunder and lightning, thanks be to God that all things
are so.

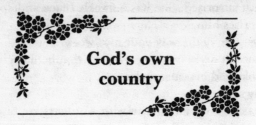

# God's own country

The plump girl from Cork City who was the editor's secretary came into the newsroom where the four of us huddled together, and said, so rapidly that we had to ask her to say it all over again: Goodness gracious, Mr. Slattery, you are, you really are, smouldering.

She was plump and very pretty and enticingly perfumed and every one of the four of us, that is everyone of us except Jeremiah, would have been overjoyed to make advances to her except that, being from Cork City, she talked so rapidly that we never had time to get a word in edgeways. She said: Goodness gracious, Mr. Slattery, you are, you really are, smouldering.

Now that our attention had been drawn to it, he really was smouldering. He sat, crouched as close as he could get to the paltry coal fire: the old ramshackle building, all rooms of no definable geometrical shape, would have collapsed with Merulius Lacrymans, the most noxious form of dry rot, the tertiary syphilis of ageing buildings, if central heating had ever been installed. Jeremiah nursed the fire between his bony knees. He toasted, or tried to toast, his chapped chilblained hands above the pitiful glow. The management of that small weekly newspaper were too mean to spend much money on fuel; and in that bitter spring Jeremiah was the coldest man in the city. He tried, it seemed, to suck what little heat there was into his bloodless body. He certainly allowed none of it to pass him by so as to mollify the three of us who sat, while he crouched, working doggedly with our overcoats and woollen scarves on. The big poet who wrote the cinema reviews, and who hadn't been inside a cinema since he left for a drink at the intermission in *Gone With The Wind* and never went back, was typing, with woollen gloves on, with one finger; and for panache more than for actual necessity he wore a motor-cycling helmet with fleece-lined flaps over his ears. The big poet had already told Jeremiah that Jeremiah was a raven, a scrawny starved raven, quothing and croaking nevermore, crumpled up there in his black greatcoat over a fire that wouldn't boil an egg. Jeremiah only crouched closer to the fire and, since we knew how cold he always was, we left him be and forgot all about him, and he might well have gone on fire, nobody, not even himself, noticing, if the plump pretty secretary, a golden perfumed ball hopping from the parlour into the hall, hadn't bounced, warming the world, being the true honey of delight, into the room.

It was the turned-up fold of the right leg of his shiny black trousers. He extinguished himself wearily, putting on, to protect the fingers of his right hand, a leather motoring-gauntlet. He had lost, or had never possessed, the left-hand gauntlet. He moved a little back from the fire, he even tried to sit up straight. She picked up the telephone on the table before me. Her rounded left haunch, packed tightly in a sort of golden cloth, was within eating distance, if I'd had a knife and fork. She said to the switch that she would take that call now from where she was in the newsroom. She was silent for a while. The golden haunch moved ever so slightly, rose and fell, in fact, as if it breathed. She said: Certainly, your Grace.
— No, your Grace.
— To the island, your Grace.
— A reporter, your Grace.
— Of course, your Grace.
— And photographer, your Grace.
— An American bishop, your Grace.
— How interesting, your Grace.
— Confirmation, your Grace.

— All the way from Georgia, your Grace

— Goodness gracious, your Grace.

— Lifeboat, your Grace.

— Yes, your Grace.

— No, your Grace.

— Next Thursday, your Grace.

— I'll make a note of it, your Grace.

— And tell the editor when he comes in from the nunciature, your Grace.

The nunciature was the place where the editor, promoting the Pope's wishes by promoting the Catholic press, did most of his drinking. He had a great tongue for the Italian wine.

— Lifeboat, your Grace.

— Absolutely, your Grace.

— Goodbye, your Grace.

The big poet said: That wouldn't have been His Grace you were talking to?

— That man, she said, thinks he's three rungs of the ladder above the Pope of Rome and with right of succession to the Lord himself.

She made for the door. The gold blinded me. She turned at the door, said to us all, or to three of us: Watch him. Don't let him make a holocaust of himself. Clean him up and feed him. He's for the Islands of the West, Hy-Breasil, the Isle of the Blest, next Thursday with the Greatest Grace of all the Graces, and a Yankee bishop who thinks it would do something for him to bestow the holy sacrament of confirmation on the young savages out there. Not that it will do much for them. It would take more than two bishops and the Holy Ghost. . . .

She was still talking as she vanished. The door crashed shut behind her and the room was dark again, and colder than ever. Jeremiah was visibly shuddering, audibly chattering, because to his bloodlessness and to the chill of the room and of the harsh day of east wind, had been added the worst cold of all: terror.

— Take him out, the big poet said, before he freezes us to death. Buy him a hot whiskey. You can buy me one when I finish my column.

As he tapped with one gloved finger and, with a free and open mind and no prejudice, critically evaluated what he had not seen, he also lifted up his voice and sang: When the roses bloom again down by yon river, and the robin redbreast sings his sweet refrain, in the days of auld lang syne, I'll be with you sweetheart mine, I'll be with you when the roses bloom again.

In Mulligan's in Poolbeg Street, established 1782, the year of the great Convention of the heroic patriotic Volunteers at Dungannon when the leaders of the nation, sort of, were inspired by the example of American Independence, I said to Jeremiah: Be a blood. Come alive. Break out. Face them. Show them. Fuck the begrudgers. Die, if die you must, on your feet and fighting.

He said: It's very well for you to talk. You can eat.

— Everybody, for God's sake, can eat.

— I can't eat. I can only nibble.

— You can drink, though. You have no trouble at all with the drink.

His first hot whiskey was gone, but hadn't done him any good that you'd notice.

— Only whiskey, he said, and sometimes on good days, stout. But even milk makes me ill, unless it's hot and with pepper sprinkled on it.

I pretended to laugh at him, to jolly him out of it, yet he really had me worried. For he was a good helpless intelligent chap, and his nerves had gone to hell in the seminary that he had had to leave, and the oddest rumours about his eating or non-eating habits were going around the town. That, for instance, he had been seen in a certain hotel, nibbling at biscuits left behind by another customer, and when the waiter, who was a friend of mine, asked him in all kindness did he need lunch, he had slunk away, the waiter said, like a shadow that had neither substance nor sunshine to account for its being there in the first place. He was no man, I had to agree, to face on an empty stomach a spring gale, or even a half or a hatful of a gale, on the wild western Atlantic coast.

— And the thought of that bishop, he said, puts the heart across me. He's a boor and a bully of the most violent description. He's a hierarchical Genghis Khan.

— Not half as bad as he's painted.

— Half's bad enough.

So I told some story, once told to me by a Belfast man, about some charitable act performed by the same bishop. It didn't sound at all convincing. Nor was Jeremiah convinced.

— If he ever was charitable, he said, be sure that it wasn't his own money he gave away.

— You won't have to see much of him, Jeremiah. Keep out of his path. Don't encounter him.

— But I'll encounter the uncandid cameraman who'll be my constant companion. With his good tweeds and his cameras that all the gold in the mint wouldn't buy. How do the mean crowd that run that paper ever manage to pay him enough to satisfy him? He invited me to his home to dinner. Once. To patronise me. To show me what he had and I hadn't. He ran out six times during dinner to ring the doorbell, and we had to stop eating and listen to the chimes. A different chime in every room. Like living in the bloody belfry. Searchlights he has on the lawn to illuminate the house on feast-days. Like they do in America, I'm told. Letting his light shine in the uncomprehending darkness. Some men in this town can't pay the electricity bill, but he suffers from a surplus. And this bishop is a friend of his. Stops with him when he comes to town. His wife's uncle is a monsignor in His Grace's diocese. Practically inlaws. They call each other by their Christian names. I was permitted and privileged to see the room the bishop sleeps in, with its own special bathroom, toilet seat reserved for the episcopal arse, a layman would have to have his arse specially anointed to sit on it. Let me tell you that it filled me with awe. When they have clerical visitors, he told me, they couldn't have them shaving in the ordinary bathroom. I hadn't the courage to ask him was there anything forbidding that in Canon Law, Pastoral Theology or the Maynooth Statutes. God look down on me between the two of them, and an American bishop thrown in for good luck. They say that in the United States the bishops are just bigger and more brutal.

— Jeremiah, I said severely, you're lucky to be out with that cameraman. He'll teach you to be a newsman. Just study how he works. He can smell news like, like . . .

The struggle for words went on until he helped me out. He was quick-witted; and even on him the third hot whiskey was bound to have some effect: to send what blood there was in his veins toe-dancing merrily to his brain.

— Like a buzzard smells dead meat, he said.

Then the poet joined us. Having an inherited gift for cobbling he had recently cobbled for himself a pair of shoes but, since measurement was not his might, they turned out to be too big even for him, thus, for any mortal man. But he had not given up hope of encountering in a public bar some Cyclopean for whose benefit he had, in his subconscious, been working, and of finding him able and willing to purchase those shoes. He carried them, unwrapped, under his arm. They always excited comment; and many were the men who tried and failed to fill them. That night we toured the town with them, adding to our company, en route, an Irish professor from Rathfarnham, a French professor from Marseilles, a lady novelist, a uniformed American soldier with an Irish name, who came from Boston and General Patch's army which had passed by Marseilles and wrecked it in the process. Outside Saint Vincent's hospital in Saint Stephen's Green a total stranger, walking past us, collapsed. He was a very big man, with enormous feet. But when the men from Boston and Marseilles, and the poet and myself, carried him into the hospital he was dead.

All that, as you are about to observe, is another story.

We failed, as it so happened, to sell the shoes.

On that corner of the western coast of Ireland the difference between a gale and a half-gale is that in a half-gale you take a chance and go out, in a gale you stay ashore.

The night before the voyage they rested in a hotel in Galway City. The wind rattled the casements and now and again blew open the door of the bar in which Jeremiah sat alone, until well after midnight, over one miserable whiskey. Nobody bothered to talk to him, not even in Galway where the very lobsters will welcome the stranger. The bar was draughty. He wore his black greatcoat, a relic of his clerical ambitions. It enlarged his body to the point of monstrosity, and minimised his head. Dripping customers came and drank and steamed and went again. When the door blew open he could see the downpours of rain hopping like hailstones on the street. The spluttering radio talked of floods, and trees blown down, and crops destroyed, and an oil-tanker in peril off the Tuskar Rock. The cameraman had eaten a horse of a dinner, washed it down with the best wine, said his prayers and gone to bed, to be, he said, fresh and fit for the morning. Jeremiah was hungry, but less than ever could he eat: with fear of the storm and of the western sea as yet unseen and of the bull of a bishop and, perhaps too, he thought, that visiting American would be no better. At midnight he drained his glass dry and afterwards tilted it several times to his lips, drinking, or inhaling, only wind. He would have ordered another whiskey but the bar was crowded by that time, and the barman was surrounded by his privileged friends who were drinking after hours. The wind no longer blew the door open for the door was double-bolted against the night. But the booming, buffeting and rattling of the storm could still be heard, at times bellowing like a brazen bishop, threatening Jeremiah. The customers kept coming and crowding through a dark passage that joined the bar and the kitchen. They acted as if they had spent all day in the

kitchen and had every intention of spending all night in the
bar. Each one of them favoured Jeremiah with a startled look
where he sat, black, deformed by that greatcoat, hunched-up
in his black cold corner. Nobody joined him. He went to
bed, to a narrow, hard, excessively white bed with a ridge up
the middle and a downward slope on each side. The rubber
hot-water bottle had already gone cold. The rain threatened
to smash the window-panes. He spread his greatcoat over his
feet, wearing his socks in bed, and, cursing the day he was
born, fell asleep from sheer misery.

Early next morning he had his baptism of salt water, not
sea-spray but rain blown sideways and so salty that it made
a crust around the lips.

— That out there, said the cameraman in the security of
his car, is what they call the poteen cross.

The seats in the car were covered with a red plush,
in its turn covered by a protective and easily washable,
transparent plastic that Jeremiah knew had been put there
to prevent himself or his greatcoat or his greasy, shiny pants
from making direct contact with the red plush.

— Did you never hear of the poteen cross?

— No, said Jeremiah.

They had stopped in a pelting village on the westward
road. The doors were shut, the windows still blinded. It was
no morning for early rising. The sea was audible, but not
visible. The rain came bellying inshore on gusts of wind.
On a gravelled space down a slope towards the sound of the
sea stood a huge bare black cross: well, not completely bare
for it carried, criss-crossed, the spear that pierced, that other
spear that bore aloft the sponge soaked in vinegar; and it was
topped by a gigantic crown of thorns. The cameraman said:
When the Redemptorist Fathers preached hellfire against the
men who made the poteen, they ordered the moonshiners,
under pain of mortal sin, to come here and leave their stills
at the foot of the cross. The last sinner to hold out against
them came in the end with his still but, there before him, he

saw a better model that somebody else had left, so he took it away with him. There's a London magazine wants a picture of that cross.

— It wouldn't, said Jeremiah, make much of a picture.

— With somebody beside it pointing up at it, it wouldn't be so bad. The light's not good. But I think we could manage.

— We, said Jeremiah.

— You wouldn't like me, he said, to get up on the cross? Have you brought the nails?

He posed, nevertheless, and pointed up at the cross. What else could he do? We saw the picture afterwards in that London magazine. Jeremiah looked like a sable bloated demon trying to prove to benighted sinners that Christ was gone and dead and never would rise again. But it was undeniably an effective picture. Jeremiah posed and pointed. He was salted and sodden while the cameraman, secure in yellow oilskins and sou'wester, darted out, took three shots, darted in again, doffed the oilskins, and was as dry as snuff. They drove on westwards.

— That coat of yours, said the cameraman. You should have fitted yourself out with oilskins. That coat of yours will soak up all the water from here to Long Island.

— Stinks a bit too, he said on reflection. The Beeoh is flying.

That was meant to be some sort of a joke and, for the sake of civility, Jeremiah tried to laugh. They crossed a stone bridge over a brown-and-white, foaming, flooded river, turned left down a byroad, followed the course of the river, sometimes so close to it that the floodwater lapped the edge of the road, sometimes swinging a little away from it through a misted landscape of small fields, thatched cabins dour and withdrawn in the storm, shapeless expanses of rock and heather, until they came to where the brown-and-white water tumbled into the peace of a little land-locked harbour. The lifeboat that, by special arrangement, was to carry the party to the island was there, but no lifeboatmen, no party. A few small craft lay on a sandy slope in the shelter of a breakwater.

Jeremiah and the cameraman could have been the only people alive in a swamped world. They waited: the cameraman in the car with the heat on; Jeremiah, to get away from him for a while, prowling around empty cold sheds that were, at least, dry, but that stank of dead fish and were floored with peat-mould terrazzoed, it would seem, by fragments broken from many previous generations of lobsters. Beyond the breakwater and a rocky headland the sea boomed, but the water in the sheltered harbour was smooth and black as ink. He was hungry again but knew that if he had food, any food other than dry biscuits, he wouldn't be able to eat it. All food now would smell of stale fish. He was cold, as always. When he was out of sight of the cameraman he pranced, to warm himself, on peat-mould and lobsters. He was only moderately successful. But his greatcoat, at least, steamed.

The rain eased off, the sky brightened, but the wind seemed to grow in fury, surf and spray went up straight and shining into the air beyond the breakwater, leaped it and came down with a flat slap on the sandy slope and the sleeping small craft. Then, like Apache on an Arizona skyline, the people began to appear: a group of three, suddenly, from behind a standing rock; a group of seven or eight rising sharply into sight on a hilltop on the switchback riverside road, dropping out of sight into a hollow, surfacing again, followed by other groups that appeared and disappeared in the same disconcerting manner. As the sky cleared, the uniform darkness breaking up into bullocks of black wind-goaded clouds, the landscape of rock and heather, patchwork fields divided by grey, high, drystone walls, came out into the light; and from every small farmhouse thus revealed, people came, following footpaths, crossing stiles, calling to each other across patches of light green oats and dark-green potatoes. It was a sudden miracle of growth, of human life appearing where there had been nothing but wind and rain and mist. Within three-quarters of an hour there were a hundred or more people around the harbour, lean hard-faced fishermen and small farmers, dark-haired laughing girls, old women in coloured shawls, talking Irish, talking English, posing in groups for the cameraman who in his yellow oilskins moved among them like a gigantic canary. They waved and called to Jeremiah where he stood, withdrawn and on the defensive, in the sheltered doorway of a fish-stinking shed.

A black Volkswagen came down the road followed by a red Volkswagen. From the black car a stout priest stepped forth, surveyed the crowd like a general estimating the strength of his mustered troops, shook hands with the cameraman as if he were meeting an old friend. From the red car a young man stepped out, then held the door for a gaunt middle-aged lady who emerged with an effort, head first: the local school-teachers, by the cut of them. They picked out from the crowd a group of twelve to twenty, lined them up, backs to the wall, in the shelter of the breakwater. The tall lady waved her arms and the group began to sing.

— Ecce sacerdos magnus, they sang.

A black limousine, with the traction power of two thousand Jerusalem asses on the first Holy Thursday, came, appearing and disappearing, down the switchback road. This was it, Jeremiah knew, and shuddered. On the back of an open truck behind the limousine came the lifeboatmen, all like the cameraman, in bright yellow oilskins.

— This is God's own country, said the American bishop, and ye are God's own people.

Jeremiah was still at a safe distance, yet near enough to hear the booming clerical-American voice. The sea boomed beyond the wall. The spray soared, then slapped down on the sand, sparing the sheltered singers.

— Faith of our fathers, they sang, living still, in spite of dungeon, fire and sword.

Circling the crowd the great canary, camera now at ease, approached Jeremiah.

— Get with it, Dracula, he said.

He didn't much bother to lower his voice.

— Come out of your corner fighting. Get in and get a story. That Yank is news. He was run out of Rumania by the Communists.

— He also comes, said Jeremiah, from Savannah, Georgia.

— So what?

— He doesn't exactly qualify as a Yankee.

— Oh Jesus, geography, said the cameraman. We'll give you full marks for geography. They'll look lovely in the paper where your story should be. If he came from bloody Patagonia, he's here now. Go get him.

Then he was gone, waving his camera. The American bishop, a tall and stately man, was advancing, blessing as he went, to the stone steps that went down the harbour wall to the moored lifeboat. He was in God's own country and God's own people, well marshalled by the stout parish priest, were all around him. The Irish bishop, a tall and stately man, stood still, thoughtfully watching the approaching cameraman and Jeremiah most reluctantly plodding in the rear, his progress, to his relief, made more difficult by the mush of wet peat-mould underfoot, growing deeper and deeper as he approached the wall where sailing hookers were loaded with fuel for the peatless island. Yet, slowly as he moved, he was still close enough to see clearly what happened and to hear clearly what was said.

The bishop, tall and stately and monarch even over the parish priest, looked with a cold eye at the advancing cameraman. There was no ring kissing. The bishop did not reach out his hand to have his ring saluted. That was odd, to begin with. Then he said loudly: What do you want?

— Your Grace, said the great canary.

He made a sort of a curtsey, clumsily, because he was hobbled in creaking oilskins.

— Your Grace, he said, out on the island there's a nonagenarian, the oldest inhabitant, and when we get there I'd like to get a picture of you giving him your blessing.

His Grace said nothing. His Grace turned very red in the face.

In increased terror, Jeremiah remembered that inlaws could have their tiffs and that clerical inlaws were well known to be hell incarnate. His Grace right-about-wheeled, showed to the mainland and all on it a black broad back, right-quick marched towards the lifeboat, sinking to the ankles as he thundered on in the soft wet mould, but by no means abating his speed which could have been a fair five miles an hour. His long coat-tails flapped in the wind. The wet mould fountained up like snow from a snow-plough. The sea boomed. The spray splattered. The great canary had shrunk as if plucked. Jeremiah's coat steamed worse than ever in the frenzy of his fear. If he treats his own like that, he thought, what in God's holy name will he do to me? Yet he couldn't resist saying: That man could pose like Nelson on his pillar watching his world collapse.

The canary cameraman hadn't a word to say.

Once aboard the lugger the bishops had swathed themselves in oilskins provided by the lifeboat's captain, and the cameraman mustered enough of his ancient gall to mutter to Jeremiah that that was the first time that he or anybody else had seen canary-coloured bishops.

— Snap them, said Jeremiah. You could sell it to the magazines in Bucharest. Episcopal American agent turns yellow.

But the cameraman was still too crestfallen, and made no move, and clearly looked relieved when the Irish bishop, tall and stately even if a little grotesque in oilskins, descended carefully into the for'ard foxhole, sat close into the corner, took out his rosary beads and began to pray silently: he knew the tricks of his western sea. Lulled by the security of the land-locked sheltered harbour, the American bishop, tall and stately even if a little grotesque in oilskins, stood like Nelson on the foredeck. He surveyed the shore of rock, small fields, drystone walls, small thatched farmhouses, oats, potatoes, grazing black cattle, all misting over for more rain. Then he turned his back on the mainland and looked at the people, now marshalled all together by the parish priest and the two teachers in the lee of the harbour wall. The choir sang: Holy God, we praise thy name. Lord of all, we bow before thee.

An outrider of the squall of rain that the wind was driving inshore cornered cunningly around harbour wall and headland, and disrespectfully spattered the American bishop. Secure in oilskins and the Grace of state he ignored it. The cameraman dived into the stern foxhole. Jeremiah by now was so sodden that the squall had no effect on him. An uncle of his, a farmer in the County Longford, had worn the same heavy woollen underwear winter and summer and argued eloquently that what kept the heat in kept it out. That soaking salty steaming greatcoat could, likewise, stand upright on its own against the fury of the Bay of Biscay. It was a fortress for Jeremiah; and with his right hand, reaching out through the loophole of the sleeve, he touched the tough stubby oaken mast, a talismanic touch, a prayer to the rooted essence of the earth to protect him from the capricious fury of the sea. Then with the bishop, a yellow figurehead, at the prow, and Jeremiah, a sable figurehead, at the stern, they moved smoothly towards the open ocean; and, having withdrawn a little from the land, the bishop raised his hand, as Lord Nelson would not have done, and said: This is God's own country. Ye are God's own people.

The choir sang: Hail Glorious Saint Patrick, dear Saint of our isle.

From the conscripted and marshalled people came a cheer loud enough to drown the hymn; and then the sea, with as little regard for the cloth as had the Rumanian Reds, struck like an angry bull and the boat, Jeremiah says, stood on its nose, and only a miracle of the highest order kept the American bishop out of the drink. Jeremiah could see him, down, far down at the bottom of a dizzy slope, then up, far up, shining like the sun between sea and sky, as the boat reared back on its haunches and Jeremiah felt on the back of his head the blow of a gigantic fist. It was simply salt seawater in a solid block, striking and bursting like a bomb. By the time

he had wiped his eyes and the boat was again, for a few brief
moments, on an even keel, there were two bishops sheltering
in the for'ard foxhole: the two most quiet and prayerful men
he had ever seen.

— On the ocean that hollows the rocks where ye dwell,
Jeremiah recited out as loudly as he could because no ears
could hear even a bull bellowing above the roar and movement
and torment of the sea.

— A shadowy land, he went on, has appeared as they tell.
Men thought it a region of sunshine and rest, and they called
it Hy-Breasil the Isle of the Blest.

To make matters easier, if not tolerable, he composed his
mind and said to himself: Lifeboats can't sink.

On this harshly-ocean-bitten coast there was the poetic
legend of the visionary who sailed west, ever west, to find the
island where the souls of the blest are forever happy.

— Rash dreamer return, Jeremiah shouted, oh ye winds of
the main, bear him back to his own native Ara again.

For his defiance the sea repaid him in three thundering
salty buffets and a sudden angled attack that sent the boat
hissing along on its side and placed Jeremiah with both arms
around the mast. In the brief following lull he said more
quietly, pacifying the sea, acknowledging its power: Night
fell on the deep amid tempest and spray, and he died on the
ocean, away far away.

He was far too frightened to be seasick, which was just as
well, considering the windy vacuum he had for a stomach.
The boat pranced and rolled. He held on to the mast, but now
almost nonchalantly and only with one arm. The sea buffeted
him into dreams of that luckless searcher for Hy-Breasil, or
dreams of Brendan the Navigator, long before Columbus,
sailing bravely on and on and making landfall on Miami
Beach. Secure in those dreams he found to his amazement that
he could contemn the snubbed cameraman and the praying
bishops hiding in their foxholes. He, Jeremiah, belonged with
the nonchalant lifeboatmen studying the sea as a man through

the smoke of a good pipe might look at the face of a friend. One of them, indeed, was so nonchalant that he sat on the hatch-roof above the bishops, his feet on the gunwale chain so that, when the boat dipped his way, his feet a few times went well out of sight in the water. Those lifeboatmen were less men than great yellow seabirds and Jeremiah, although a landlubber and as black as a raven, willed to be with them as far as he could, for the moment, go. He studied on the crazy pattern of tossing waters the ironic glint of sunshine on steel-blue hills racing to collide and crash and burst into blinding silver. He recalled sunshine on quiet, stable, green fields that he was half-reconciled never to see again. He was on the way to the Isle of the Blest.

Yet it was no island that first appeared to remind him, after two hours of trance, that men, other than the lifeboat's crew and cargo, did exist: no island, but the high bird-flight of a dozen black currachs, appearing and disappearing, forming into single file, six to either side of the lifeboat, forming a guard of honour as if they had been cavalry on display in a London park, to escort the sacerdotes magni safely into the island harbour. Afterwards Jeremiah was to learn that lifeboats could sink and had done so, yet he says that even had he known through the wildest heart of that voyage it would have made no difference. Stunned, but salted, by the sea he arose a new man.

The parish church was a plain granite cross high on a windy, shelterless hilltop. It grew up from the rock it was cut from. No gale nor half-gale, nor the gates of hell, could prevail against it.

To west and south-west the land sank, then swept up dizzily again to a high bare horizon and, beyond that there could be nothing but monstrous seacliffs and the ocean. To east and north-east small patchwork fields, bright green, dark green, golden, netted by greystone walls, dotted by white and golden cabins all newly limewashed and thatched for the coming of the great priests, sloped down to a sea in the lee of the island and incredibly calm. The half-gale was still strong. But the island was steady underfoot. Far away the mainland, now a bit here, now a bit there, showed itself, glistening, out of the wandering squalls.

— Rock of ages cleft for me, he hummed with a reckless merriment that would have frightened him if he had stopped to reason about it, let me hide myself in thee. He was safe in the arms of Jesus, he was deep in the heart of Texas. The granite cruciform church was his shelter from the gale, providing him, by the protection of its apse and right arm, with a sunny corner to hide in and smoke in. He was still giddy from the swing of the sea. He was also, being, alas, human and subject to frailty, tempted to rejoice at the downfall and humiliation of another. He hath put down the mighty, he began to chant but stopped to consider that as yet there was little sign of the lowly being exalted.

This corner of the cross was quiet. One narrow yellow grained door was securely shut. All the bustle, all the traffic was out around the front porch: white-jacketed white-jerseyed islanders sitting on stone walls, women in coloured shawls crowding and pushing, children hymn-singing in English, Irish and Latin, real Tower of Babel stuff, the cameraman photographing groups of people, and photographing the bishops from a safe distance, and the church from every angle short of the one the angels saw it from. He was no longer a great clumsy canary. He was splendid in his most expensive tweeds. He was, nevertheless, a cowed and broken man.

For back at the harbour, at the moment of disembarkation, it had happened again.

The two bishops, divested of oilskins, tall and black but not stately, are clambering up a ladder on to the high slippy quayside, and they are anything but acrobatic. Jeremiah, a few yards away, is struggling to tear from his body his sodden greatcoat, to hang it to dry under the direction of an islandman, in the lee of a boathouse where nets are laid to dry.

The cameraman has jocosely snapped him. Then he directs the camera on the clambering bishops only to be vetoed by a voice, iron and Irish and clanging.

— Put away that camera, the Irish voice says, until the opportune time.

— Why Peter, says the American voice, that would make a fun picture.

— In Ireland we don't want or need fun pictures of the hierarchy. We're not clowns.

It is arguable, Jeremiah thinks. He recalls that archbishops, on their own territory and when in full regimentals, are entitled to wear red boots. But he keeps his back turned on the passing parade in sudden terror that his eyes might reveal his thoughts. He hears the cameraman say: Your Grace, there is on the island the oldest inhabitant, a nonagenarian. I'd like to . . .

But there is no response. The procession has passed on. Fickle, Jeremiah knows, is the favour of princes, particularly when, like the Grand Turk, they are related to you. But whatever or how grievous the cause of offence had been that led to these repeated snubs, Jeremiah feels for the first time, burning through empty belly and meagre body, the corps-spirit of the pressman. Who in hell, anyway, is a bishop that he won't stand and pose like any other mortal man? All men are subject to the camera. Face up to it, grin, watch the little birdie. Only murderers are allowed to creep past, faces covered. If he won't be photographed, then to hell with him. He will be scantily written about, even if he is Twenty Times His Grace. And to hell also with all American bishops and Rumanian Reds, and with all colour stories of confirmations and of simple island people who, more than likely, spend the long winter nights making love to their own domestic animals which, as far as Jeremiah is concerned, they have a perfect right to do.

So here in the corner of the granite cross he had found peace. He didn't need to see the nonsense going on out there.

When the time came to type, as no doubt it would, the Holy Ghost would guide his fingertips. The moment on the quayside mingled with the moment in the shelter of the church and he realised, for the first time since anger had possessed him, that he had left his greatcoat still drying with the nets. He had been distracted by a call to coffee and sandwiches intended to keep them from collapsing until the show was over. But to hell, too, he decided with all greatcoats; a man could stand on his own legs. He smoked, and was content, and heard far away the voices of children, angels singing. Then the narrow, yellow, grained door opened, a great venerable head, a portion of surpliced body, appeared, a voice louder than the choirs of angels said: Come here, pressman.

Jeremiah went there.

— On the alert I'm glad to see, His Grace said. Waiting to see me. What can I do for you?

Jeremiah, to begin with, bent one knee and kissed his ring. That little bit of ballet enabled him to avoid saying whether he had or had not been on the alert, waiting for an interview.

— You must be starved, His Grace said. That was a rough journey.

They were in the outer room of the sacristy. The walls were mostly presses all painted the same pale yellow, with graining, as the narrow door. In an inner room the American bishop, head bowed, was talking to two tiny nuns. From one of the presses His Grace took a bottle and a half-pint tumbler and half-filled the tumbler with Jameson neat.

— Throw that back, he ordered. 'Twill keep the wind out of your stomach.

He watched benevolently while Jeremiah gasped and drank. The whiskey struck like a hammer. How was His Grace to know that Jeremiah's stomach had in it nothing at all, but wind? Jeremiah's head spun. This, he now knew, was what people meant when they talked about the bishop's bottle. His Grace restored bottle and glass to the press.

— We mustn't, he said, shock the good sisters.

He handed Jeremiah a sheaf of typescript. He said: It's all there. Names. History. Local lore. All the blah-blah, as you fellows say. Here, have a cigar. It belongs to our American Mightyship. They never travel without them. God bless you now. Is there anything else I can do for you?

Jeremiah's head had ceased to spin. His eyes had misted for a while with the warmth of the malt on an empty stomach, but now the mist cleared and he could see, he felt, to a great distance. The malt, too, had set the island rocking but with a gentle soothing motion.

— There's a man here, he said, the oldest inhabitant, a nonagenarian. The cameraman who's with me would like a picture.

— No sooner said than done, oh gentleman of the press. That should make a most edifying picture. I'll call himself away from the nuns. We'll just have time before the ceremony.

But, for reasons never known to me or Jeremiah, he laughed all the time as he led the way around the right arm of the cross to the front of the church; and brought with him another cigar for the cameraman, and shook hands with him, and offered him his ring to be kissed.

Apart from Jeremiah and the cameraman and the island doctor it was a clerical dinner, the island parish priest as host, a dozen well-conditioned men sitting down to good food, and wines that had crossed from Spain on the trawlers without paying a penny to the revenue.

— One of the best men in the business, said His Grace, although he'd sell us all body and soul to the News of the World.

He was talking about the cameraman, and at table, and in his presence. But he was laughing, and inciting the gathering to laughter. Whatever cloud there had been between the relatives had blown away with the storm, or with Jeremiah's diplomacy. So Jeremiah felt like Tallyrand. He was more than

a little drunk. He was confirmed and made strong by the sea
and the bishop's whiskey. He was hungry as hell.

— And Spanish ale, he muttered, shall give you hope, my
dark Rosaleen.

His mutter was overheard, relayed around the table, and
accepted as unquestionable wit. He was triumphant. He ate.
He fell to, like a savage. He drank, he said afterwards —
although we suspected that he had conned the names from
a wine merchant's list, red and white Poblet, and red Rioja,
and red Valdapenas, and another wine that came from the
plain to the west of Tarragona where the Cistercians had a
monastery: the lot washed down with Fundadór brandy which
the American bishop told him had been the brandy specially
set aside for the Conclave of Pope John the Twenty-third.

— Thou art Peter, said Jeremiah, and upon this rock.

Once again the remark was relayed around the table.
Awash on the smuggled products of Spain, Jeremiah was in
grave danger of becoming the life and soul of the party.

A boy-child had that day been born on the island. The
American bishop had asked the parents could he baptise the
child and name it after himself.

— Episcopus Americanus O'Flaherty, said Jeremiah.

Pope John's Fundadór circled the board. The merriment
knew no bounds. His Grace told how the great traveller,
O'Donovan, had dwelt among the Turkomans of ancient
Merv, whom he finally grew to detest because they wouldn't
let him go home, but who liked him so much they called all
their male children after him: O'Donovan Beg, O'Donovan
Khan, O'Donovan Bahadur, and so on.

— It was the custom in ancient Merv, said His Grace, to
call the newborn babes after any distinguished visitor who
happened to be in the oasis at the time.

— It was not the custom in Rumania, said Jeremiah.

Renewed merriment. When the uproar died down, the
American bishop, with tears in his eyes, said: But this is
God's Own Country. Ye are God's Own People.

Jeremiah got drunk, but nobody minded. Later, outside a bar close by the harbour, he was photographed feeding whiskey out of a basin to a horse. The horse was delighted. The picture appeared in a London magazine, side-by-side with a picture of the nonagenarian flanked by bishops.

— You got him to pose, said the cameraman, when he rusted on me.

He meant, not the horse, but the bishop.

— Jer, he said, you'll make a newsman yet.

So, as Jer, a new man, eater of meat and vegetables, acknowledged gentleman of the press, he came back from the Isle of the Blest, sitting on the hatch above the bishops, feet on the gunwale chain. He was not beyond hoping that the swing of the sea and the tilt of the boat might salt his feet. It didn't. The easy evening sway would have lulled a child in the cradle.

— Episcopus Americanus O'Flaherty, he said to the lifeboatman who sat beside him and who had enough Latin to clerk Mass.

— True for you, said the lifeboatman. Small good that christening will do the poor boy. As long as he lives on that island he'll never be known as anything but An Teasbog Beag – the Little Bishop. If he goes to the States itself, the name could follow him there. His sons and even his daughters will be known as the Little Bishops. Or his eldest son may be called Mac an Easboig, the Son of the Bishop. They'll lose O'Flaherty and be called Macanespie. That's how names were invented since the time of King Brian Boru who bate the Danes.

Behind them the island stepped away into the mist: the wanderer, crazed for Hy-Breasil, would never find it. The rain would slant for ever on rocks and small fields, on ancient forts and cliffs with seabirds crying around them, on currachs riding the waves as the gulls do. Visitors would be enthralled by ancient ways, and basking sharks captured. But as long as winds rage and tides run, that male child, growing up to be a lean tanned young man in white jacket and soft pampooties, leaning into the wind as he walks as his forebears have always done, courteous as a prince but also ready to fight at the drop of a half-glass of whiskey, sailing with the trawlers as far away as the Faroes, will continue, because of this day, to be known as the Little Bishop.

In the foxhole underneath Jeremiah, the American bishop was telling the Irish bishop and the cameraman that in the neighbourhood of the Okeefenokee Swamp, out of which the Suwannee River drags its corpse, and generally in the state of Georgia, there were many Southern Baptists with Irish Catholic names.

The water in the land-locked harbour was deadly still, and deep purple in the dusk. Sleepy gulls foraged on the edge of the tide, or called from inland over the small fields. Jer's greatcoat was still on the island, dry by now, and stiff with salt. He never wanted to see it again.

Shadowy people gathered on the harbour wall. The choir sang: Sweet Sacrament Divine, dear home of every heart.

— Ye are God's own people, said the American bishop. This is God's own country.

— Fuck, said the cameraman and in a painfully audible voice.

He had sunk over the ankles in soggy peat-mould, losing one shoe. But while he stood on one leg and Jer groped for the missing shoe, the bishops and the people and the parish priest and the choir, and the cameraman himself, all joked and laughed. When the shoe was retrieved they went on their way rejoicing.

In Galway City Jer ate a dinner of parsnips and rare roast meat and sauté potatoes that would have stunned an ox; and washed it down with red wine.

Far away the island gulls nested on his discarded greatcoat.

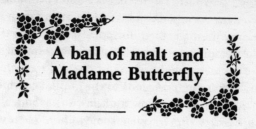

# A ball of malt and Madame Butterfly

On a warm but not sunny June afternoon on a crowded Dublin street, by no means one of the city's most elegant streets, a small hotel, a sort of bed-and-breakfast place, went on fire. There was pandemonium at first, more panic than curiosity in the crowd. It was a street of decayed Georgian houses, high and narrow, with steep wooden staircases, and cluttered small shops on the ground floors: all great nourishment for flames. The fire, though, didn't turn out to be serious. The brigade easily contained and controlled it. The panic passed, gave way to curiosity, then to indignation and finally, alas, to laughter about the odd thing that had happened when the alarm was at its worst.

This was it.

From a window on the top-most floor a woman, scantily clad, puts her head out and waves a patchwork bed coverlet, and screams for help. The stairway, she cries, is thick with smoke, herself and her husband are afraid to face it. On what would seem to be prompting from inside the room, she calls down that they are a honeymoon couple up from the country. That would account fairly enough for their still being abed on a warm June afternoon.

The customary ullagone and ullalu goes up from the crowd. The fire-engine ladder is aimed up to the window. A fireman begins to run up the ladder. Then suddenly the groom appears in shirt and trousers, and barefooted. For, to the horror of the beholders, he makes his bare feet visible by pushing the bride back into the room, clambering first out of the window, down the ladder like a monkey although he is a fairly corpulent man; with monkey-like agility dodging round the ascending fireman, then disappearing through the crowd. The people, indignant enough to trounce him, are still too concerned with the plight of the bride, and too astounded to seize him. The fireman ascends to the nuptial casement, helps the lady through the window and down the ladder, gallantly offering his jacket which covers some of her. Then when they are halfways down, the fireman, to the amazement of all, is seen to be laughing right merrily, the bride vituperating. But before they reach the ground she also is laughing. She is brunette, tall, but almost Japanese in appearance, and very handsome. A voice says: If she's a bride I can see no confetti in her hair.

She has fine legs which the fireman's jacket does nothing to conceal and which she takes pride, clearly, in displaying. She is a young woman of questionable virginity and well known to the firemen. She is the toast of a certain section of the town to whom she is affectionately known as Madame Butterfly, although unlike her more famous namesake she has never been married, nor cursed by an uncle bonze for violating the laws of the gods of her ancestors. She has another, registered, name: her mother's name. What she is her mother was before her, and proud of it.

The bare-footed fugitive was not, of course, a bridegroom, but a long-established married man with his wife and family and a prosperous business in Longford, the meanest town in Ireland. For the fun of it the firemen made certain that the news of his escapade in the June afternoon got back to Longford. They were fond of, even proud of, Butterfly as were many other men who had nothing at all to do with the quenching of fire.

But one man loved the pilgrim soul in her and his name was Pike Hunter.

Like Borgnefesse, the buccaneer of St. Malo on the Rance, who had a buttock shot or sliced off in action on the Spanish

Main, Pike Hunter had a lopsided appearance when sitting down. Standing up he was as straight and well balanced as a man could be: a higher civil servant approaching the age of forty, a shy bachelor, reared, nourished and guarded all his life by a trinity of upper-middle-class aunts. He was pink-faced, with a little fair hair left to emphasise early baldness, mild in his ways, with a slight stutter, somewhat afraid of women. He wore always dark-brown suits with a faint red stripe, dark-brown hats, rimless spectacles, shiny square-toed brown handmade shoes with a wide welt. In summer, even on the hottest day, he carried a raincoat folded over his arm, and a rolled umbrella. When it rained he unfolded and wore the raincoat and opened and raised the umbrella. He suffered mildly from hay fever. In winter he belted himself into a heavy brown overcoat and wore galoshes. Nobody ever had such stiff white shirts. He favoured brown neckties distinguished with a pearl-headed pin. Why he sagged to one side, just a little to the left, when he sat down, I never knew. He had never been sliced or shot on the Spanish Main.

But the chance of a sunny still Sunday afternoon in Stephen's Green and Grafton Street, the select heart or soul of the city's south side, made a changed man out of him.

He had walked at his ease through the Green, taking the sun gratefully, blushing when he walked between the rows of young ladies lying back in deck-chairs. He blushed for two reasons: they were reclining, he was walking; they were as gracefully at rest as the swans on the lake, he was awkwardly in motion, conscious that his knees rose too high, that his sparse hair – because of the warmth he had his hat in his hand – danced long and ludicrously in the little wind, that his shoes squeaked. He was fearful that his right toe might kick his left heel, or vice versa, and that he would fall down and be laughed at in laughter like the sound of silver bells. He was also alarmingly aware of the bronze knees, and more than knees, that the young ladies exposed as they leaned back and relaxed in their light summer frocks. He would honestly have liked to stop and enumerate those knees, make an inventory – he was in the Department of Statistics; perhaps pat a few here and there. But the fearful regimen of that trinity of aunts forbade him even to glance sideways, and he stumbled on like a winkered horse, demented by the flashing to right and to left of bursting globes of bronze light.

Then on the park pathway before him, walking towards the main gate and the top of Grafton Street, he saw the poet. He had seen him before, but only in the Abbey Theatre and never on the street. Indeed it seemed hardly credible to Pike Hunter that such a man would walk on the common street where all ordinary or lesser men were free to place their feet. In the Abbey Theatre the poet had all the strut and style of a man who could walk with the gods, the Greek gods that is, not the gods in the theatre's cheapest seats. His custom was to enter by a small stairway, at the front of the house and in full view of the audience, a few moments before the lights dimmed and the famous gong sounded and the curtain rose. He walked slowly, hands clasped behind his back, definitely balancing the prone brow oppressive with its mind, the eagle head aloft and crested with foaming white hair. He would stand, his back to the curtain and facing the house. The chatter would cease, the fiddlers in the orchestra would saw with diminished fury. Some of the city wits said that what the poet really did at those times was to count the empty seats in the house and make a rapid reckoning of the night's takings. But their gibe could not diminish the majesty of those entrances, the majesty of the stance of the man. And there he was now, hands behind back, noble head high, pacing slowly, beginning the course of Grafton Street. Pike Hunter walked behind him, suiting his pace to the poet's, to the easy deliberate rhythms of the early love poetry: I would that we were, my beloved, white birds on the foam of the sea. There is a queen in China or, maybe, it's in Spain.

They walked between the opulent windows of elegant glittering shops, doors closed for Sunday. The sunshine had drawn the people from the streets: to the park, to the lush green country, to the seaside. Of the few people they did meet, not all of them seemed to know who the poet was, but those who did know saluted quietly, with a modest and unaffected reverence, and one young man with a pretty girl on his arm stepped off the pavement, looked after the poet and clearly whispered to the maiden who it was that had just passed by the way. Stepping behind him at a respectful distance Pike felt like an acolyte behind a celebrant and regretted that there was no cope or cloak of cloth of gold of which he could humbly carry the train.

So they sailed north towards the Liffey, leaving Trinity College, with Burke standing haughty-headed and Goldsmith sipping at his honeypot of a book, to the right, and the Bank and Grattan orating Esto Perpetua, to the left, and Thomas Moore of the Melodies, brown, stooped and shabby, to the right; and came into Westmoreland Street where the wonder happened. For there approaching them came the woman Homer sung: old and grey and, perhaps, full of sleep, a face much and deeply lined and haggard, eyes sunken, yet still the face of the queen she had been when she and the poet were young and they had stood on the cliffs on Howth Head, high above the promontory that bears the Bailey Lighthouse as a warning torch and looks like the end of the world; and they had watched the soaring of the gulls and he had wished that he and she were only white birds, my beloved, buoyed out on the foam of the sea. She was very tall. She was not white, but all black in widow's weeds for the man she had married when she wouldn't marry the poet. Her black hat had a wide brim and, from the brim, an old-fashioned veil hung down before her face. The pilgrim soul in you, and loved the sorrows of your changing face.

Pike stood still, fearing that in a dream he had intruded on some holy place. The poet and the woman moved dreamlike towards each other, then stood still, not speaking, not saluting, at opposite street corners where Fleet Street comes narrowly

from the East to join Westmoreland Street. Then still not
speaking, not saluting, they turned into Fleet Street. When
Pike tiptoed to the corner and peered around he saw that
they had walked on opposite sides of the street for, perhaps,
thirty paces, then turned at right angles, moved towards each
other, stopped to talk in the middle of the street where a shaft
of sunlight had defied the tall overshadowing buildings. Apart
from themselves and Pike that portion of the town seemed to
be awesomely empty; and there Pike left them and walked in
a daze by the side of the Liffey to a pub called The Dark
Cow. Something odd had happened to him: poetry, a vision
of love?

It so happened that on that day Butterfly was in the Dark
Cow, as, indeed, she often was: just Butterfly and Pike, and
Jody with the red carbuncled face who owned the place and
was genuinely kind to the girls of the town, and a few honest
dockers who didn't count because they had money only for
their own porter and were moral men, loyal to wives or
sweethearts. It wasn't the sort of place Pike frequented. He
had never seen Butterfly before: those odd slanting eyes, the
glistening high-piled black hair, the well-defined bud of a
mouth, the crossed legs, the knees that outclassed to the
point of mockery all the bronze globes in Stephen's Green.
Coming on top of his vision of the poet and the woman, all
this was too much for him, driving him to a reckless courage
that would have flabbergasted the three aunts. He leaned on
the counter. She sat in an alcove that was a sort of throne for
her, where on busier days she sat surrounded by her sorority.
So he says to Jody whom he did not yet know as Jody: May
I have the favour of buying the lady in the corner a drink?

— That you may, and more besides.

— Please ask her permission. We must do these things
properly.

— Oh there's a proper way of doing everything, even
screwing a goose.

But Jody, messenger of love, walks to the alcove and formally asks the lady would she drink if the gentleman at the counter sends it over. She will. She will also allow him to join her. She whispers: Has he any money?

— Loaded, says Jody.

— Send him over so. Sunday's a dull day.

Pike sits down stiffly, leaning a little away from her, which seems to her quite right for him as she has already decided that he's a shy sort of man, upper class, but shy, not like some. He excuses himself from intruding. She says: You're not inthrudin'.

He says he hasn't the privilege of knowing her name.

Talks like a book, she decides, or a play in the Gaiety.

— Buttherfly, she says.

— Butterfly, he says, is a lovely name.

— Me mother's name was Trixie, she volunteers.

— Was she dark like you?

— Oh, a natural blonde and very busty, well developed, you know. She danced in the old Tivoli where the newspaper office is now. I'm neat, not busty.

To his confusion she indicates, with hands moving in small curves, the parts of her that she considers are neat. But he notices that she has shapely long-fingered hands and he remembers that the poet had admitted that the small hands of his beloved were not, in fact, beautiful. He is very perturbed.

— Neat, she says, and well-made. Austin McDonnell, the fire-brigade chief, says that he read in a book that the best sizes and shapes would fit into champagne glasses.

He did wonder a little that a fire-brigade chief should be a quotable authority on female sizes and shapes, and on champagne glasses. But then and there he decided to buy her champagne, the only drink fit for such a queen who seemed as if she came, if not from China, at any rate from Japan.

— Champagne, he said.

— Bubbly, she said. I love bubbly.

Jody dusted the shoulders of the bottle that on his shelves had waited a long time for a customer. He unwired the cork. The cork and the fizz shot up to the ceiling.

— This, she said, is my lucky day.

— The divine Bernhardt, said Pike, had a bath in champagne presented to her by a group of gentlemen who admired her.

— Water, she said, is better for washing.

But she told him that her mother who knew everything about actresses had told her that story, and told her that when, afterwards, the gentlemen bottled the contents of the bath and drank it, they had one bottleful too many. He was too far gone in fizz and love's frenzy to feel embarrassed. She was his discovery, his oriental queen.

He said: You're very oriental in appearance. You could be from Japan.

She said: My father was, they say. A sailor. Sailors come and go.

She giggled. She said: That's a joke. Come and go. Do you see it?

Pike saw it. He giggled with her. He was a doomed man.

She said: Austin McDonnell says that if I was in Japan I could be a geisha girl if I wasn't so tall. That's why they call me Butterfly. It's the saddest story. Poor Madame Butterfly died that her child could be happy across the sea. She married a sailor, too, an American lieutenant. They come and go. The priest, her uncle, cursed her for marrying a Yank.

— The priests are good at that, said Pike who, because of his reading allowed himself, outside office hours, a soupçon of anticlericalism.

Touched by Puccini they were silent for a while, sipping champagne. With every sip Pike realised more clearly that he had found what the poet, another poet, an English one, had called the long-awaited long-expected spring, he knew his heart had found a time to sing, the strength to soar was in his spirit's wing, that life was full of a triumphant sound and death could only be a little thing. She was good on the nose, too. She was wise in the ways of perfume. The skin of her neck had a pearly glow. The three guardian aunts were as far away as the moon. Then one of the pub's two doors – it was a corner house – opened with a crash and a big man came in, well drunk, very jovial. He wore a wide-brimmed grey hat. He walked to the counter. He said: Jody, old bootlegger, old friend of mine, old friend of Al Capone, serve me a drink to sober me up.

— Austin, said Jody, what will it be?

— A ball of malt, the big man said, and Madame Butterfly.

— That's my friend, Austin, she said, he always says that for a joke.

Pike whose face, with love or champagne or indignation, was taut and hot all over, said that he didn't think it was much of a joke.

— Oh, for Janey's sake, Pike, be your age.

She used his first name for the first time. His eyes were moist.

— For Janey's sake, it's a joke. He's a father to me. He knew my mother.

— He's not Japanese.

— Mind your manners. He's a fireman.

— Austin, she called. Champagne. Pike Hunter's buying champagne.

Pike bought another bottle, while Austin towered above them, swept the wide-brimmed hat from his head in a cavalier half-circle, dropped it on the head of Jody whose red carbuncled face was thus half-extinguished. Butterfly giggled. She said: Austin, you're a scream. He knew Trixie, Pike. He knew Trixie when she was the queen of the boards in the old Tivoli.

Sitting down, the big man sang in a ringing tenor: For I knew Trixie when Trixie was a child.

He sipped at his ball of malt. He sipped at a glass of Pike's champagne. He said: It's a great day for the Irish. It's a great day to break a fiver. Butterfly, dear girl, we fixed the Longford lout. He'll never leave Longford again.

The wife has him tethered and spancelled in the haggard. We wrote poison-pen letters to half the town, including the parish priest.

— I never doubted ye, she said. Leave it to the firemen, I said.

— The Dublin Fire Brigade, Austin said, has as long an arm as the Irish Republican Army.

— Austin, she told Pike, died for Ireland.

He sipped champagne. He sipped whiskey. He said: Not once, but several times. When it was neither popular nor profitable. By the living God, we was there when we was wanted. Volunteer McDonnell, at your service.

His bald head shone and showed freckles. His startlingly blue eyes were brightened and dilated by booze. He said: Did I know Trixie, light on her feet as the foam on the fountain? Come in and see the horses. That's what we used to say to the girls when I was a young fireman. Genuine horsepower the fire-engines ran on then, and the harness hung on hooks ready to drop on the horses as the firemen descended the greasy pole. And where the horses were, the hay and the straw were plentiful enough to make couches for Cleopatra. That was why we asked the girls in to see the horses. The sailors from the ships, homeless men all, had no such comforts and conveniences. They used to envy us. Butterfly, my geisha girl, you should have been alive then. We'd have shown you the jumps.

Pike was affronted. He was almost prepared to say so and take the consequences. But Butterfly stole his thunder. She stood up, kissed the jovial big man smack on the bald head and then, as light on her feet as her mother ever could have been, danced up and down the floor, tight hips bouncing, fingers clicking, singing: I'm the smartest little geisha in Japan, in Japan. And the people call me Rolee Polee Nan, Polee Nan.

Drowning in desire, Pike forgot his indignation and found that he was liking the man who could provoke such an exhibition. Breathless, she sat down again, suddenly kissed

Pike on the cheek, said: I love you too. I love champagne.
Let's have another bottle.

They had.

— Rolee Polee Nan, she sang as the cork and the fizz
ascended.

— A great writer, a Russian, Pike said, wrote that his ideal
was to be idle and to make love to a plump girl.

— The cheek of him. I'm not plump. Turkeys are plump.
I love being tall, with long legs.

Displaying the agility of a trained high-kicker with hinges
in her hips she, still sitting, raised her shapely right leg, up
and up as if her toes would touch the ceiling, up and up until
stocking-top, suspender, bare thigh and a frill of pink panties,
showed. Something happened to Pike that had nothing at all
to do with poetry or Jody's champagne. He held Butterfly's
hand. She made a cat's cradle with their fingers and swung
the locked hands pendulum-wise. She sang: Janey Mac, the
child's a black, what will we do on Sunday? Put him to bed
and cover his head and don't let him up until Monday.

Austin had momentarily absented himself for gentlemanly
reasons. From the basement jakes his voice singing rose above
the soft inland murmur of falling water: Oh my boat can
lightly float in the heel of wind and weather, and outrace the
smartest hooker between Galway and Kinsale.

The dockers methodically drank their pints of black porter
and paid no attention. Jody said: Time's money. Why don't
the two of you slip upstairs. Your heads would make a lovely
pair on a pillow.

Austin was singing: Oh she's neat, oh she's sweet, she's a
beauty every line, the Queen of Connemara is that bounding
barque of mine.


He was so shy, Butterfly said afterwards, that he might have
been a Christian Brother and a young one at that, although
where or how she ever got the experience to enable her to
make the comparison, or why she should think an old Christian

Brother less cuthallacht than a young one, she didn't say. He told her all about the aunts and the odd way he had been reared and she, naturally, told Austin and Jody and all her sorority. But they were a kind people and no mockers, and Pike never knew, Austin told me, that Jody's clientele listened with such absorbed interest to the story of his life, and of his heart and his love-making. He was something new in their experience, and Jody's stable of girls had experienced a lot, and Austin a lot more, and Jody more than the whole shebang, and all the fire-brigade, put together.

For Jody, Austin told me, had made the price of the Dark Cow in a basement in Chicago. During the prohibition, as they called it, although what they prohibited it would be hard to say. He was one of five brothers from the bogs of Manulla in the middle of nowhere in the County of Mayo. The five of them emigrated to Chicago. When Al Capone and his merry men discovered that Jody and his brothers had the real true secret about how to make booze, and to make it good, down they went into the cellar and didn't see daylight nor breathe fresh air, except to surface to go to Mass on Sundays, until they left the U.S.A. They made a fair fortune. At least four of them did. The fifth was murdered.

Jody was a bachelor man and he was good to the girls. He took his pleasures with them as a gentleman might, with the natural result that he was poxed to the eyebrows. But he was worth more to them than the money he quite generously paid after every turn or trick on the rumpled, always unmade bed in the two-storeyed apartment above the pub. He was a kind uncle to them. He gave them a friendly welcome, a place to sit down, free drink and smokes and loans, or advances for services yet to be rendered, when they were down on their luck. He had the ear of the civic guards and could help a girl when she was in trouble. He paid fines when they were unavoidable, and bills when they could no longer be postponed, and had an aunt who was reverend mother in a home for unmarried mothers and who was, like her nephew, a kindly person. Now and again, like the Madame made immortal by Maupassant, he took a bevy or flock of the girls for a day at the seaside or in the country. A friend of mine and myself, travelling into the granite mountains south of the city, to the old stone-cutters' villages of Lackan and Ballyknockan where there were aged people who had never seen Dublin, thirty miles away, and never wanted to, came upon a most delightful scene in the old country pub in Lackan. All around the bench around the walls sat the mountainy men, the stone-cutters, drinking their pints. But the floor was in the possession of a score of wild girls, all dancing together, resting off and on for more drink, laughing, happy, their gaiety inspired and directed by one man in the middle of the floor: red-faced, carbuncled, oily black hair sleeked down and parted up the middle in the style of Dixie Dean, the famous soccer centre-forward, whom Jody so much admired. All the drinks were on generous Jody.

So in Jody's friendly house Pike had, as he came close to forty years, what he never had in the cold abode of the three aunts: a home with a father, Austin, and a brother, Jody, and any God's amount of sisters; and Butterfly who, to judge by the tales she told afterwards, was a motherly sort of lover to him and, for a while, a sympathetic listener. For a while, only: because nothing in her birth, background, rearing or education, had equipped her to listen to so much poetry and talk about poetry.

— Poor Pike, she'd say, he'd puke you with poethry. Poethry's all very well, but.

She had never worked out what came after that qualifying: But.

— Give us a bar of a song, Austin. There's some sense to singing. But poethry. My heart leaps up when I behold a rainbow in the sky. On Linden when the sun was low. The lady of Shalott left the room to go to the pot. Janey preserve us from poethry.

He has eyes, Jody told Austin and myself, for no girl except Butterfly. Reckon, in one way, we can't blame him for that. She sure is the smartest filly showing in this paddock. But there must be moderation in all things. Big Anne, now, isn't bad, nor her sister, both well-built Sligo girls and very cooperative, nor Joany Maher from Waterford, nor Patty Daley from Castleisland in the County Kerry who married the Limey in Brum but left him when she found he was as queer as a three-dollar bill. And what about little Red Annie Byrne from Kilkenny City, very attractive if it just wasn't for the teeth she lost when the cattleman that claimed he caught gonorrhoea from her gave her an unmerciful hammering in Cumberland Street. We got him before he left town. We cured more than his gonorrhoea.

— But, Austin said, when following your advice, Jody, and against my own better judgment, I tried to explain all that to Pike, what does he do but quote to me what the playboy of the Abbey Theatre, John M. Synge, wrote in a love poem about counting queens in Glenmacnass in the Wicklow mountains.

— In the Wicklow mountains, said Jody. Queens? With the smell of the bog and the peat smoke off them.

Austin, a great man, ever, to sing at the top of his tenor voice about Dark Rosaleen and the Queen of Connemara and the County of Mayo, was a literary class of a fireman. That was one reason why Pike and himself got on so well together, in spite of that initial momentary misunderstanding about the ball of malt and Madame Butterfly.

— Seven dog days, Austin said, the playboy said he let pass, he and his girl, counting queens in Glenmacnass. The queens he mentions, Jody, you never saw, even in Chicago.

— Never saw daylight in Chicago.

— The Queen of Sheba, Austin said, and Helen, and Maeve the warrior queen of Connacht, and Deirdre of the Sorrows and Gloriana that was the great Elizabeth of England and Judith out of the Bible that chopped the block of Holofernes.

— All, said Jody, in a wet glen in Wicklow. A likely bloody story.

— There was one queen in the poem that had an amber belly.

— Jaundice, said Jody. Or Butterfly herself that's as sallow as any Jap. Austin, you're a worse lunatic than Pike.

— But in the end, Jody, his own girl was the queen of all queens. They were dead and rotten. She was alive.

— Not much of a compliment to her, Jody said, to prefer her to a cartload of corpses.

— Love's love, Jody. Even the girls admit that. They've no grudge against him for seeing nobody but Butterfly.

— They give him a fool's pardon. But no doll in the hustling game, Austin, can afford to spend all her time listening to poetry. Besides, girls like a variety of pricks. Butterfly's no better or worse than the next. When Pike finds that out he'll go crazy. If he isn't crazy already.

That was the day, as I recall, that Butterfly came in wearing the fancy fur coat – just a little out of season. Jody had, for some reason or other, given her a five-pound note. Pike knew nothing about that. And Jody told her to venture the five pounds on a horse that was running at the Curragh of Kildare, that a man in Kilcullen on the edge of the Curragh had told him that the jockey's wife had already bought her ball dress for the victory celebration. The Kilcullen man knew his onions, and his jockeys, and shared his wisdom only with a select few so as to keep the odds at a good twenty to one.

— She's gone out to the bookie's, said Jody, to pick up her winnings. We'll have a party tonight.

Jody had a tenner on the beast.

— She could invest it, said Austin, if she was wise. The day will come when her looks will go.

— Pike might propose to her, said Jody. He's mad enough for anything.

— The aunts would devour him. And her.

— Here she comes, Jody said. She invested her winnings on her fancy back.

She had too, and well she carried them in the shape of pale

or silver musquash, and three of her sorority walked behind her like ladies-in-waiting behind the Queen of England. There was a party in which even the dockers joined, but not Pike, for that evening and night one of his aunts was at death's door in a nursing home, and Pike and the other two aunts were by her side. He wasn't to see the musquash until he took Butterfly on an outing to the romantic hill of Howth where the poet and the woman had seen the white birds. That was the last day Pike ever took Butterfly anywhere. The aunt recovered. They were a thrawn hardy trio.

Pike had become a devotee. Every day except Sunday he lunched in Jody's, on a sandwich of stale bread and leathery ham and a glass of beer, just on the off-chance that Butterfly might be out of the doss and abroad, and in Jody's, at that, to her, unseasonable hour of the day. She seldom was, except when she was deplorably short of money. In the better eating places on Grafton Street and Stephen's Green, his colleagues absorbed the meals that enabled higher civil servants to face up to the afternoon and the responsibilities of State: statistics, land commission, local government, posts and telegraphs, internal revenue. He had never, among his own kind, been much of a mixer: so that few of his peers even noticed the speed with which, when at five in the evening the official day was done, he took himself, and his hat and coat and umbrella, and legged it off to Jody's: in the hope that Butterfly might be there, bathed and perfumed and ready for wine and love. Sometimes she was. Sometimes she wasn't. She liked Pike. She didn't deny it. She was always an honest girl, as her mother, Trixie, had been before her – so Austin said when he remembered Trixie who had died in a hurry, of peritonitis. But, Janey Mac, Butterfly couldn't have Pike Hunter for breakfast, dinner, tea and supper, and nibblers as well, all the livelong day and night. She still, as Jody said, had her first million to make, and Pike's inordinate attachment was coming between her and the real big business, as when, say, the country cattle

men were in town for the market. They were the men who
knew how to get rid of the money.

— There is this big cattle man, she tells Austin once, big he
is in every way, who never knows or cares what he's spending.
He's a gift and a godsend to the girls. He gets so drunk that
all you have to do to humour him is play with him a little in
the taxi going from pub to pub and see that he gets safely to
his hotel. The taximen are on to the game and get their divy
out of the loot.

One wet and windy night, it seems, Butterfly and this
philanthropist are flying high together, he on brandy, she
on champagne, for which that first encounter with Pike has
given her a ferocious drouth. In the back of the taxi touring
from pub to pub, the five pound notes are flowing out of your
man like water out of a pressed sponge. Butterfly is picking
them up and stuffing them into her handbag, but not all of
them. For this is too good and too big for any taximan on a
fair percentage basis. So for every one note she puts into her
handbag she stuffs two or three down into the calf-length boots
she is wearing against the wet weather. She knows, you see,
that she is too far gone in bubbly to walk up the stairs to her
own room, that the taximan, decent fellow, will help her up
and then, fair enough, go through her bag and take his cut.
Which, indeed, in due time he does. When she wakes up,
fully clothed, in the morning on her own bed, and pulls off
her boots, her ankles, what with the rain that had dribbled
down into her boots, are poulticed and plastered with notes
of the banks of Ireland and of England, and one moreover of
the Bank of Bonnie Scotland.

— Rings on my fingers, she says, and bells on my toes.

That was the gallant life that Pike's constant attendance
was cutting her off from. She also hated being owned. She
hated other people thinking that she was owned. She hated
like hell when Pike would enter the Dark Cow and one of
the other girls or, worse still, another man, a bit of variety,
would move away from her side to let Pike take the throne.

They weren't married, for Janey's sake. She could have hated
Pike, except that she was as tender-hearted as Trixie had
been, and she liked champagne. She certainly felt at liberty
to hate the three aunts who made a mollycoddle out of him.
She also hated, with a hatred that grew and grew, the way
that Pike puked her with poethry. And all this time poor Pike
walked in a dream that he never defined for us, perhaps not
even for himself, but that certainly must have looked higher
than the occasional trick on Jody's rumpled bed. So dreaming,
sleep-walking, he persuaded Butterfly to go to Howth Head
with him one dull hot day when the town was empty and
she had nothing better to do. No place could have been more
fatally poetic than Howth. She wore her musquash. Not even
the heat could part her from it.

— He never let up, she said, not once from the moment we
boarded the bus on the quays. Poethry. I had my bellyful.

— Sure thing, said Jody.

— Any man, she said, that won't pay every time he
performs is a man to keep a cautious eye on. Not that he's not
generous. But at the wrong times. Money down or no play's
my motto.

— Well I know that, Jody said.

— But Pike Hunter says that would make our love
mercenary, whatever that is.

— You're a great girl, said Austin, to be able to pronounce it.

— Your middle name, said Jody, is mercenary.

— My middle name, thank you, is Imelda. And the cheek
of Pike Hunter suggesting to me to go to a doctor because he
noticed something wrong with himself, a kidney disorder, he
said. He must wet the bed.

— Butterfly, said Austin, he might have been giving you
good advice.

— Nevertheless. It's not for him to say.

When they saw from the bus the Bull Wall holding the
northern sand back from clogging up the harbour, and the
Bull Island, three miles long, with dunes, bent grass, golfers,

bathers and skylarks, Pike told her about some fellow called Joyce – there was a Joyce in the Civic Guards, a Galwayman who played county football, but no relation – who had gone walking on the Island one fine day and laid eyes on a young one, wading in a pool, with her skirts well pulled up; and let a roar out of him. By all accounts this Joyce was no addition to the family for, as Pike told the story, Butterfly worked out that the young one was well under age.

Pike and Butterfly had lunch by the edge of the sea, in the Claremont Hotel, and that was all right. Then they walked in the grounds of Howth Castle, Pike had a special pass and the flowers and shrubs were a sight to see if only Pike had kept his mouth shut about some limey by the name of Spenser who landed there in the year of God, and wrote a poem as long as from here to Killarney about a fairy queen and a gentle knight who was pricking on the plain like the members of the Harp Cycling Club, Junior Branch, up above there in the Phoenix Park. He didn't get time to finish the poem, the poet that is, not Pike, for the Cork people burned him out of house and home and, as far as Butterfly was concerned, that was the only good deed she ever heard attributed to the Cork people.

The Phoenix Park and the Harp Club reminded her that one day Jody had said, meaning no harm, about the way Pike moped around the Dark Cow when Butterfly wasn't there, that Pike was the victim of a semi-horn and should go up to the Fifteen Acres and put it in the grass for a while and run around it. But when, for fun, she told this to Pike he got so huffed he didn't speak for half an hour, and they walked Howth Head until her feet were blistered and the heel of her right shoe broke, and the sweat, with the weight of the musquash and the heat of the day, was running between her shoulder-blades like a cloudburst down the gutter. Then the row and the ructions, as the song says, soon began. He said she should have worn flat-heeled shoes. She said that if she had known that he was conscripting her for a forced march

over a mountain she'd have borrowed a pair of boots from
the last soldier she gave it to at cut-price, for the soldiers,
God help them, didn't have much money but they were more
open-handed with what they had than some people who had
plenty, and soldiers didn't waste time and breath on poetry:
Be you fat or be you lean there is no soap like Preservene.

So she sat on the summit of Howth and looked at the
lighthouse and the seagulls, while Pike walked back to the
village to have the broken heel mended, and the sweat dried
cold on her, and she was perished. Then when he came back,
off he was again about how that white-headed old character
that you'd see across the river there at the Abbey Theatre,
and Madame Gone Mad McBride that was the age of ninety
and looked it, and known to all as a roaring rebel, worse than
Austin, had stood there on that very spot, and how the poet
wrote a poem wishing for himself and herself to be turned into
seagulls, the big dirty brutes that you'd see along the docks
robbing the pigeons of their food. Butterfly would have laughed
at him, except that her teeth by this time were tap-dancing
with the cold like the twinkling feet of Fred Astaire. So she
pulled her coat around her and said: Pike, I'm no seagull. For
Janey's sake take me back to civilisation and Jody's where I
know someone.

But, God sees, you never knew nobody, for at that
moment the caveman came out in Pike Hunter, he that was
always so backward on Jody's bed and, there and then, he
tried to flatten her in the heather in full view of all Dublin
and the coast of Ireland as far south as Wicklow Head and
as far north as where the Mountains of Mourne sweep down
to the sea.

— Oh none of that, Pike Hunter, she says, my good
musquash will be crucified. There's a time and a place and
a price for everything.

You and your musquash, he tells her.

They were wrestling like Man Mountain Dean and Jack
Doyle, the Gorgeous Gael.

— You've neither sense nor taste, says he, to be wearing a fur coat on a day like this.

— Bloody well for you to talk, says she, with your rolled umbrella and your woollen combinations and your wobbly ass that won't keep you straight in the chair, and your three witches of maiden aunts never touched, tasted or handled by mortal man, and plenty of money and everything your own way. This is my only coat that's decent, in case you haven't noticed, and I earned it hard and honest with Jody, a generous man but a monster on the bed, I bled after him.

That put a stop to the wrestling. He brought her back to the Dark Cow and left her at the door and went his way.

He never came back to the Dark Cow but once, and Butterfly wasn't on her throne that night. It was the night before the cattle-market. He was so lugubrious and woebegone that Jody and Austin and a few merry newspaper men, including myself, tried to jolly him up, take him out of himself, by making jokes at his expense that would force him to come alive and answer back. Our efforts failed. He looked at us sadly and said: Boys, Beethoven, when he was dying, said: Clap now, good friends, the comedy is done.

He was more than a little drunk and, for the first time, seemed lopsided when standing up; and untidy.

— Clap now indeed, said Jody.

Pike departed and never returned. He took to steady drinking in places like the Shelbourne Hotel or the Buttery in the Hibernian where it was most unlikely, even with Dublin being the democratic sort of town that it is, that he would ever encounter Madame Butterfly. He became a great problem for his colleagues and his superior officers in the civil service, and for his three aunts. After careful consultation they, all together, persuaded him to rest up in Saint Patrick's Hospital where, as you all may remember, Dean Swift died roaring. Which was, I feel sure, why Pike wasn't there to pay the last respects to the dead when Jody dropped from a

heart attack and was waked in the bedroom above the Dark
Cow. The girls were there in force to say an eternal farewell
to a good friend. Since the drink was plentiful and the fun
and the mourning intense, somebody, not even Austin knew
who, suggested that the part of the corpse that the girls knew
best should be tastefully decorated with black crepe ribbon.
The honour of tying on the ribbon naturally went to Madame
Butterfly but it was Big Anne who burst into tears and cried
out: Jody's dead and gone forever.

Austin met her, Butterfly not Big Anne, a few days afterwards
at the foot of the Nelson Pillar. Jody's successor had routed
the girls from the Dark Cow. Austin told her about Pike and
where he was. She brooded a bit. She said it was a pity, but
nobody could do nothing for him, that those three aunts had
spoiled him for ever and, anyway, didn't Austin think that he
was a bit astray in the head.

— Who knows, Butterfly? Who's sound or who's silly?
Consider yourself for a moment.

— What about me, Austin?

— A lovely girl like you, a vision from the romantic east,
and think of the life you lead. It can have no good ending.
Let me tell you a story, Butterfly. There was a girl once in
London, a slavey, a poor domestic servant. I knew a redcoat
here in the old British days who said he preferred slaveys to
anything else because they were clean, free and flattering.

— Austin, I was never a slavey.

— No Butterfly, you have your proper pride. But listen: this
slavey is out one morning scrubbing the stone steps in front of
the big house she works in, bucket and brush, carbolic soap
and all that, in one of the great squares in one of the more
classy parts of London Town. There she is on her bended
knees when a gentleman walks past, a British army major in
the Coldstream Guards or the Black Watch or something.

— I've heard of them, Austin.

— So this British major looks at her, and he sees the
naked backs of her legs, thighs you know, and taps her on

the shoulder or somewhere and he says: Oh, rise up, lovely maiden and come along with me, there's a better life in store for you somewhere else. She left the bucket and the brush, and the stone steps half-scrubbed, and walked off with him and became his girl. But there were even greater things in store for her. For, Butterfly, that slavey became Lady Emma Hamilton, the beloved of Lord Nelson, the greatest British sailor that ever sailed, and the victor of the renowned battle of Trafalgar. There he is up on the top of the Pillar.

— You wouldn't think to look at him, Austin, that he had much love in him.

— But, Butterfly, meditate on that story, and rise up and get yourself out of the gutter. You're handsome enough to be the second Lady Hamilton.

After that remark, Austin brought her into Lloyd's, a famous house of worship in North Earl Street under the shadow of Lord Nelson and his pillar. In Lloyd's he bought her a drink and out of the kindness of his great singing heart, gave her some money. She shook his hand and said: Austin, you're the nicest man I ever met.

Austin had, we may suppose, given her an image, an ideal. She may have been wearied by Pike and his sad attachment to poetry, but she rose to the glimmering vision of herself as a great lady beloved by a great and valiant lord. A year later she married a docker, a decent quiet hard-working fellow who had slowly sipped his pints of black porter and watched and waited all the time.

Oddly enough, Austin told me when the dignity of old age had gathered around him like the glow of corn-stubble in the afterwards of harvest.

He could still sing. His voice never grew old.

— Oddly enough, I never had anything to do with her. That way, I mean. Well you know me. Fine wife, splendid sons, nobody like them in the world. Fine daughters, too. But a cousin of mine, a ship's wireless operator who had been all round the world from Yokohama to the Belgian Congo and back again, and had had a ship burned under him in Bermuda and, for good value, another ship burned under him in Belfast, said she was the meanest whore he ever met. When he had paid her the stated price, there were some coppers left in his hand and she grabbed them and said: give us these for the gas-meter.

But he said, also, that at the high moments she had a curious and diverting way of raising and bending and extending her left leg – not her right leg which she kept as flat as a plumb-level. He had never encountered the like before, in any colour or in any country.

# Down then
# by Derry

The first time Tom Cunningham ever saw Sadie Law's brother, Francie, that brother was airborne between the saddle of a racing bicycle and a stockade filled with female lunatics. Francie is not the chief part of this story, nor is his sister, but since he has been mentioned, it might be fair to his fame and memory to say who he was and what he was doing in the air in that odd place.

A resident medical officer in the district's mental hospital had, years before, been a believer in athletics as curative therapy for the crazy: running and jumping and the lord knows what. So he set those who were out of cells and strait-jackets, and otherwise capable, at the running and jumping, barring, for good reasons the throwing of the hammer or the discus, or the tossing of the caber – which can be dangerous occupations even for the sane. Then the medical officer, to introduce a sanative, competitive spirit, organised an annual sports meeting, with cups, shields and lesser prizes. The thing grew and grew. That medical officer died and went to Valhalla. The annual meeting continued to grow until it was one of the most notable sporting events in that part of the country. Professionals competed. The crazy men and women, those of them who could be out and about, were now only two small corralled sections among the spectators. They had been pushed back into the shouting or gibbering shadows where everybody, except the man in Valhalla, thought they belonged.

Francie Law was a famous track cyclist. That was how

he came to be there in the air. There was one bad corner
on the packed cinder track. This day there was a pile-up
and Francie was catapulted clean, to land among the lunatic
ladies. He survived. It was as a hero-worshipper bearing
grapes to Francie's hospital bedside – Francie, wherever he
was, always smelled of embrocation – that Tom Cunningham
first met Francie's sister, Sadie, who was almost as famous as
her brother, but not for track-cycling.

— She's Number One, according to all the talk, Tom
said to his favourite friend who was five years younger
than him.

Tom was nineteen.

— And she liked me, Tom said. We have a date. She
wore a black leather coat with a belt. There was a good
warm smell off it. Like the smell of the plush seats at the
back of the cinema where all the feeling goes on. Hot stuff,
boy. Also the smell of embrocation. Rub it up good. Frank
Mullan told me she was okay and easy to get, if you once got
to know her. And the May devotions are on the way. Long
evenings. Warm grass. And Frank Mullan should know. He
knows them all.

Of course it goes without saying that the devotions on May
evenings in the parish church, with the high, limping, Gothic
spires, went away back to something far before the worship of
holy purity and the blessed virgin, to some pagan festival of
the rites of spring. This he found out afterwards by reading,
and by much dull talk, in more sophisticated places, heaven
help us, than his own native town. But in the spring of that
year he neither knew nor worried about such things, as he
knelt beside Tom Cunningham in the side aisle to the left
hand of the high altar.

Oh, those brown angels cut in wood of a slightly lighter
colour than the wood of the beams to which they provided a
figurehead finish. They swooped out towards each other over
the nave and eyed the praying people. Once he had tried to
write a poem about them:

> In church the angels cut in wood,
> In row on row arranged,
> Stand always as before they stood,
> And only I am changed.

But it wouldn't work. The angels weren't standing, for God's sake, they had no legs or feet to stand on, or, if they had, those legs were buried in the wood of the beams from which winged torsos and long-haired oaken heads seemed to have instantaneously, ecstatically, emerged. Times, he still saw those angels in his dreams, soaring, in a sort of a way, over altar, incense, monstrance, praying priest, responding mumbling people, over Tom Cunningham in the side aisle making cute sideways eyes and secret signs at Sadie Law who knelt with her favourite friend directly under the angels in the nave. Whatever about bullshit talk and the rites of spring, the devotions on May evenings was where you met people for good or evil; and all around the church, high on a hill with its hopalong spires, the rolling country was rich in deep grass and the birds were making mocking calls along hidden lovers' lanes. The high grassy embankments along the railways that went out of the town to the Donegal sea at Bundoran, or to Dublin or Belfast, or down then by Derry to the northern sea, were a sort of secret world where only lovers went in the long evenings. No respectable girl would be seen walking along the railway. The art was in not being seen.

His daughter, who was eighteen years of age, said to his mother who admitted to being eighty-five: Dad must have been happy here in this town in his schooldays. He's always singing a song. Well, not singing exactly. It has no particular tune. No beat. Dad's a bit of a square. It goes more like an African chant.

— Wallawalla boom boom, said his son who was fourteen.

— John, said the daughter, mind your manners. Granny doesn't dig Swahili. No granny. The song begins like this.

Thrice happy and blessed were the days of my childhood and happy the hours I wandered from school, by green Mountjoy's forest, our dear native wildwood, and the green flowery banks of the serpentine Strule.

— Mountjoy forest, he said, was part of the estate of Lord and Lady Blessington. Back in the days of the great Napoleon. That was an old song.

— He was a good scholar, his mother said. He was very fond of reading poetry out loud. In the mornings after breakfast. Before he went to school.

As if he wasn't there at all. His daughter giggled.

He was accustomed to his mother rhapsodising in this way, talking about him to other people in his presence. Once she had said to a friend of his: He would be the best man in Ireland if it wasn't for the little weakness.

Afterwards his friend had said with great good humour: with you standing there I couldn't very well ask her which weakness she meant.

Another time and under similar circumstances she had said to the same friend: His father, God rest him, put on some weight when he passed forty, but he never swelled like that.

Pointing to him. As if, by God, the son, had had a dropsical condition.

To her grand-daughter and grandson she said: He read Shelley. If Winter comes can Spring be far behind. I liked that. Shelley was a good poet. Although my own mother could never understand about Tennyson and the brook. She used to say: Poor fellow, could nobody stop him. I think she thought it was about some unfortunate man that had something astray with his bowels. Then there was one poet that droned on and on about Adam and Eve and the fall of Satan.

She spat mildly and politely towards the fireplace where, winter or summer, there was always a fire. She preserved many old country customs. One was to spit when, by inadvertence or necessity, one mentioned a name of the devil – and his names were legion.

Twenty-eight years later he was still a little ashamed that he had inflicted on his mother's patient ears the monotony of Milton, even to the utter extremity of the Latin verses.

— Milton, he said, a bit of a bore.

But nobody paid the least attention to him. So he closed his eyes and his mind to the lot of them: the mother, old, wrinkled, wearing a battered old felt hat that looked like a German helmet, but with an eye as bright and inquisitive as it must have been when she was a lively singing country girl, and the man she was to marry was walking round and round the South African veldt; and he himself wasn't even a fragment of an imagination, or a gleam or a glint in his father's eye; the daughter, pert, small, lively, endlessly talkative; the son, tall, easy-going, slouching when he walked – as his grandfather had done. It was uncanny to observe such resemblances.

Since not one of the three of them paid any attention to him he shut his eyes and his mind to them and went on his own through the town, and back to the past that had made the town and him.

The two tall limping Gothic spires rose high above the hilly narrow streets. Those two spires and the simple plain spire of the Protestant church – that would be Church of Ireland, for the Methodists and Presbyterians did not rise to spires – could be seen for a distance of ten miles. They soared, they were prayers of a sort, over the riverine countryside.

The taller spire was all of two hundred and thirty feet high, thirty of that being for the surmounting cross. To climb up the inside of that spire you went first by a winding stone stairway to the organ loft, then by a steep straight wooden stairway to the shaky creaky platform where the sexton stood when he pulled the bell-rope, then up a series of perpendicular ladders to the place where the two bells were hung, sullen and heavy, but ready at the twitch of a rope to do their duty. From that eminence, one hundred and fifty feet up, you could look down on everything. The town was almost flat, no longer all humps and hills and high ridged roofs and steep narrow streets. Down there was the meeting place of two rivers, the Camowen and the Drumragh: a sparkling trout-water, a sullen pike-water. Who could comprehend the differences there were between rivers, not to speak now of the Amazon and the Seine and the Volga and the Whang-ho and the Ohio, but even between neighbouring rivers destined to marry and to melt into one? United, the waters of Drumragh and Camowen went on under the name of the Strule, sweeping in a great horseshoe around the wide holm below the military barracks, tramping and tossing northwards to meet yet another river, the Fairywater, then to vanish glistening into a green-and-blue infinity.

Except you were the sexton, or some lesser person authorised by him, you were not, by no means, supposed to be up there at all. Dusty boards, with crazy, dizzy gaps between them, swayed and bent under your feet. Vicious jackdaws screeched. The blue-and-green infinity into which the sparkling water vanished was the place where Blessington's Rangers had once walked, speaking Gaelic, great axes on shoulders. They cut down the trees to make timber for war against Bonaparte, and money to keep Lord and Lady Blessington, their daughter, and the ineffable Count D'Orsay gallivanting.

One day coming home from school alone – that was a time of the day when it wasn't easy to be alone but, with cunning, it could be managed – he had found the door at the foot of the stone stairway open and had taken the chance that it was open by accident. It was. He made the climb. He saw the world. He was alone with the jackdaws and the moan of the wind. Then on the way down the perpendicular ladders he had missed a rung, slipped, screamed with the jackdaws, grabbed desperately and held on. Just about where the sexton would stand to pull the bell-rope he had vomited a sort of striped vomit that he had never seen before. Even in boyhood there was the fear of death.

Nobody, thank God, had ever found out who had thus paid tribute, made offertory, in the holy place. For weeks afterwards he had felt dizzy even when climbing the stairs to his bedroom.

When the war was over and Boney beaten, the gallivanting lords and ladies had no more use for the woodsmen of Mountjoy. For the last time they walked down there below in the old Flax Market that hadn't changed much since 1820: in their rough boots and frieze coats, axes on shoulders, speaking a guttural language that was doomed almost to die, singing, drinking, fighting among each other, but standing shoulder to shoulder or axe to axe against the world. The paltry townsmen and shopkeepers must have breathed easily when the woodsmen went north to Derry to board the American boat.

As a boy he had known of them and walked among their shadows in the Old Market: No more will we see the gay silver trouts playing, or the herd of wild deer through its forest be straying, or the nymph and gay swain on its flowery bank straying, or hear the loud guns of the sportsmen of Strule.

On those May evenings the steeplejacks were swinging on the spires, tiny black dwarfs sitting in wooden chairs at the ends of ropes. They were pointing the stones, which meant that they smeared in fresh cement, netted the soaring prayers in nets of new white. Snug and secure in deep warm grass on a railway embankment from which there was a view both of the tips of the roofs of the town and of one deep curve of the slow pike-infested Drumragh River, Tom and Sadie, Tom's friend and Sadie's friend, lay on their backs and watched the dwarfs on the steeples.

— Why, Angela said, did they not build one steeple as long as the other?

— As high, he said, you mean.

— High or long, she said, what's the difference?

She had a wide humorous mouth that, some evening, with the help of God, he would get around to kissing.

— It all depends, Tom said, on which way you're going. Like up or down or sideways.

— Why, she repeated.

She was a stubborn girl. He held her hand.

— In this life, Tom said, there is nothing perfect.

— No, he said.

Because he knew.

— Two men were killed on the smaller steeple. So they stopped.

— Brian, said Tom, always has a better story. Say us a poem, Brian.

— That's no story. It's gospel truth.

Tom and Sadie were kissing, gurgling. Angela tickled his palm.

— That's a job, he said, I wouldn't have for all the tea in China.

He meant being a steeplejack.

Tom surfaced. He said: I'm not so sure. I wouldn't mind being able to get up as high as that.

Sadie said: You could always try.

With her left hand she gently massaged Tom's grey-flannelled crotch.

He watched Sadie's small moving hand. He wondered how many people within a ten-mile radius, in the town, in villages, from farmhouse doorways, walking along laneways, or fishing, or lying on grass, were watching the steeplejacks on the spires.

For no reason that he could explain he thought it would be exciting to see that face again, the wide humorous mouth, the brown hair that curled like two little brown horns over her temples, the plump fresh cheeks. The hair, though, wouldn't be brown any more. Don't forget that. Look for something older. Three years older than yourself: a reasonable gap of years, once upon a time, for a girl who could teach and a boy who was willing, even afraid, to learn.

— That woman, his daughter said, who writes you those letters from Indiana. What part of this town did she live in? When she was a girl, I mean.

The three of them were walking down the steep High Street.

Behind and above them, where two narrower streets met to form the High Street, was the eighteenth-century courthouse, high steps before it and Doric columns, dominating the long undulations of High Street and Campsie Avenue until the houses ended and the point of vision was buried in deep trees.

He told them that there had once been in the town a policeman so lazy that he hated to walk. So he sat all day, when the day was sunny, on the courthouse steps. When his superior officers asked him what he thought he was at, he defended himself by saying that he had the whole town under observation.

This grey day, the last sad day but one of the old year, would have been no day for sitting on the steps.

They laughed at the memory of the lazy policeman, and descended the steep street. The daughter said: You never met her, all the times you were in the States?

— I never even met her, I only saw her, when we were young together here in this town. She's a shadow, a memory.

— Shadows, she said precisely, don't write letters. Memories might.

— One time last year, he said, I had hoped to meet her. I was, so to speak, passing that way. That is, within a few hundred miles or so of where she lives. That's not far, out there.

— Just next door, his son said.

— It was in March, he said, and I was on the way north to give a lecture in Minnesota. I crossed Indiana.

— See any Injuns dad, said the son.

— No, what I mostly remember about Indiana is big barns and ducks, the big ducks that we call Muscovy ducks. Never saw so many Muscovy ducks, anywhere else in the world.

— But then dad, his daughter said, you never were in Muscovy.

— Or if he was, said the son, he never told us.

In March in Indiana the endless flat brown land still shivered. The harness-racing tracks by the roadside were soggy and empty. The last of the snow lay here and there in sordid mounds. Cattle, with a certain guilty look about them, foraged among the tall battered corn-stalks of last year's harvest. There was ice at the fringes of creeks and rivers that looked far too small to negotiate such interminable expanses of flat land. Great round-roofed barns stood aloof from, yet still dwarfed, the neat houses. Flat and sombre the land went every way to a far horizon . . .

— A small American penny, his daughter said, for your wandering thoughts.

He told her that in one small field near the city of Lafayette he had seen a flock of more than two hundred Muscovy ducks. The field had been between a railway and a line of power pylons.

— Nothing, he explained, more emphasises distance in flat land than a line of pylons striding on and on for ever, giants marching, carrying cables on their shoulders, until they vanish east or west.

— Or north or south, his son said.

— Now, she said sweetly, we know all about electricity. Dad, you're such a dear old bore. We couldn't care less about ducks or pylons. We want to know about the woman who writes you those marvellous letter from Indiana.

— She was an orphan, he said. In an orphanage. In Derry City.

— So far so good, his son said.

— She was taken out of the orphanage by this woman and reared in this town. She suffered a lot from illness. She wore a leg-splint when she was a child. She grew up. She read books. My father used to talk a lot about her. He used to say: You should meet that young woman. She's a wonder.

— But I was in college in Dublin, by that time coming and going and somehow or other I never did get the opportunity of speaking to her. My memory is of a rather long beautiful face, sort of madonna, and fair hair. Framed like an old picture in glass and wood, against a background of coloured magazines and paperbacked books. Because my last recollection of her is that she was working in the bookstall in the railway station. During the war she went off to London, married an American. Then seven or eight years ago she read something I'd written and wrote to me. That's the whole story.

She had written: You may have a vague recollection of who I am when you read my name. Then again you may not. It's been a long time. About thirty years. But I remember you very well, indeed: on your way to school, to church, walking the roads around our town, always, it seemed to me, alone.

That would be a romantic young girl confusing an average sullen lout of a fellow with her private image of Lord Byron.

— We rarely said more than hello. We lived in the same town all our growing years. We walked the same roads, knew the same people, and didn't meet at all. We might have shared a common interest. I loved books, poetry, music, but had little opportunity to enjoy any of them. I did manage to read quite a lot, and to remember poetry, and get a little music on an old radio. I walked, and thought of the books I'd read, and repeated the poetry to myself, and could hear the music again along the quiet roads. Thus I survived the town I was born in. Though mostly I remember it with love, because of Margaret, the woman who reared me. She was gentle, poor, uneducated, but with a lively mind and kind to all things living – especially to me when she took me from the nightmare of the orphanage in Derry, haunting me even now with its coldness, the crooked hilly streets of Derry, the jail, the Diamond, the wide Foyle which is really our own Strule, and the ships.

— Another penny for your thoughts, his daughter said. Or a measly nickel.

They turned right from the Market Street along the Dublin Road, past a filling station and a Presbyterian church, a toy-like gasworks, the old white houses of Irishtown. Beyond

Irishtown, he told them, was the Drumragh River and the old humped King's Bridge where James Stuart, falling back from the walls of Derry, had watched the town burn behind him.

Then they were ascending through a pleasant affluent suburb.

— No, he said, this wasn't the part of the town she lived in. We're not going that way just at the moment.

They were, in fact, walking to say a prayer at his father's grave. Everywhere he went he carried with him for luck a white stone from the grave. A white stone from the grave of a kind man would have to be lucky, wouldn't it, if there was the least pick of reason in the universe? But in a drunken moment in Dublin City he had loaned the stone to a man who ran greyhounds, and this particular greyhound had won, and the man had begged to be allowed to keep the stone. Today he would say his prayer and take away with him another white stone.

The Protestants lay to the left of the cemetery's main avenue, the Catholics to the right, and between them, on a slight rise, the stone oratory, cold and draughty, where on harsh days the last prayers were said over the coffins. He never remembered the wind around the corners of that oratory as being, even in summer, anything but bitterly cold. This last dead day, but one, of the year it was unbearable. Bravely the boy and girl knelt on the damp earth and prayed. He knelt with them, not praying, talking without words to the man under the clay, or somewhere in the air around him, and around him wherever in the world he went: the dead hover for ever over the living.

Low dark clouds travelling, or being forced to travel, fast, bulged with rain. To the lee of the empty oratory the three of them stood and looked over the forest of obelisks and Celtic crosses, Sacred Hearts and sorrowing mothers, at the distant sweep of the flooded Drumragh, at where the railway line used to cross it by a red metal bridge. The bridge was gone and the railway too – sold for scrap. But three hundred yards to the east of the river, there was still the stone bridge under the embankment – it looked like a gateway into an old walled city – and the lovers' lane that led into the fields, and across the fields to the wooded brambly slope above one of the deepest, most brooding of the river's pike-pools.

Would it be sin or the beginning of living to touch the hidden flesh of Angela? His dream of fair women was all about the creeping hand, the hair, the warmth. That was all that Tom and the other boys talked about.

She lay on her back in the brambly wood – the pike hovering in the pool below them – and he fumbled fearfully, and tickled her, his hand timidly outside her dress. But when she reached for him he rolled away. She laughed for a longer time than seemed necessary. From the far side of a clump of bushes he heard Tom say to Sadie: There must be nothing in Brown's house that doesn't smell of embrocation.

— The grave was very weedy, the daughter said.

— So I noticed. Your grandmother pays good money to have it kept clean and covered with white stones. On the way out I'll call to the caretaker's house and talk to him.

The clay in the centre of the grave had sunk. He was glad that neither son nor daughter had noticed that. It would be so painful to have to explain to young people, or even to oneself, that clay sank so when the coffin underneath had collapsed.

The hotel they stopped in was a mile outside the town, a domed mid-nineteenth-century house, miscalled a castle, on a hill top with a view of the heathery uplands the Camowen came from, and quite close to a park called the Lovers' Retreat, but known to the soldiers in the barracks as Buggers' Den.

The aged mother was safely at home in bed, in her small house across the narrow street from those gigantic limping spires. She liked to be close to the quietness of the church, the glowing red circle around the sanctuary lamp where she remembered and prayed for and to the dead man.

Leaving her in peace they had walked through the lighted crowded town, along a quiet dim suburban road, over a bridge that crossed the invisible talkative Camowen – there was a good gravelly trout pool just below that bridge. They dined late in a deserted dining-room. Along a corridor there was the noise of merriment from the bar. His son asked him which room had been the haunted room in the days when the hotel had been a castle.

— For the sake of the ghost, the daughter said, let's hope it wasn't where the bar is now.

— Ghosts, he told her, might like company.

— Not mine I pray, she said.

— Fraidy cat, the son said. A ghost couldn't hurt you.

— That ghost, he told them, couldn't hurt anyone. The story was that the people who lived here called in the priest and he blessed the room and put the ghost in a bottle.

— Poor ghost, she said.

— But where, she wondered, did the priest put the bottle.

— On the river, the son said. And it floated over the sea, to England, and somebody found it and opened it, and got a ghost instead of a message.

He saw them to their rooms. No ghost could survive in such up-to-date comfort. No ghost could rest in peace in any of the coloured bottles in the bar. The noisy local drinkers had gone home, taking their din with them. A few commercial men, talking of odds and ends, drinking slowly but with style, sat in an alcove. He joined them.

— Did you like it out there, they asked him.

— You were a friend of Tom Cunningham, they said.

— It's good out there. Fine people. Hospitable. The sort of people I meet.

— Tom went into the Palestine police after the war, they said. Then he went farther east. Never heard of since.

— Chasing the women in China, they said.

— But the crime in America, they said. Did you ever come up against that?

— It's there. But I never came up against it. Except in the newspapers.

— By God, they said, they have picturesque murders out there. We never have anything here except an odd friendly class of a murder. But out there. That fellow in Chicago and the nurses. And the young fellow that made the women in the beauty parlour lie down like the spokes of a wheel and then shot the living daylights out of them.

— The one that sticks most in my mind . . .

They were all attention.

. . . was the girl in the sump. This sump is an overflow pond at the back of a dry-cleaning plant. One morning a man walking by sees a girl's leg standing up out of the water.

— Clothed in white samite, they said. Mystic, wonderful.

— Seems she had been by day a teller in a bank and by night a go-go dancer in a discotheque. One day she walks out of the bank with a bagful of thousands of dollars. She is next encountered in the sump, one leg surfacing, her hands tied behind her back, her throat cut, the bag and the dollars gone. A barman from the discotheque is also missing.

— All for love, they said.

The long cold day, the search for the past, the drink, the warm company, had made him maudlin.

— When I read the newspapers today there are times I think I was reared in the Garden of Eden.

— Weren't we all, they said.

But it hadn't been the Garden of Eden for one waif of a girl, now a woman in far-away Indiana. From Atlanta, Georgia, where he had been for two years he had remailed to her the local newspapers that had come to him from this town.

She had written: That photograph of the demolition of the old stone railway bridge at Brook Corner saddened me. I recall that bridge with affection. When I'd spent about fourteen months flat on my back in the County Hospital, and was at last permitted up on crutches, I headed, somewhat shakily, under that bridge to begin the first of many walks. I still remember the bridge framing the road beyond like a picture, and the incredible green of the fields, the flowering hedges, the smell of hawthorn. The bridge became for me a gateway: to happy solitude. When I had trachoma and thought I might go blind my bitterest thought was that I might never again see the world through that bridge. Margaret's brother, Fred, was my companion and consolation in those dark days. He had been hired out at the age of six to work with a farmer and Margaret remembered seeing the golden-curly-haired child going off in the farmer's trap.

— Perhaps that was why Fred never cared to work. He hadn't, for about twenty-five years before he died, not because he couldn't but simply because he didn't want to. Oh, on a number of occasions he worked, briefly, for farmers at harvest time, was rarely paid in cash but in kind; and only on condition that his dog, Major, could accompany him. Major barked all day, every day, as though indignant at his master's labours, and much to the chagrin of the other workers and the farmer. But since, when he wanted to, Fred could work as well as the others, his services were always desired and he was permitted to stay, dog and all.

— He was a strange silent man who sat by the fire all day with a far-off look in his eyes. He had very blue eyes. He rarely spoke to anybody outside the house. He was my sole companion during many long hours when I was confined to bed. I would read to him and ask him to spell and he would deliberately mis-spell and would be delighted when I would sharply correct him. I never knew how much I loved him until he died.

— Margaret housekept for Morris, the lawyer, who lived in the Georgian house beside the church with the high spires, and that left Fred and me a lot alone, and Fred would cook for me. Once, after I had been with Margaret several months, some sadistic neighbour woman told me that I was being sent back to the orphanage. So terrified was I that I hobbled up

to the church and stood for hours across the street from the
lawyer's house, waiting, the wind moaning away up in the
spires in the darkness, until Margaret came and comforted me,
led me home by the hand to Fred and Major and numerous
cats, and a one-legged hen who had a nest in the corner and
who was infuriated if another hen ever came to the back door
in search of scraps.

His room was haunted, sure enough. He had sat too late,
drunk too much, perhaps released the ghosts from the bottles.
Oaken angels sang from the ceiling. A tearful crippled girl
waited in the darkness at the foot of spires lost also in the
windy darkness, no longer magic towers from which one could
see the world. The leg of a girl who had stolen for love stood
up like a stump of wood out of stagnant water.

Very cautiously he had asked his mother: Do you remember
a family called Law? Are they still in the town? One of them,
I think, was a famous racing cyclist.

Cautiously: because in her eyes there were times when he
was still fourteen or less and there were people that he wasn't
supposed to know.

— Oh, I remember the Laws. They were famous, indeed.

Around the house she had a fancy for dressing as if
she were a pirate chief. Or perhaps it was a gipsy queen.
Sometimes instead of the helmet-shaped hat she wore a white
gipsy head-handkerchief; and a long red dressing-gown and a
Galway shawl with the corners tucked back under her oxters
and pinned behind.

— One of them called in to see me one morning after
Sunday mass. A Law or a half-Law or a quarter-Law or a
by-Law. You wouldn't have much time for the like of them.
Not condemning anyone for the weakness, but there were more
distant cousins in that clan than was natural. Or godly.

That seemed to be that.

— You wouldn't have exacted much of the Laws, she
said. But it's heartrending to see the fate of some families

that had every chance that God and man could give them.

— Like who, for instance?

— Like many I've seen. Like the Glenshrule family, for one.

The red bull of Glenshrule roared through his haunted dreams.

— Glenshrule's sold, she said, and in the hands of strangers.

The bull, he supposed, had been sold to make bovril.

Two private roadways led into the old house at Glenshrule, one from the steep by-road along which the crippled girl had hobbled to find peace, one from the road that led west to the Donegal sea. To either hand on either road it was all Glenshrule land, green, bountiful, a little unkempt, cattle country, little tillage. The three bachelor brothers of Glenshrule were gentlemen farmers: which meant whipcord breeches and booze and hunting horses. But they were frank, reckless, generous, easy in their money and good breeding, and made no objection to the townspeople using their private roads for circular walks on Sunday afternoons. Roving boys used those roads all the time, and the fields around them, and the only prohibiting notice to be seen told you to beware of the red bull.

— Christ, look at the size of him, Tom cried with an artist's enthusiasm. Boy, if you were built like that you'd be welcome anywhere.

They sat on a five-barred iron gate. Between them and the bull's private meadow was the additional fortification of a strong wooden gate. He was an unruly bull. His red coat shone. He had a head near as big as the head of the mouldy bison they had seen in the Old Market in Bostock and Wombell's travelling menagerie. He rooted at the ground with one fore-foot. The great head rose and fell. He didn't roar. He rumbled all the time like a train, far away, going into a tunnel.

— There's a lot to be said, Tom said, for being a bull.

— Everybody puts up with your tantrums.

— There's more to it than that.

Then the lady of Glenshrule, the one single sister of the three bachelor brothers, rode by on a bay mare. To acknowledge that they existed she raised her riding-crop, she smiled and said: Don't tempt him. Don't enter the meadow. Bulls eat boys.

— Boys, Tom muttered.

He was very bitter.

— There's also a lot to be said, he said, for being a bay mare.

She was bareheaded. She was blonde. She was twenty-five. She was blonde, she was blonde, she was blonde and calm-faced, and all the officers in the barracks pursued her. Years afterwards – altering the truth, as memory always does – he thought that he had then thought about queen and huntress, chaste and fair. But he hadn't. He had been too breathless to think of anything except, perhaps, that Sadie and Angela, lively and provoking as they could be, were still only in the servant-maid class.

She rode on towards the Donegal road. The sound of hooves died away. The red bull, calmed, had lain down on grass.

— One Sunday evening I sat beside her in the church, Tom said. My right leg against her left. It burned me. I can feel it still.

He rubbed his right thigh slowly, then sniffed his hand.

— I swear to God, he said, she pressed her thigh against mine. It made short work of the holy hour.

That was the year Tom and himself had been barred from the town's one cinema because Tom, ever an eager and enquiring mind, had discovered the anti-social use of hydrogen sulphide. A few sizzling test-tubes planted here and there in the darkness could have tumultuous effects on the audience. Old Mr. Pritchard – he was so old that it was suspected he had fought in the Zulu war – was heard to say in a barracks-square voice that some bloke here needed a purge of broken bottles. But three burly ushers simply purged Tom and his companion from the audience, two of them to hold Tom, the other to herd the companion before him.

Such a splendid deed and its consequences gave the two of them the glory of outlaws among their contemporaries. And to be barred from the delights of Eddy Cantor's Rome, or of Broadway with its gold-diggers, or of Wallace Beery's Big House, meant more nights in the Old Flax Market. That was fair enough, because the Old Flax Market was the place for outlaws. Black-uniformed constables patrolled the streets but, unless there was very audible drunken disorder, they left the Old Flax Market alone. No flax was ever sold there any more.

— The ghosts of the woodsmen are still here, he told Tom. This was their place when they came to town.

— You and those bloody woodsmen. You're a haunted man.

The unpaved three acres of the Old Market were sodden and puddled. A sharply defined half-moon cut like a cleaver through wispy running clouds. He shouted at the moon: No more will the fair one of each shady bower hail her dear boy of that once happy hour, or present him again with a garland of flowers that they oft times selected and wove by the Strule.

— And poetry, boy, will be your ruination. Poetry will get you nowhere with Angela. Move in man. Angela demands action.

The moon, even if it was only half a moon, was useful to outlaws in a land of outlaws. For there were only three gas-lamps in the whole of the Old Flax Market and gas-lamps were little use on windy nights or when somebody, for fun or hellery, wished to quench them. One lamp was on a wall-bracket at the corner of a rowdy dance hall. It lighted, when it was allowed to, the wooden stairway to the door of the dance hall, and the people ascending or descending or standing in groups making noise. One lamp lighted the covered cobbled entry-way from the High Street. The third lighted the muddy uncovered exit to a dark riverside walk from which an irate lover had, about that time, heaved his fancy into the river.

— Let's have a look, Tom said, at the Jennett's corner. You'll see things there you never saw at the pictures.

— But look, he said, there goes the Bluebottle, her legs like elevenpence marked on a new bucket.

The drum boomed, the horn blared from the dance hall. The half-moon coldly shone on the Strule waters that flowed by one side of the Old Market.

— If your woodsmen ever walked here you can bloody well guess what they were after.

A tall thin girl in a blue coat was being eased into the shadows by a drunken man.

— Would you believe it, Tom said, she fought like a cat here one night with one of the Fighting McDermotts. The one with the dinge in his temple where some decent man brained him with a bottle of port-wine. When she wouldn't go with him he shouted he'd tell her father that sent her out for money, and her uncle that broke her in. She tore the red face off him.

— He rings the bell, her uncle.

— They say he rang the bell for her when she was thirteen.

There then was the terror of the dark walk by the river. The uncle who rang the bell as one of the last town-criers was a figure out of a German fairy-tale, a pied piper, tall hard hat, tailed coat, long grey moustache, a small man with a voice of thunder, swinging his handbell, shouting out fragments of news: that a group of strolling players would perform in the town hall, that the water supply would be turned off – for repairs to pipes in this or that part of the town, that such and such a house property would be auctioned. Was it credible that a comic fairy-tale figure should also be a part of some sniggering story? The Bluebottle vanished ahead of them into some riverside bushes. Where the river made an elbow bend a group of smoking muttering men waited at the Jennet's corner. Her shady bower was a wooden shelter put there by the town council to protect Sunday walkers from sudden showers. The council had not intended to cater for the comfort of the Jennet and her customers. She was a raw-boned red-headed country girl whose husband was in the mental hospital.

— Good natured and charges very little, Tom said. Some of the shadowy courtiers called after them.

— But, boy, a little bit too open to the general public for men of taste like ourselves. Take me back to sweet sinful Sadie. Or the lady of Glenshrule on her bay mare.

She rode on to the Donegal road, the hooves dancing clippety-clop, and the bull lay down in the meadow.

— What went wrong there, he said to his mother. They had everything.

— What would go wrong but debt and drink and the want of wit. The three brothers fled to Canada.

— They followed the woodsmen.

His mother didn't hear him.

— And my, she said, she looked lovely when she rode out astraddle on that bay mare.

— Tom Cunningham would have agreed with you.

— Oh, Tom Cunningham was a rare one. Very freckled when he was a little boy. And curly-haired. I'm amazed you remember him. He went to the war and never came back when it was over. But then you always had a good memory.

— I always had.

— She lived alone after the brothers left, and she never married, and went on drinking. There was a bit of scandal, too. But I never paid much attention to that sort of talk. She died in the ambulance on the way to hospital. But not, thank God, without the priest. For one of the curates was driving past just at that moment.

On the road she had ridden over on the bay mare.

— The Lord, his mother said, has everything mixed with mercy.

— He must have a lot of mercy for orphans, he said.

— Tell granny that story, dad, about the girl in the

rain. The woman who writes to you. When she was a child, I mean.

She could still be outside there, the ghost of a frightened child, standing in the darkness at the foot of the spires. But one day in the orphanage playground she had broken out in rebellion.

— A sudden storm came up. The nuns called us in. We were to shelter, cold and miserable, in a sort of arcade or cloister. I started in with the rest, but suddenly I stopped and ran back to the playground. It was pouring. I was alone. The nuns called me. I wouldn't come. I danced around that playground in my bare feet, hair and dress soaking wet. Repeated calls failed to move me. Two nuns came after me. I ran and danced from one side to the other, dodging the hands that tried to clutch me. I laughed and danced in the wind and rain. I'd wait until they got close and then I'd run like the wind. Their long robes were heavy with water. They were exhausted. But I was exhilarated. Until suddenly I collapsed and was dragged inside. Mute and terrified and expecting to be lashed. I don't know why, but my defiance was forgiven.

— It was a ballet, his daughter said. The truant in the rain.
— Nuns on the run, said the son.

The German poet, long ago, went walking in the botanical gardens, saw plants, that elsewhere he had seen only in pots or under glass, growing cheerfully under the open sky. Might he not discover among them, the original plant from which all others are derived? After all, the poet thought, it must exist, the innermost nucleus.

A crazy idea. A wise old woman dressed like a gipsy or a pirate chief. A pert young girl curious about the American woman who had once been an orphan child in this town. Sadie Law with her leather coat and the smell of embrocation. A blonde horse-riding queen and huntress dying of drink in the back of an ambulance. Two sad creatures, nicknamed, one

for the colour of her only coat and the hard meagre shape of
her body, the other because it was said, with sniggers, that
she was hopeless of progeny and disreputable in her ancestry.
Angela running hand in hand with him on a wet Saturday
afternoon through the Old Flax Market.

The place was empty that day. Not even the ghosts of the
woodsmen walked in the grey light and the rain. He couldn't
remember where Sadie and Tom had been at that time. The
Jennet's corner was also empty. In the wooden shelter, hacked
with names and odd obscenities and coy references to local
love affairs, they sat on a creaky seat and kissed and fumbled.
Then around a corner of the shelter came the Jennet herself,
leading a staggering cattle-drover, his ash-plant in his hand.

— Wee fellow, he said with great camaraderie, I suppose
you're at the same game as myself.

— He's too bashful, Angela said.

— He'll live to learn, the Jennet said. They all do.

The rain ran down her bony face. Wet yellow hair stuck
out from under a red tam o'shanter. Her eyes were of such
a bright blue as to make her seem blind.

— The good book, the drover said, says that the wise man
falls seven times. And, as sure as my name is Solomon, I'm
going to fall now.

So the wee fellow retreated from the shelter, dragging
Angela with him for a little way until she dug her heels
into the muddy ground. The river was a brown fresh, taking
with it broken branches and hay from flooded meadows,
sweeping on, down then by Derry our dear boys are sailing.
Now he remembered that that day Angela had been wearing
a sou'wester and Sadie's black coat, a little big for her but a
stronghold against the rain.

— What do we need to run for? You might learn something.

He said nothing.

— Wee boy, she said. I'm going back for a peep.

He stood alone looking at the turbulent river, looking across
the river at the limping spires, one proud and complete, one for

ever unfinished, a memory of defeat and death. What would a wild woodsman have done? Down along the river valley it was said that there were trees on which the woodsmen, just before they left, had carved their names so strongly that the letters could still be read. But that must be a fable, a memory out of the old song: Their names on the trees of the rising plantation, their memories we'll cherish, and affection ne'er cool. For where are the heroes of high or low station that could be compared with the brave boys of Strule?

— That was as good as a circus, Angela said. You've no idea in the world what you missed.

At breakfast in the hotel in the morning the chatty little waitress shook his belief in himself by saying to him and his children that she had never heard of anybody of his name coming from this town.

— The great unknown, his daughter said.

— Fooling us all the time, the son said. He came from Atlanta, Georgia.

But then it turned out that the waitress came from a smaller town twenty miles away and was only eighteen years of age.

— Off we go now, said the daughter, to see where granny came from.

— Bring no whiskey to Claramore, his mother said. There was always too much whiskey in Claramore. Returned Americans coming and going.

The son and the daughter wished her a happy new year.

— Drive down the town first, she said. I owe a bill I must pay.

— Won't it wait?

She was dressed in high style: widow's black coat, high hat and veil, high buttoned boots for walking in country places.

— Never begin the new year in debt was a good maxim. I'll stick to it while I have breath.

Her grand-daughter sitting beside her in the back of the hired car, giggled. Sourly he accepted the comments, one unconscious, one conscious, of two other generations on his own finances.

He drove down the High Street. They waited for her outside a hardware shop. The sky was pale blue, cloudless, and last night's unexpected white frost lay on the roofs and spotted the pavements. His daughter said: Granny never heard of a credit card.

More sordidly the son said: Nor hire purchase. Nor a post-dated cheque.

— It was a different world, mes enfants. They paid their way or went without.

But he knew that he had never worked out where – in the world that he had grown into – that terrifying old-fashioned honesty had gone: no debt, no theft, no waste. Beggars were accepted, because Joseph and Mary and the Child Jesus had gone homeless into Egypt. But debt was a sort of sin.

— Eat black bread first, she would say. But let no man say you're in his debt.

He had never taken to black bread. He hadn't told her that in a briefcase in the boot he had two bottles of Jack Daniels as a gift for his cousin – and for himself. A decent man could not with empty hands enter a decent house, and two bottles of American whiskey would be a fit offering to a house that had sent so many sons and daughters to the States.

She was back in the car again, settling herself like a duchess, her small red-headed grand-daughter helping her to tuck a rug around her knees. She refused to believe that a moving vehicle could be heated like a house.

It was a twelve-mile drive, first down the Derry road, over the steep hill that, in spite of all the miracles of macadam, was called, as it had been called in the eighteenth century, Clabber Brae. Then west, over the Drumquin railway crossing. There was no longer any railway to cross. Once upon a time the crossing-keeper's daughter had been as famous as Sadie Law. Then by Gillygooley crossroads where, one June day, Tom and himself, coming tired from fishing perch in the

Fairywater, had seen Angela climbing a gate into a ripe meadow just opened for the mower. Her companion was a stocky-shouldered blackavised soldier. That much they could see. A hundred yards ahead, Tom rested from his cycling and was silent for a long time. Then he said: Boy, I'd leave that one alone for the future.

— She's leaving me alone. Who's she with?

— The worst in the barracks. Fusilier Nixon. And he'll never rank higher.

— Why so?

— Four years ago when he came back from India he was all but drummed out for raping a slavey in the soldiers' holm.

— There's a great view of the holm from the tall spire.

— If you had been up there you could have seen the fun. His bacon was saved by a major whose life he saved, or something, in India. And God help the slaveys. The offspring of that bit of love at first sight is now toddling around Fountain Lane. I'll point him out to you some day. You'd have something in common.

They cycled on.

— I'll tell Sadie, Tom said, what we saw. Sadie has some sense. She wouldn't want to be seen in the company of Fusilier Nixon.

Their bicycles bumped over the railway crossing. The keeper's daughter waved, and called: Hello, Tom Cunningham.

— Cheer up, boy. You'll get another girl.

— I suppose I will.

— From here to China the world's full of them.

— I liked Angela.

He found it hard not to sob. Angela peeping around a corner at the animals in the circus. Angela in the clutches of a black-chinned brute. He had, too, really liked her. More than thirty years later he foolishly looked for her face on the streets of the old town and the face he looked for could not, in reason, ever be there. He would see, instead, a Madonna

– whom, also, he had never known – against a background of the coloured covers of magazines.

Now as he drove on, he looked at the gate that Angela had climbed into the meadow. But one gate was very like another and, under white frost, all meadows were the same. Although this valley to him would always be summer holiday country. Every mile of it he had walked or cycled. A hay-shed by a prosperous farmhouse meant for him mostly the sultry July hush before the rain came, the smell of sheds and barns, heavy rain on tin roofs, or soda bread and strong tea by peat fires on open hospitable hearths.

There now across the stilled, white fields was the glint of water at the pool where Tom and himself would first strike the Fairywater. The road climbed here, up over the stony place of Clohogue, then switchbacked for miles in and out of hazel glens, over loud rough brooks, then on to a plateau, high, very high; and visible in such clear frosty air, and a good seventy miles away by the edge of the Atlantic, the pigback of Muckish Mountain, the white cone of Mount Errigal, the Cock of the North. Claramore was just below the plateau. It was a place of its own, in a new valley.

From the Barley Hill beyond the old long white farmhouse you could also see those two far-away mountains and, in the other direction and looking down the valley of the Fairywater, the tips and crosses of the two limping Gothic spires, but not the smaller plain spire of the Protestant church.

— On a calm evening, his cousin said, they seem so close that you'd imagine you could hear the bell ringing for the May devotions.

He asked his cousin: Do the young people still climb Drumard in autumn to pluck the blayberries?

— We've heard a lot about those same blayberries, his daughter said. To pluck and eat them, dad says, was a memory of some ancient pagan feast.

— The young people, his cousin said, have their own pagan feasts.

The four of them walked on the boreen that crossed the Barley Hill to the place where the men were building a house for his cousin's son and the bride he would bring home with him in three months' time. Hard frost had slowed up the building work. Among the men, half-loitering, working just enough to keep warm, keeping as close as possible to an open brazier, his cousin passed round one of the bottles of bourbon. They drank from cracked cups and tin mugs, toasted the health of the visitors, of the bride-to-be, wished luck for ever on the house they were building. High above a jet plane, westward-bound out of Prestwick, made its mark on the cold pale blue.

— They'll be in New York before you, his son said.

The drinking men, circling the brazier, saluted the travellers in the sky and raised a cheer. It was only a few hours to New York from the Barley Hill or the pagan blayberries of Drumard. Breath ascended in puffs as white as the jet's signature. On the far side of the hill from the long farmhouse the Fairywater, glittering black, looped through frosted bottom-land.

— Phil Loughran, that used to work for you, he said. He was about my age. Where did he go?

The Black Stepping Stones were at that bend of the Fairywater, the seventh bend visible from where they stood; and above the Black Stones the pool where the country boys went swimming. Willows drooped over it. The bottom was good yellow sand. The water had the brown of the peat and was nowhere more than four feet deep. It was an idyllic place, had been an idyllic place until the day he had that crazy fight with Phil Loughran.

— He went to Australia, his cousin said. We hear he's doing well. The family, what's left of them, are still living here on my land.

Even to this day, and in the frosty air, he blushed to think of the lies he had told to Phil Loughran down there by the Black Stones – blushed all the more because, country boys being so much more cunning than towny boys, Phil almost certainly hadn't believed a word he said. Phil as he listened would have secretly laughed.

— So her name is Angela, he said.

Phil was a squat sallow-faced young fellow, dressed in rough corduroys and heavy nailed boots, his brown hair short-cropped, his eyes dark brown and close together. There was always a vague smell of peat smoke, or stables or something, from those corduroys.

— Angela the walking angel, he said.

They were dressing after a swim. Three other boys splashed and shouted in the pool. A fourth hung naked from a trailing willow, swinging like a pendulum, striking the water with his feet.

— So you tell us, Phil, you had the little man out of sight.

He made a sideways grab, as Angela had done on the wooded brambly slope above the pike-pool on the Drumragh. He was laughing. He said: Little man, you've had a busy day.

Then the two of them were rolling on the grass, swiping at each other, Phil still laughing, he sobbing, with temper, with the humiliation of having his tall tales of conquest made mockery of. Four naked dripping boys danced and laughed and shouted around them. It was the last day but one that he had been at the Black Stones. He had come second best out of that fight but he had a mean miserable sort of vengeance on his very last visit to the place.

Phil in his best corduroys – since it was Sunday – is crossing the water, stepping carefully from stone to stone, in his right hand the halter with which he is leading a love-stricken Claramore cow to keep her date with a bull on the farm on the far side of the river. So he calls to Phil to mind his Sunday-go-to-meeting suit and Phil, turning round to answer, is off his guard when the restive beast bolts. It is, fair enough, his turn to laugh, sharp, clear and cruel, as Phil, bravely holding on to the halter is dragged through the shallow muddy water below the stones. There are seventeen in Phil's family, and he is the eldest, and those corduroys will not be easily replaced.

Over the hard frosted fields his own laughter came back to him.

— I'm glad to hear he did well in Australia.

— They were a thrifty family, his cousin said. A sister of his might visit us this evening, the youngest of the breed, a god-daughter of mine.

The trail of the jet was curdling in the cold sky. The men had gone back to work. For penance he told his cousin and son and daughter how he had laughed on the day the cow dragged Phil through the muddy water. They stood by a huge sycamore a little down the slopes from the unfinished house. Icicles hung from bare branches. He said nothing about how James had mocked his boasting.

— Weren't you the beast, dad, his daughter said.

— But it was funny, the son said.

— The young, his cousin said, can be thoughtless. Present company excepted.

For the daughter, the face of a good mimic distorted with mock fury, was dancing towards the cousin to stab him with an icicle broken from the sycamore.

— No, but seriously, he said when they had played out their pantomime of fury and terror: a grey man over sixty with a restful singing sort of voice and a pert little girl of sixteen.

— Seriously. Look at the sycamore. It was planted here more than a hundred years ago by an uncle of mine who was a priest. He died young, not long after ordination. He planted this tree on the day he was ordained, and blessed the earth and the sapling. You may recall, when you were young yourselves, some of his books were still about the house. Mostly Latin. Theology. Some novels. I told you about one of them and you rushed to get it. The *Lass of the Barns*, you thought I said. But, man alive, were you down in the mouth when you discovered it was the *Last of the Barons*.

— Oh dad, his daughter said.

— But I know the age of this tree by checking on the date

on the priest's tombstone in Langfield churchyard. And my son says to me: We'll cut it down. It'll spoil the view from the new house. So I said: The house may fall, but this tree will stand while I do. The old have a feeling for each other.

— Lucky tree, the daughter said, that has somebody to stand up for it.

They went, laughing, back down the Barley Hill towards the warmth of the great kitchen of the farmhouse. Under the pall of the white frost it seemed as if nothing here would ever change: not the sycamore, not his cousin, nor the ancient sleeping land. Nothing would change, no matter how many airliners swept westwards up there, leaving nothing behind them but a curdling dissolving mark on the sky. All the ships that had carried all those people westwards, even so many sons and daughters of this house, and the ocean was still unmarked and the land here as it had been. It was elsewhere in the world the changes happened.

— But this fatal ship to her cold bosom folds them. Wherever she goes our fond hearts shall adore them. Our prayers and good wishes will still be before them, that their names be remembered and sung by the Strule.

The pond at the corner of the avenue was frozen over. He had fallen into it once, climbing the fence above and beyond it to chase a wandering bullock out of a field of young oats. The fence-post he had been holding on to had broken. The water, he had always imagined, had tasted of duck-dirt. But then how in hell would one be expected to know what duck-dirt tasted like? The fence-post, he noticed, was now made of iron, and that might be some indication, even here, of change. But not much.

The ash-grove to the left before you came to the stables – in that grove he had once criminally broken a young sapling to make a fishing rod – was now a solid wall of grown strong trees, a windbreak on days of south-westerly gales.

Would the horses in the stables be the same, with the same names, as they had been thirty years ago? He was afraid to ask, to be laughed at, to be told what he knew: that even here, even loved familiar farmhorses didn't live for ever. The dogs seemed the same – collies, with more sprawling pups underfoot than had ever seemed natural. The pattern of farming though, had changed somewhat, he had been told: more barley, more pigs fed on the barley, less oats, less root crops, more sucking calves bred in season on the open pasture, taken early from their mothers and sold to be fattened somewhere in confinement, and slaughtered.

In the house ahead of them somebody was playing a melodeon, softly, slowly, and that was something that hadn't changed, because in the past in that house there had been great country dances to pipe, fiddle and melodeon. That was before so many of his cousins, all much older than himself, had gone to the States.

His mother had enjoyed herself. She was red in the face and moist-eyed from sitting by the open hearth with its high golden pyramid of blazing peat; from remembering, for the instruction of a younger generation, the comic figaries of her dear departed dowager of a sister, Kate, who, as a widow in her thirties, had ruled not only Claramore but half the countryside; and from, let it be admitted, sipping at the bourbon. For while she was a great one to lecture about the dangers of drink, she was liable the next minute to take from her sideboard a bottle of brandy and a bottle of whiskey, to ask what you were having, and to join you herself, and she instinctively thought the worst of a man who neither smoked, drank, swore, nor rode horses.

— The young people, she said, are growing up well, God bless them. They haven't forgotten the old ways. That house was never without music and dancing.

The Claramore people had stood around the car, under a frosty moon, and sang Auld Lang Syne as their guests departed.

— That Loughran girl was a good hand at the melodeon. Did you all see her making up to the widow man, the returned American?

She poked him between the shoulder-blades as he drove slowly over the icy plateau.

— She sat on your knee, dad, the daughter said.

He could still feel the pressure of the underparts of the girl's thighs. She was conventionally slim and dark and handsome, with wide brown eyes; in appearance most unlike her eldest brother. She had sat on his knee in the dancing kitchen to tell him that Phil, in every letter he wrote from Australia, enquired about him. She stayed sitting there while his cousin sang: Then was once a maid in a lonely garden when a well-dressed gentleman came passing by.

— Was that story true granny, the son asked. The one about the lone bush.

— Would I tell it if it wasn't.

They descended into the first hazel glen. Over the rushing of its brook they could hear the roaring of another jet, out of Prestwick, bound for New York.

— They're lining up to get into America, the son said.

— To get out of it too, son.

Six hours or so to the bedlam of Kennedy airport: but now our bold heroes are past all their dangers. On America's shores they won't be long strangers. They'll send back their love from famed Blessington's Rangers to comrades and friends and the fair maids of Strule.

People who travelled by jet left no shadows in old market-places. Generations would be born to whom the ache and loneliness in the old songs of exile would mean nothing.

— Jordan Taggart the cobbler, as I said, had his house on the road from Claramore to Carrickaness, and a small farm to boot. Against the advice of all, even against Father Gormley the priest that cured people, he cut down a whitethorn that grew alone in the middle of his meadow and, at nightfall, he dragged it home behind him for kindling. In the orchard before his house he saw two small children, dressed in white, and he spoke to them but they made no answer. So he told his wife and his three sons, who were also cobblers, that there were two shy children waiting, maybe for mended shoes in the orchard. But when two of the sons went out and searched they saw nothing. Then Jordan ate the supper of a healthy man and went to bed and died in his sleep.

— But he wasn't really dead, the son said.

— No, the white children took him. God between us and all harm.

In the darkness in the car she spat, but slightly and politely, and into her handkerchief.

The daughter said nothing. They were back again in the meadow country where Angela had climbed the gate and, except for one last meeting, had climbed out of his life for ever. They bumped over the Drumquin crossing where there was no longer any railway to cross, no easy girl to call longingly after Tom Cunningham who was chasing girls in China and never wrote to enquire about anybody.

The daughter was alert again. She was giggling. She said: Dad, Granny wants to do something about the way you dress.

— I was only thinking about his own good, his mother said.

Although he was carefully driving the car over Clabber Brae, he knew by the way she talked that he was no longer there.

— But when I was by the seaside at Bundoran I saw these young fellows wearing loose coloured patterned shirts outside their trousers. I was told it was an American fashion, and I was sure that he would be wearing one of them when he came home.

He said: I'm no young fellow.

— What I thought was that it would cover his middle-aged spread.

As they descended by the military barracks into the town the daughter's giggles rocked the car.

— A maternity shirt, she said.

— For how could he expect anyone to look at him at his age and with a stomach like that.

Castle Street went up so steeply that it seemed as if it was trying to climb those dark grotesque spires.

— A young one, for instance, like that Loughran girl who sat on his knee because the chairs were scarce.

— That one, he said. All that I remember about the Loughrans is that her bare-footed elder brothers were always raiding Aunt Kate's cherry trees and blaming the depredation on the birds.

In the hotel bar only two of the commercial men were left. They said: What do you think now of your happy home town?

— How do you mean?

— Last night's tragic event, they said. Didn't you hear? Didn't you read the paper?

— I was in the country all day.

Back in the past where one didn't read the newspapers.

— A poor man murdered, they said. What your American friends would call a filling-station attendant.

— Robbed and shot, they said. Just when we were sitting here talking about murder.

The grandfather clock in the hallway chimed midnight.

— The New Year, he said. May it be quiet and happy.

In the ballroom in the far wing of the hotel the revellers were clasping hands and singing about old acquaintance.

— We should be there singing, he said.

— The second murder here this year, they said. The other was a queer case, two young men, a bit odd. Things like that usen't to happen. This town is getting to be as bad as Chicago.

It isn't as big or as varied.

They laughed. They agreed that the town was still only in a small way of business. He asked them was the park called the Lovers' Retreat still where it had been.

— If that's the way you feel, it is.

More laughter.

— But it's gone to hell, they told him. It's not kept as it used to be. The young compulsory soldiers in national service wreck everything. They haven't the style of the old Indian army, when the empire was in its glory. Children's swings uprooted now. Benches broken. One of the two bridges over the millrace gone completely. The grass three feet long.

— Nothing improves, they said.

When they left him he sat on for a long time, drinking alone. Was it imagination, or could he really hear the sound of the Camowen waters falling over the salmon leap at the Lovers' Retreat? That place was one of the sights of the town when the salmon were running: the shining curving bodies rising from the water as if sprung from catapults – leaping and struggling upwards in white foam and froth. But one year the water was abnormally low, the salmon a sullen black mass in the pool below the falls – a temptation to a man with Tom Cunningham's enterprise. The water-bailiff and his two assistants and his three dogs came by night and caught Tom and his faithful companion with torch and gaff and one slaughtered salmon. But since the bailiff, a bandy-legged amiable man, was also the park-keeper he said not a word to the police on condition that the two criminals kept the grass in the park mowed for a period of six months.

— Hard labour, by God, boy. He has us by the hasp. The Big House with Wallace Beery. You be Mickey Rooney.

The bad news travelled and was comic to all except the two mowers. Then one day from the far side of the millrace that made one boundary to the park they heard the laughter of women, and saw Sadie and Angela, bending and pointing.

— Two men went to mow, they sang, went to mow the meadow.

— Grilled salmon for all, they called.

Tom crossed the millrace by leaping on to the trunk of a leaning tree that was rooted on the far bank. Sadie, laughing, screaming in mock terror, and Tom in pursuit, vanished into the bluebell woods. Tom's companion crossed the millrace

prosaically by one of the wooden footbridges. Was it the one that
the wild young resentful compulsory soldiers had destroyed?
She didn't run. She wasn't laughing any more. Her brown
hair no longer curled in little horns on her temples but was
combed straight back. But the wide mouth, in spite of the
black fusilier, was to him as inviting as ever. She said: You're
a dab-hand at mowing. You've a future in cutting grass.

He said: I never see you any more.

— Little boys should take what's offered to them, when
it's offered. Go back to your scythe.

— Go back to the fusilier, he said.

He went back to his scythe by climbing along the trunk of
the leaning tree and leaping the millrace. The grass that fell
before his scythe was crimson in colour and swathed in a sort
of mist. The swing of the scythe moved with the rhythm of the
falling water sweeping on to meet the Drumragh, to become
the Strule, to absorb the Fairywater and the Derg and the
Owenkillew, to become the Mourne, to absorb the Finn, to
become the Foyle, to go down then by Derry to the ocean,
taking with it the shadows of the woodsmen, the echoes of the
brass and pipes and tramping feet of the army of a vanished
empire, the stories of all who had ever lived in this valley.

He knew he was drunk when he heard the woman's voice
speak respectfully to him and saw her through the crimson
mist through which long ago he had seen the falling grass.
She said: You wouldn't remember me, sir.

He didn't. She wore the black dress, white collar and cuffs
of the hotel staff. She would be sixtyish. She said: We saw you
on the teevee one night and I said to Francie who you were.
But he said he didn't know you. He knew your elder brother
better.

— My brother was well known.

— Francie's my brother. You might remember he used to
ride racing bicycles. I saw you in the dining-room. I work in
the kitchen. I knew it was you when I saw your son, and from
the teevee.

— You're Sadie Law.

— I didn't like to intrude on you and the children.

He said there was no intrusion. They shook hands. He asked her how her brother was.

— He's in a chair all the time. He broke his back at the tomfool cycling. But he does woodcarving, and I work here. We manage. I never married.

Her face did not remind him of Sadie Law, but then he found that he could not remember what Sadie Law's face had looked like.

— Nobody, he said, could replace Tom Cunningham.

She neither smiled nor looked sorrowful. Her face remained the same. She said: Oh, Tom was a card. He went away.

Some revellers from the ballroom came in, drunk, singing, wearing paper hats. She said: I must be off.

— I'll see you in the morning.

— I'm off duty then. Because of the late dance tonight. But we hope you'll come back often to see the old places.

— Do you ever remember, he asked, a Fusilier Nixon, a wild fellow.

She thought: No. But there were so many fusiliers. A lot of them we'll never see again.

— We'll look out for you on the teevee, she said.

They shook hands again.


They said goodbye to his mother and drove away. His daughter said: Dad, this isn't the Dublin road.

— There's a place I want to see before we leave.

It was the place that Tom and himself used to go to when they considered that the mental strain of school was too much for them. For it was an odd thing that in all the comings and goings of that railway station nobody ever thought of asking a pair of truants what they were doing there. Everybody thought that everybody else was waiting for somebody else, and there were always porters and postmen who knew what you were at, but who kept the knowledge to themselves, and

would share talk and cigarettes with runaway convicts, let alone
reluctant schoolboys. No police hunted for drifters or loiterers
as in American bus stations: and the sights were superb and
you met the best people. They had spent several hours one
day with Chief Abidu from southern Nigeria and his Irish
wife and honey-coloured brood. He danced on broken glass
and swallowed fire in a wooden booth in the Old Market,
and, beating on his breast, made the most wonderful throaty
noises; and came, most likely, from Liverpool.

— I understand, she had written, that the railway station
is closed now. Only the ghosts of those who passed through it
abide there. Some were gentle, some were violent men, morose
or gay, ordinary or extraordinary. I had time to watch them
passing by. It is pain that they died so young, so long ago.

The tracks were gone, the grass and weeds had grown
high through the ballast. The old stone buildings had been
turned into warehouses. Two men in dusty dungarees kept
coming and going, carrying sacks of meal, at the far end of
the platform. But if they spoke to each other they were too far
away for their voices to be heard, and the cold wind moved as
stealthily in grass and weeds as if it were blowing over some
forlorn midland hillside. Where the bookstall had been there
was just a scar on the granite wall, where she had stood,
framed against coloured books and magazines, and watched
the soldiers coming and going.

— The young English poet you mention, I knew briefly.
He came to buy books. At first he had little to say, simply
polite, that's all. Then one day he and another young man
began to talk. They included me. But mostly I listened. It
was fascinating. After that, when he came he talked about
books. He asked questions about Ireland. He was uneasy
there, considered it beautiful but alien, felt, I think, that the
very earth of Ireland was hostile to him, the landscape had
a brooding quality as though it waited.

— He was five or six months garrisoned in our town. They
told me he could be very much one of the boys, but he could

also be remote. He treated me kindly, teased me gently. But he and a brilliant bitter Welshman gave me books and talked to me. Sometimes they talked about the war.

— It was only after he was reported missing in Africa that I learned he was a poet. But I think I knew anyway.

— I never heard if the Welshman survived. I had several long letters from him and that was all.

Ghosts everywhere in this old town.

— Now I have a son who may pass through a railway station or an airport on his way to war.

He said to his daughter: That's where the bookstall was.

— Will you go to see her, dad? In the States, I mean.

— In a way I've seen her.

He was grateful that she didn't ask him what on earth he was talking about.

— As the song says, I'll look for her if I'm ever back that way.

The ghost of his father stood just here, waving farewell to him every time he went back after holidays to college in Dublin.

They walked through the cold deserted hall, where the ticket offices had been, and down the steps, grass-grown, cracked, to the Station Square, once lined with taxis, now empty except for some playing children and the truck into which the dusty men were loading the sacks. From the high steeple the noonday angelus rang.

— How high up is the bell? his son asked.

He told him, and also told him the height of the spire and of the surmounting cross, and why one spire was higher than the other, and how he had once climbed up there, and of the view over the valley, and of how he had almost fallen to doom on the way down, and of the vertigo, the fear of death, that followed.

— And a curious thing. Once, on top of the Eiffel Tower, that vertigo returned. And once over the Mojave desert when I thought the plane was going to crash. But I didn't see Paris or the Mojave desert. I saw that long straight ladder.

The bell ceased. The spires were outlined very clearly in the cold air, looked as formidable as precipices. Around them floated black specks, the unbanishable jackdaws.

— Once I got a job from the parish priest because I was a dab hand with a twenty-two. The job was to shoot the jackdaws, they were pests, off the spires. It was going fine until the police stopped me for using a firearm too close to a public highway. The sexton at the time was a tall man in a black robe down to his feet, more stately than a bishop. One day, when he was watching me at work, a bird I shot struck one of those protruding corner-stones and came soaring, dead, in a wide parabola, straight for the sexton. He backed away, looking in horror at the falling bird. But he tripped on his robe, and the bird, blood, feathers, beak and all got him fair in the face. At that time I thought it was the funniest thing I had ever seen.

— Grisly, his daughter said.

— But once upon a time I laughed easily. It was easy to laugh here then.

High Street, Market Street, the Dublin Road. A stop at the grave where the caretaker's men had already done their job. The weeds were gone, the sad hollow filled, new white stones laid.

Then on to Dublin, crossing the Drumragh at Lissan Bridge where, it was said, Red Hugh O'Donnell had passed on his way back from prison in Dublin Castle to princedom in Donegal and war with Elizabeth of England. The wintry land brooded waiting, as it had always done, and would do for ever.

He sang at the wheel: There was once a maid in a lovely garden.

— Oh dad, his daughter said.

So he thought the rest of it: Oh, do you see yon high high building? And do you see yon castle fine? And do you see yon ship on the ocean? They'll all be thine if thou wilt be mine.

# There are meadows in Lanark

The schoolmaster in Bomacatall or McKattle's Hut was gloved and masked and at his beehives when his diminutive brother, the schoolmaster from Knockatatawn, came down the dusty road on his high bicycle. It was an Irish-made bicycle. The schoolmaster from Knockatatawn was a patriot. He could have bought the best English-made Raleigh for half the price, but instead he imported this edifice from the Twenty-six into the Six Counties and paid a mountain of duty on it. The bike, and more of its kind, was made in Wexford by a firm that made the sort of mowing-machine that it took two horses to pull. They built the bikes on the same solid principle. Willian Bulfin from the Argentine who long ago wrote a book about rambling in Erin had cycled round the island on one of them and died not long afterwards, almost certainly from over-exertion. There was a great view from the saddle. Hugh, who was the son of the schoolmaster from Bomacatall, once on the quiet borrowed the bike and rode into the side of a motor-car that was coming slowly out of a hedgy hidden boreen. He was tossed sideways into the hedgerow and had a lacework of scratches on his face. The enamel on the car was chipped and the driver's window broken. The bike was unperturbed.

The little man mounted the monster by holding the grips on the handlebars, placing his left foot on the extended spud or hub of the back wheel and then giving an electrified leap. This sunny evening he dismounted by stepping on to the top rail of the garden fence at Bomacatall. He sat there like a gigantic rook, the King Rook that you hear chanting base barreltone in the rookery chorus. He wore a pinstriped dark suit and a black wide-brimmed hat. He paid no attention to the buzzing and swarming of the bees. The herbaceous borders, the diamond-shaped beds at Bomacatall would blind you. There was a twisting trout stream a field away from the far end of the garden. To his brother who was six feet and more the little man said: I have a scheme in mind.

From behind the mask the big man said: Was there ever a day that God sent that you didn't have a scheme in mind?

— It would benefit the boy Hugh. *Ce an aois é anois?*

That meant: What age is he now?

— Nine, God bless him.

— Time he saw a bit of the world. Bracing breezes, silvery sands, booming breakers, lovely lands: Come to Bundoran.

That was an advertisement in the local newspaper.

— You could sing that if you had a tune to it, said the man behind the mask.

— The holiday would do him good, the King Rook said, and for three weeks there'd be one mouth less to feed.

That was a forceful argument. The master from Knocka-tatawn, or the Hill of the Conflagrations, was a bachelor. Hugh was midways in a household of seven, not counting the father and mother.

The bees settled. The bee-keeper doffed the mask and wiped the sweat off a broad humorous face. He said: James, like St Paul you're getting on. You want another to guide you and lead you where thou would'st not.

— John, said the man on the fence, in defiance of Shakespeare, I maintain that there are only three stages in a man's life: young, getting-on, and not so bad-considering. I've a sad feeling that I've got to the third.

The nine-year-old, as he told me a long time afterwards, was all for the idea of Bundoran except that, young as he was, he knew there was a hook attached. This was it. At home on the Hill of the Conflagrations there wasn't a soberer man than the wee schoolmaster, none more precise in his way of life and his teaching methods, more just and exact in the administering of punishments or rewards. But Bundoran was for him another world and he, when he was there, was another man. He met a lot of all sorts of people. He talked his head off, behaved as if he had never heard of algebra or a headline copy-book, and drank whisky as if he liked it and as if the world's stock of whisky was going to run dry on the following morning. Yet, always an exact man, he knew that his powers of navigation, when he was in the whisky, were failing, that – as Myles na Gopaleen said about a man coming home from a night at a boat-club dance in Islandbridge – he knew where he was coming from and going to, but he had no control over his lesser movements. He needed a pilot, he needed a tug, or both combined in one: his nephew. There was, also, this to be said for the wee man: he was never irascible or difficult in drink, he went where the pilot guided him and the tug tugged him. He was inclined to sing, but then he was musical and in the school in Knockatatawn he had a choir that was the terror of Féis Doire Cholmcille, the great musical festival held in Derry in memory of St Colmcille. He even won prizes in Derry against the competition of the Derry choirs – and that was a real achievement.

So for one, two, three, four years the nephew-and-uncle navigational co-operation worked well. The nephew had his days on the sand and in the sea. He even faced up to it with the expert swimmers at Roguey Rocks and the Horse Pool. By night while he waited until his uncle was ready to be steered back to the doss he drank gallons of lemonade and the like, and saw a lot of life. With the natural result that by the time the fifth summer came around, that summer when the winds were so contrary and the sea so treacherous that the priest was drowned in the Horse Pool, the nephew was developing new interests: he was looking around for the girls. At any rate, Bundoran or no Bundoran, he was growing up.

Now this was a special problem because the schoolmaster from Knockatatawn had little time for girls, for himself or anybody else and, least of all, for his nephew who, in the fifth summer, had just passed thirteen.

One of the wonders of the day on which they helped the schoolmaster from Knockatatawn to the hotel and happed him safely into bed by four o'clock in the afternoon was that Hugh saw a woman, one of the Scotchies, swimming at her ease in the pool where the priest had been drowned. She was a white and crimson tropical fish, more blinding than the handsomest perch in the lake at Corcreevy or the Branchy Wood: white for arms, shoulders, midriff and legs; crimson for cap and scanty costume. Women were not supposed to be in the Horse Pool on any account but so soon after the drowning, the usual people were shunning it, and that woman either didn't know or didn't care. The Scotchies who came to the seaside to Bundoran in the summer had a great name for being wild.

In the hotel bedroom the sun came in as muted slanted shafts through the cane blinds. The shafts were all dancing dust. Carpet-sweepers weren't much in use in that hotel. They helped the wee man out of his grey sober clothes and into a brutal pair of blue-and-white striped pyjamas. He was a fierce hairy wee fellow. Arms long like an ape and a famous fiddler when he was sober. The big purple-faced schoolmaster from Lurganboy said: Begod, you're like a striped earthenware jar of something good.

The little man waved his arms and tried to sing and once slipped off the edge of the bed and sat on the floor and recited word-perfect:

> A Chieftain to the Highlands bound
> Cries: Boatman, do not tarry,
> And I'll give thee a silver crown
> To row me o'er the ferry.

The lot of it, every verse, all about how the waters wild swept o'er his child and how Lord Ullin's daughter and her lover were drowned. The drowning of the priest must have put it into his mind. The purple-faced man from Lurganboy, rocking a little, listened with great gravity, his head to one side, his black bushy eyes glistening, his thick smiling lips bedewed with malt. He said: In the training college he was renowned for his photographic memory. And for the fiddle.

Hugh said nothing. He was sick with delight. His uncle was a blue-and-white earthenware jar of Scotch whisky, as full as it could hold. He always drank Scotch in Bundoran, out of courtesy, he said, to the hundreds of Scotchies who came there every year on their holidays and spent good money in the country. The music of hurdy-gurdies and hobby-horses and the like came drifting to them from the strand, over the houses on the far side of the town's long street. This blessed day the blue-and-white jar could hold no more. He would sleep until tomorrow's dawn and Hugh was a free man, almost fourteen, and the world before him.

— He'll rest now, said the red-faced master from Lurganboy.

They tiptoed out of the room and down the stairs.

— What'll you do now, boy?

— Go for a walk.

— Do that. It's healthy for the young.

He gave Hugh a pound, taken all crumpled out of a trouser pocket. Then nimbly, for such a heavy man, he sidestepped into a raucous bar and the swinging doors, glass, brass and mahogany, closed behind him. It was an abrupt farewell yet Hugh was all for him, and not only because of the crumpled pound, but because in him, man to man and glass for glass, the schoolmaster from the Hill of the Conflagrations had for once taken on more than his match. Several times as they helped the little man towards his bed the unshakeable savant from Lurganboy had said to Hugh: Young man, you are looking at one who in his cups and in

his declining years can keep his steps, sir, like a grenadier
guard.

He had the map of his day already worked out in his head.
The Scotchy girl wouldn't be sitting on the high windowsill
until seven o'clock. She was there most evenings about that
time. She and God knew how many other Scotchies, male
and female, lived in a three-storeyed yellow boarding-house
at the east end of the town. There was a garden in front
of it, a sloping lawn but no fence or hedge, and the two
oval flower-beds were rimmed with great stones, smoothed
and shaped by the sea, tossed up on the beach at Tullaghan
to the west, gathered and painted and used as ornaments
by the local people. This Scotchy girl was one that liked
attention. The way she went after it was to clamber out of
a bedroom window on the third floor and to sit there for
an hour or more in the evening kicking her heels, singing,
laughing, pretending to fall, blowing kisses, and shouting
things in unintelligible Scottish at the people in the street
below, throwing or dropping things, flowers, chocolates, little
fluttering handkerchiefs and once, he had heard, a pair of
knickers. He had only seen her once at those capers when
one evening he navigated past, tug before steamship, with his
uncle in tow. But a fella he knew slightly told him she was to
be seen there at that time most evenings. She sure as God was
there to be seen. It wouldn't have been half the fun if she'd
worn a bathing-suit, but a skirt with nothing underneath
was something to tell the fellas about when he got back to
Bomacatall. Not that they'd believe him, but still.

Behind her in the room there must have been 30 girls.
They squealed like a piggery. That was a hell of a house.
A randyboo, the wee master called it. Bomacatall, Knockatatawn and Corcreevy all combined never heard the equal
of the noise that came out of that house. On the ground
floor the piano always going, and a gramophone often at the
same time, and a melodeon and pipes, and boozy male voices

singing Bonny Doon and Bonny Charlie's noo awa' and Over
the sea to Skye and Loch Lomond and The Blue Bells of
Scotland and Bonny Strathyre and Bonny Mary of Argyle
and, all the time and in and out between everything else:

> For I'm no awa tae bide awa,
> For I'm no awa tae leave ye,
> For I'm no awa tae bide awa,
> I'll come back an' see ye.

— They work hard all year, the wee master said. In the
big factories and shipyards of Glasgow. Then they play hard.
They're entitled to it. The Scots are a sensitive generous
people and very musical.

This was the map that was in Hugh's mind when the red- or
purple-faced master from Lurganboy left him outside the
swinging doors of the saloon bar. That Lurganboy man was
a wonder to see at the drink. When he moved, Hugh thought,
he should make a sound like the ocean surf itself with the
weight of liquid inside him. He had also said something
remarkable and given Hugh a phrase to remember. For
as they'd steered the Knockatatawn man round a windy
corner from the promenade to the main street, a crowd, ten
or eleven, of Scotchy girls had overtaken them, singing and
shouting, waving towels and skimpy bathing-suits, wearing
slacks and sandals, bright blouses, short skirts, sweaters with
sleeves knotted round their waists and hanging over rumps
like britchens on horses.
— This town, said the master from Lurganboy, is hoaching
with women.
That was the northern word you'd use to describe the way
fingerlings wriggle over and around each other at the shallow
fringes of pools on blinding June days.
— Hoaching. Hoaching with women, Hugh said to himself
as he set out to follow the map he had drawn in his mind

that would bring him back at seven o'clock to the place where the daft girl kicked her heels and more besides on the windowsill.

From the house of glass to the Nuns' Pool by way of the harbour where the fishing boats are. It isn't really a house of glass. This shopkeeper has a fanciful sort of mind and has pebbledashed the front wall of his place with fragments of broken glass. The shop faces east, catching the morning sun, the whole wall then lives and dances like little coloured tropical fish frisking, hoaching, in a giant aquarium. Hugh can look down on it from his window which is right on top of the hotel across the street. Some people say the wall is beautiful. Some people say the man is crazy. The seer from Knockatatawn says that's the way with people.

Westward the course towards the Nuns' Pool. Passing the place where the sea crashes right into the side of the street, no houses here, and only a high strong wall keeps it from splattering the traffic. Here in the mornings when the tide is ebbed and the water quiet a daft old lady in a long dress walks out along rocks and sand, out and out until she's up to her neck in the water, dress and all, and only her head and wide-brimmed straw hat to be seen. Then she comes calmly out again and walks home dripping. Nobody worries or bothers about her. The bay is her bath tub. She lives here winter and summer.

This day the harbour is empty, a few white sails far out on the bay, pleasure boats. He sits on the tip of the mole for a while and looks down into the deep translucent water. On the gravelly bottom there are a few dead discarded fish, a sodden cardboard box, and fragments of lobster claws turned white. If he could clamber around that sharp rock headland and around two or three more of the same he could peep into the Nuns' Pool and see what they're up to. Do they plunge in, clothes and all, like the mad woman in the morning? It's hard to imagine nuns stripping like the Scotchy in the pool where the priest was drowned. Surely the priests and the nuns should share the one pool and leave Roguey Rocks and the Horse Pool to the men and the wild Scotchies. The strand and the surf are for children and after five summers he knows he's no longer a child.

But he's also alone and he knows it. Tugging and steering his mighty atom of an uncle has taken up all his time and cut him off from his kind. On the clifftop path by the Nuns' Pool there are laughing girls by the dozen, and couples walking, his arm as tightly around her as if she had just fainted and he is holding her up. In corners behind sod fences there are couples asprawl on rugs or on the naked grass, grappled like wrestlers but motionless and in deep silence. Nobody pays the least attention to him. Fair enough, he seems to be the youngest person present. Anyone younger is on the sand or in the surf. Or going for rides on donkeys. He is discovering that, unless you're the tiniest bit kinky, love is not a satisfactory spectator sport.

Steep steps cut in rock go down to the Nuns' Pool. Was it called after one nun or gaggles of nuns, season after season? It must have been one horse. But what was a horse ever doing out there on rocks and seaweed and salt water? He sees as he walks a giant nun, a giant horse. The steep steps turn a corner and vanish behind a wall of rock as big as Ben Bulben mountain. Only God or a man in a helicopter could see what goes on in there. Do they swim in holy silence, praying perhaps, making aspirations to Mary the Star of the Sea? He listens for the sort of shouts and music and screaming laughs that come from the house where the girl sits on the windowsill. He hears nothing but the wash of the sea, the wind in the cliffside grass, the crying of the gulls. What would you expect? It is ten minutes to five o'clock.

He has time to walk on to the place where the Drowes river splits into two and goes to the sea over the ranked, sea-shaped stones of Tullaghan, to walk back to the hotel by the main road, feast on the customary cold ham and tomatoes and tea, bread and butter, wash his hands and face and sleek his hair with Brylcreem and part it up the middle, and still be on good time and in a good place for the seven o'clock show. He does all this. He is flat-footed from walking and a little dispirited. On the stony strand of Tullaghan there isn't even a girl to be seen. If there was he could draw her attention to the wonderful way the sea forms and places the stones, rank on rank, the biggest ones by the water line and matted with seaweed, the smallest and daintiest right up by the sand and the whistling bent-grass. They are variously coloured. The tide has ebbed. Far out the water growls over immovable stones.

He rests for a while by the two bridges over the Drowes river. If there was a girl there he could tell her how the river flows down from Lough Melvin, and how the trout in the lake and the trout in the river have the gizzards of chickens and how, to account for that oddity, there's a miracle story about an ancient Irish saint. There is no girl there. A passing car blinds him with dust. Has the evening become more chilly or is that just the effect of hunger? He accelerates. He knows that while a Scotchy girl might show some interest in stones shaped and coloured into mantelpiece or dressing-room ornaments, she would be unlikely to care much about trout or ancient miracles. In the hotel the master is sound asleep in blue-and-white bars, the bed-clothes on the floor. He doesn't snore. Hugh eats four helpings of ham and tomatoes, two for himself, two for the recumbent fiddler from the Hill of the Conflagrations.

The evening is still ahead of him and the fleshpots delectably steaming. There is no glitter from the house of glass. The hot tea and ham, the thought of the kicking girl on the high windowsill have done him a lot of good. In the evening most of the children will be gone from the strand, the Palais de Danse warming up, the hoaching at its best.

* * *

He wasn't the only one watching for the vision to appear, and right in the middle, like a gigantic rugby-football forward holding together a monumental scrum, was the purple-faced man from Lurganboy. The Assyrian, Hugh thought, came down like a wolf on the fold and his cohorts were gleaming in purple and gold. He wasn't his uncle's nephew for nothing, even if he wasn't quite sure what a cohort meant. As he told me long afterwards in the Branchy Wood, or Corcreevy, if his literary education had then advanced as far as *Romeo and Juliet* he would have been able, inevitably, to say: But soft what light through yonder window etc. The man with the face as purple as cohorts saw it differently. To the men that ringed him round he said: Lads, I declare to me Jasus, 'tis like Lourdes or Fatima waiting for the lady to appear. All we lack is hymns and candles.

— We have the hymns, one voice said, she has the candles.

— *Ave ave*, said another voice.

The laughter wasn't all that pleasant to listen to. They were a scruffy enough crowd, Hugh thought, to be in the company of a schoolmaster that had the benefit of education and the best of training; the master from Bomacatall, kind as he was, would have crossed the street if he'd seen them coming. Shiny pointy toes, wide grey flannels, tight jackets, oiled hair; the man from Lurganboy must, at last, like the stag at eve, have drunk his fill or he wouldn't, surely to God, be in the middle of them. Hugh dodged. There was a fine fat flowering bush, white blossoms, bursting with sparrows when the place was quiet, right in the middle of the sloping lawn. He put it between himself and the waiting watching crowd. His back was to the bush. He was very close to the high yellow house. The din was delightful, voices male and female, a gramophone playing a military march, somebody singing that there are meadows in Lanark and mountains in Skye – and he was thinking what a wonderful people the Scots were and what a hell and all of a house that must be to live in, when the high window went up with a bang and there she was, quick as a sparrow on a branch, but brighter, much brighter.

He had heard of a bird of paradise but never had he, nor has he up to the present moment, seen one. But if such a bird exists then its plumage would really have to be something to surpass in splendour what Hugh, in the dying western evening, saw roosting and swinging on the windowsill. Far and beyond Roguey Rocks the sun would be sinking in crimson. The light came over the roofs of the houses across the street, dazzled the windows, set the girl on fire. Long red hair, red dress, pink stockings, red shoes with wooden soles. She was so high up, the angle was so awkward, the late sunlight so dazzling, that he could find out little about her face except that it was laughing. The scrum around the Lurganboy man cheered and whistled. He knew she was laughing, too, because he could hear her. She was shouting down to the Lurganboy contingent, the *caballeros*, but because of the noise from the house and the street he couldn't pick out any words and, anyway, she would be talking Scottish. Nor could he be certain that he had been correctly informed as to what, if anything, she wore underneath the red dress although when he got home to his peers in McKattle's Hut or Bomacatall he sure as God wouldn't spoil a good story by unreasonable doubts.

All told it was an imperfect experience. She twisted and tacked so rapidly, agile as a monkey, that a man could see nothing except crimson. He couldn't even have known that her red shoes had wooden soles if it hadn't been that, with the dink of kicking, one of them came unstuck, and landed as surely as a cricket-ball in his cupped palms where he stood in hiding behind the bush. It was in the pocket of his jacket before he knew what he was doing. Cinderella lost her slipper. He was off through the crowd in a second and nobody but the girl saw him go. The eyes of Lurganboy and his men were on the vision. She screamed high and long. From the far end of the crowd he glanced back and saw her pointing towards him. But nobody bothered to look the way she was pointing. The map of his evening was as clear in his mind as the strand before him, as sure as the shoe in his pocket, and hunt-the-slipper was a game at which anything might happen.

The people in this place have, like the tides, their own peculiar movement. Evening, as he expected, draws most of the children away from the strand to a thousand boarding-house bedrooms. The promise of the moon draws the loving couples, the laughing and shouting groups away from the westward walk by the Nuns' Pool to dry sheltered nooks between strand and dunes, to the hollows in the grassy tops of the high cliffs above Roguey, to the place where later the drums will begin to feel their way in the Palais de Danse. Every night, including Sunday, in the palais there is not only a dance but a few brawls and a talent competition.

No moon yet. No drums yet. The last red rays are drowned in the ocean. The light is grey. The strand is pretty empty and a little chilly, the sea is far out. But as he runs, ankle deep in churned sand, down the slope from the now silent motionless hobby-horses and hurdy-gurdies, he sees a slow, silent procession of people coming towards him around the jagged black corner of Roguey Rocks. The sea washes up almost around their feet. They step cautiously across a shelf of rock, then more rapidly and boldly along the slapping wet sand by the water's edge. Four men in the lead are carrying something. He runs towards them, all girls forgotten. What-ever chance, anyway, he had of meeting a girl during the day he can only have less now in this half-desolate place. The red shoe will be his only souvenir, yet still something to show to the heathens in Bomacatall. Halfways across the strand a distraught woman in shirt and cardigan, hair blowing wild stops him. She says: Wee boy, see if it's a wee boy with fair hair. He's missing for an hour and I'm distracted. Jesus, Mary and Joseph protect him. I'm afraid to look myself.

But it isn't a wee boy with fair hair. It isn't even the crimson-and-white Scotchy girl who had been swimming in the Horse Pool and whom the sea might have punished for sacrilege, for surely a dead drowned priest must make some difference to the nature of the water.

What he sees is nothing that you could exactly put a name to. The four men carry it on a door taken off its hinges. It's very large and sodden. There's nothing in particular where the face should be – except that it's very black. A woman looks at it and gasps. Somebody says: Cover that up, for God's sake.

A tall red-headed man throws a plastic raincoat over the black nothing in particular. Hugh walks back to the woman in the skirt and cardigan. He tells her that it isn't a wee boy with fair hair. She thanks God.

— It's a big person that must have been a long time in the water.

But she has moved away and isn't listening. He falls in at the tail of the procession. People leave it and join it, join it and leave it. It's a class of a funeral. An ambulance comes screaming down the slope from the long town and parks beside the stabled silent hobby-horses. Two civic guards come running, a third on a bicycle. Behind on the strand one single man in a long black coat walks, fearing no ghosts, towards Roguey Rocks. No couples or laughing groups are to be seen, even on the grassy clifftops. He fingers the shoe in his pocket to remind him of girls. A drum booms, a horn blares from the Palais de Danse which is halfways up the slope towards the town. He gets in, and for free, simply by saying that he's singing in Irish in the talent competition.

The hall was already crowded because the evening had turned chilly and the threat of rain was in the air. He found a seat in a corner near the ladies where he could watch the procession coming and going. They came and went in scores and for all the attention any of them paid to him he might have been invisible. He was grateful for the anonymity. He was too weary to carry on with the hopeless chase and that grim vision on the beach had given him other things to think about. It was still fun to sit and watch the women, all shapes and sizes and colours, and moods. They went in demure and came out giggling. That was because most of them, he had heard, kept noggins of gin and vodka concealed in the cloakroom. It was a great world and all before him. The band was thunderous, the floor more and more crowded until somebody thumped a gong and everybody who could find a chair sat down: girls who couldn't sitting recklessly on the knees of strangers, nobody on his. So he stood up and gave his chair to a girl who didn't even say thanks. The band vanished. A woman sat at the piano, a man with a fiddle and a young fellow with a guitar stood beside her. This was the talent competition.

A grown man long afterwards in the Branchy Wood, or Corcreevy, he couldn't remember much of it. The time was after eleven, he had been on foot all day, his eyes were closing with sleep. A man with long brown hair and long – the longest – legs and big feet came out, sang in a high nervous tenor about the bard of Armagh, then tripped over the music stand and fell flat on his face. That act was much appreciated. A little girl in a white frock and with spangles or something shining in her hair, tiptoed out, curtsied, holding the hem of her skirt out wide in her hands, danced a jig to the fiddle, then sang a song in Irish that meant: There are two little yellow goats at me, courage of the milk, courage of the milk. This is the tune that is at the piper, Hielan laddy, Hielan laddy. And more of the same. A fat bald man sang: While I'm jog jog jogging along the highway, a vagabond like me. Then there were tin whistles and concertinas, six sets of Scottish and two of Irish or Uillean pipes, piano accordions, melodeons, combs in tissue paper and clicking spoons, cornet, fiddle, big bass, drum, something, something and euphonium. As the song says.

He lost interest. His insteps ached. He would unnoticed have slipped away only a crowd and girls hoaching was always better than a lonely room. Surveying the crowd from China to Peru he saw in the far corner the man from Lurganboy, like the old priest Peter Gilligan, asleep within a chair, his legs out like logs, hands locked over splendid stomach and watch-chain and velvet waistcoat, chin on chest, black hat at a wild angle but bravely holding on to his head. No angels, as in the case of Peter Gilligan, hovered over him, none that Hugh could see. Five other adults sat in a row beside him, all awake except Lurganboy. Angels that around us hover, guard us till the close of day. Singing that, the Knockatatawn choir had once won a first prize in Derry city.

As Hugh watched, Lurganboy awoke, pulled in his legs, raised his head, gripped the arms of his chair and hoisted himself to sit erect. The ballroom was silent. Was it the oddness of the silence made the sleeper awake? No, not that, but something, Hugh felt, was going to happen. The drummer was back on the stage. He struck the drum a boom that went round the room, echoing, shivering slowly away. Then the compère said: Ladies and gentlemen.

He said it twice. He held up his right hand. He said again: Ladies and gentlemen, while the judges, including our old, true, tried and stalwart friend from Lurganboy are making up their minds, adding up points, assessing the vast array of talent, not to mention grace and beauty, we will meet again an old friend, a man who needs no introduction, a man who many a time and oft has starred on this stage and who, in days gone by but well remembered has worn more laurels for music than –

The cheers hit the roof, and out on the stage like a released jack-in-the-box stepped the wee master from Knockatatawn, sober as a judge, lively as a cricket, dapper as a prize greyhound, fiddle in one fist, bow in the other. When the cheering stopped he played for fifteen minutes and even the gigglers, resurfacing after gin and vodka, kept a respectful silence. Lord God Almighty, he could play the fiddle.

It could be that the way to get the women is to be a bachelor and play the fiddle, and drink all day and pay no attention to them. For I declare to God, the schoolmaster from Corcreevy said long afterwards, I never saw anything like it before or since, flies round the honeypot, rats round a carcase, never did I see hoaching like that hoaching, and in the middle of it and hopping about on the stage like a wound-up toy, a monkey on a stick, the red Scots girl from the windowsill, and her shoe in my pocket. Radar or something must have told her where it was. She saw me, isolated as I was, standing like a pillar-box in the middle of the floor, for the crowd was on the stage or fighting to get on the stage, and the drum was booming and the compère shouting and nobody listening. She came towards me slowly and I backed away and then ran for the beach, and then stopped. The moon was out between clouds. There was a mizzle of rain.

He stopped running and looked at the moon and the moon-light on the water. This was destiny and he had no real wish to run from it. The moon shines bright, on such a night as this. As he is now, a moonlit beach always reminds him of loneliness, a crowded beach of faceless death. She was a little monkey of a girl and she crouched her shoulders and stooped when she talked. Her red hair was down to her hips. She said: Wee laddie, will ye no gie me backma shoe?

He was learning the language.

— I'm as big as ye are, yersel.

— Will ye no gie me back ma shoe?

She wasn't pleading. She wasn't angry. He knew by her big eyes that it was all fun to her, all part of the holiday. She really wasn't any taller than himself and her foot fitted into his pocket.

— It's no here. It's in ma room.

— You'll bring it tae me.

— For sure. It's no awa tae bide away.

— Guid laddie. Do ye dance?

— Thon's my uncle wi' the fiddle.

— Ye're like him. Ye were quick away wi' ma shoe. I'll no tell him ye're here.

The red shoe was his ticket of admission to the wild happy house. Nothing much, naturally, came of that except a lot of singing and some kisses in the mornings from a sort of elder sister. He learned to talk and understood Scots and to this day, and in his cups, can sing that he's no awa tae bide awa with the best Glaswegian that e'er cam doon frae Gilmour hill. Like his uncle he enjoyed his double life. Not for years, though, not until he had been through college and had his own school, in Corcreevy or the Branchy Wood, did he tell the tale to the old man who by that time was retired and able to drink as he pleased. The old fellow, mellow at the time, laughed immoderately and said: Seemuldoon, I always hold, is a land of milk and honey if you keep your own bees and milk your own cow.

That was a favourite and frequently irrelevant saying of his. Seemuldoon, meaning the dwelling-place of the Muldoons, was, in all truth, the place he came from, and not Knockatatawn. Nor did the man from Lurganboy really come from Lurganboy: I used the name just because I like it, and when people ask me to go to Paris and places like that I say no, I'll go to Lurganboy. Because you don't *go* to Lurganboy, you find yourself there when you lose the road going somewhere else.

# Bluebell meadow

When she came home in the evening from reading in the park that was a sort of an island the sergeant who had been trounced by the gipsies was waiting to ask her questions about the bullets. He had two of them in the cupped palm of his right hand, holding the hand low down, secretively. His left elbow was on the edge of the white-scrubbed kitchen table. The golden stripes on his blue-black sleeve, more black than blue, were as bright as the evening sunshine on the old town outside. He was polite, almost apologetic, at first. He said: I hate to bother yourself and your aunt and uncle. But it would be better for everybody's sake if you told me where you got these things. People aren't supposed to have them. Least of all girls in a convent school.

There had been six of them. The evening Lofty gave them to her she had looked at them for a whole hour, sitting at that table, half-reading a book. Her uncle and aunt were out at the cinema. She spread the bullets on the table and moved them about, making designs and shapes and patterns with them, joining them by imaginary lines, playing with them as if they were draughts or dominoes or precious stones. It just wasn't possible that such harmless mute pieces of metal could be used to kill people. Then she wearied of them, put them away in an old earthenware jug on the mantelpiece and after a while forgot all about them. They were the oddest gifts, God knew, for a boy to give to a girl. Not diamonds again, darling. Say it with bullets.

* * *

This is how the park happens to be a sort of an island. The river comes out of deep water, lined and overhung by tall beeches, and round a right-angled bend to burst over a waterfall and a salmon leap. On the right bank and above the fall a sluice-gate regulates the flow of a millrace. A hundred yards downstream the millrace is carried by aqueduct over a rough mountain stream or burn coming down to join the river. Between river and race and mountain stream is a triangular park, five or six acres, seats by the watersides, swings for children, her favourite seat under a tall conifer and close to the corner where the mountain stream meets the river. The place is called Bluebell Meadow. The bluebells grow in the woods on the far side of the millrace.

When the river is not in flood a peninsula of gravel and bright sand guides the mountain stream right out into the heart of the current. Children play on the sand, digging holes, building castles, sending flat pebbles skimming and dancing like wagtails upstream over the smooth water. One day Lofty is suddenly among the children just as if he had come out of the river which is exactly what he has done. His long black waders still drip water. The fishing-rod which he holds in his left hand, while he expertly skims pebbles with the right, dips and twiddles above him like an aerial. The canvas bag on his back is sodden and heavy and has grass, to keep the fish fresh, sticking out of the mouth of it. One of the children is doing rifle-drill with the shaft of his net. She has never spoken to him but she knows who he is.

When she tires of reading she can look at the river and dream, going sailing with the water. Or simply close her eyes. Or lean back and look up into the tall conifer, its branches always restless and making sounds, and going away from her like a complicated sort of spiral stairway. She has been told that it is the easiest tree in the world to climb but no tree is all that easy if you're wearing a leg-splint. She is looking up into the tree, and wondering, when Lofty sits beside her. His waders are now dry and rubbery to smell. The rod, the net and the bag are laid on the grass, the heads of two sad trout protruding, still life that was alive this morning. Her uncle who keeps greyhounds argues that fishing is much more cruel than coursing: somewhere in the happy river are trout that were hooked and got away, hooks now festering in their lovely speckled bodies. She thinks a lot about things like that.

Lofty sits for five minutes, almost, before he says: I asked Alec Quigley to tell you I was asking for you.

— He told me.

— What did you say?

— Did he not tell you?

— He said you said nothing but I didn't believe him.

— Why not?

— You had to say something.

— If I said anything Alec Quigley would tell the whole town.

— I daresay he would.

— He's the greatest clatter and clashbag from hell to Omagh.

— I didn't know.

— You could have picked a more discreet ambassador.

The words impress him. He says: It's a big name for Alec Quigley. I never thought of him as an ambassador.

— What then? A go-between? A match-maker? A gooseberry?

They are both laughing. Lofty is a blond tall freckled fellow with a pleasant laugh. He asks her would she like a trout.

— I'd love one. Will we cook it here and now?

— I can roll it in grass for you and get a bit of newspaper in McCaslan's shop up at the waterfall.

— Who will I tell my aunt and uncle gave me the trout?

— Tell them nothing. Tell them you whistled and a trout jumped out at you. Tell them a black man came out of the river and gave you a trout.

He left his bag and rod where they were and walked from the apex of the triangular park to the shop at the angle by the waterfall. He came back with a sheet of black parcelling paper and wrapped up the trout very gently. He had long delicate hands, so freckled that they were almost totally brown. The trout, bloody mouth gaping, looked sadly up at the two of them. Lofty said: I'd like to go out with you.

— I'm often out. Here.

So he laughed and handed her the trout and went on upstream towards the falls, casting from the bank at first, then wading knee-deep across a shallow bar of gravel and walking on across a green hill towards the deeps above the falls. She liked his long stride, and the rod dipping and twiddling above him, and the laden bag – even though she knew it was full of dead gaping trout. She knew he was a popular fellow in the town. Yet she didn't tell her aunt and uncle who exactly it was had made her a gift of the trout. She said it was an elderly man and she wasn't quite sure of his name, but she described him so that they'd guess he was a wellknown fisherman, a jeweller by trade and highly respected in the town. Not that Lofty and his people were disrespectable.

The gipsies who trounced the sergeant hadn't been real romany gipsies but tinkers or travelling people from the west of Ireland, descendants, the theory was, of broken people who went on the roads during the hungry years of the 1840s and hadn't settled down since. Five of them, wild, ragged, rough-headed fellows came roaring drunk out of a pub in Bridge Lane. The pub was owned by a man called Yarrow and the joke among those literate enough to appreciate it was about Yarrow Visited and Yarrow Revisited. There was also an old English pishroge about girls putting Yarrow, the plant, between two plates and wishing on it and saying: Good morrow, good morrow, good yarrow, thrice good morrow to thee! I hope before this time tomorrow thou wilt show my true love to me.

One of the five fell with a clatter down the three steps from the door of the pub. In their tottering efforts to pick him up two of the others struck their heads together and began to fight. The remaining two joined in and so, when he was able to stand up, did the fellow who had fallen down the steps. The sergeant was walking past and was fool enough to try to stop them. In the west of Ireland the civic guards had more sense and stood as silent spectators until the tinkers had hammered the fight out of each other.

The five of them, united by foreign invasion, gave the sergeant an unmerciful pounding. He had just enough breath left to blow his whistle. More police came running. More tinkers came shouting, men, women and children, out of the pub, out of dark tunnels of entryways between houses, out of holes in the walls. The battle escalated. More police came. The tinkers made off on two flat carts. One old man was so drunk he fell helpless off a cart and was arrested. The police followed in a tender.

At their encampment of caravans a mile outside the town the tinkers abandoned the carts and took in the darkness to the fields and the hedgerows and even, it was said, to the tops of the trees. The police wisely did not follow, but set a heavy guard on the camp, caravans, carts, horses, scrap metal and everything the tinkers owned. Sober and sheepishly apologetic they reappeared in the morning and gave themselves up and half a dozen of them went to jail. But for a long time afterwards when the sergeant walked the town the wits at the street-corner would whistle: Oh, play to me gipsy, the moon's high above.

Thanks to Arthur Tracy, known as the Street Singer, it was a popular song at the time.

In spite of all that, the sergeant remained an amiable sort of man, stout, slow-moving, with a large brown moustache and a son who was a distinguished footballer.

Yarrow is a strong-scented herb related to the daisies. It has white or pink flowers in flat clusters.

One Sunday in the previous June in an excursion train to Bundoran by the western sea she had overheard Lofty's mother telling funny stories. As a rule Protestants didn't go west to Bundoran but north to Portrush. The sea was sectarian. What were the wild waves saying: At Portrush: Slewter, slaughter, holy water, harry the papishes every one, drive them under and bate them asunder, the Protestant boys will carry the drum. Or at Bundoran: On St Patrick's day, jolly and gay, we'll kick all the Protestants out of the way, and if that won't do we'll cut them in two and send them to hell with their red, white and blue.

Nursery rhymes.

She sat facing her aunt in the train and her uncle sat beside her. They were quiet, looking at all the long beauty of Lough Erne which has an island, wooded or pastoral, for every day in the year. Her aunt, a timid little woman, said now and again: Glory be to God for all his goodness.

Her uncle said just once: You should see Lake Superior. No end to it. As far as the human eye can see.

Then they were all quiet, overhearing Lofty's mother who had no prejudices about the religion of the ocean and who, with three other people, sat across the corridor from them, and who had a good-natured carrying voice and really was fun to listen to. She was saying: I'm a Protestant myself, missus dear, and I mean no disrespect to confession but you must have heard about the young fellow who went to the priest to tell him his sins and told him a story that had more women in it than King Solomon had in the Bible and the goings-on were terrible, and the priest says to him, Young man are you married?, and the young fellow says back to him, dead serious and all, Naw father but I was twice in Fintona.

The train dived through a tunnel of tall trees. The lake vanished. Sunlight flashing and flickering through leaves made her close her eyes. Everybody on the train, even her aunt, seemed to be laughing. A man was saying: Fintona always had a bit of a name. For wild women.

Lofty's mother said, I was born there myself but I never noticed that it was all that good, nobody ever told me.

* * *

She opens her eyes and the sunlight flickers down on her through the spiralling branches of the great conifer. There's a book in the public library that has everything, including pictures, about all the trees of Great Britain and Ireland. Lofty is on the very tip of the peninsula of sand and gravel, demonstrating fly-casting to half a dozen children who are tailor-squatting around his feet. She is aware that he's showing off to impress her and the thought makes her warm and pleased, ready to laugh at anything. But to pretend that she's unimpressed she leans back and looks up into the tree in which the sunlight is really alive, creeping round the great bole, spots of light leaping like birds from one branch to another. She thinks of the omú tree which grows on the pampas of South America. Its trunk can be anything up to 40 or 50 feet thick. The wood is so soft that when cut it rots like an over-ripe melon and is useless as firewood. The leaves are large, glossy and deep green like laurel leaves – and also poisonous. But they give shade from the bare sun to man and beast, and men mark their way on the endless plains by remembering this or that omú tree. She has read about omú trees. Her own tree is for sure not one of them. She sits up straight when her book is lifted from her lap. Lofty is sitting by her side. The children are pointing and laughing. He must have crept up on hands and knees pretending to be a wild animal, a wolf, a prowling tiger. He's very good at capers of that sort. His rod and net lie by the side of the burn.

It was April when he first sat beside her. It is now mid-June. Her school will close soon for the holidays and she will no longer be compelled to wear the uniform: black stockings, pleated skirt of navy-blue serge, blue gansey, blue necktie with saffron stripes, blue blazer with school crest in saffron on breast-pocket, blue beret, black flat-heeled shoes. Even Juliet, and she was very young, didn't have to wear a school uniform. If she had Romeo wouldn't have looked at her.

Not that they are star-crossed lovers or Lofty any Romeo.

They haven't even crossed the millrace to walk in the bluebell woods as couples of all ages customarily do. She isn't shy of walking slowly because of the leg-splint but she knows that Lofty hasn't asked her because he thinks she might be: that makes her feel for him as she might feel, if she had one, for a witless younger brother who's awkward. And a bit wild: for a lot of Lofty's talk doesn't go with the world of school uniforms mostly blue for the mother of God. What the saffron is for, except variety of a sort, she can't guess. Lofty's rattling restless talk would lift Mother Teresa out of her frozen black rigidity.

Lofty with great good humour fingers the saffron stripes and says that, in spite of everything, she's a wee bit of an Orangewoman. They hold hands regularly. Lofty can read palms, a variant reading every time. They have kissed occasionally, when the children who are always there have been distracted by a water-hen or rat or leaping fish or a broken branch or an iceberg of froth from the falls.

— Don't look now, he says one day, but if you swivel round slowly you'll see my three sisters in action.

Beyond the millrace and against the fresh green of woods she can see the flash of coloured frocks, the glint of brass buttons and pipe-clayed belts. In those days it was only the wild ones who went with the soldiers: it wasn't money and security they were after.

— They're hell for soldiers, he says, between the three of them they'd take on the Germans.

Lofty himself reads a lot of military books, campaigns and generals, Napoleon and Ludendorf, all the way from Blenheim to the Dardanelles. When he doodles as he often does on the writing-pad she always carries with her – to make notes on her reading, to transcribe favourite poems – he doodles uniforms, every detail exact. Yet he listens to her when she reads poetry or the splendid prose of a volume of selected English essays, Caxton to Belloc.

— They're advancing on us, he says. They have us surrounded, enfiladed, debouched and circumnavigated.

— We'll tell Maryanne, the three sisters say, that you're with another.

Two of them, Mildred and Rosemary, are plump, laughing, blonde girls, and Mildred who is the youngest is as freckled as her brother. Gertie, the eldest, is olive-faced, with jet-black hair, wrinkles on the forehead and around the eyes like her mother. She is never to see the father of the family but the gossip of the town is to tell her that he's away a lot in Aldershot and India and that Lofty's mother, that merry woman, is friendly with more soldiers than the one she's married to.

The three British soldiers who are with the sisters are, one of them from Sligo, one from Wexford and one actually from Lancashire, England. They all talk and laugh a lot and she likes them. The Lancashire lad climbs right up to the top of the tree and pretends to see everything that's going on in the town and tells them about it: he has a lurid imagination. Then they go away towards the waterfall, still laughing, calling back about telling Maryanne. She asks him who Maryanne is. Lofty who clearly likes his sisters is not in the least embarrassed by the suggestion that he has another woman.

— Oh Maryanne's nobody or nobody much.

— She has a name. She must be somebody.

She's not really jealous, just curious.

— Maryanne's a girl I met one day on the road beyond McCaslan's shop.

— You met nobody on the road?

— She was wheeling a pram.

— She's married to Mr Nobody?

— It wasn't her pram. She's the nursemaid in Mooney's, the fancy-bread bakery. There was a lovely smell of fresh bread.

— Had you a good appetite, apple-jelly, jam-tart?

But since the rest of that rhyme to which children, Protestant and Catholic, rope-skip on the streets, is tell me the name of your sweetheart, she doesn't finish it and finds herself, to her annoyance, blushing. Lofty doesn't seem to notice.

— There were twins in the pram. I pushed it for her up

the hill to the main road. Then she said I bet you wouldn't do that for me if it was in the town on the court-house hill where everybody could see you. I said why not and she said Christian Brothers' boys are very stuck-up, I've met some that would do anything they could or you'd let them if they had a girl in the woods or in the dark, but that wouldn't be seen talking to her on the street, maids aren't good enough for them. I didn't tell her I was a Presbyterian and went to the academy.

— Why not?

— She mightn't like a Presbyterian pushing her pram.

They laugh at that until the playing children turn and look and laugh with them. Cheerful voices call from beyond the millrace where soldiers and sisters are withdrawing to the woods.

— We have girls at the academy, on the house, what Harry Cassidy and Jerry Hurst and the boys don't have at the Brothers. Harry and the boys are mad envious when we tell them about the fun we have feeling Daisy Allen under the desk at school. All lies of course.

— I hope Daisy Allen doesn't hear that.

— Och Daisy, she's well handled anyway, she's going about with a bus-driver and he's a married man as well, he ruined a doctor's daughter in Dungannon. Harry and the Catholic boys think the Protestant girls are wilder because they don't have to tell it all in confession. That isn't true either.

One other funny story she had heard Lofty's mother telling that day as the train in the evening left Bundoran station and the great romantic flat-topped mountains diminished into the distance. This time the story-teller faced her aunt and sat beside her uncle who had been talking about jerry-building in a new housing estate. Lofty's mother agreed with him. She had a shopping-bag of sugar to smuggle back into the Six Counties where it cost more. The sugar was tastefully disguised under a top-dressing of dulse. With content and triumph Lofty's mother sang a parody popular at the time:

South of the border down Bundoran way, that's where we get
the Free State sugar to sweeten our tay.

She was great fun. She had bright blue eyes and a brown
hat with a flaring feather, and a brown crinkly face. She said:
Those houses are everything you say and worse. Fancy fronts
and ready to fall. When you flush the lavatory in them the
noise is heard all over the town. Only the other day the lady
who lives in number three sent down to River Row for old Mr
Hill, the chimney-sweep, and up he came and put the brush
up the chimney and then went out, the way sweeps do, to see
if the brush was showing out of the top of the chimney. No
brush. In he went and screws on another length of handle on
the brush and pushes for dear life, and out again to look, but
no brush. In again and screws on the last bit of handle he has,
and he's pushing away when the lady from number eleven
knocks on the door. Have you the sweep in, missus dear, she
says. I have, missus dear, says the lady from number three.
Then please ask him to be careful, missus dear, she says, that's
twice now he's upset our wee Rosy from the lavatory seat.

Because of her happy carrying voice passers-by in the
corridor stop to join the fun. The smuggled sugar is safely
across the border.

Remembering Lofty's laughing mother makes it easier still
to like Lofty. The three sisters also look as if they'd be good
for a lot of laughs.

Her uncle is a tall broad-shouldered man with a good grey
suit, a wide-brimmed hat, two gold teeth and a drawl. Years ago
he was in the building trade in the United States and knows a lot
about jerry-building. He gets on very well with Lofty's mother.

It was well on towards the end of August when the black
man sat on the bench beside her. She was looking sideways
towards the bridge over the millrace, and laughing: because
two big rough young fellows were running like hares before Mr
McCaslan's boxer dog. Mr McCaslan who owned the shop was
also water-bailiff and park-keeper. The rough fellows had been

using, brutally, one of the swings meant for small children, so brutally that the iron stays that supported it were rising out of the ground. Mr McCaslan had mentioned the matter to them. They had been offensive, even threatening, to the old rheumatic man so he hobbled back to his shop and sent the boxer dog down as his deputy. The pair took off as if all hell were behind them. It was funny because the dog didn't bark or growl or show hostility, didn't even run fast, just loped along with a certain air of quiet determination and wouldn't (as far as she knew) savage anybody. But he was a big dog even for a boxer and the retreat of the miscreants was faster than the Keystone Cops. She laughed so much that the book fell on the grass. The black man picked it up and sat down beside her.

She thought of him as a black man not because he was a Negro but because her uncle had told her that he was a member of the black preceptory which was a special branch of the Orange Order. She had seen him walking last twelfth of July in the big parade in memory of the battle of the Boyne, which happened a long time ago, and in honour of King William of Orange who was a long time dead and had never been in this town. He had worn the black sash, with shining metallic esoteric insignia attached, as had the other men who marched beside him. The contingent that followed wore blue sashes and were supposed to be teetotallers but her uncle said that that was not always so. One of the blue men, a red-faced red-headed fellow was teetering and might have fallen if he hadn't been holding on to one of the poles that supported a banner.

The drums drummed, the banners bellied in the breeze, the pipes and fifes and brass and accordions played:

> It is old but it is beautiful
> And its colours they are fine,
> It was worn at Derry, Aughrim,
> Enniskillen and the Boyne.
> My father wore it in his youth,
> In bygone days of yore,

And on the Twelfth I'll always wear
The sash my father wore.

The name of the black man who sat beside her was Samuel
McClintock and he was a butcher. It was said about him for
laughs that if the market ran out of meat the town could live
for a week on McClintock's apron: blue, with white stripes.
That August day and in the public park he naturally wasn't
wearing the apron. He had a black moustache, a heavy blue
chin, a check cloth-cap, thick-soled boots, thick woollen
stockings and whipcord knee-breeches. The Fomorians, the
monsters from stormy seas had, each of them, one arm, one leg
and three rows of teeth. He said: The dog gave those ruffians
the run.

The way he said it took the fun out of it. She said: Yes,
Mr McClintock.

She wished him elsewhere. She half-looked at her book. She
was too well reared to pick it up from her lap and ostentatiously
go on reading. The river was in a brown fresh that day, the
peninsula of sand and gravel not to be seen, nor Lofty, nor
the children. The black man said: Plenty water in the river
today.

She agreed with him. It was also a public park in a
free-and-easy town and everyone had a right to sit where he
pleased. Yet this was her own seat under the tall tree, almost
exclusively hers, except when Lofty was there. The black man
said: The Scotchies have a saying that the salmon's her ain
when there's water but she's oor's when it's oot.

He explained: That means that often they're easier to catch
when the water's low.

He filled his pipe and lighted it. The smell of tobacco
was welcome. It might have been her imagination but until
he pulled and puffed and sent the tobacco smell out around
them she had thought that the resinous air under the tree
was polluted by the odours of the butcher's shop and apron.
He said that the salmon were a sight to see leaping the falls

when they went running upstream. She said that she had often watched them.

— I'm told you're very friendly with a well-known young fisherman of my persuasion.

— Who, for instance?

— You know well. That's what I want to talk to you about. It's a serious matter.

— Being friendly with a fisherman?

— Don't play the smarty with me, young lassie. Even if you do go to the convent secondary school. Young people now get more education than's good for them. Lofty at the academy and you at the convent have no call to be chumming it up before the whole town.

— Why not?

But it occurred to her that they hadn't been chumming-up or anything else before the whole town. What eyes could have spied on them in this enchanted island?

— His uncle's a tyler, that's why.

— I never knew he had an uncle.

— His mother's brother is a tyler and very strict.

— What's a tyler?

— I shouldn't repeat it, lassie. But I will, to impress on you how serious it is. A tyler he is and a strict one. Wasn't it him spoke up to have Lofty let into the B Specials?

— Don't ask me. I never knew he was a B Special.

But one day for a joke, she remembered, he had given her a handful of bullets.

— The nuns wouldn't tell you this at school but the B Specials were set up by Sir Basil Brooke to hold Ulster against the Pope and the Republic of Ireland.

The nuns, for sure, hadn't told her anything of the sort: Mother Teresa who was very strong on purity and being a lady and not sitting like a man with your legs crossed had never once mentioned the defensive heroisms of the B Specials who, out in country places, went about at night with guns and in black uniforms, holding up Catholic neighbours and asking them their names and addresses – which they knew very well to begin with. The Lofty she knew in daylight by this laughing river didn't seem to be cut out for such nocturnal capers.

— If his uncle knew that the two of you and you a Catholic girl were carrying-on there'd be hell upon earth.

— But we're not carrying-on.

— You were seen kissing here on this bench. What's that but carrying-on?

— What does he level?

— What does who level?

— The uncle who's a leveller or whatever you called him.

— Speak with respect, young lassie. A tyler, although I shouldn't tell you the secret, is a big man in the Order at detecting intruders. His obligation is this: I do solemnly declare that I will be faithful to the duties of my office and I will not admit any person into the lodge without having first found him to be in possession of the financial password or without the sanction of the Worshipful Master of the Lodge.

Then after a pause he said with gravity: And I'm the worshipful master.

He was the only one of the kind she had ever met or ever was to meet and she did her best, although it was all very strange there by the river and the rough stream and under the big tree, to appear impressed, yet all she could think of saying was: But I'm not interfering with his tyling.

Then she was angry and close to tears, although it was also funny: For all I care he can tile the roofs and floors and walls of every house in this town.

The big man hadn't moved much since he sat down, never raised his voice, but now he shouted: Lassie, I'll make you care. The B Specials are sworn to uphold Protestant liberty and beat down the Fenians and the IRA.

— I'm not a Fenian nor an IRA.

— You're a Roman Catholic, aren't you? And there isn't any other sort. Sir Basil Brooke says that Roman Catholics are 100 per cent disloyal and that he wouldn't have one of them about the house.

— Sir Who's It?

— No cheek, lassie. Didn't he sit up a tree at Colebrook all night long with a gun waiting for the IRA to attack his house? Didn't he found the B Specials to help the police to defend the throne and the Protestant religion?

What was it to her if Sir Somebody or Other spent all his life up a tree at Colebrook or anywhere else? The Lancashire soldier had climbed her tree and been as comic as a monkey up a stick. The black man calmed himself: Your own clergy are dead set against mixed marriages.

— We weren't thinking of marriage.

— What of then? Silliness and nonsense. The young have no wit. What would Mother Teresa say if she heard you were keeping company with a Protestant?

— Who would tell her?

— I might. For your own good and for Lofty.

He knocked the ash out of his pipe and put it away. The pleasant tobacco smell faded. She smelled blood and dirt and heard screams and knew, with a comical feeling of kindness, that she had been wrongly blaming him for bringing with him the stench of the shambles. There was a piggery at the far end of the field beyond the river and the wind was blowing from that direction.

— That's the piggery, she said. It's a disgrace.

— Time and again I've said that on the town council. You must have read what I said in the papers. It's a sin, shame and scandal to have a piggery beside a beauty spot. Not that I've anything against pigs, in my business, in their own place.

He stood up and patted her on the shoulder. He was really just a big rough friendly man: You don't want him put out of the Specials or the Lodge itself.

— Why should he be?

— These are deep matters. But they tell me you read a

lot. You've the name for being one of the cleverest students in this town, Protestant or Catholic. So I'll talk to you, all for the best, as if you were a grown-up and one of my own. It is possible but very difficult for a convert to be accepted as a member of the Orange Order.

He was as good as standing to attention. He was looking over her head towards the waterfall.

— A convert would have to be of several years standing and his background would have to be carefully screened. His admission would have to be authorized by the Grand Lodge. They'd have to go that high, like Rome for the Catholics. No convert can get into the Black Preceptory if either of his parents is still living, in case the Roman Catholic Church might exert pressure on a parent.

He was reciting. Like the sing-song way in which in school the children learned the Catechism.

Q: What are the seven deadly sins?
A: Pride, covetousness, lust, gluttony, envy, anger and sloth.
Q: What are the four sins that cry to heaven for vengeance?
A: Wilful murder, sodomy, oppression of the poor and defrauding the labourer of his wages.

Dear Sacred Heart it was a cheery world.

— A convert who was even a Protestant clergyman was blacked-out because one of his parents was still living, and there is automatic expulsion for dishonouring the Institution by marrying a Roman Catholic.

The great tree creaked its branches above them. The brown water tumbled on towards the town.

— You see what I mean, lassie.

She supposed she saw. In a way she was grateful. He was trying to help. He shook her hand as if they were friends forever. He went off towards the waterfall so that, without turning around, she could not see him walking away and he could not, thank God, see her face laughing, laughing. For, sweet heart of Jesus fount of love and mercy to thee we come thy blessings to implore, but it was comic to think of him marching up the convent grounds (he should wear his black sash and have a fife and drum before him) holy white statues to left and right and a Lourdes grotto as high as Mount Errigal, to relate all about the love-life of Lofty and herself to Mother Teresa who had a mouth like a rat-trap — and a mind. A worshipful master and a most worshipful reverend mother and never, or seldom, the twain shall meet. She was an odd sort of a girl. She sat around a lot and had read too many books. It was funny, also, to think of his daughter, Gladys, a fine good-natured brunette with a swinging stride, a bosom like a Viking prow, and a dozen boy friends of all creeds and classes. Nothing sectarian about Gladys who was one of his own kind and the daughter of a worshipful master. Somebody should tell the tyler to keep an eye on her. But she was too clever to be caught, too fast on her feet, too fast on her feet.

Walking slowly past the Orange hall on the way home she thought that the next time she met him she would have a lot to tell to lazy, freckled, lovable Lofty. The Orange hall was a two-storeyed brownstone building at a crossroads on the edge of the town. High on its wall a medallion image of William of Orange on an impossibly white horse rode forever across the Boyne. The two old cannon-guns on the green outside had been captured from the Germans in the Kaiser war. In there, Lofty's lodge met and it was a popular joke that no man could become a member until he rode a buck goat backways up the stairs. Sometimes in the evenings bands of music played thunderously in there, practising for the day in July when they marched out, banners flying. It was crazy to think that a man on a white horse, riding across a river 200 years ago could now ride between herself and Lofty. Or for that matter — although Mother Teresa would have a fit if she thought that a pupil of hers could think of such things — another man on a chair or something being carried shoulder-high in the city of Rome.

All this she meant to mention to Lofty the next time he came to the seat under the tree. But all she could get around to saying was: Lofty, what's a tyler?

He had no rod and net and was dressed, not for fishing, in a new navy-blue suit. The children called to him from the gravel but he paid no attention to them. At first he didn't pretend to hear her, so she asked him again. He said that a tyler was a man who laid tiles. That was the end of that. Then it was winter. One whole week the park was flooded. She couldn't exactly remember when it was that Lofty had given her the bullets.

It was also crazy to think that Lofty's laughing mother could have a brother who went about spying on people and nosing them out. What eyes had spied on Lofty and herself on the enchanted island? What nosy neighbour had told somebody who told somebody who told the sergeant that she had bullets in the earthenware jug?

— If you don't tell me, the sergeant says, it will be awkward for all concerned. What would Mother Teresa think if she thought you had live bullets in an earthenware jug?

It wasn't possible to control the giggles. What, in the holy name of God, would Mother Teresa think, if the sergeant and the worshipful master descended on her simultaneously, what would she say, how would she look? Keeping live bullets in a jug must be one of the few things that she had not warned her girls against.

— You'll have to come down to the barracks with me. I'll walk ahead and you follow just in case the people are passing remarks. They might think I'm arresting you.

— What are you doing?

— Och, I'd just like you to make a statement. It's not a crime to have bullets. Not for a young lady like you who wouldn't be likely to be using them. But we have a duty to find out where they came from. My son Reggie speaks highly of you, Reggie the footballer you know.

She knew. It was a town joke that the sergeant couldn't speak to anybody for ten minutes without mentioning Reggie who parted his hair up the middle, wore loud scarves and played football very well: it was clear that the sergeant thought that to be thought well of by Reggie was a special distinction.

Old low white houses line the hill that goes up from the brook and the co-operative creamery to the centre of the town. The sergeant plods on, twenty yards ahead of her. The town is very quiet. His black leather belt creaks and strains to hold him together. The butt of his pistol, his black baton case shine. She has never noticed before that Lofty has a stutter. Another sergeant sits behind a desk in the dayroom and makes notes. Two young constables are laughing in the background. The black man comes in and says: I warned the two of them.

Her own sergeant says: There wasn't much harm in it.

— Not for the girl, says the man behind the desk. But for him a breach of discipline.

Lofty has surely never stuttered when he talked to her by the meeting of the waters.

— Did you tell them I gave you the bullets?

— Dear God, it wasn't a crime to give me bullets.

— Did you tell them?

— I did not.

— They said you did.

— So.

Her own sergeant looks ashamed and rubs his moustache. The other sergeant says: Case closed.

Then her uncle walks in, and so hopping mad that he seems to have a mouthful of gold teeth. He talks for a long time and they listen respectfully because he's a famous man for keeping running dogs which he feeds on brandy and beef. He says over and over again: You make a helluva fuss about a few bullets.

— A breach of discipline, says the man behind the desk.

— My ass and yours, says her uncle. A helluva fuss.

And repeats it many times as they walk home together.

— But all the same they'll put him out of the Specials, he says. And I dare say he shouldn't have been assing around giving away government issue.

Over the supper table he remembers the time he had been a policeman in Detroit: Some Negro trouble then and this rookie policeman from Oklahoma was on patrol with a trained man. The rookie has no gun. So they're rushed by twenty black men and the first rock thrown clobbers the trained man unconscious. But the Oklahoma guy he stoops down, takes the pistol out of the other man's holster and shoots six times and kills six black men, one, two, three, four, five, six. He didn't waste a bullet.

— Sacred Heart have mercy, says her aunt.

— What did the other black men do, uncle?

— They took off for home and small blame to them. He was a cool one, that rookie, and a damned good shot. Here in this place they make a helluva fuss over a few bullets. I told them so.

Lofty came never again to the tall tree. They met a few times on the street and spoke a few words. She left the town after a while and went to work in London. Once, home on holidays, she met Lofty and he asked her to go to the pictures, and she meant to but never did. The Hitler war came on. She married an American and went to live in, of all places, Detroit. Her uncle and aunt and the sergeant and the worshipful master and the tyler and, I suppose, Lofty's mother and old McCaslan and his dog died.

Remembering her, I walked, the last time I was in the town to revisit Bluebell Meadow. The bridge over the millrace was broken down to one plank. Rank grass grew a foot high over most of the island. The rest of it was a wide track of sand and gravel where the river in fierce flood had taken everything before it. The children's swings and all the seats were gone,

smashed some time before by reluctant young soldiers from
the North English cities doing their national service. Repair
work had been planned but then the bombings and murders
began.

No laughing Lancashire boy in British uniform will ever
again climb the tall tree. For one thing the tree is gone. For
another the soldiers go about in bands, guns at the ready, in
trucks and armoured cars. There are burned-out buildings in
the main streets – although the great barracks is unscathed –
and barricades and checkpoints at the ends of the town. As a
woman said to me: Nowadays we have gates to the town. Still,
other towns are worse. Strabane which was on the border and
easy to bomb is a burned-out wreck. And Newry, where the
people badly needed shops and factories, and not ruins. And
Derry is like Dresden on the day after.

When I wrote to her about this she said, among other
things, that she had never found out the name of that tall
conifer.

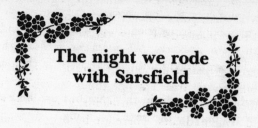

# The night we rode with Sarsfield

That was the house where I put the gooseberries back on the bushes by sticking them on the thorns. It wasn't one house but two houses under one roof, a thatched roof. Before I remember being there, I was there.

We came from the small village of Dromore to the big town of Omagh, the county town of Tyrone, in the spring of 1920, bad times in Ireland (Violence upon the roads/Violence of horses) particularly bad times in the north-east corner of Ulster. There have been any God's amount of bad times in the north-east corner of Ulster. There were no houses going in the big town and the nearest my father could find to his work was three miles away in the townland of Drumragh and under the one roof with Willy and Jinny Norris, a Presbyterian couple, brother and sister. They were small farmers.

That was the place then where I put the gooseberries back on the bushes by impaling them on the thorns. But not just yet because I wasn't twelve months old, a good age for a man and one of the best he's ever liable afterwards to experience: more care is taken of him, especially by women. No, the impaling of the gooseberries took place seven to eight years later. For, although we were only there six or so months until my father got a place in the town – in the last house in a laneway overlooking the green flowery banks of the serpentine Strule – we went on visiting Willy and Jinny until they died, and my father walked at their funeral and entered their church and knelt with the congregation: a thing that Roman Catholics were not by no means then supposed to do. Not knelt exactly but rested the hips on the seat and inclined the head: Ulster Presbyterians don't kneel, not even to God above.

It was a good lasting friendship with Willy and Jinny. There's an Irish proverb: *Nil aitheantas go haontigheas.* Or: You don't know anybody until you've lived in the one house with them.

Not one house, though, in this case but two houses under one roof which may be the next best thing.

Willy and Jinny had the one funeral because one night the house burned down — by accident. Nowadays when you say that a house or a shop or a pub or a factory burned down, it seems necessary to add — by accident. Although the neighbours, living next door in our house, did their best to rescue them and to save the whole structure with buckets of water from the spring-well which was down there surrounded by gooseberry bushes, they died, Willy from suffocation, Jinny from shock, the shock of the whole happening, the shock of loneliness at knowing that Willy was dead and that the long quiet evenings were over. However sadly and roughly they left the world, they went, I know, to a heaven of carefully kept harvest fields, and Orange lilies in bloom on the lawn before the farmhouse, and trees heavy with fruit, and those long evenings spent spelling out, by the combined light of oil-lamp and hearth fire, the contents of *The Christian Herald.* My three sisters who were all older than me said that that was the only literature, apart from the Bible, they had ever seen in the house but, at that time, that didn't mean much to me.

The place they lived in must have been the quietest place in the world. This was the way to get there.

The Cannonhill road went up from the town in three steps but those steps could only be taken by Titans. Halfways up the second step or steep hill there was on the right-hand side a tarred timber barn behind which such of the young as fancied, and some as didn't, used to box. My elder brother, there, chopped one of the town's bullies, who was a head-fighter, on the soft section of the crown of his head as he came charging like a bull, and that cured him of head-fighting for a long time. Every boy has an elder brother who can box.

The barn belonged to a farmer who would leave a team of horses standing in the field and go follow a brass band for the length of a day. Since the town had two brass bands, one military, one civilian, his sowing was always dilatory and his harvests very close to Christmas. He owned a butcher shop in the town but he had the word, Butcher, painted out and replaced by the word, Flesher, which some joker had told him was more modern and polite but which a lot of people thought wasn't exactly decent.

If you looked back from Cannonhill the prospect was really something: the whole town, spires and all, you could even see clear down into some of the streets; the winding river or rivers, the red brick of the county hospital on a hill across the valley, and beyond all that the mountains, Glenhordial where the water came from, Gortin Gap and Mullagharn and the high Sperrins. Sometime in the past, nobody knew when, there must have been a gun-emplacement on Cannonhill so as to give the place its name. Some of the local learned men talked vaguely about Oliver Cromwell but he was never next or near the place. There were, though, guns there in 1941 when a visit from the Germans seemed imminent and, indeed, they came near enough to bomb Belfast and Pennyburn in Derry City and were heard in the darkness over our town, and the whole population of Gallowshill, where I came from, took off for refuge up the three titanic steps of the Cannonhill road. It was lovely June night, though, and everybody enjoyed themselves.

If any of those merry refugees had raced on beyond the ridge of Cannonhill they would have found themselves, Germans or no Germans, in the heart of quietness. The road goes down in easy curves through good farmland to the Drumragh River and the old graveyard where the gateway was closed with concrete and stone long before my time, and the dead sealed off forever.

There's a sort of stile made out of protruding stones in the high wall and within – desolation, a fragment of a church wall that might be medieval, waist-high stagnant grass, table tombstones made anonymous by moss and lichen, a sinister hollow like a huge shellhole in the centre of the place where the dead, also anonymous, of the great famine of the 1840s were thrown coffinless, one on top of the other. A man who went to school with me used to call that hollow the navel of nothing and to explain in gruesome detail why and how the earth that once had been mounded had sunk into a hollow.

That same man ran away from home in 1938 to join the British navy. He survived the sinking of three destroyers on which he was a crew member: once, off the Faroes; once, for a change of temperature, in the Red Sea; and a third time at the Battle of Crete. It may be possible that the crew of the fourth destroyer he joined looked at him with some misgiving. A fellow townsman who had the misfortune to be in Crete as a groundsman with the RAF when the Germans were coming in low and dropping all sorts of unpleasant things to the great danger of life and limb, found a hole in the ground where he could rest unseen, and doing no harm to anybody, until he caught the next boat to Alexandria.

When he crawled into the hole who should be there but the thrice-torpedoed sailor reading *The Ulster Herald*. He said hello and went on reading. He was a cool one, and what I remember most about him is the infinite patience with which he helped me when, impelled by a passion for history, I decided to clean all the table tombstones in old Drumragh and recall from namelessness and oblivion the decent people who were buried there. It was a big project. Not surprisingly it was never completed, never even properly commenced, but it brought us one discovery: that one of the four people, all priests, buried under a stone that was flat to the ground and circled by giant yews, was a MacCathmhaoil (you could English it as Campbell or McCarvill) who had in history been known as the Sagart Costarnocht because he went about without boots or socks, and who in the penal days of proscribed Catholicism had said Mass in the open air at the Mass rock on Corra Duine mountain.

For that discovery our own parish priest praised us from the pulpit. He was a stern Irish republican who had been to the Irish college in Rome, had met D'Annunzio and approved of him and who always spoke of the Six Counties of north-east Ulster as *Hibernia Irredenta*. He was also, as became his calling, a stern Roman Catholic, and an antiquarian, and in honour of the past and the shadow of the proscribed, barefooted priest, he had read the Mass one Sunday at the rock on Corra Duine and watched, in glory on the summit like the Lord himself, as the congregation trooped in over the mountain from the seven separate parishes.

This ground is littered with things, cluttered with memories and multiple associations. It turns out to be a long three miles from Gallowshill to the house of Willy and Jinny Norris. With my mother and my elder sisters I walked it so often, and later on with friends and long after Willy and Jinny were gone and the house a blackened ruin, the lawn a wilderness, the gooseberry bushes gone to seed, the Orange lilies extinguished – miniature suns that would never rise again in that place no more than life would ever come back to the empty mansion of Johnny Pet Wilson. That was just to the left before you turned into the Norris laneway, red-sanded, like a tunnel with high hawthorn hedges and sycamores and ash trees shining white and naked. My father had known Johnny Pet and afterwards had woven mythologies about him: a big Presbyterian farmer, the meanest and oddest man that had ever lived in those parts. When his hired men, mostly Gaelic speakers from West Donegal, once asked him for jam or treacle or syrup or, God help us, butter itself, to moisten their dry bread, he said: Do you say your prayers?

— Yes, boss.

They were puzzled.

— Do you say the Lord's prayer?

— Yes, boss.

— Well, in the Lord's prayer it says: Give us this day our daily bread. Damn the word about jam or treacle or syrup or butter.

When he bought provisions in a shop in the town he specified: So much of labouring man's bacon and so much of the good bacon.

For the hired men, the imported long-bottom American bacon. For himself, the Limerick ham.

He rose between four and five in the morning and expected his men to be already out and about. He went around with an old potato sack on his shoulders like a shawl, and followed always by a giant of a gentleman goat, stepping like a king's warhorse. The goat would attack you if you angered Johnny Pet, and when Johnny died the goat lay down and died on the same day. Their ghosts walked, it was well known, in the abandoned orchard where the apples had become half-crabs, through gaps in hedges and broken fences, and in the roofless rooms of the ruined house. Nobody had ever wanted to live there after the goat and Johnny Pet died. There were no relatives even to claim the hoarded fortune.

— If the goat had lived, my father said, he might have had the money and the place.

— The poor Donegals, my mother would say as she walked past Johnny Pet's ghost, and the ghost of the goat, on the way to see Willy and Jinny. Oh, the poor Donegals.

It was a phrase her mother had used when, from the doorstep of the farmhouse in which my mother was reared, the old lady would look west on a clear day and see the tip of the white cone of Mount Errigal, the Cock o' the North, 60 or more miles away, standing up and shining with shale over Gweedore and the Rosses of Donegal and by the edge of the open Atlantic. From that hard coast, a treeless place of diminutive fields fenced by drystone walls, of rocks, mountains, small lakes, empty moors and ocean winds the young Donegal people (both sexes) used to walk eastwards, sometimes barefoot, to hire out in the rich farms along the valley of the Strule, the Mourne and the Foyle – three fine names for different stages of the same river.

Or the young people, some of them hardly into their teens, might travel as far even as the potato fields of Fifeshire or Ayrshire. They'd stand in the streets at the hiring fairs to be eyed by the farmers, even by God to have their biceps tested to see what work was in them. The last of the hiring fairs I saw in Omagh in the early 1930s but by that time everybody was well dressed and wore boots and the institution, God be praised, was doomed. There was a big war on the way and the promise of work for all. But my mother, remembering the old days and thinking perhaps more of her own mother than of the plight of the migratory labourers, would say: The poor Donegals. Ah, the poor Donegals.

Then up the sheltered red-sanded boreen or laneway – the Gaelic word would never at that time have been used by Ulster Presbyterians – to the glory of the Orange lilies and the trim land and in the season, the trees heavy with fruit. Those gooseberries I particularly remember because one day when I raided the bushes more than somewhat, to the fearful extent of a black-paper fourteen-pound sugar-bag packed full, my sisters (elder) reproved me. In a fit of remorse I began to stick the berries back on the thorns. Later in life I found out that plucked fruit is plucked forever and that berries do not grow on thorns.

Then another day the three sisters, two of them home on holidays from Dublin, said: Sing a song for Jinny and Willy.

Some children suffer a lot when adults ask them to sing or recite. There's never really much asking about it. It's more a matter of get up and show your paces and how clever you are, like a dancing dog in a circus, or know the lash or the joys of going to bed supperless.

Or sometimes it's bribery: Sing up and you'll get this or that.

Once I remember — can I ever forget it? — the reverend mother of a convent in Dublin gave me a box of chocolates because in the presence of my mother and my cousin, who was a nun, and half the community I brazenly sang:

> Paddy Doyle lived in Killarney
> And he loved a maid named Bessy Toole,
> Her tongue I know was tipped with blarney,
> But it seemed to him the golden rule.

But that was one of the exceptionally lucky days. I often wondered, too, where the reverend mother got the box of chocolates. You didn't expect to find boxes of chocolates lying around convents in those austere days. She dived the depth of her right arm for them into a sort of trousers-pocket in her habit, and the memory of them and of the way I won them ever after braced me in vigour (as the poet said) when asked to give a public performance.

— Up with you and sing, said the eldest sister.

Outside the sun shone. The lilies nodded and flashed like bronze. You could hear them. On a tailor's dummy, that Jinny had bought at an auction, Willy's bowler hat and sash were out airing for the Orange walk on the twelfth day in honour of King William and the battle of the Boyne. The sash was a lovely blue, a true blue, and the Orangemen who wore blue sashes were supposed to be teetotallers. Summer and all as it was the pyramid of peat was bright on the hearth and the kettle above it singing and swinging on the black crane, and Jinny's fresh scones were in three piles, one brown, one white, one spotted with currants and raisins, on the table and close to the coolness of the doorway.

— Sing up, said the second sister. Give us a bar.

— Nothing can stop him, said the third sister who was a cynic.

She was right. Or almost. Up I was and at it, with a song
learned from another cousin, the nun's brother, who had been
in 1920 in the IRA camp in the Sperrin mountains:

> We're off to Dublin in the green and the blue,
> Our helmets glitter in the sun,
> Our bayonets flash like lightning
> To the rattle of the Thompson gun.
> It's the dear old flag of Ireland, boys,
> That proudly waves on high,
> And the password of our order is:
> We'll conquer or we'll die.

The kettle sputtered and spat and boiled over. Jinny dived
for it before the water could hit the ashes and raise a stink, or
scald the backs of my legs where I stood shouting treason at
Willy and the dummy in the bowler and the teetotaller's blue
sash. It may have been a loyal Orange kettle. Willy was weeping
with laughter and wiping the back of his left hand sideways
across his eyes and his red moustache. In the confusion, the
eldest sister, purple in the face with embarrassment, said: If
you recited instead of singing. He's much better at reciting.

So I was and proud of it. Off I went into a thundering
galloping poem learned by heart from the *Our Boys*, a magazine
that was nothing if not patriotic and was produced in Dublin
by the Irish Christian Brothers.

> The night we rode with Sarsfield out from Limerick
>     to meet
> The waggon-train that William hoped would help in
>     our defeat
> How clearly I remember it though now my hair is
>     white
> That clustered black and curly neath my trooper's cap
>     that night.

This time there was no stopping me. Anyway Willy wouldn't
let them. He was enjoying himself. With the effrontery of one of
those diabolical little children who have freak memories, even
when they don't know what the words mean, I let them have
the whole works, eight verses of eight lines each, right up to
the big bang at Ballyneety on a Munster hillside at the high
rock that is still called Sarsfield's Rock.

It is after the siege of Derry and the battle of the Boyne
and the Jacobite disaster at the slope of Aughrim on the
Galway road. The victorious Williamite armies gather round
the remnants of the Jacobites locked up behind the walls of
Limerick. The ammunition train, guns, and wagons of ball and
powder, that will end the siege rumble on across the country.
Then Sarsfield with the pick of his hard-riding men, and led
by the Rapparee, Galloping Hogan, who knows every track
and hillock and hollow and marsh and bush on the mountains
of Silver Mine and Keeper and Slieve Felim, rides north by
night and along the western bank of the big river:

> 'Twas silently we left the town and silently we rode,
> While o'er our heads the silent stars in silver beauty
> glowed.
> And silently and stealthily well led by one who knew,
> We crossed the shining Shannon at the ford of Killaloe.

On and on from one spur of the mountains to the next,
then silently swooping down on the place where, within a
day's drag from the city's battered walls, the well-guarded
wagons rest for the night. For the joke of it the Williamite
watchword is Sarsfield:

> The sleepy sentry on his rounds perhaps was musing o'er
> His happy days of childhood on the pleasant English
> shore,
> Perhaps was thinking of his home and wishing he were
> there

> When springtime makes the English land so wonderfully
>     fair.
> At last our horses' hoofbeats and our jingling arms he
>     heard.
> 'Halt, who goes there?', the sentry cried. 'Advance and
>     give the word.'
> 'The word is Sarsfield,' cried our chief, 'and stop us he
>     who can,
> 'For Sarsfield is the word tonight and Sarsfield is the man.'

Willy had stopped laughing, not with hostility but with
excitement. This was a good story, well told. The wild riders
ride with the horses' shoes back to front so that if a hostile
scouting party should come on their tracks, the pursuit will
be led the wrong way. The camp is captured. Below the rock
a great hole is dug in the ground, the gun-powder sunk in it,
the guns piled on the powder, the torch applied:

> We make a pile of captured guns and powder bags and
>     stores,
> Then skyward in one flaming blast the great explosion
>     roars.

All this is long long ago – even for the narrator in the
poem. The hair is now grey that once clustered black and
curly beneath his trooper's cap. Sarsfield, gallant Earl of
Lucan, great captain of horsemen, is long dead on the plain
of Landen or Neerwinden. Willy is silent, mourning all the
past. Jinny by the table waits patiently to pour the tea:

> For I was one of Sarsfield's men though yet a boy in years
> I rode as one of Sarsfield's men and men were my
>     compeers.
> They're dead the most of them, afar, yet they were
>     Ireland's sons
> Who saved the walls of Limerick from the might of
>     William's guns.

No more than the sleepy sentry, my sisters never recovered from the shock. They still talk about it. As for myself, on my way home past the ghosts of Johnny Pet and the gentleman goat, I had a vague feeling that the reason why the poor girls were fussing so much was because the William that Sarsfield rode to defeat must have been Willy Norris himself. That was why the poem shouldn't be recited in his house, and fair play to him. But then why had Willy laughed so much? It was all very puzzling. Happy Ulster man that I then was I knew as little about politics and the ancient war of Orange and Green as I knew about the way gooseberries grew.

It wasn't until after my recital that they found out about the black-paper fourteen-pounder of a sugar-sack stuffed full of fruit. The manufacturers don't do sacks like that any more in this country. Not even paper like that any more. It was called crib-paper, because it was used, crumpled-up and worked-over and indented here and bulged out there to simulate the rock walls of the cave of Bethlehem in Christmas cribs.

For parcelling books I was looking for some of it in Dublin the other day, to be told that the only place I'd come up with it was some unlikely manufacturing town in Lancashire.

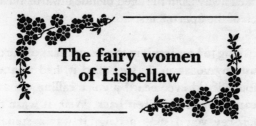

# The fairy women of Lisbellaw

If it hadn't been for an elderly blonde that I saw sitting in the sun in a bikini on a lawn in Atlanta, Georgia, I'd never have remembered him again. She was a good 40 paces away from me as I stepped out with two friends from the door of my yellow-brick apartment building. Her back was towards us. She was the only object that disturbed the green grass, and very green it was to grow up out of the red clay of the dry sunny south.

She swivelled her head, left to right, and looked around at us. Although I didn't know who she was and had never even seen her before or, at any rate, had never seen that much of her, I waved my right hand. For beyond her, although in reality there was nothing but the street called Ponce de Leon where it ceases to be suburbia and becomes a stretch of rooming-houses and heavy traffic, and black girls washing cars, and a good Greek restaurant on the far side of the traffic, I saw clearly the Atlantic rolling in on the cliffs of Donegal, and the dark rocks of Roguey under which only the most courageous ever venture to swim.

So Gene asked me who the blonde on the grass was and I said I didn't know.

— But you waved at her.

— Wouldn't you wave at any girl in a bikini?

— A girl, Dolores said.

— I waved at the past.

— You sure did, Gene said. She's 90. You crazy Irish.

— We're a friendly people, I said.

We walked away from the aged blonde towards the car-park at the back of the apartments.

I gave up trying to be a Jesuit in the second year of the novitiate not because my vocation, as we called it, had weakened – I gravely doubt if I'd ever heard a voice calling me anywhere – but because I had a broken back. Well, it wasn't exactly broken the way you'd snap a twig. It was a spinal lesion, an injured spot on which the bacillus that lurks in all of us settled to make it difficult for me to bend if I was straight or to straighten up if I was bent, and to make me feel that some unseen demon stabbed now and again, slowly and carefully, with a thin red-hot knitting-needle about the region of the third lumbar lump. Eighteen months of Christian patience it took to exorcise that demon.

The Atlantic breakers, white and blue and green, and flashing a lot of colours I could put no name to, came trampling and tumbling up Bundoran strand. The surf was crowded with happy shouting bathers. Little children, grave with excitement, rode slowly on tiny brown hairy donkeys, and one enterprising entertainer had even introduced a baby elephant. The hurdy-gurdy at the hobby-horses and chairaplanes was squeezing the last drop of melody out of the tune that went to the words about the old rustic bridge by the mill:

'Twas oftimes, dear Maggie, when years passed away,
And we plighted lovers became . . .

The town was a long thin line along the coast behind me as I left the red strand and climbed the steep short-grassed slope to the top of the cliffs above Roguey Rocks. Golfers, like jerky clockwork toys, moved, bent with no pain, drove with the intensity of cyclones, on the windy links around Bundoran's grandest hotel. That wind was strong and salty. Behind the town the flat-topped mountains, all the way from Rossinver Braes to bare Ben Bulben, lay like sleeping purple animals.

The straps that held my back-splint in place were cutting into my armpits and crotch. My shiny black jacket, that had fitted well enough when I went into the hospital eighteen months previously, had a hard job now to keep buttoned because of the back-splint and a slight stomach spread developed in hospital. In that place of rolling ocean and salt shouting wind, purple mountains, hurdy-gurdies and near-naked bathers, I was, and felt I was, a cheerless sombre figure.

This clifftop walk was my path of escape. It brought me away from the happy all-together crowds that seemed so nastily to emphasize my own isolated predicament. Beyond Roguey the cliffs – flung spray rising high above them, high as they were, and spattering the rocks – swung directly eastwards and so, unavoidably did the path. It brought me by the bowl-shaped fresh-water spring, clear as crystal against solid rock, that was one of the wonders of those cliffs. It brought me by an even more wonderful wonder, the Fairy Bridges, where the sea had moled its way through weaknesses in the dark rock and, far back from the dangerous slanting edge of the cliffs, you could look down into deep terrifying cauldrons of boiling froth. Tragedies were always happening there: daring young people clambering down the sides of the cauldrons, to what purpose God alone knew, and losing foothold or handhold, and falling down where not all the lifeguards in the world could be of the least assistance to them.

Beyond those fatal Fairy Bridges the holiday crowd had vanished. There was an odd courting couple, snug from the wind behind a fence of green sods or a drystone wall, grazing nimble goats who sometimes attacked people; and inland, protected from the cliffs by walls and fences, easy grazing cattle. The great flat mountains were still visible, but the eye and imagination were taken now by the long rising-and-falling range of highlands far across the bay.

Poems had been written about this place: that vision of highlands, strand and sea, and far away the estuary of the River Erne. The strand was perilous with quicksands and so generally deserted.

From Dooran to the Fairy Bridge
And down by Tullan Strand,
Level and long and white with waves,
Where gull and curlew stand . . .

The wooden shelter that I sat and read in was as near to being my own exclusive property as made no difference. It was roofed with red tiles, and had no sides, and a cruciform wooden partition held up the roof and divided the structure into four parts so that no matter from what airt the wind did blow, myself and my book always had shelter. There I sat reading, daydreaming, I was nineteen, remembering. Remembering now and again the Jesuit novitiate where, inexplicably, I had been happy in a brief fit of religious frenzy that was to be my ration ever since. A classical rectangular house that had once belonged to a great lord and, with red carpet on the main avenue, given welcome to an English king, sheltered in deep pine woods in the sleepy Irish midlands. Bells divided the holy day. Black-gowned neophytes made their meditations, walked modestly, talked circumspectly. Wood pigeons cooed continuously, and there were more bluebells and daffodils and red squirrels in those woods than I have ever seen anywhere else in the world.

But, to be honest, I was never quite sure what I was doing there and, if I was happy, it was happiness in a sort of trance that I felt uneasily must have its end. My lumbar spine made up my mind for me, and eighteen months surrounded by fresh and pleasant young Irish nurses convinced me that there were certain things that Jesuits were not normally supposed to have. So that my memories in the cruciform shelter were less about the Ignatian spiritual exercises than about dreams of fair women in blue-and-white uniforms. They were all there, around the corner by Ben Bulben and off through Sligo on the high road to Dublin. To the rocks and the seawind I repeated the names of the seven or eight of them I had fallen in love with: Lane, Devlin, Brady, Love, Callaghan, Mullarkey, O'Shea, Rush and Moynihan. On a recount: nine.

Far away a black-sailed boat that seemed scarcely to be moving came down the sand-channel of the Erne estuary to the sea. In the privacy of the shelter I eased the crotch-straps of the back-splint. It was made of good leather stretched on a light steel frame, it travelled from the neck to the buttocks, it smelled of horse-harness.

— Head out to sea, I said, when on your lee the breakers you discern. Adieu to all the billowy coasts and the winding banks of Erne.

The tide, the bathers, the children, the donkeys, and even the baby elephant, had withdrawn for a while from the red half-moon of Bundoran Strand. Far out the frustrated breakers were less boisterous. The hurdy-gurdy was silent and the hobby-horses resting at their stalls, and in hotels and boarding-houses the evening meal was being demolished. In Miss Kerrigan's old-fashioned whitewashed Lios na Mara, or the Fort, God help us, by the sea, my mother looked up from her ham salad to say that I was late as usual.

— Sara Alice, leave him be, Miss Kerrigan said. He's thinking long. Waiting for the happy day when he gets back to his studies. Looking forward to his ordination, God bless him, the holy oil, the power to bind and loose.

Listening to her I kept my thoughts fixed on red squirrels flashing in bluebell woods, on the wasps' nest at the foot of the Spanish chestnut tree close to the croquet court, on the dark silent file of neophytes, eyes cast down, obeying the holy bell and walking to the chapel to morning oblation – along cold corridors and down a stairway up which unholy royalty had once staggered to bed. For I felt if my thoughts were on laughing young nurses, Lane, Devlin, Brady, Love, Callaghan, Mullarkey, O'Shea, Rush and Moynihan, my nine blue-and-white Muses, Miss Kerrigan's sharp brown eyes would discover those thoughts and betray the old Adam hiding behind the shiny black suit.

— Thinking long, she said again.

She was very fond of me and I wouldn't have hurt her for the world. Lios na Mara, too, was a place that caught the fancy as the average seaside boarding-house most certainly did not. It stood well back from the town's one interminable street, under a stone archway, secure and secluded in a grassy courtyard that overlooked the toy harbour where the fishing-boats and the seagulls were. It wasn't New York or Liverpool but it was the first harbour I ever saw and, as a child, I had actually thought that ships might sail from that harbour to anywhere or Antananarivo.

— This, said Miss Kerrigan, is Master McAtavey.

He had come into the room silently while, with my back to the door, I was fumbling with a napkin and sitting down to attack my ham. It was a surprise to find anyone except my mother and Miss Kerrigan who were girlhood friends, and myself, of course, by right of inheritance, in that small private parlour. The other guests ate elsewhere and did not presume.

— My only sister's son, said Miss Kerrigan.

— From the Glen of Glenties, said my mother who was hell all out for geography.

He was still standing, very tall and awkward, three paces away from the table.

— Sit down, Eunan dear, said my mother. Don't be shy.

She disliked shy people. She suspected them of dishonesty.

— He teaches school, said Miss Kerrigan.

— In the Vale of Dibbin, said my mother. A heavenly place. You know it, she said to me.

Then he blushed. Never before or since have I seen a blush like it. He had fair curly hair that was cropped too short and his eyes were a startlingly bright and childish blue. His navy-blue pinstripe was too short in the sleeves and, above strong square hands, the knobs on his wrists were as large as golfballs. He had taken two paces forward abruptly as if he were a sentry under command, towards his provender, so that the lower half of him was hidden by the table and I couldn't see whether the legs of his pants, like his sleeves, were too short. Not that I, with my shiny coat of clerical black straining to meet around my back-splint, was in any position to criticize. His blond skin – once it must have been blond – was so beaten by the heathery wind of the Glen of Glenties, and burned by the same sun that shines both on Glenties and Georgia, that even experts on the matter would have considered it quite impossible for him to blush.

But he did. The blush went upwards in little leaps or spurts, an inch or so at a time, from the tight white collar that squeezed his long neck, up and up, spreading, intensifying until his whole face shone, as the man said about the sunset, like a forge. He was a very shy master and let me say, to my credit, that I leaped up, offered him a chair, seated him at his ham salad, sat down again and talked non-stop for half an hour about the Vale of Dibbin and the Glen of Glenties. He choked over his ham, and played back to me the occasional yes or no, and I wasn't sure whether he was grateful or resentful. But I didn't care much, for I did know the places I talked about and to talk about them was a pleasure in itself.

The town of Glenties, I told them, was always bright with paint and so spotlessly clean that a scrap of paper or cigarette butt wasn't to be seen on the street, and a bluebottle fly, invading from some less-regulated town, wouldn't last for five minutes. A few miles away, the sands, under clear water where the Gweebarra River turned salt, shone like silver. In the Vale of Dibbin the neat white-washed farmhouses stood along the breast of the mountain and the clean fields sloped steeply down to a trout stream, all white cataracts and deep populated pools. On which river I had fished with my brother and a fat man called Joe Maguire who had fought at the Dardanelles and who wore a bowler hat even when he was fishing.

The life and times of Joe Maguire could have kept me going for half a day, but time was passing and I prized the private hours ahead when I would sit in my room and read and look down on the harbour and across the water at the happy company on the strand. They couldn't see me but I could see them and that, in some way or other, helped my morale. When I stopped to draw breath and chew ham I was glad to see that his blush had faded.

Miss Kerrigan listened, and watched me with loving brown eyes that were set deeply in a long wrinkled yellow face. She continuously rubbed her feet on the floor in a nervous way she had. That nervousness increased when she went to whist-drives and it was said that once, when she was running hard for first prize, she had rubbed a hole in the uncarpeted floor of the cardroom in a parish hall in a neighbouring town. She always dressed in black, in mourning for her father and mother who had died within the one week 30 years ago, and she was six feet two inches in height.

— What a memory, she said.

— A powerful man to tell stories, said my mother, like his father before him.

— A blessed gift, Miss Kerrigan said, and will stand to him well after ordination.

She must have meant something else, for no one could have suspected Miss Kerrigan of anti-clericalism.

— In the pulpit I mean, she said.

That didn't make it any better.

— I'll go for a walk now, said Eunan McAtavey.

Those were the first words I'd heard him say. They began as a whispering squeak and then spread out like a shout. They had clearly cost him premeditation and effort. He stood up. He didn't overturn his chair. He did drop his napkin. I picked it up for him.

— Bernard will go with you, Miss Kerrigan said.

— Bernard, my mother said, Eunan was never here before. He doesn't know his way around.

There went my private hours, but politeness compelled me and, at any rate, the ladies had me trapped.


Three lovely old ladies lived in that block of yellow-brick apartments. Taken all-together they were a sort of sign that something remained in a place where everything was rapidly changing.

They lived in a world of their own and had memories that had nothing whatsoever to do with the neighbours. Forty years ago, when they had come to live there, those apartments had been new and quite the thing. But suburbia in automobiles had swept far beyond them. The district decayed. The old ladies stayed on because they were too old, perhaps too poor, to move. Their neighbours now were myself, and the withered blonde whoever she was, and rowdy students who had lively parties and were occasionally evicted because the landlord would find six living in an apartment he had rented to two. To evict one such group his workmen had to take the door off the hinges. A few decent quiet linotype men lived there. The paper they had worked for in a more southern city had folded and they had come north to Atlanta to find work. A flock of go-go girls who were working down the street stayed for a while, brightened the lawn with bodies more naked than had ever startled Eunan McAtavey on Bundoran Strand, then flew off elsewhere. Their place was taken one evening by a fat oily bald man. From their windows the students made offensive noises. Two burglars who lived in another part of the city rented one of the yellow apartments to keep their loot in. The police came and were a whole afternoon carrying out and counting miscellaneous objects. My next-door neighbour was a girl from Nashville who was married at fifteen and whose husband dressed up as the tiger in the tank at a filling-station. He walked out every morning in his costume, his own head showing, the tiger's head grinning in his hand.

Gene drove down the slope. We passed the hotel where the black girl, coming to fill her fifth date for the night, had changed her mind and tried to steal the cash register instead, and had been shot dead by the night porter. We passed three liquor stores, an army induction centre, a Sears Roebuck, a waste-patch that had once been a ball-park and would, any day henceforth, sprout skyscrapers. The twenty black girls washing cars were, to keep cool, squirting water over each other. We passed a Yarab shrine, a Presbyterian centre, a motel, three churches, a pop place painted all purple, saloons, and shops, and one skyscraper hotel at the corner of Peachtree Street. Dolores was on the way to a suburban shopping centre to buy shoes.

That was the first of seven walks, dull enough, silence mostly between us, our chief activities just walking, or tossing driftwood back into the tide, or simply sitting and gazing out to sea. He couldn't swim and I because of my third lumbar lump and my back-splint, wasn't allowed to. Now and again, to break the silence, I played courier and pointed out the estuary, named the mountains and quoted the poetry. He showed no interest. He would walk stolidly beside me, and I had a crazy feeling that his arms swung together, both before him at the same time, both behind him at the same time, if you know what I mean. The pinstripe trousers were, indeed, too short, and the feet were considerable. When he put away the pinstripe – he said it was his Sunday-best and that the salt air faded dark cloth – and put on grey flannels with a dangerous crease, they also were too short. His oatmeal tweed jacket creaked from the shop and my back-splint answered. We were a fine pair to be seen on any gay promenade. He never nonchalantly put his hands in his pockets. When he stood up they hung by his side as if he had no control over them.

On the fifth walk I talked about the Jesuits and the novitiate and the weedy lake where boating and bathing were allowed, depending on the weather, on major Christian festivals. He responded by telling me, in broken spurts and mumbles, how he had spent two years of hell in a teachers' training college in Dublin, and that he might as well, for all the college ever taught him about life, have been incarcerated, he used that word, in Mountjoy Jail. That reference to life should have warned me.

On the sixth walk I mentioned the nurses and litanied the nine magic names and, growing reckless with wishful thinking, hinted at nights of love under dimmed lights. On the seventh walk he stopped in the sunshine, on a path through the dunes beyond Tullan Strand, and raised his stiff right arm to indicate

the curves and hollows of the dry sand, the sleek comfort of the
bent grass, and said hoarsely: This would be a bloody great
place to have a woman.

— True enough, I said and felt guilty before his awkward
innocent passion.

For by day in the shelter when the crotch straps were eased,
by night in bed when my black garments were laid aside, I had
skipped in fantasy up and down those same dunes, a satyr in
pursuit of nine nymphs, or lurked in grassy corners to cut off
unclad stragglers.

— The way you talk about the place I come from, he said,
you'd think it was Blackpool or the Land of Youth.

It took me until the following day to appreciate that juxtaposi-
tion but, on reflection in the quietude of my room, it seemed
reasonable. The poets don't tell us, but there must have been
beaches and bathing beauties in the land to which Niamh led
Oisin. Eunan, clearly, had given the matter long thought.

— It's lovely country, I said. A home for poets. The fishing's
good.

— I don't fish. The only poetry I ever learned off by heart
was this.

He stood up stiff as a guardsman, filled his lungs with
seawind and let fly: Bracing breezes, silvery sands, booming
breakers, lovely lands. Come to Bundoran.

It didn't occur to me, I remember, to be surprised at
this display of eloquence. Being talkative myself, I must
have assumed that there was as much talk in everyone, that
it was welling up in him and that some day the dam would
burst.

— I learned that out of an advertisement in the newspaper
because it was my intention to come here to Bundoran for the
women. I'd heard time and again that the place was hoaching
with them during the Scottish holiday season.

Hoaching was the word we used to describe the way finger-
ling fish, in low water and warm weather, would swarm together at the mouths of pools. It was an evocative sultry word.

— What's holding you up? I said. They're everywhere to
be seen.

Even in the lonely dunes that was true. Couples sprawled
in sheltered corners. When they couldn't be seen they could be
heard: muffled voices, and shrills of laughter quickly stifled, to
remind the horseman passing by that love was all. The path
we followed skirted the barbed wire of a military camp, went
down a slope past an ancient churchyard to join the main road
to Ballyshannon, Enniskillen, Omagh and Donegal town. Four
green soldiers stood where the path joined the roadway and
bantered and jackacted with six girls with bright flaring skirts
and Glasgow accents.

— A surplus of two, she said. The soldiers have all the luck.
You were lucky, too, with all those nurses. You struck it lucky.
All good things. They say the nurses are the best. They know
everything.

If I had not already come close to believing that my own
imaginings were reality I might have had an attack of conscience
for all the tall tales I had told him.

— My trouble, Bernard, is that I can't talk to women. Even
your mother and Miss Kerrigan frighten me. I never had the
training. Where would I get it? With mountainy women as wild
as the mountain sheep? Hands on them as hard as flagstones. I
never got a bloody chance. Even in Dublin. The priests in the
college wouldn't let you see daylight. The Vincentians.

— No, I said, I suppose the Vincentians wouldn't be so
good at that. It wouldn't be on the curriculum.

It worried me a little that he didn't laugh at the idea.
He looked straight in front of him. His mouth, and it was
a small tight one for such a large man, was tightly closed –
now that his talking was over for the moment. Muscle stood
out on the point of his left jaw as if he had his teeth clenched
on his grievance. The hard sidewalk, crowded with women, I
suppose there must have been men there too, was hot under
our feet, the long town ahead. He had touchingly used my
name for the first time and so made me his ally, his sworn

brother sweet, his voice when it came to putting chat on the women.

He was so awkward on his feet that he came into the class of men who can be described as getting in their own way. Walking beside him had all sorts of problems. It wasn't so bad when he was silent, as he seldom was after he had confessed to me his true reason for coming to Bundoran. For when he was silent he could follow a straight course as well as any man. But when he talked he moved, inch by inch as his blush did, sideways in little spurts towards his listener, and to emphasize his point he jabbed with his elbows. Or they did the jabbing all on their own, for of all the men I've ever known, he had the least control over his hands and elbows and feet. To make his feet more noticeable he purchased and wore a pair of those rubber-and-corduroy pampooties known to the civilized world as brothel creepers. They didn't go with the iron crease of his grey flannels nor the creaking jacket of honest oatmeal tweed. They were also too big for him, although that seemed impossible, but the toes certainly flopped when he walked or stumbled along sideways, elbowing, so that every 50 yards or so I had to dodge to the other side of him to save myself from bruises and correct our course. We were the rarest-looking pair of Romeos that ever walked out to rummage and ruin the girls, Scottish or Irish, that hoached in that summery pool.

— You're a man of the world, he said. You can talk to people.

Nobody had ever said that to me before. Nobody has ever said it since, although two months later, as a student in Dublin walking home by night, I picked up a little girl with a blue beret and a brown belted coat and protruding teeth, and kissed her good-night at her garden gate. She breathed deeply. She said: Boy, you've got technique.

Afterwards the risks I took with more sophisticated college lasses, to establish my claim to a technique of which until then I had been quite innocent, must have earned me an odd sort of reputation. But breathing bracing breezes, walking silvery sands, listening to, because I was unable to plunge into, booming breakers, it was up to me, as a man of the world, to do something for my hapless mountainy man. It wasn't going to be easy.

— Not that one, Bernard. She's as bold as brass by the cut of her.

— Isn't that what we're after, Eunan?

— She would talk the ass out of a pot. And the laughs of her.

The plump girl in orange swimsuit and blue bathing-cap ran, leaping and laughing, into the surf. Her thin blonde companion, in red suit and no cap, trotted demurely behind her, squeaking a little now and again. Little did the plump girl know how close she had come to the arms of Eunan McAtavey. He looked after her for a long time. He fancied her but he was afraid of her laughter.

— Not that one, Bernard, You couldn't get near her for lipstick.

This was a tall redhead, long flying red hair, who went round and round riding sidesaddle and flashing thighs on the hobby-horses. Her crimson mouth was, indeed, a size larger than nature, but only a man who had more on hand than he could deal with, would have faulted her for that. For a man who had nothing at all, nor ever had, Eunan of the Glen was mighty choosey. He feared laughter. He feared lipstick. He didn't want to spend money.

— Not that one, Bernard. She's a chain-smoker. Look at the butts on the ground around her. A bank manager couldn't keep her in cigarettes.

The thin girl in dark slacks and dark woollen sweater sat on a bench outside the Hamilton Hotel and blew out smoke as if she meant to blind the passers-by. She was gone beyond her first bloom but there was something appealingly wistful, and promising, about her dark steady eyes, and cheeks that hollowed as she sucked smoke.

— Not that pair, Bernard. They remind me of the mountainy girls at home.

They were sisters, two country girls, bright red berets, damp tails of hair straggling out from under the berets, belted fawn raincoats. Like ourselves and a hundred others, they had raced for shelter from an Atlantic squall to play the machines in hurdy-gurdy country. They stamped with delight in the deep churned discoloured sand. For fun, they shouldered each other like county footballers while they both grabbed for the one arm of the one bandit. They laughed so as to be heard above the noise of a crowd of people crushed suddenly into a small space, even above the steam-organ hurdy-gurdy noises. The hobby-horses, all mounted, circled, the redhead sidesaddle. The rising-and-falling mountain range beyond the bay was hidden by a pitch-black cloud that came down like a smothering curtain. Then the curtain was split by forked lightning and the thunder came before the flash had faded. Under the wooden roof of the place of hobby-horses and bandits it was then so dark that one of the showmen switched on the lights. More lightning, the thunder seemed to come closer. A woman screamed and more children than you could count or kill began to cry. The elder of the two laughing sisters turned round and looked at us, and began to laugh as if she had just learned the secret. No question or doubt about it, nor was there any point in mentioning the matter to Eunan – but she was laughing at us.

Dolores is a slender sensitive woman who paints well and exhibits and sells her paintings. Gene, in spite of an English surname, has Arab blood in him that makes him look like a non-aggressive, even affable, slightly smaller version of General Nasser. On Saturday afternoons Rich's in Lennox Square in Atlanta, Georgia, is as good a field as I've ever seen for the wholehearted bird-watcher. Gene and Dolores couldn't see him, but Eunan of the Glen, lost to me long ago by the Donegal sea, was beside me on the escalator on the way up to the shoe department. He was so real to me that day, for the first time in 27 years, that I was ready to speak to him out loud, ready to hear him say: No, Bernard, not that one. She couldn't be a

modest girl. Look at the bare back of her. Be the holy, if the
parish priest saw the like of that on a teacher's wife in the Glen
of Glenties, there'd be a new teacher in the school before the
end of the month if not sooner.

Yet Eunan — it must have been something he read — had
desired, I think, silks and perfumes with the sins he imagined
and feared: and the silks and perfumes were all here. It was
the women of his own mountainy place and people that he
feared most. He told me of a girl who grabbed his hand in the
darkness of the schoolhouse at a travelling movie show: She
had a palm, Bernard, as hard as a whinstone rock. It would
frighten you. A woman shouldn't be like that. A woman should
be gentle. And true. Terrible things, Bernard, can happen to
country schoolmasters. A man I heard tell of got into trouble
with the girls in the school, two of them, and one was jealous
of the other, and she told. The country girls are deceitful. And
if you married the wrong one your job's ruined.

Looking up the escalator at the bare-backed beauty ahead
of us, I said that you could play the zither on the knuckles of
her spine.

She was a tall olive Amazonian, with her right shoulder
arrogantly bare, and white pants so tight that her bottom
looked like an outsize meringue; and a crimson waistcoat all
front and no back, that was a miracle of cantilever.

But it was Gene, not Eunan, that heard. Bundoran was 27
years away, and 4,000 miles.

— Hardly worth while, he said, for her escort to take her
home. Nothing more left to see. Billy Graham says that it's okay
for girls to wear miniskirts if there is no intention of provoking
sensual desire.

Oh Eunan McAtavey where are you now?


Failure after failure, he wouldn't take the jump, so there was
nothing for it now but the Palais de Danse. As a man I know
says: If you want to get it you must go where it is.

Miss Kerrigan would say to me: You're more cheerful now,

Bernard, since Eunan came. You're not thinking long any more. I'm so glad the two of you get along together. Good healthy walks, bracing breezes, silvery sands.

Everybody in the bloody place seemed to know that jingle off by heart.

— Booming breakers, lovely lands, rhymed my mother.

— That's real poetry, she said smugly and just to madden me for she knew that I kept hidden in my room above the harbour the steadily accumulating collected works: three developing epics, one on Barac, Deborah and King Sisera in the *Book of Judges*, one on the Easter Rising of 1916, one on the lighting by St Patrick, on the Hill of Slane, of Ireland's first-ever Pascal fire. Apart of course, from many shorter pieces of an intense lyricism, inspired by one or other or all of the chosen nine: Could I into that silent shrine advance, to where the sacred flame makes all things plain, what joy were mine to find engraven there my name.

— Good healthy walks, said Miss Kerrigan. But don't overdo it. Think of your back and all that lying down and standing up for ordination.

She was right: I mean about the thinking long. For I had now an interest in life outside myself, and was more anxious that Eunan should find his woman, and find engraven there his name, than he was himself. He had nothing: my hoard or pocket of nine nurses was in Dublin beyond the mountains, I could afford to be generous. For to be afflicted by desire for hoaching Scottish lasses, and yet not be able to say a blessed preliminary word to any one of them must have been pain beyond pain. Once in a while he would whisper, spluttering sideways into my ear, gripping my bicep hard enough to hurt, as if he were trying to hold himself back from leaping on the lady there and then: That one, Bernard. That's the ticket. God, it would be something to give her a run for it in the sandhills.

Nearly always the desired one was pale, golden-haired, prim, modestly dressed and an obvious member of the Children of Mary. This puzzled me for a while until I realized sadly that

Eunan, perhaps subconsciously, was attracted to young women whose appearance would please the parish priest. When I managed to put chat on one of these votaresses Eunan was no help at all: arms dangling, mouth like a vice, gaze at a tangent – towards the breakers, or the bulk of Truskmore concealing Ben Bulben, or the cliffs of Slieve League across the bay. So there was nothing for it but the Palais de Danse where not even a shy buck like Eunan would have a chance of escape, for far and wide the place was notorious for frenzied women. Even the boom-thump-boom-thump-boom of it, echoing night after night from the sea to the hills and back again was the cause of protests and letters to the local paper.

— See it, Eunan, you must. If you went back to Glenties and said you'd never seen the inside of the palais they'd laugh at you. They'd do worse. They'd worry about you.

The palais had also the name for being a rough class of a place. There was a long-nosed man I knew from my own town, who kept the entire works of Edgar Wallace in a tin trunk under his bed, and had got mildly drunk one night in the palais and had bones broken by the gorillas. Not a word of this did I tell to Eunan, he was nervous enough as it was, nor was I all that happy myself: shiny tight black suit and creaking back-splint smelling like horseharness weren't exactly standard equipment for the palais. What would I say to the first girl who put her arm around me to convince her that I wasn't made of leather or wood, or about to perish with a petrifying disease?

We crossed the strand. A mist-swollen moon was coming up slowly from behind Truskmore. The surf shone, the cliff-shadows were jet-black on the sand, the small stream that dribbled across the strand was silver. The glaring lights, the boom-thump-boom of the palais were sacrilege. Restive Eunan at any moment might turn and bolt like a colt running from harness and, if he did, I'd have no power to halt him. For now that I was face-to-face with the palais I was damned near as nervous as he was, and not much more of a man of the world. Nearer and nearer. The entering crowd shuffled around a doorway guarded by

the two gorillas who had beaten up the long-nosed devotee of
Edgar Wallace. The lights were blinding, the noise deafening.
Eunan was moving more slowly, had, indeed, almost come to
a halt, when a woman's voice said clearly into my ear: Is it
going to say Mass you are, your reverence? Or has somebody
had a sudden heart-attack?

It was the laughing girl. She was still laughing. So was her
sister. They were linked, and leaning against each other with
unaffected gaiety.

— It's no place for a clerical student, the elder sister said.

— An ex-clerical student.

— A clerical error, then.

They laughed fit to fall at the ancient joke and I couldn't
but laugh with them, while Eunan stood there as stiff as my
back-splint.

— There was a fight in there already, she said.

The younger sister, as I recall, never spoke, but only laughed.

— Drunken animals. The civic guards took away two that
you couldn't see for blood.

She took my arm: Let's go for a walk to Tullaghan. There's
a lovely moon.

Tullaghan was two miles to the side of the town away
from the Fairy Bridges and my four-cornered wooden shelter.
A concrete pathway led along the tops of low cliffs, the sea to
the right, quiet residential hotels to the left. Beyond the rock
bathing-pool that was reserved for nuns the hotels ended and
there was nothing but grass, grey-white under the moon, and
the moon shining on the water.

— I'm Ellen, she said. That there behind is Madge, my
sister. We'd be twins only she's two years younger.

Behind us in the salty moonlight Madge was laughing
gently but continuously, Eunan wasn't making even a grunt,
and it was a wonder to God to me that he had come walking
at all: except to escape from the more certain horrors of the
palais.

— She's very like you. Except that she laughs more.

— We both laugh a lot. But Madge laughs more because she's shy.

— She's in proper company this blessed night.

— He does look shy, too. Where's he from?

— The hills of Donegal.

— All night and day I'm dreaming, she sang, of the hills of Donegal.

Then she said: We're from the meadows of Fermanagh, from Lisbellaw.

Lisbellaw I knew, as I knew even then the half of Ireland: Lisbellaw, and the sleepy lake shore and grass meadows all around. The map shows a filigree pattern of blue, Upper Lough Erne, on a field of flat green: restful country, quiet towns, little harbours with long names where you could idle away ten life-times fishing spoon or spinning minnow for pike and perch and bream. It made me warm to her right away that she came from a countryside meant for laziness or, since I was literary then, lotus-eating. She swung easily on my arm, and sometimes went one, two, three and a one, two, three on the tips of her toes as if she were readying to dance the Walls of Limerick. So I slipped my arm around her waist and felt like the hell of an ex-cleric, and hoped I was giving good example to Eunan lumbering along behind us.

She was wearing a green sort of dress, not a raincoat as when she had first surfaced in the place of the one-armed bandits. She had a small golden-coloured harp as a clasp at the cleavage, no beret, her dark hair dry and shampoo-shiny, and held in place by a golden-coloured snood; nor did she smell of peat smoke as it was generally said that rural beauties did. Thus, we came to the old square tower that guards the eel-weir at Bundrowes, where the Drowes, which is a magic river, meets the sea, and all the wonder of Tullaghan Strand was before us: no ordinary level of sand where people went bathing, but rank upon rank of oval stones that the sea had shaped. They shone, between salt and moonshine, like gigantic jewels. All along the country roads out of Bundoran, into Donegal and Leitrim and

Sligo, you could see Tullaghan stones painted all colours and making borders for beds in flower gardens.

Ellen and myself sat in the shadow of the tower and looked out on the flashing Drowes where the trout have the gizzards of chickens because of a miracle performed by a saint back there at Lough Melvin where the river comes from. She said that when she and Madge went back to Lisbellaw they'd take Tullaghan stones with them, and paint them striped, and keep them as souvenirs of this lovely night. That set us kissing and grappling merrily in the shadows. When we came up for air she asked: Where are they?

Oh, there they were, sure enough, not rolling on the grass or wrestling in the shadows but standing 50 yards from us on the bank of the Drowes, and five yards from each other: Eunan, a dark statue, arms by its side, that looked as if it had been there as long as the tower. They were too far away for us to hear if Madge were still laughing. Since there was nothing, short of roping them together, that we could do about it, we kissed and grappled again and when we had surfaced again they were exactly as we had last seen them, enchanted to stone by magic river and sea and moon. Ellen breathed a long breath and slowly let it loose again. She said: They'd never credit it in Lisbellaw.

— Ellen, I know a song about Lisbellaw.

— Sing it, for God's sake.

— It's in Irish.

— Sing it in Irish.

So I sang in Irish the verse that mentions Lisbellaw.

— What does it mean?

— Something like this: I met a fairy woman down at Lisbellaw and asked her would any key unlock the lock of love. In low and kind and gentle voice she answered me: When love locks the heart the lock will never be loosened.

— It would be grand, she said, but I doubt if it's true.

We kissed again, quietly and without grappling. She stood up and smoothed down the green dress and said we'd better walk home before Madge froze to death or leaped in the Drowes for lack of anything better to do.

The fighting was over for the night in the Palais de Danse. The long moonlit town, painted all colours for the holiday season, was asleep, it seemed, and silent, except that you could guess that here and there and everywhere it was still a holiday and the fun was going on. We left the sisters at the door of their boarding-house. Because of Eunan, or rather because of Madge, I forbore kissing Ellen good-night, but she understood, and gripped my hand hard, and dug her nails into my palm, and said we'd meet tomorrow night by the hobby-horses, and hoped that the moon would be out again.

Eunan and myself walked wordless home along the bright empty street. It wasn't until we were at Miss Kerrigan's door that he spoke: Bernard, she had a very hard hand.

I said nothing.

— That one, Bernard, was laughing at me all night.

— Not at you, Eunan. She was laughing because she's young and on her holidays.

After a while I added: And walking out with a young man by the bright silvery light of the moon.

— Bernard, ever since the first day I went to school country girls have been laughing at me.

Up in my silent room I couldn't even read myself to sleep, feeling sorrier then for lonely Eunan than out at Tullaghan I had felt for laughing Madge.

The morn was breaking fresh and fair and the lark sang in the sky, and it was as lovely a day as you would expect after such a night of moonlight. Eunan and myself walked like automatons across the strand. What, I asked myself, are the wild waves saying, for Eunan hadn't a word to throw to land or ocean, nor could I think of anything to say that wouldn't make the poor man more miserable than he obviously was already. In sad silence we came to the two high flights of wooden steps that went up from a moist cliff-shadowed corner of the strand to the top of Roguey. Eunan climbed up ahead of me – as blithely as a man climbing to the scaffold. He had his pinstripe on and his trousers, God help me, seemed to have shrunk. Up above us there was music and dancing and singing voices. The local branch of the Gaelic League kept an open-air dancing-floor at that point on the clifftop, and all day long, Maryanne, weather permitting, the young people were at it hammer and tongs: slip jig and hornpipe and fourteen-hand reel, the Walls of Limerick, the Waves of Tory, Saddle the Pony, the Mason's Apron and the Chaffpool Post. It was such a lively place and such a beautiful morning. Far out, wisps of mist drifted over dark-blue unbroken water. There was autumn in the air. The flat-topped mountains were still hidden. Because of the noise of the music and dancing the cries from the strand were inaudible, so that the silent movements of the people on the edge of the surf, and of the donkeys and the baby elephant, seemed completely senseless. White mist, too, drifted in bundles over the golf-links, and the clockwork figures stepping out of the mist, vanishing into it again were crazily comic.

It was part of the mood of the morning that I should at that moment see the blonde and purple woman, 50 yards away, higher up the slope on the path to the Fairy Bridges. She sat quite close to the cliff's edge. She waved and I waved in return.

— Who is that? says Eunan.

— What we're after, Eunan. Scottish and glamorous. Look at that purple dress, that blonde hair.

The blonde hair shone in the morning. She waved again.

— That there's no laughing country girl, Eunan. Perfume, I'd say, that would flatten a regiment. If there was a wind this morning we'd get the perfume already.

Side-by-side, keeping step, we advanced up the slope. Behind us the dancing and music went on as if we never had been. His big feet beside me were no longer flopping in brothel creepers but solid and determined in square-toed black shoes. The woman was reading a book, her head turned away from us. At 60 paces it was clear that I had been right about the perfume.

— Good-morning, I said.

It was an irreproachable and perfectly accurate remark.

She turned her head and looked at us and said: To whom have I the honour of speaking?

It wasn't that she was old: remembering her now I suppose she couldn't have been more than 60. She wore red shoes and purple stockings, and her short purple dress, tucked up to allow her to squat in comfort, showed fat knees with pads of surplus flesh to the insides of the kneecaps. It wasn't that she was ugly. It was the desperate effort to defeat ugliness that made me feel that life could be a losing battle. She wore a loose purple jacket about as long as the dress, and a striped blouse – I can't remember the colour of the stripes – and a foamy sort of syllabubbly chiffon scarf emerging from the neckline of the dress, which was cut like a schoolgirl's gym-frock. That now was what she wore, for she was the sort of woman that you looked first at the radiant clothes before you came face to face with her face. On her left hand she seemed to wear two wedding rings and an engagement ring and a keeper. She had fine plump hands. But the face was a mask, with long false lashes and, below the eyes, radiating black streaks that looked as if they had been done with a sharp knife dipped in cobbler's dye. The eyes, which were not unkind, moved almost audibly when they moved at all. It wasn't that we were disappointed in her, it was my awful feeling that she too had her dreams and that the pair of us did not fulfil them.

Her voice, I will confess, was a little shrill and she had, in so far as I could judge, a Lancashire way of speaking which is fine in its own way but you want to know English very well to keep up with it. To this day I can see her quite clearly, apart from the colours of the stripes in her blouse, and I remember her with interest and a great curiosity. I can even hear her talking – about her husband who was coming to Bundoran to join her. She was a fit rival for the mysterious Atlantic which was at that moment her background: oceans of woman, all waiting for daring young mariners.

But Eunan, like Bishop Berkeley, thought otherwise. He was already ten yards away and moving fast while I was preparing to squat beside her, even though squatting in a back-splint was a trick that took some rehearsing.

— My husband, she said, had a special sort of tandem bicycle built all to his own specifications. We frequently take trips on it.

At least that's what I thought she said. But what between the Lancashire accent and the state of confusion in which Eunan's retreat left me, I could have imagined the words: they didn't seem very likely. There he went, his arms stiff as logs, his trouser-bottoms halfways to his knees.

— What's wrong with your friend? she said. Was he short-taken?

She laughed fit to frighten the gulls and, since I couldn't think of anything to say and couldn't laugh with her, I fled. Her laughter followed me. My back-splint seemed to have slipped its moorings, but that also was imagination. Truskmore was pushing one jagged rocky shoulder out of the mist. Come and cover me, oh mist, hide me from that laughter, and hell run away with Eunan McAtavey who could at least have stood his ground until, with dignity, we retreated together. But when I came on him in the crowd by the dancing-floor he looked so hapless that I could find no word of reproach.

— An error of judgement, Eunan, I said, She looked all right from a distance.

— They all do.

The dancers were having the time of their lives. Nobody paid the least attention to us.

— That's the sort of woman, he said, that you're warned against in the catechism.

— You're from a different diocese, Eunan. The catechism where I came from never mentioned the likes of her.

— She was mentioned somewhere if it wasn't in the catechism.

We walked on by the freshwater spring and the Fairy Bridges and the four-cornered shelter in which, to my annoyance, there was a young couple holding hands and gazing out to sea: Head out to sea when on your lee the breakers you discern. Oh, adieu to all the billowy coasts.

We crossed Tullan Strand with its gulls and curlews, and crossed the sand-dunes and walked the long street to Lios na Mara and didn't swap a word all the way. Up in my room I opened my neglected books, took notebook and pencil and set to the reading: this was my business, I was a frost and a failure as a man of the world and, as a pimp, quite preposterous. He was so silent at lunch and again at high tea, ham salad, that I knew Miss Kerrigan and my mother thought we had had a row, but were too polite to say anything about it; and that night there was no moon and no Eunan.

The morning mist had dissolved into mizzling rain. He hadn't even told Miss Kerrigan that he was going. Without any feeling in her voice my mother said: I hope you weren't rude to him. He was so shy.

The lights around the hurdy-gurdies were bleary weeping eyes. The hobby-horses, riderless, went round a few times, then halted hopelessly, and their music stopped and there was no sound between the sea and the mountains but the boom-thump-boom of the palais. I wore a heavy black cloth coat and a black hat and looked, Ellen said, like a parish priest on the run. With a rain-coated girl on each arm I walked as far as the four-cornered shelter. The weather was telling us that the holidays were over and that everything came to an end.

— He ran away from us, Ellen said. He was afraid of the fairy women of Lisbellaw.

When I told them about the purple blonde on the clifftop they laughed for ten minutes, and went on laughing at the idea of Eunan, suitcase in hand, legging it back to the mountainy safety of the Vale of Dibbin. In the four-cornered shelter I profited by his absence and made gentle love to the two of them. Oh, it was all very harmless: running from one corner to another, grappling, kissing, with two girls who couldn't stop laughing; discovering that shy Madge was far and away the more ardent of the two. We walked back through rising wind that blew the clamour of the palais off towards Lough Melvin. The town was a long line of weeping lights. When we came as far as the hobby-horses, the music – although the animals were at rest – was playing about the old rustic bridge by the mill, and Ellen and Madge sang:

> But one day we parted in pain and regret,
> Our vows then we could not fulfill.

— Too true, Ellen said, We're off tomorrow.
— But you'll write, Madge said.
— And we'll meet again next year, Ellen said.
— Maybe, said Madge, you might come to see us in Lisbellaw.
Although I meant to write, I never did: Dublin and the nine, and other things, distracted me. The next year I wasn't in Bundoran; and although ten years later I passed briefly through Lisbellaw, there was another woman with me and I never even thought of Madge and Ellen. As I said, if it hadn't been for the ancient blonde on the green in Atlanta I'd never even have remembered Eunan.

A beautiful blonde girl sat in a chair and in the most queenly fashion allowed herself to be fitted with pink shoes. A serious youth; he couldn't have been more than eighteen, knelt at her feet and did the fitting. She was searching for a shoe of a colour that would match some detail in the dress she wore. Patiently the young fellow eased the dainty foot into shoe after shoe after shoe. We marvelled at his restraint.

— What, Gene said, is behind the American rape epidemic?
That had been a joke between us, not a very good one, ever since we had seen the question printed on the cover of a lurid magazine, and with it the picture of a man with billiard-ball eyes roping a buxom, and quite unconcerned, lady to a chair.

We were still guessing at answers, and watching the young
kneeling troubadour and the girl of the pink shoes, when Dolores
returned. We drove back to my place. The aged blonde was
gone from the green.

On that very day my mother was writing me a letter. That
sort of coincidence is common. For instance, on a day in a
college in Virginia when a student was asking me about a
friend of mine, a singer, he, in Chicago, was mailing me his
newest long-player.

My mother wrote:

Miss Kerrigan, whom you may recall, died recently and I
went to Bundoran to the funeral. May she rest in peace. She
was a dear woman, albeit a little eccentric, and thought the
world and all of you, and thought in her final doting days
that you were a priest and wondered why you never came
to see her. I always told her you were far away on the
foreign missions and that the Jesuits were very strict and
didn't allow you home often. It wasn't much of a lie, and
I feel that God and even the Jesuits would forgive me. She
prayed for you every night. But who should be at the funeral
only your companion of long ago, Eunan McAtavey, with his
wife and nine children, a car-load of them. They seemed very
happy. He was asking for you. He said he read everything
you wrote, in newspapers and even in books.

On what dusty lovely Donegal roadway, walking home from
school or Mass or market-day shopping, did he, or how did he,
manage to tell a girl that he loved her?

They seemed very happy, she said. He was asking for me.
He had read everything I had written. Ah well, his memory
was better than mine. He couldn't very well explain to my
mother and his wife why he ran, or what he ran, or thought he
was running, from. What ever became, I wonder, of the fairy
women of Lisbellaw?

# Your left foot
# is crazy

The stout man whose wife and two daughters run the school of ballroom-dancing doesn't sleep with his wife and tells me so almost every Monday and Thursday. Can I be the only man he confides in? He wears an expensive dark-brown suit with a darker stripe. And wide-toed, handsewn brown shoes. He is bald but with dark tufts at the ears. He has thick blackrimmed spectacles with golden arms, three rectangular perforations in each arm. All this gives him a scholarly appearance. He doesn't dance. He's the business manager. Or perhaps the clerk. His wife, stout and motherly but in an authoritative sort of way, doesn't dance but she supervises the dancing while he seldom or never puts a foot on the dancing-floor. He sits behind a desk in a sort of ante-room but it isn't too easy to see what exactly he does beyond just sitting behind the desk: he smokes, he reads, he shuffles sheets of paper with lists of names but the fees are paid in advance at the beginning of a season and paid to his wife on the dancing-floor after a brusque lecture about the rules of the Academy; the rules are brief, no booze, no big boots or hobnails, proper dancing pumps and formal clothes, no sweaters, no denims, this is a dancing academy not a shipyard, not tails exactly, although they're not prohibited, nor tuxedos nor claw-hammer coats or what you will, but respectable suits, preferably dark-brown or navy-blue and, for the ladies, long dresses not all the way to the waxed floor but well below the knee, no slacks, no summer shorts, no mini-skirts, no disorderly behaviour. This is a very civilized dancing-school.

Who is the maid on the dancing-floor, he hums to himself,

and since I know that song, which Sidney McEwan has sung so well, I can go on with the words in my mind and wonder what he's really thinking of and why he doesn't sleep with his wife. He never tells me why. Like foam on the wavetop, foam on the wavetop, who is the maid on the dancing-floor, who but the bride came sailing. Is that what's in his mind as he hums?

The two daughters demonstrate and teach, God of the dance do they demonstrate, and their two young men in impeccable tails to help them. The ante-room glitters with the cups the four of them have won in competitions in Ireland, England, Scotland, Wales and the Isle of Man. One of the daughters is a brunette who mostly wears whites and greens, the other, a blonde, favours pinks and mauves. Mostly they demonstrate tangoes because most of the cups are tributes to their undeniable ability to tango, but tangoes are very advanced stuff for students and far beyond the powers of Peter who dances as if he had two wooden legs or was a little snub-nosed bear doing his paces on a hot plate: and it is Peter's plight and his falling in love that have me in a dancing academy for the first and, I promise myself, the last time in my life. Tangoes are not for me, so I sit in the ante-room with the father of those female dervishes and he tells me that he doesn't sleep with his wife, but never tells me why or why not, and I tell him about Buckrambak who taught dancing in South Tyrone in the early part of the nineteenth century. We also talk about football and fishing and women. We are at the back part of the fourth floor of a corner-house on the quays above the Liffey. At the front the music plays and the dancers dance, and who are the maids on the dancing-floor? Nobody pays the least attention to us: nobody ever pays any attention, that I notice, to him, and my fees are paid for the term or season and nobody gives a fiddler's flute whether I tango or trot or fly through the air with the greatest of ease.

It was the time in the history of Europe when American troops in large numbers and in uniform appeared on the streets of

Dublin for the first and, so far, the only time. British soldiers did not so appear. Even, or especially, Irishmen in British uniform. Because of history? Because of the hardness of our hearts? But American troops were different. General Mark Clark was Irish, wasn't he? Most American troops were Irish, weren't they? This was Spencer Tracy and the Fighting 69th alive and well and walking about in Dublin. So they were to be seen all over the place and everybody was very glad to see them, and glad they were to be there to be seen, and glad that the war was over. Peter and myself used to watch them out of the high corner-window at which we spent a lot of our time. We were minor civil-servants, which is a nice way of putting it, and had an easy-going boss who spent a lot of his time in a pub across the street, the door of which was visible from the high window, so we sat and smoked and watched the door and the street and the traffic and the people, and the American troops because there were so many of them about, and one day Peter said: I want to dance. I must dance.

And I said: Dance and be damned and enjoy yourself. He's over in the pub.

And he said: But I can't put a foot under me.

Which in a way wasn't to be wondered at.

Peter was just out of a seminary, having made up his mind that he wasn't fit for martyrdom, red or white, on the foreign missions. Or had his mind made up for him: he was hesitant in speech and action. There are priests and nuns, postulants, neophytes and novices who can dance like David. Peter wasn't one of them. He had entered the seminary from a strict home where dancing had been discouraged. Dancing meant drink and women and dark corners. As well as which he wasn't made for dancing. To glide was not in his nature. He hopped. In a later style of dancing, if you could call it that, he might have managed. He was also shy: the strict home and the seminary had made their marks. A small snub-nosed man with close-cropped hair and a tight jacket.

The brass-ornamented swing-doors of the pub across the

street opened and our boss stepped out. A poet I know wrote
that ancient Celtic monks prayed in dark stone cells so that
when they came out into the sunlight they really knew whether
God was. He blinked. Rubbed his eyes. Stretched himself,
actually stretched himself, a senior civil servant, on the public
street, and yawned, then placed his right hand round or about
his navel and, I'd say, belched. We stubbed our cigarettes,
buttoned our jackets. Peter always had some difficulty with that
operation. Not because of corpulence but because the jacket,
brown tweed, must have predated the black, now discarded,
jacket or jackets he had worn in the seminary. We prepared
ourselves for our desks. But wait. He's not making a move to
cross the street towards the office. He's facing right, staring
with interest. Seeing God? He was a very stout man.

— Running on oil, Peter said.

Then into our field of vision, as they call it, came the tall,
strong, blackhaired whore, one of two wild-eyed sisters from
the County Roscommon who had taken off for town when they
heard of, or sensed, the passing of a part of the great army. By
her side and with his arm around her waist (a man may allow
himself a few liberties when away from his own home town:
that's a quotation) walked a tall, thin, blond, American soldier.
He looked shaken. Drink, perhaps, and a wild night with that
wild woman in one of the lodging-houses opposite the railway
station up the street. He could have been embracing her just
to keep himself from collapsing. Harder on him, I thought,
than the Battle of the Bulge. But, because of Peter, I didn't
say that out loud. She smiled at the boss. She and her sister
were friendly girls and had a wide acquaintance. He stood to
attention and gave a fair imitation of a military salute. Which
the soldier courteously returned. That must have cost him an
effort. They walked on out of our field of vision. He looked
after them and smiled at nothing and rubbed the back of his
head, then disappeared again through the swinging doors. We
lit two more cigarettes.

— Peter, I said, beware of the women.

— That's it. That's the trouble. The way it is I'm walking out with one of a set of twins and she dances.

— Let her dance with her twin.

— She's a girl, too.

— It has been known to happen. I'm told you see them at it in all the dance-halls.

— It's no joke. You've no notion how awkward I feel.

— I'll give your condition deep thought.

— If I take Brenda out Joan comes too. They link each other and smile sideways at me. Like meeting yourself twice in a mirror. If I was able to dance I'd get one of them on her own.

— Which is which?

— Brenda is which.

— You've no complaint. Two for the price of one.

— If you would help out.

— Anything for a friend.

— And if you'd come with me to a school of ballroom dancing, on the quiet like, not telling the twins, I want to surprise Brenda some night by taking her to a ballroom.

— And I'll surprise Joan.

— You're a friend indeed.

— Is a friend in need.

The boss resurfaced, looked east and west expecting another vision. Not finding one he began to cross the street. We went back to work.

From the far side of the river Liffey the Room or School of Ballroom Dancing, high in a fine red-brick building and with wide windows looks, in the dusk or the dark, like a garden of delights; coloured paper lampshades like kingsize concertinas, swaying, undulating shadow-shapes that must be something nobler than men and women, and, on warm evenings, the sound of music on the water.

— An oriental garden, I say.

We are very young. We lean with our backs against the

parapet of the bridge and look up at the coloured windows, the dancing shadows, and he sings, a daring song for a modest man: There's a soldier in the garden and with him I will run for my heart's filled with pleasure and I won't be a nun, I won't be a nun and I shan't be a nun . . .

— They wouldn't have you, one of the girls says. You're the wrong shape.

They have come up beside us, crossing the bridge on their way to the tango which they are quite capable of performing in a robust, rural fashion. They are not the twins nor yet the wild sisters, the courtesans from Roscommon. They most certainly do not look like twins, they are not even sisters and one of them comes from Ballyvourney in West Cork, and the other from Nenagh in Tipperary. They dance together when they feel like it, although not quite with the approval of the lady of the house. But they'll dance with anybody and they dance well, would even dare to match their style with the two elegant boyfriends of the beautiful dervishes: and why they bother coming to the school at all we cannot well make out. One is small and dark and round as a pudding, a very tasty pudding. The other tall and redheaded and you'd see her if you closed your eyes and for a long time after, and that evening on the bridge she says to me: Why don't you dance? I'd like to dance with you. I fancy you.

Admittedly, that's flattering. But somewhat to the amazement of Peter, who has never heard the story before, I tell her about the broken ankle that has never properly set; limp a little to prove it too as we climb the stairs and the beat of the music grows louder. It's a lie, not the music but the spiel about the ankle. Because even from Peter I have to conceal that I know as much about the theory of dancing as he does, and as for the practice . . . Well in that as in other things I may be a disgrace to my family, for while they are all elegant dancers I'm no better at it than the renowned Clarence McFadden who, in a song my mother used to sing, went to a dancing-academy to study the waltz: One, two, three, come balance like me, you're a fairy but you have your faults. When your right foot is lazy your left one is crazy, but don't be unaisy I'll larn you to waltz.

And in the summer Gaelic College in the Rosses of Donegal the whirls and thuds of the dusty stampedes of the Irish dances, the Walls of Limerick, the Siege of Ennis, the High Caul Cap, have simply made me dizzy, when I had the nerve to join them at all: so that my talks with the good man who never tells me why he doesn't sleep with his wife are for me a refuge and a haven. They keep me from being out on that there waxy floor making a bloody fool of myself. On which dangerous floor the daughters and the boy friends go round and round like seraphim on the wing and sway backward and forward like the saplings bent double by the gale when the wood is in trouble on Wenlock Edge.

We get on splendidly together. He seems to be happy when we talk and, because of that, his wife who is kindly, if authoritative, leaves both of us at peace and, as Dr. Johnson might have put it, compels me to no gyrations. That is, doesn't force me to dance nor try to, and I am at ease. Or was until the tall redhead told me she fancied me. Her company would be most desirable. But, oh God, at what a price: and inside the dance goes on and outside the two of us sit, heads together, cigarette smoke rising, two veterans in an ingle talking of lost wars.

— I'm going to write a book, I tell him, about William Carleton. He wrote novels in the nineteenth century.

To write that book is my honest intention.

— Bully for you, he says. I look forward to reading it. Why Carleton, more than anybody else?

— Well for one thing he was a novelist and so am I. I mean I will be.

— 'Tis in reversion that you do possess.

The quotation takes the harm out of it. We roar laughter into our cloud of smoke. It is an odd place for Shakespeare, or perhaps it isn't. Beatrice was born under a dancing star.

The tall redhead who fancies me comes out from the music
and movement of the inner room, stands in the doorway and
looks at us for a while, then says to us that some people have
all the fun.

— Join us, he says, and make the fun better.

She does. That doesn't make me teetotally happy. She has
told me that she fancies me and she's lovely to look at: it's
the sort of thing that sooner or later affects a young fellow.
But to respond to her may mean that I'll end up in agony
out there on the slippery floor and, unlike Peter, I am not as
yet goaded on by the desperation of love.

— For another thing, he came from Tyrone and so do I.

She asks me who I'm talking about but with the din from
the dancing-floor I can pretend not to hear her and still be
polite.

— For a third thing, I was as good as reared on him.
I'm deeply devoted to him and his people. They're my own
people, not much changed over a century.

Looking at his most professorial, he says that that's the
best reason yet: and again she asks me who I'm talking
about. This time I allow myself to hear her. The flattery
of her open-mouthed interest is pleasant. Not open-mouthed
exactly. She's too beautiful to gape. Just lips a little moist and
slightly parted. Othello felt the way I feel, in the early stages
that is, when he charmed her ears and all with tales of antres
vast and deserts idle, and cannibals that eat each other, the
Anthropophagi, and men whose heads do grow beneath their
shoulders. But look, oh Lord, where the flattery of an open-
mouthed attention led Othello.

— And one of the great experiences of my early boyhood
was to read his novel *Fardorougha the Miser* in serial form in
the *Ulster Herald*. It was more exciting to read it that way.
You had to wait a week for the next movement. As people
used to wait for the next of Dickens.

She blinks a little: well, I am talking to impress. A civil
servant can be as learned and literary as any professor and,

moreover, it is my intention, when I have enough money stashed, to get out of that job and back to college.

— And one of the funniest characters he ever wrote about was a teacher of ballroom-dancing. Buckramback. That was his name.

— Buckramback, he says. Fancy that.

He laughs until he chokes and coughs and has to take off his glasses to wipe his eyes.

What, I wonder, is he thinking of.

— But Buckramback, she says, that's a comical name.

Thereafter there's a fourth person with us while, with the help of William Carleton, I try to explain to them about Buckramback, to set him curtseying and prancing on the floor before us: while inside the music sounds and the tango goes round and round and Peter hops and hops towards the wild moment when he will have Brenda cut off from the herd and all on his very own.

— They called him Buckramback because he had been for a time a drummer in the British Army. He didn't like soldiering. He deserted so often and was caught so often and flogged so often that his back was cartaliginous. As hard as buckram, that is.

But they know what I mean.

— He was a dapper light little fellow with a Tipperary accent crossed by a lofty strain of illegitimate English he had picked up in the army.

— Tipperary, she hums, never more will I roam from my dear native home, Tipperary, so far away.

He compliments her on her singing voice and she is obviously pleased: he has such a way of humouring the ladies that it's a continual wonder to me why he doesn't sleep with his wife: she's not as young as she used to be but she goes out and round in all the right places. And is well perfumed.

— He wore tight secondhand clothes, shabby-genteel, and his face was as secondhand and tight-skinned and wrinkled as his clothes. And tight breeches, and high, brightly-polished high boots, also cracked, and white stockings, and a tall hat and coloured gloves: and small as he was he would take on to fight any man. But he was also and always a gentleman to the ladies.

— The image of yourself, she says.

And sounds as if she means it, the bit, that is, about being a gentleman to the ladies, and I try not too well to pretend that I haven't heard.

— He kept his dancing-school in a roadside cabin, and the country-girls around him in all their frocks and ribbons, and the young fellows in knee-breeches and green-tailed coats.

— Like a postcard for St. Patrick's Day, she says, Paddy and the pig, and the pig running wild and twisting the rope round Paddy's legs.

— But dancing was the least part of what Buckramback had to teach. He could teach the country boys and girls how to enter a drawingroom in the most fashionable manner alive. They that never saw or would see a drawingroom.

— You never know, she says. You should see me at work. Even if it's not my own drawingroom.

— He taught the whole art of courtship with all the politeness and success as it was practised in Paris during the last season.

She says that she would give her heart and soul to see Paris and Gene Kelly and Leslie Caron and all the dancing. And singing.

— And how to write valentines and love-letters as Napoleon wrote them to his wife or his two wives.

He says that Buckramback would be a useful little man to have about any well-ordered house: and, if I hadn't been swept away by my own eloquence and learning and the elation of owning an audience, I would have known that the mention of valentines would set her humming: I'll be your sweetheart if you will be mine.

— And teach the ladies how to curchy and the young gentlemen how to shiloote the ladies.

Curchy, she knew, was curtsey.

— But shiloote, she says. Did he mean salute? I've heard old countrymen say shiloote.

— He meant salute.

— Like soldiers in the army. All present and correct.

She stands up, our four eyes fixed on her, and performs in a way to warm the heart of any sergeant-major, or any other man.

— No, he meant kissing. To shiloote was to kiss.

— Amo, amas, amat he says. Followed by osculo, osculas, osculat. Or perhaps osculo comes before amo.

— Amo I know, she says. L'amour.

Her eyes glow. This is perilous country. This could lead me out there, and in the company of this maid, to the dancing-floor where she, but not her spavindy partner, would move like foam on the wavetop, foam on the wavetop.

In my secret and poltroon's heart I knew that I wanted to be her partner. But not out there under coloured lights, in jostling crowds and perpetual motion, and contrasting comically with the prizewinning boyfriends. Or even with Peter who must by now be picking up something. The shadows I craved, green secrecy and silence: and I didn't need a man who didn't sleep with his wife to tell me (which he politely did when she had left us for a while to do a routine tango with her tasty pudding of a friend), didn't need him to tell me, I repeat, that it was an odd way to make love to a girl, to talk on and on about a character from an author dead and at rest in Mount Jerome cemetery for the better part of a century. And what young fellow in love was ever afraid to go dancing with the loved one? The primitive country-boys in caubeens, knee-breeches and green-tailed coats, were more daring. Clarence McFadden, awkward and all, was a better man than I was: he tried. Peter was a better man: he was trying. And this was the middle of the twentieth century and the streets full of heroes returning from an ended war: and faint heart never won, and all the rest of it. My friend and confidant was kindly and fatherly. It wasn't in him to be otherwise. But in the cloud of smoke that bound us together he was concerned and critical. It would have been no satisfaction to me, even if I had had the gall to do it, to *tu quoque* him and tell him that he didn't even sleep etc. For my own good he was talking, I knew. He was telling the truth. At every stage of development or decline, love, it occurred to me, had its special problems.

But I want to tell you about the twins, Peter's twins. Brenda and Joan.

They lived in Donnybrook in a quiet side-street of bay-windowed houses built at the turn of the century out of good red brick from Somerset. The Joycean ship that came into Dublin out of Bridgewater with bricks carried across the Irish Sea the walls of most of those houses. The side-street led to, still leads to, the beauty of Herbert Park. So on a bright Sunday morning after Mass the four of us met for the first time between the lake and the bandstand in the corner of the park by the Ballsbridge bakery wall. All very pure and proper, and shaded and pleasantly fanned by noble trees: the faint odour of fresh bread an added intimacy. The band would not be out until the afternoon.

It was the season in which the ducks walked the grass, parading their ducklings. Two Muscovy ducks, like boozed geese with the whiskey-drinker's crimson horse's-collar round their necks, stood on the concrete rim of a small leafy island and scowled at the water and the world. They always kept the same place and everybody, the other ducks I mean, left them alone. They looked both dirty and dangerous.

One of them affected, as we'd have said in another century, bright colours. I'm talking now about the twins. The other went abroad in more demure shades. Brenda was the bright one. They were handsome girls, both of them: if one was the other almost had to be. They spoke well, the good, clear, unaccented (almost) English of the Dublin middle-class: as in Bernard Shaw. They had dark-blue berets and brown eyes that were always smiling. They were good-humoured but never laughed out loud, not, at any rate, while we were with them. They were self-assured, capable I'd say, good managers, good housekeepers, the pride and joy of their parents, and right-away I could see how they had Peter rattled. One of them would have rattled a veteran. Two was, or were, by much too much or too many.

Twice round the entire park we walked slowly. That, roughly, would be three miles.

First we headed north across the lime-lined road that cuts the park into two portions. By the happy corner where there's a toy railway for children, seesaws, a long-armed tree that God grew to pleasure pygmy climbers. By the back of the tennis-courts: where, out of respect for Peter's pure passion, I looked ahead, keeping my eyes from the strong thighs of the girls leaping about in short skirts. Brenda went on Peter's arm, Joan went on mine, and with such military force and precision that those who met with us were forced unto the grass. By the bowling-green where stout ladies and elderly gentlemen in white peaked caps were doing the Francis Drake. Where do they come from, the good people who join bowling-clubs? Four-deep, we looked at them over the precisely clipped hedge and I made the inevitable remark about my bias running against the bowl, then had to explain what the hell I was talking about.

Diagonalwise across grass that was half-white with fluff from the maples. Back again across the dividing roadway and along a pillared walk that showed us the splendid planned vista of the lake. All around the sporting-grounds where roaring youths were enraged at soccer, Gaelic football and hurling. In another happy corner there was a whirligig for children, and chutes, and twenty little girls on twenty swings were rising and falling in rhythm and singing the same chirping song. To our right was the river Dodder, then high trees and big houses and, a few miles away, the blue Dublin-Wicklow mountains to which,

Peter wildly proposed, we would some Sunday go cycling. But also cunningly: it isn't so easy to maintain on bicycles the four-deep flying formation. Somewhere in Wicklow heather he meant to have his will, whatever it was.

But back for now to the empty bandstand and the corner by the Ballsbridge bakery wall. Then round the course once again, clockwise, except that the second time round we didn't stop to look over the hedge at the bowlers and I did peep sideways at the stout thighs of the girls playing tennis: as I was riding on the outside, if you follow me, and could pretend to be looking at Peter who was hugging the rails. Four deep all the time. Four at a table we had poisonous coffee at a lounge-bar in Ballsbridge. Then Peter and myself took a bus into town. The two young ladies walked home across the park. Because their parents mightn't like to see them escorted home so early on a Sunday morning. Better, I savagely thought, than late and drunk on a Saturday night. Not one word can I now remember that anybody said on the walk or at the coffee-table. Nor could remember even on the very next day. Apart from that bit about the bias and the bowl.

Only pity kept me from telling Peter what I thought. Only sheer force of friendship brought me out again on safari: second-time to a cinema where we sat four abreast and no scuffling took place. Chocolates were consumed. The twins didn't smoke and didn't fancy the smell of smoke. There was much whispering and crinkling of tinfoil. An elderly gentleman in the row in front asked us, loudly, to be quiet, and the usherette shone her lamp on the elderly gentleman and asked him to be quiet, and voices all over the place asked everybody else to be quiet: this was long before the days when cinemas became so infested with riotous ten-year-olds that you couldn't even hear the uproar of Star Wars.

Afterwards, we had coffee and sweet-cakes in a green-walled green-carpeted restaurant where I knew all the waitresses: principally Josie who was tall, wide-mouthed, most affable always to me; and Marie who was only gorgeous and had a married lover who wore a fur-coat and walked the streets leading a big dog on a silver chain. Something odd about chaps who wear fur-coats and lead big dogs on silver chains. He and the dog came in that evening and were introduced to Peter and the twins. Who liked style and dogs. Who were so impressed that on the way home we walked two-by-two at a distance of almost twenty paces. And hand-in-hand. Peter held Brenda's hand. Joan held my hand. My heart, I now knew, was elsewhere. Off the bus at Ballsbridge. Along the river-walk to Donnybrook. The Dodder, ten feet below us, whispered of all sorts of things.

To Joan I told how somewhere in the mountains and along the upper waters of that river, perhaps in Glenasmole or the Glen of the Thrushes, might be the spot where, in mythology, had stood the hostelry of Da Derga. How the King, Conaire the good, had been murdered there by Irish outlaws and marauding sea-rovers: and the hostelry burnt. How the murdering marauders or the marauding murderers had camped on Lambay island and sailed in, under darkness, to Merrion or Sandymount strand where James Joyce had set Stephen Dedalus walking between the markings of high and low tide. How Conaire went to his doom because he had had the ill-luck on the way to the hostelry to break all his geasa or taboos. How one of those geasa was: Do not let two reds [redheads] go before you to the house of a red.

She listened with exemplary, if obvious, patience. Some-where else, I said to myself, and to the sound of music and dancing, I would find a livelier, more lovable listener for one of the greatest of all stories. Yet that thing about the taboo got to wherever her head was. She repeated it over and over again: Do not let two reds go before you to the house of a red.

We leaned against the park railings, the park closed and the dark behind us. Across the narrow water great trees stood up like clouds: the lights of the mansions on Anglesea Road shone through them. Music came to us over the water from the dance-pavilion in the grounds of the rugby-football club.

We whispered and kissed. Peter kissed Brenda: believe it or not but I saw him at it. Joan kissed me and I kissed her in return: fair's fair. The thin red line had been broken by the symbolism of a man in a fur-coat, with a gorgeous, only gorgeous, mistress, and a big dog on a silver chain.

On the Dodder bridge at Donnybrook Peter stood as proud as a turkey-cock, and said: Have the rothar [bicycle] oiled for next Sunday. We're off for the mountains. Brenda wants to see the Devil's Glen.

Looking out of high city-windows any more you don't see as much as you used to, for the odd reason that the streets and sidewalks are more crowded. More people, in Dublin at any rate, more cars, too much wood, fewer distinctive trees. People I saw then from our spy-window and smoking-room I can see quite clearly to this day. As well as that there was a darkhaired young woman who worked in our office: lonely, hollow-cheeked, slightly sallow but lovely, who sometimes when the boss was across in the pub used to stand with us at the window and, while we smoked, sip tea. A cup held delicately between finger and thumb, never a saucer, and we never saw her brew the tea nor knew where. She brooded. She was mysterious. She went away to be a nun and it pains me still to think that, in her presence and all unwittingly, Peter used to sing his daring song: There's a soldier in the garden, etc.

His daring song! Far below us the soldiers from the war returning walked up and down. She sipped her tea and talked little and was one of those people I can see as clearly now as I did then.

Gobnait, the red, comes out to us. She is flushed from the dance. Through rings of smoke like the rings round Saturn we contemplate her beauty. She is, I am now convinced, the most beautiful woman I have ever seen. She is called Gobnait because, as I've said, she comes from Ballyvourney and that odd name (say it with a vee) is the name of the patron saint of that place: a consecrated virgin, Gobnait of the Bees, who cooled the ardour of a chieftain, who would have explored her virginity, by unleashing at him a hive of honeybees: sweets to the sweet, farewell. She stands in stone, cut by the great sculptor Seamus Murphy, above the holy well at that place, and bees, cut in stone, circle forever around her chaste feet.

Gobnait knows all about Gobnait and can stand still and mime the statue and with pursed lips make a noise so like swarming bees that you'd run for cover. Nobody but a born actress could compress such a mouth to a thin colourless line. Through the smoke two sour chieftains look at her and, speaking for myself, lust and wonder: foam on the wavetop, foam on the wavetop. Her tasty plump little pudding of a friend sits at a distance and is clearly very happy. She's a jolly girl, would be most attractive if Gobnait were not standing there and the bees buzzing around her. They are very fond of each other, Gobnait and the jolly girl.

Gobnait has absorbed every word I've said about Buckramback. One evening she mimes him. It's uncanny, even a little alarming, how a tall redhead with so much about her that you can't take your eyes off even when your eyes are shut, can become a dapper light little fellow with secondhand clothes, shabby-genteel, tight breeches, brightly-polished high boots, white stockings, a tall hat, coloured gloves. She bows and scrapes to the ladies and in a roadside cabin, long-gone, kisses laughing rural beauties, long-dead. He lilts: One two three, come balance like me.

She, or Buckramback or Clarence McFadden, waltzes to the lilting. Marcel Marceau himself couldn't do better. The music in the inner room has ceased. Peter is standing in the doorway mopping his brow. Behind him the crowd is gathering, even the motherly lady herself and the dervishes and their boyfriends, tails and all: and when the lilting and miming stop, the applause and laughter begin, and one of the boyfriends waltzes Gobnait round the room, her hair flying. For the only time in my life I feel weak and sick because I'm a disgrace to a family who are all good dancers.

Peter and myself walk Gobnait and her friend to the last Enniskerry bus. They work in a big house there and that's twelve miles away. There's no time for coffee in the green restaurant. She takes my arm, holds it close to her, she is very warm and my knees are weak. She says: I'd love to have seen him. Buckramback. I'd love to have gone to those dancing classes.

So I tell her that while I'm not able to enable her to see Buckramback I can bring her and her friend some Thursday afternoon, which is afternoon-off for domestics, to the national gallery to show her the portrait of the man who created or remembered Buckramback. The friend's name is Pauline which I don't know until that moment. She is one of those amiable girls who didn't seem to need a name: I ask her also to come to the gallery because through sudden fright I crave the safety of numbers. In contrast to Peter.

It is the first time that I have looked real love in the face.

When the last bus has gone off towards Enniskerry and the dark mountains Peter says to me: Tonight I danced my first tango.

Christ keep Brenda when he gets her in the mountains, and if he finds her in the glen her blood will stain the heather.

No, we never did get as far as the Devil's Glen. It was a windy day with showers blowing up all the way from Ballyvourney, a place I now thought of all the time. No matter in what direction you faced, that wind was against you. Cycling was slavery. The best we could do was make the secrecy of Calary lake to the right of the high road from Enniskerry to Roundwood. To the east the Sugarloaf stood up sharply over the moor. To the west, and high above us, the gloom of the woods and Djouce mountain into which, about that time, a French plane had crashed because the pilot hadn't been speaking to the navigator. Down there in the woods the long lake hugged itself, arms tightly folded.

We walked along the west of it, then across at the dam and sluice-gate, then along the east of it and back again, and across again and back along the west of it: you could sing that. Joan and myself in the lead and hand-in-hand, Brenda and Peter ten paces in the rear and stepping well. On a carpet of damp pine-needles we picnicked. Neither God nor St. Patrick intended Ireland for picnics. Murderous midges came around us in the damp and fed on us. We fed on ham sandwiches and lukewarm tea. Then halfway up Djouce mountain, searching for and not finding the wreck of the French plane: and talking about nothing else. Those girls were dull and so was Peter. Not their fault that day, perhaps. For as we walked I kept repeating: Bosomed high in tufted trees, bosomed high in tufted trees.

To the wonderment of all.

Because on the far side of Enniskerry, where the road falls steeply to the bridge over the Dargle, was the mansion in which Gobnait worked. And Joan. Just like that: bosomed high in tufted trees.

To the dripping woods I proclaimed: Where perhaps some beauty lies, the cynosure of neighbouring eyes.

They were used to me now. They made no comment.

No bums disturbed, no blood stained the damp pine-needles. Segregation went only so far.

But the sun came out in the evening and, homeward bound, we could see, faint and faraway, the outline in Ulster of the Mourne mountains.

In Enniskerry I sneaked a secret half-whiskey and a pint. Badly needed. Those girls were deadly. Courage for the dreary walk, pushing bicycles up that hill.

Halfway up the wonder happened. Two on one bike they came down like the wind. A man's bike. Pauline on the bar, Gobnait in the saddle, hair flying. They called my name. And Peter's name. They didn't stop. Out of sight round a corner and down to the bridge and the village. Bosomed high in tufted trees.

Brenda asked what that was.

— Girls from the office, I told her.

For Peter's sake: to preserve the secret of the school ballroom dancing. That first fine careless tango.

The mizzling rain came on again and kept us company all the way to Donnybrook.

Peter never could have been described as passionate and I had only gone with him to balance the boat, as I take care to explain to Gobnait on the following Thursday afternoon.

— Pushing up the hill, she says, you all looked so woebegone it was funny.

She laughs so happily, right before the portrait of the man who had created or remembered Buckramback. There he sits: a long, strong, heavy, northern face, hair going grey and thinning over the temples, a respectable black coat, a quill in the right hand, an elbow resting solidly on a copy of *The Traits and Stories of the Irish Peasantry*.

— And a fine man indeed, she says. Very like my father. A fine countryman. You might look like that when you're growing old. You might look distinguished. We'll wait and see.

She has come without Joan. We walk hand-in-hand on the polished slippery floor. We stand for a long time before the battle of the Boyne, and the merriment and mayhem and writhing limbs around the nuptials of Eva and Strongbow: my arm is around her waist; the gallery is as secret as the woods of Djouce mountain to which some day when the sun is shining we will go together. Her hair is on my shoulder:

The zoological museum is noisy with school-children.

— But, she says, children I love and all these things are better than just pictures.

Skeletons of whales, apes, male and female, with all found and every hair numbered: and the Rathcannon elk about which

I am the greatest living authority as, on that day and being inspired, I am about many other things: no longer even has the dancing-floor any terrors for me, foam on the wavetop, foam on the wavetop, and I tell her that my father's father and the Rathcannon elk came from the same place. She says that there's a definite family resemblance. She stands back and studies me and the high proud skeleton.

— Your father's father wasn't so tall. What was he?

— A policeman.

— They made them bigger then.

— They found him in a marsh in 1824.

— Your father's father?

— And dug him up.

— Not a pick on his bones.

— From his toes to the tip of his antlers he's ten feet and four inches.

— Your father's father's people were a fine body of men. You take after them.

We kiss to clinch our happiness in the presence of the Rathcannon elk and his two skeletal companions, one female. Passing children giggle. The man at the turnstile bar scratches his old beard. We are past caring. We aren't laughing any more. Round the corner then to Stephen's Green to sit on a bench in the sun and look at the lake. We talk little, we don't need to. Then to tea in the Country Shop with all the delicacies a minor civil servant can afford. She laughs again when I tell her about the ham sandwiches and lukewarm tea in the wood under Djouce mountain. When we go there together the fare will be better. She promises.

Even to please Peter there was little point in pretending much longer with the twins: Joan or Brenda. For a while we went on parading in the park, cuddling mildly at the movies, sipping coffee in the all-green restaurant, chatting to the affable Josie and the gorgeous Marie who was having some trouble with the lover with the fur-coat and the big dog on a silver chain. We stood regularly in the shadows on the river-walk by the Dodder, and kissed a bit and whispered. Peter may have been well content. His ambitions went no further. Joan and myself stood here. Brenda and Peter stood there, twenty paces away, regulation distance. Or did they? For I had begun to suspect something peculiar. That the twins changed their clothes, swapped I mean, and their colours. Was it taste, was it touch, was it odour?

It couldn't have been sight. They looked alike. Or hearing. They talked alike. Poor Peter I thought: and tested and tricked them with the magic formula from the tale of the death of King Conaire the Good: Do not let two reds go before you to the house of a red.

Joan couldn't remember the words. It wasn't Joan. For three nights later she was word-perfect, and without prompting. That was Joan. Three nights later she hadn't a clue. That was Brenda. Poor Peter. They tasted the same. And sounded and looked etc. They were playing a game and the stakes weren't high, they hadn't even bothered to do their homework, they stood to lose nothing and we, sure as God, had nothing to gain. Never knew if Peter ever knew and, as in two little girls in blue, we drifted apart: and Gobnait and Pauline made the newspapers, not the headlines exactly but not a brief paragraph neither.

They got two and a quarter inches, single-column, provincial papers please copy, and I kept the clipping for a long time. And that was that, the man's bicycle one in the saddle one on the bar, brakes that snapped and the stone bridge at the foot of that precipice of a hill: foam on the wavetop.

On my last visit to the dancing-academy we talked about it through the smoke.

Now and again I communed with the Rathcannon elk and thought of Buckramback and Clarence McFadden.

Peter and myself never did take Brenda and Joan to a dance: and four years later I met Brenda, or so she said, on a street near Ballsbridge. She was married and happy and wheeling a pram and halfways to filling another, and I wondered, but was too polite to ask, was her sister similarly situated. Of course it could have been Joan. How was I to know? They tell me there's only one sure way for a man to find out.

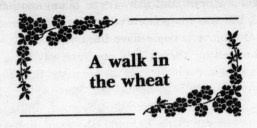

# A walk in
the wheat

Three swans flew above us, very high and swift for swans, before we turned off the highway. They flew northeast towards the big, islanded, windy trout-lake that fused the borders of three counties. We followed a byroad towards the village in the lost valley. The old man who had been reared in that valley shaded his eyes and looked up at the swans. Looked after them until they were no longer white magic birds but black specks drifting in the haze of a Spring morning. We thought of reeds and water over shore-stones and dirty grey cygnets growing into snowy beauty. He said: In my boyhood here it was a saying that it was a lucky day you saw three swans flying.

We marched down the red byway: the American woman in green slacks and white Aran sweater, the old man and myself.

I love red roads where basic sandstone glows up through the thin surface of tar or, better still, untarred roads in mountain valleys where the rain-puddles are the colour of rich chocolate.

In blue, morning mist this was no midland country of lakes and low green hills. For the lakes were steaming cauldrons and the hills were elevated by haze into floating Gothic palaces the height of the Rocky Mountains. Four miles we had walked from the fishing hotel in the triangular market-town where draughty gusts of Spring wind set the pictures dancing on the walls: where all the photographs in the hotel lounge and dining-room were of a lavish white wedding that had happened in Buenos Aires.

— From these parts, said the old man returning to his native place, they emigrated mostly to the Argentine. Not to

New York or Boston or Chicago. There was a reason for that. A famous Irish missionary priest who had gone ahead of them to the pampas. They mingled Spanish and Irish names and blood.

The panelling in the hallway of the hotel had been damaged when a terrified whitehead bullock had invaded the place on the last fairday. We were surrounded by good, midland grass building beef into red cattle. Behind hedges and orchard trees, chickens sheltered from the ruffling wind.

— There was a man in these parts in my youth, he said, was reputed to own a hen laid three times a day. And one of the three eggs was invariably three-cornered. But I must myself admit that I never saw one of those miraculous eggs.

The gloss of the strengthening sun was on the young hawthorn leaves. Clipped tree-stumps were phosphorescently white. Ash trees, slim as young girls, stood up on their own above the ranked hawthorns.

— My father had green fingers, he said. I'll show to you strangers an avenue of trees he planted.

The old woman with the silvery can in her hand met us just where the narrow road twisted, dipped suddenly, and we had our first sight of the wall and tower of the ancient abbey-ruin. She was tiny, with brown wrinkled face and blue eyes: and the eyes brightened and the face came to life when she saw our guide. She reached out her hand to him. She wore a black shawl with tassels and trimmings, a black skirt, an apron made out of a well-washed potato-sack, a pair of men's boots. She held his hand for a long time. She said: Dermot, you're welcome back to your own place.

— If it was still my own place.

— The ground doesn't change, she said.

The silvery can held goats' milk, and if we stepped with her into her cottage by the side of the road we could share the midmorning tea with herself and her husband. She explained, not to Dermot but to the woman and myself: If you haven't supped tea with goats' milk then you don't know what tea is.

So we went with her to help her carry the milk and, ourselves, to break the morning. Her husband, not quite as old as herself, gillied on the lakes for visiting fishermen, and the rafters under the thatched roof of the cottage were laced with rods and the handles of gaffs and nets. She sang for us, standing with her back to the hearth fire, her hands tightly locked behind her back, her eyes raised but tightly closed, and a young smile on her face. So sweetly, too, she sang a song about the lakes and hills, the valley, the ancient abbey, the monks who once upon a time had chanted and prayed there, the miracles wrought by the patron of the place, the holiness of the last hermit who had lived in the valley: and about a tyrant king who, after the manner of Holofernes, had been tricked and killed by the decent people. The words went haltingly to Tom Moore's melody about the harp that once through Tara's halls. Those words had been written by an old flame of hers who had long since emigrated to the land of the gauchos. When he had been gone for ten years and was showing no sign of returning she married another and tried to forget the song-writer: who afterwards married a half-Spanish woman and died among strangers.

Her husband tapped his pipe on the hob and said: I never did think much of it as a song. There was a young school-master by Granard in the County Longford made a song was twice as good. There was more history in it. And a tune he didn't borrow but made it up out of his own head.

She said, sadly enough, yet still with the sauciness of a young girl: The old tunes were the best.

She put some of the goat's milk in an empty whiskey-bottle and gave it to the green-legged woman. With her blessing hovering about us, and the taste of strong tea flavoured with goats' milk in our mouths, we went down into the valley.

— That song she sang, Dermot said, was a fair resumé of the history of the locality. The people of this place were breastfed on legends and wonders. Miracle springs and miracle mills. Wood that won't burn. Water that won't boil. Water that flows uphill. There now is the wood that won't burn.

Ten yards from the road, in a marshy field, yellow with mayflowers, stood a bare, three-armed thorn bush. We crossed a shaky stone stile and went towards it. Rags and rosary beads hung from the withered arms. A small well, spotted with green scum, nestled down at the twisted roots, and through the shallow, particoloured water we could see coins and holy medals lying on the bottom. Abandoned sticks and crutches decayed with age, and one metal-and-leather leg-brace, were piled to one side.

— Three arms to the bush, he said. For the Father, the Son and the Holy Ghost. The water of the well won't boil. The wood of the bush won't burn.

The woman, sceptical and literary, quoted: Said the wicked, crooked, hawthorn-tree.

— By all accounts the saint wanted it so, he said. It was his holy well.

He had his hat in his hand. He was a big man, still handsome. But the fair locks of youth had gone and his clean, wellshaven chin and shiny, washed baldness, and around his eyes some freckles that lingered from boyhood summers, gave him at times the glow of childish, innocent enthusiasm.

— Did anybody ever try, said the woman. I mean boiling and burning.

— Oh woman, he said, of green shanks and little faith and foreign origins.

Then he covered his head and laughed loudly. He said: Not to my personal knowledge and belief. But the tradition is that anyone who ever tried to boil the water or burn the wood regretted it. And the sick were cured here. Faith made the dry bush blossom.

Faith it was, too, that made the water run uphill and confounded the sceptical miller.

— Look to the right hand now, he said.

We had regained the road.

— That there is the Hermit's Rock. Beyond that rock and the steep hill it stands on, there's one of the loveliest of the lakes of Ireland. And look to the left now.

The width of two fields away and close to the ruined abbey was a shapeless heap of grey stones.

— Over there, the saint built a mill. And no sign of water next or near it. A miller passing the way mocked him. In the legends millers were always mockers.

The water will come, said the Saint. And he blessed the mill and the millstones. And here where we stand by the side of the road the water burst out and flowed past the mill as you see it to this day. It leaves the lake on a lower level. Flows under the earth and under the hermit's rock. Comes back here to the daylight. The story says the mocking miller died of shock.

— You could see his point, she said.

The water fountained up by the roadside, spread out in a weedy shallow pool, then narrowed to make a stream. A man watered a horse in the miracle pool. Geese paddled by the horse's head. Lambs with black noses grazed on the steep slope that went up to the hermit's rock.

— Before God, said Dermot, it's my old friend, the Stone Man. I thought he was dead and gone years ago.

Together the daughter and myself said: Another miracle. A man of stone.

He came towards us, leading the horse. Small, hunched and lame-legged, he splashed through the shallow water, scattering the paddling geese.

— Dermot, he said. I couldn't mistake you. You've come back at last. To see the old places.

— No longer mine, said Dermot. But I've brought a visitor from Dublin. And my daughter.

— So I see. So I see.

The horse grazed the roadside grass. The geese, again at peace, returned to the weedy water. A poet's words came into my head, a lazy description of a Connacht village: Where seven crooked crones are tied all day to the tops of seven listening halfdoors, and nothing to be heard or seen but the drowsy dropping of water and the ganders on the green.

— You're welcome, girl, said the Stone Man. You're also a sort of a wonder. The first woman, I'd say, ever to wear trousers in this valley. Three thousand shaven celibate men once chanted prayers here. They wouldn't have welcomed the likes of you.

— But they might have, she said. As a change from chanting.

We walked through the village of seven houses and a pub, and a small village-green with an old worn stone cross. The place was still asleep. To the right hand the Hermit's Rock towered above us. To the left, across the valley and beyond the ruins of the abbey, was a graceful conical hill, green of grass, gold of furze, topped by a head of stone.

— My hill, Dermot said. If it hadn't been for an aging man in love and a designing young woman. My father's first family were left with nothing.

— I'll walk with you to the summit, said the Stone Man. If you wait till I hand the horse to the servant-boy.

He led the horse down an entry by the side of one of the seven houses.

He has a name I suppose, she said. A real name.

— He has the name he got at the font. But nobody ever uses it. Old as I am, he's older. He came to this valley, a journeyman stonecutter, when I was sixteen. The year my father married again. The year before he died and the new woman put us out. A local landlord and the parish priest and the Protestant rector paid him to come to restore the abbey. So that the occasional learned visitor could look at it in some comfort. Up to that it was all weeds and dead scaldy jackdaws and stones scattered all over the place. Morning to night he was there like a leprechaun, hammer and chisel tinkling, working by the light of a hurricane lamp in old cloisters that nobody here would go near after dusk. Then he married a woman of the place and stayed here. And was a journeyman no longer. But the jokers said it wasn't the woman he married but the old stones of the abbey.

— Will we walk by the abbey path, the Stone Man said. Or by the church and the schoolhouse?

He had ornamented himself with a grey tailed coat and an ancient bowler. He supported his limp on a varnished blackthorn.

— By the church and the schoolhouse, Dermot said. That's the path I knew best as a boy.

The low, grey, cruciform church had a separate bell tower. To ring the bell you swung on a huge iron wheel. The whitewashed, oblong box of a schoolhouse had narrow, latticed windows.

— My uncle taught there, Dermot said. A tyrant with black sidewhiskers. And more severe on me than on any boy in the valley. He was a cattledealer, too, and thought more of bullocks than of boys. He had a gold watchchain thick as a ship's cable. And a green velveteen waistcoat. He went every week to the cattlemarket in Dublin. Once he came back and by my father's hearth solemnly told us how a young woman. A daring hussy with paint on her face, he said. How she had had the temerity to address him, outside the City Hotel on the north-side. Where the cattlelairs were. But, he said, with one glance I froze her to silence. Listening to him I thought sadly of a poor painted Red Indian squaw petrified like Lot's wife. So I asked him, uncle, why did you freeze her with a glance. Dermot, he said, she was a loud woman. Or that was what I thought I heard. Long after I realized he said lewd. But it puzzled me at the time.

— Mayhap she was loud, too, said Greenshanks. Singing. Or swearing. Or playing the guitar.

— Yet I will say this for my uncle. He did his damnedest to fight when my father died. And that woman took the land from us. And threw my brothers and sisters and myself out on the ways of the world.

—Jack Dempsey, said the Stone Man, nor the best counsellor ever took snuff or wore a wig could not fight the sort of marriage agreement they make in this part of Ireland. They could teach lessons to the French.

By a masspath that went under blossoming hawthorn and skirted the edge of a field of young oats we began to ascend. Then, crossing a wooden stile, we were on another narrow road, going up steeply, screening stones loose under our feet. In his boyhood the children used to gather at the foot of the hill and, with cheers, help the horse with the peat-cart, heavy from the bog, to make the grade. His step quickened, his shoulders bent, he was a child among cheering children, digging heel-and-toe in the pebbles, approaching home in the evening. As we ascended we saw more and more of the sights that had remained with him when, faraway in exile, he'd close his eyes and recall beginnings: white crosses in a graveyard above a small lake: the sheen of clipped horses, free and running, manes flying, in the fields: the pebbly way going between red beech hedges: the sun gold on the little lake like a path you could walk on: scrubby, wintry, hillside land beginning to flame with blossoming furze: slopes holy and haunted by the shadows of monk and hermit.

— A tireless wonder to quote both poetry and prose your uncle was.

That was the Stone Man.

— We knew the Readamedaisy by heart, Dermot said. The name of the book as written was *Reading Made Easy*. He had the stonebreakers by the roadside quoting Byron and Burke. Stop, for thy tread is on an empire's dust. It is now seventeen years since I saw the queen of France. And the impeachment of Warren Hastings.

Suddenly the Stone Man is standing up like an orator, asking us to look down from this height on the beauty of his abbey, the square tower, the round columbarium to the left. And, in a voice grating like rusty metal, reciting from the repertoire of the dead schoolmaster: Where the ivy clings to the ruin and the moss to the fallen stones, where the wild ash guards the crumbling gable and the brook goes babbling, where the quiet of ages has settled down on green fields and purple hills, there is the faithfulest memorial of a past that is dead.

Paying no heed to him Dermot strides onward. He opens one half of a creaking iron gate. He says: My father planted that avenue of trees. I told you he was a green-fingered man.

The reverent breathing of the trees, the devotion of a dead man who had digged and planted and loved, for a second time foolishly and late, was with us. Green beech, copper beech, ash coming tardily to leaf, they whispered to us of the man who had helped to give them life. They were, also, his children. Rooted in the ground. Not to be cast out.

— Her one son lives in that bungalow on the slope, he said. He never married. We won't call on him.

I ventured. He's your half-brother.

— He may be. But I'm no brother of his. Half nor whole.

He strode on heavily, leading us between the trees.

— He might have the gall to tell me I was a trespasser. He has the land, legally, that rightfully belongs to us. But it always half-consoled me that he never had the harvest of son or daughter to leave it to. The sheaves in the field wouldn't feel the same in his hands, as in mine. He wouldn't know how ready and willing the ground is to yield. He wouldn't know what these trees are saying.

The road began slightly to descend. Older trees, giant oaks and sycamores, were among the ash and beech his father had planted. From a branch of one of the sycamores a thrush had sung to the good days of his boyhood. Always he had thought, the same brave cock guarding his territory with music. One bird to one tree. A propertied male proud on his own land. That bird would be long gone, his place taken by a younger cock, and another, and another. The trees, the green silence, deepened around us. We were on what had once been a clear cobbled square, now badly weedgrown, in front of a long, low cottage, the old abandoned farmhouse in which he had been born.

— She grew grand, he said, and left the old place to the cattle and hens.

— No, it wasn't that, the Stone Man said. She claimed she smothered living among trees. Some people are like that. So the new house was built up the hillside.

Chickens picked and fluttered and squawked around us. Close to the sagging doorway cattle had softened and muddied the ground. We followed him into the shadowy dung-smelling room that had once been a large kitchen. He had his hat in his hand again. He didn't speak for a long time. The woman took a ballpoint from the bag she carried and wrote her name on one white speck of wall. Then handed me the ballpoint so that I could sign myself beside her.

— Outside there, he said. That garden hedge gone wild. It made a magic circle around my childhood. It spread its leaves and shade over me on mornings like this. I'd peep out through it and see the world. I've seen a lot of the world since then. But nothing as sad to me as the spectacle of this house. This day.

— Things change, dad, the woman said.

Every rafter in this kitchen had a special name I'd given it. And the polished mantel beam was King of them all.

The woman said again that things change.

— I was born in that bedroom below, he said. And when I was small and in bed, the moon would shine in on me through that door. When I lost the door I lost the moon.

— It's somewhere still, she said.

— And outside in the evening the rocktop of the hill above was a giant's head. Eyes and all. And the green slope was the giant's cloak floating off towards the west.

— We'll go to the summit, the Stone Man said. And study the view. Five counties you can see from the crown of the giant's head.

We could feel his anger, or pain, growing as he led us up to the summit. The Stone Man, to ease the strain, talked of the view we could see, the coloured prospect of five counties and a dozen lakes: and talked of the tyrant of a Dane who had been killed by the decent people. And of the hermit who had lived in the valley. He joked at the woman about her green legs. And about the three thousand celibate men who wouldn't have allowed her into the valley.

— You'd have shattered all the rules of cloisura, he said. Why; women weren't allowed into the saint's mill. It was reckoned to be as holy as any church he ever built.

— It could be, she said, that he was afraid they'd find fault with his baking. If he could bake his own flour that is. Old bachelors never like women near their kitchens.

— Two miles away, said Dermot, there's a place called Hangman's Hollow. A landlord in the eighteenth century had a man hanged there for stealing a loaf of bread.

— The tyrant Dane, said the Stone Man, had a more subtle method. Every year he exacted from every house in his territory an ounce of gold. If he didn't get it he cut off the nose of the defaulter. So they called it Nose Money. But he had a weakness for the girls.

— Green legs, she said.

— History is silent. He demanded that a local chieftain should send him his daughter for diversion. So she came. And with her twelve beardless youths wearing skirts. And when the poor man was drunk they stuffed him in a barrel and drowned him in a lake.

— If he had been a bible-reading Christian, she said, he'd never have fallen for the old beardless youth trick.

On top of the hill we sat down and drank the goats' milk that the singing woman had given us.

— There's a man walking over there, Greenshanks said.

She pointed across the valley to the slope below the Hermit's Rock. But try as we might we could see nobody.

— The ghost of the last hermit, the Stone Man said.

Visible only to a woman who has tasted the magic milk of the white goat. They say he broke his vow in the end. He was a hunting gentleman who gave up the world. And lay in a hole in that rock. With his proctors, as they were called, ranging the country for him. Bringing back corn and eggs, geese, turkeys, hens and sheep. He ate like the quality. It was the chief part of his holiness that he was never to stir out of the cave. But this fatal day he heard the hounds and the horn. Too much for him it proved to be. Off he went on a neighbour's mount. Broke his neck at the first stone wall.

— The man's gone now, she said.

She stood up hurriedly.

— There are ticks in the grass.

White marl fringed the two small lakes at the foot of the hill and shone up at us like silver from underneath the water.

Surveying the carpet of counties Dermot said: My father used to walk a lot around the rock. He said it was holy ground.

— This entire valley is holy, the Stone Man said. Look through the chancel arch of the abbey when the furze blossom is out in all its glory. It's as if you were looking at the light of the heaven.

He led us down by another path so that he could display to us the arches, the cloisters, the cool stones of the love of his heart. We crossed a whole field of clover and yellow pimpernel, then followed a gravelly, slippery goatpath through the furze. The blue air above us was cut by the whinnying sound of flying snipe. Far below, where the stream went on from the saint's mill to join the great lake the swans had flown to, three boys and a dog followed the twisting course of the water. The boys threw sticks and stones. They crossed and recrossed the narrow stream. The dog barked and leaped in the air, plunged in to rescue floating sticks. Their actions had a happiness isolated from time.

— Spring was always a glory in this place, he said.

Then, loudly enough to be heard four fields away, he shouted a verse of a poem: Tomorrow Spring will laugh in many waters, ever the ancient promise she fulfills. Tomorrow she will set the furzebloom burning along my father's hills.

Where the furze ended we crossed a stile, the woman leading. Before us lay a broad flat field bursting with the promise of young wheat.

— Walk round the edge, I called to her. Don't trample the man's crop.

— Sink him to the pit, Dermot roared. Who owns this land?

He went across the field, sinking his heels deeply for purchase and possession. Soft clay spurted up behind him. Tender green shoots lay crushed on his path. With savage steps he wrote out on the land the story of his long-thwarted passion for the lost thing of his own. We followed him, stepping carefully, as if we feared that the stalks might cry out.

That was a late year for the ash. So there were four great ash trees, still bare, but proud and defiantly independent of decoration, on the green in the triangular market-town. Within the square they formed, stood the old collapsing market-house built by an eighteenth-century landlord to resemble a miniature St. Paul's. In its cellars, rebels in 1798 had been flogged and otherwise tortured before the dragging-out to death. Or so the Stone Man told us. He had come with us for a farewell night of drink and talk and song.

The rough Spring wind of the morning had died. The pictures no longer danced in draughts on the walls of the hotel's hallway. During the day a carpenter had repaired the damage done by the whitehead bullock. The gentle lady who owned the hotel told us about that white wedding she had attended in Buenos Aires, about the fantastic length of the bride's train. She showed us some sombre religious prints she had brought back with her. Spanish and Irish faces looked at us from the walls of the dining-room.

Then out in the public bar the people were gathered to

say welcome to the returned exile and his daughter. A girl in a red dress, without urging or invitation, sang a song about a Donegal beauty called the Rose of Arranmore. There was a great willingness in the people to sing. The Stone Man, elevated, threw his blackthorn and bowler into a corner, roared to the barmaid: Give me, girl, as the tinkers used to say, a glass of Geneva wine and a wisp for the ass.

Then in a voice like the sawing of old branches he sang the song the woman of the goats' milk had sung that morning.

Greenshanks whispered to me: My father loved that hill.

— One tiger to one hill, I said. One singing cockthrush to one sycamore.

We left the crowded bar and walked down the long yard between byres and stables at the back of the hotel. A pig nosed at a cartchain. There were nettles and abandoned motor-tyres, rusty lengths of corrugated iron, the twitter of evening birds. And slow sparse raindrops. In the bar behind us Dermot had raised his voice and was singing that his boat could lightly float in the teeth of wind and weather and outrace the smartest hooker between Galway and Kinsale.

She said: Since I was a child I always liked him to sing. That was always his favourite song.

She said that he had hurt himself when he hurt the wheat and the ground: And I felt nothing. Nothing at all. Except that it might be cute to have a summer cottage in such a heavenly place. To get away from New York in the heat. That worries me that I felt nothing. That he was a stranger to me.

— He never spoke to me much about this place, she said. As you'd think a father might.

— The subject was too painful. The dispossession. Diaspora.

— He had one funny story, though. About a funeral. And the mourners stopped at a pub and left the coffin and corpse on a stone wall outside. They said, sure God rest him, what would be the point in bringing him in. 'Twould only vex him.

She was laughing and crying.

— But I did see a man walking round the Hermit's Rock. The
hunting hermit? Or my grandfather walking on holy ground:
Or the shadow of a cloud on the grass? But I saw something
that nobody else could see. One woman in a valley with the
ghosts of three thousand celibate men. Wasn't it a sign to
show that, in spite of them, I belonged to the place?

# The python

When the wine and the after-dinner cognac dies he wakes from the glutton's stupor, sniffs the dark room, knows exactly who has stopped in the place before him. The air-conditioning makes for most of the time like the noises of a Gipsy Moth: then, every four or five minutes, clanks as if a chained man inside were trying to get out. It pumps humid air into an atmosphere already oozing: and odorous. The man who has left that odour behind him has not slept here on his own. Not even in this easygoing hotel do tomcats sign the register on their own. But pets are permissible and somewhere in the world there is a noseless man or woman, or a pair without noses and thinking that a tomcat is a pretty pet.

In the odorous dark he listens to the little man from Paris who says that it is an octopus, so the little man pulls out his knife and opens his eyes, then thinks it's a dream, then thinks that it isn't, that the octopus is reality and is draining him with its suckers: but, no, it is simply the dreadful humid heat: he is sweating, he says, he had gone to sleep about one o'clock, then at two the heat had waked him, he had plunged into a cold bath and back into bed without drying himself and right away the furnace roars again under his skin, and he is sweating again, and he dreams the house is on fire and says that this is more than mere heat, this is a sickness of the atmosphere, the air is in a fever, the air is sweating: and more of the same.

The little man from Paris is writing about humid heat.

At four in the morning the telephone begins to ring, and rings and rings. The crazy woman will just now be leaving the hotel-bar. She calls him from the payphone outside the door of the gents. That woman could clear a bar-counter quicker than the Black Death. But he answers the phone in the end. And will go to her room to get away from the smell of the tomcat. Also: her air-conditioner works. And there may be other reasons. She has long dark glossy hair, and prominent glistening American teeth: and her craziness is not menacing, only gentle and amorous.

When he switches on the light he finds it hard to believe that there is no cat to be seen: yet if a cat may vanish and leave a smile behind it, then another cat may vanish and leave a smell. The book in which the little man from Paris laments about the humid heat lies open on the other, unused bed. He checks his memory against the text. Not bad, not bad at all: for this clinging, sticky, smelly heat might very well affect a man's memory. But that cold plunge and that crawling back untowelled onto the bed was a bloody bad idea: the little man, a philosopher too, might have killed or crippled himself with rheumatics.

A quick shower now, a quick brisk towelling, helps and cannot harm: go glistening to the gentle crazy woman with the glistening teeth and the glossy hair: and as he combs his hair he thinks that the week that has just passed has been, the papers say, the bloodiest week of this warm season in little old New York. The paper is there on the dressing-table and still saying it: Fiftyeight murders, three young drug-addicts executed on a rooftop, they get a few lines on a backpage: Mafia boss murdered, that makes the front page for Mafia murders are as popular as baseball: and a most poetic policeman says take a poor guy, it's sweltering, he don't have an air-conditioner, he takes a few beers, there's no place to go, he gets mad at something, then all of a sudden it bursts out, he grabs a knife.

The knife is farandaway the most favoured weapon for warm nights.

He does have an air-conditioner. Puff, puff, puff, a

wonderful breath of foul air. Clank, clank, clank, jealous Vulcan is trapped in the crater, let me outa here. Dear dark woman with such hair too, I come, I come my heart's delight.

He has never carried a knife.

Or if he had been carrying a knife he would have attacked the python yesterday when the musician draped it around Judith's neck. Young women should not wear pythons around the neck. He recalled then with a shudder a story he had read about an Irish lord who when he was a young man in Oxford kept a python as a pet. He does not trust pythons. He, that is, not the noble lord who was lunatic enough to keep in his lodgings on the High a python fourteen feet long. Tame, he thought. Tame? But didn't like strangers. Nothing is tame that doesn't like strangers. So the landlady's daughter opens the box that the python lives in, and the python coils round and round the landlady's daughter, bruising her to the extent of thirty-five pounds sterling which was big money in the year of the Franco-Prussian war: and the python is banished to the zoo, a proper place for pythons.

All of which he tells the musician who laughs at him and says: Landladies' daughters in Oxford, England, should know better than to poke pythons.

He is not content until Judith and the two girls in her company are away from that python and out of that zany penthouse: all fixed up with blooms and screaming birds like a tropical jungle, and with fish in glass tanks that dance, the fish not the tanks, when the musician plays the piano. A sort of dance: swishing round and round, Boccaccio's seven young ladies and three young gentlemen barefoot in the crystal water and with naked arms engaging in various games. What games? But the piranha fish do not dance. Four of them in a tank which they share with a small black shark, all so dangerous to each other that they leave each other alone. The shark seems to sleep. The piranha deliberately, like the Eleventh Hussars, do not dance. They are small fellows with buck teeth. They stare out through the glass wall and say: If we had you in the Amazon.

Being fair judges of fleshmeat it is to be assumed that they stare hardest at Judith and Marion and Barbara, blooming American belles just turned twenty, fit any morning to play games in Boccaccian streams: not at myself, nor at Murtagh, lean, longjawed sports writer over from Dublin to witness and comment on an ancient Celtic stickball game in a field in the Bronx: nor, by God, at the musician, tough and brown and bald and wrinkled. Even piranha fish may prefer tender meat.

Life is much more liveable in the bar and restaurant on the ground floor. And tolerably cool, too. No puffs, no clanks, but currents of real air reminding me again of Boccaccio in the Italian mornings, and the middle-ages dead and done with, and love and laughter in the air: and the cool water fringed by smooth round stones and verdant grasses.

To the three young women Murtagh explains the nature of the stickball game: No, not curling. Hurling. Curling is something you do on ice. Like sliding a flatiron along ice. We don't have enough ice in Ireland. No, this is hurling. And it's not at all like the stickball I saw the Puerto Rican kids play around the corner there in an alley off Seventh. That's a sort of pelota or handball with a broomstick. No, hurling is hurling. Hurling is different. There's an Irish, Gaelic, word for it, but that wouldn't interest you. It goes back into history. It's the most natural thing in the world, for a man to hit a ball with a stick. There's something like it in Japan, I've heard. Though perhaps I'm confusing shinto and shinty. That's what they call it in Scotland. Shinty. Something like hurling. But then the Scots would have borrowed it from us. Great men to borrow, the Scots. Two teams. Fifteen a side. On one pitch, just like American football. The stick's about three feet long with a smooth curving blade. The best ash, cut with skill. The clash of the ash, they say. The ball's the size of two fists clasped. Like that . . .

He shapes the delicate white hands of Marion to resemble

the ball. Cute man Murtagh. He is pleased with these young
American women to whom last night I introduced him.

— That's the way the game is organized nowadays. Long
ago it used to be played by mobs. All the men of one clan
or parish against all the men of another clan or parish. And
the pitch was unconfined. Over hedges and ditches and bogs
they were bound, as the song said. But in the game, nowadays,
we have rules and limits. Even in Ireland we have rules and
limits. Anyway, you'll see it all in the Bronx. Tipperary vee
New York. And what are you all having to drink?

In honour of the heat outside it is mostly cold white wine.
Manolo, the Spanish barman, brings the drinks and olives and
celery stalks, and impeccable good manners. Piped music, but
very mildly, plays a flamenco tune. The musician has stayed
aloft, playing to the toucans and the python, and the black
shark and the staring piranha.

— Some night, Murtagh says, the piranha will come out
and get him. You couldn't feel easy with those brutes about
the house. Not a laugh in them from start to finish.

The young ladies from Boccaccio, Pampinea, Fiammetta,
Filomena laugh into their cool tinkling drinks. Faraway in the
sunny south and in a womens' college he has sat with the three
of them and nine hundred and ninety-seven others, in the great
dining-hall and over his Hawaiian salad (cherry), reflected
that Lord Byron could never stand, or sit, to see a woman
eat. That sad-crazy mother of his must have been sloppy over
her soup. Or it may just have been that Byron preferred his
women otherwise engaged: at falconry, or the careful stitching
of samplers, or at the dance, or at playing on the virginals.

— But what, saith the fair Pampinea from Tennessee, did
you expect to find in a womens' college if not women.

— A point well made. But knowing from faraway, from
the far side of the Atlantic, that a womens' college is full
of women, and finding yourself at dinner, one man among a
thousand women, are two different things. Not that I object.
Now that the first shock is over, I rather like it.

The three young women who have asked him to sit with them at their circular table thank him merrily.

— Sometimes, they say, the chaplain joins us.

— Let us hope we never need a chaplain.

Lord Byron, he reflects again and with increasing wonder, could not have endured to be in that fine, old, southern, circular, timbered dining-hall watching and listening to one thousand healthy females, hungry and unashamed, by no means walking in beauty like the night. Noble lord and all as he was, one thousand pairs of parents might have had qualms to hear that he was aprowl on the campus and, on faculty row, in possession of his own private lair into which he might entice or drag his prey.

— Belshazzar, from thy banquet turn he says, nor in thy sensual fullness fall.

And has to explain himself at some length. These are serious women. And curious.

Between bites and sups Fiammetta talked of St. Exupery and Kafka and wonders, God bless the girl's digestion, what effect Schopenhauer and Kierkegaard had on Kafka. She was, and is, a thin, intense, freckled girl with spectacles and, in those days, she did most of her study in the reading-room attached to the chapel.

— Because, she said, there is always the crucifix on the wall. You can look at it when you are depressed.

Filomena, who was then plump and writing a paper on American pragmatism, said: There is always tea.

She is trying to slim but she found that strict dieting interfered with her ability to write papers.

Fiammetta said that the chaplain was a devout Calvinist and that one could talk to him about anything except religion. To most questions he returned as answer one and the same question: Cannot we know God.

Filomena said that she had been detailed in the forenoon to cheer up three depressed freshmen. The cause of their depression was not homesickness. But that so far they had had no dates. So she said: Consider, sisters, that somewhere there must be three or thirty young men with the same problem. That cheered them up.

— Hope, she said, there is always hope. Don't I know. Fat girls always know.

That was four to five years away back from this day of the python and hurling and humid heat: and heat or no heat, Murtagh says, duty calls him to the Bronx and we don't have to go with him unless we want to see the hurling. So to hell with the heat and the five of us head for the Gaelic Park in the Bronx.

— Filomena has problems, Fiammetta says. She has a situation. She has three situations. I've asked her to ask you about them. You were once so helpful to me.

This is in the subway to the Bronx: which, the subway, is nothing more nor less than a noisy putrid horror. She shrieks the message into my ear. Her voice has become as thin and shrill as herself. But because of the surrounding noise nobody except myself hears her. Nobody bothers to hear her because of the heat. Murtagh has fallen in love or something with Pampinea. All this is so strange to him. The other day on Lexington Avenue he looked up in boyish wonder and said that never again would he mention Liberty Hall which is Dublin's one skyscraper, lopsided and all of seventeen floors: skies are low, mostly, over the islands. Even the heat is, to Murtagh, a happening. Then to crown it all he has met a genuine belle from Tennessee: Boccaccio himself had never by any crystal Italian stream imagined better. Murtagh whispers into the ear of Pampinea who listens, enchanted, to his brogue. He is as exotic to her as she is to him: and somewhere there may be the prospect of a room with an air-conditioner where they may gather even closer without dissolving into a dew. Filomena is asleep or feigns sleep. Even if she hears, it doesn't matter, for Fiammetta is consulting me, the wiseman, with her permission. What was it that I ever did or said to help Fiammetta? With the heat and the noise I cannot remember: and the situation is, or the situations are, three men, two of them married and all contestants for the hand, by metonymy, of Filomena who, now that she has slimmed, is a mighty attractive proposition.

Next Sunday the pattern at home will be keeping and the young active hurlers the field will be sweeping . . .

It is some time in the eighteenth century and in the prison in the town of Clonmel in the County Tipperary a young man sits and waits to be hanged.

How sad is my fortune and vain my repining, the strong rope of fate for this young neck is twining . . .

And he remembers his home and the boys at the hurling in some sunlit pasture on the lovely sweet banks of the Suir. Who was he? What deed had he done? Who wrote the sad song about him? Burning with enthusiasm to explain the nature of hurling, and much else, to Pampinea, Murtagh sings the old song in the over-crowded cab that carries them, sweating from the train to the playing-pitch: and far far from green Suirside grass is the rectangle of American scorched earth on which fifteen men from Tipperary, sticks in hand, do battle with fifteen Irish expatriates who, similarly armed, have taken it upon themselves to represent the city of New York. The game itself, and not just its finer points, is lost in clouds of acrid American dust. Every time a hoof or a stick or a ball or a body strikes the earth a spiralling sandstorm, devil of the desert, arises.

But back of the stands and terraces, in bars and in restaurants, several vintages of Irish-America have thrown their hats at the invisible game and are making certain sure that the heat will not dry nor the dust choke their throttles. Joining them, I find that I am among my own and far away from those awe-inspiring moments when the sun catches the tops of the buildings on, say, Seventh and I am shaken into asking myself why did man ever challenge the heavens by building such Babylonian towers.

Out on the pitch the desert devils move here and there. Here in the tents the corks pop and the stout and whiskey flow. The jovial din is only stupendous and, in the middle of it all, two nuns, one young, one old, sit on chairs and confidently shake collection boxes: and Filomena snuggles close and tells me of her three situations, two of them married, one Irish and single and works in a bank, one an airline pilot and English, one an American academic, all for one and one for all, and all together in New York on this warm day.

— And to think, she says, that once upon a time I counselled freshmen who were hardup for dates.

To think, indeed. The years and dieting have made her most desirable, and one solution for three situations is to find a fourth that will cancel out the other three. So he turns the topic by talking to her about poetry, about that same convict of Clonmel pining in his prison, and how nobody knows who he was, nor who the poet was who wrote about him in the Irish. Which he quotes mellifluously, and in full, in the cab on the way back to Manhattan. And how the Irish was translated into English in the nineteenth century by a lonely sort of a poet called Jeremiah J. Callanan whose spirit responded to that cry from the past: At my bedfoot decaying my hurlbat is lying, through the boys of the village the goal-ball is flying. My horse 'mong the neighbours neglected may fallow, while I languish in chains in the jail of Cluainmeala.

Which he tells her means Honeymeadow, a lovely name, a handsome town, a lovely river valley, romantic Ireland is not dead and gone but alive and well in the back of a cab in the humid heat in New York: and back in Manolo's Spanish bar and restaurant they are mysteriously alone or together, and Murtagh is somewhere with Pampinea, and Fiammetta has gone somewhere else alone so as to be able to catch an early morning flight to somewhere: and the three situations have been for the moment forgotten about for the poetic sake of the young man pining in the deathcell and sadly remembering his horse and the hurling in green meadows: With the dance of

fair maidens the evening they'll hallow, while this heart once
so warm will be cold in Cluainmeala.

But during dinner the vision fades and the situations
relentlessly return, as later they are expected to do for drink
and a discussion.

Her father is an episcopalian clergyman in Detroit.

— But it is not because I feel that life should be sinless.
Or can be. Life should be simpler. Or plain simple.

He is prepared to agree. They hold hands across the table.
She sips a tiny sip of his wine: then kisses the glass. One, two,
three add up to complications. Four is as simple as a May
morning. True love is an even number.

— Some things I want to buy, she says, in the supermarket.

So, after dinner, she goes for a while, leaving him
gloating like a sultan, and returns with a plastic bag full of
the things.

— My studio isn't fifty yards away.

They walk the fifty yards. He carries the plastic bag. It
is a long walk in the sweating heat and the things in the
bag are surprisingly heavy. Cans grind against each other.
Somewhere on Sixth they find a doorway and one of those
straight New York stairways. There is no elevator. The studio
is on the fifth floor. He grunts and sweats. He fardels bears.
Green meadows are forgotten, and crystal streams. Boccaccio
was a liar.

She paints. He has already known that. There is something
on the easel. An Andy Warhol prospect of a can of Sprite.
There are other things on the walls. But even before the
door opens he smells them. Not the Andy Warhol nor the
things on the walls, but three of the largest cats it has ever
been his misfortune to, he was about to think, see. A Manx,
near neighbour to a Dublinman, tabby and tigerstriped. An
Iranian: long hair sweeping the floor, tail like a living bush.
A Thailander: slender as a snake, not sweet as a pawpaw in
May nor lovely as a poppy, but mean and snarling behind
a black mask. She takes from him the plastic bag. The cans

are cans of catfood. He sits and watches while she feeds the
jealous brutes on three separate willow-pattern platters and
from different cans. She loves them. They love her. There is
a camp-bed in the corner. For the cats or Filomena, or all in
together this humid weather? She sits on it and they talk, he
and Filomena, across a room crowded by cats. The cats stare
at him. Could they outstare the musician's piranha fish? After
a while Filomena and himself go back to the Spanish bar.

On the way to which he tells her the tale of Big Joe who
played the clarinet. In the orchestra in a mammoth cinevariety
theatre in Dublin. He was very handsome. He could run like
Ronnie Delaney. He had need. He had seven mistresses.

— Knew three of them to talk to and two more by sight.

Because Big Joe was married the most he could manage
was to see one of the girls one night each week after the
late show. Told each girl he could manage only one night a
week because his wife was jealous. Told his wife, to explain
about the two hours, that he was having a drink with the
boys. Which worked. He possessed man's greatest blessing:
a complacent wife. Anyway she had him the rest of the time,
when he wasn't playing the clarinet. Satisfactory. All present
and correct.

There was one problem. In the interval between the second
show and the late show, and when the movie was on the screen,
every one of the seven wished to meet Joe somewhere or other
for a chat and a drink or a cup of tea. He couldn't have them all
in the same place so he, like a general, stationed one here, one
there, around the central city, sentries, single spies, redoubts:
and ran on foot, the quickest method of transport in crowded
places, and sat and sipped and talked and kissed, and so on
and on, and then back to the pit to blow the clarinet.

— Joe, I said, rationalize, rationalize. Not the breath of
Leviathan could stand the strain.

— And I worried about him.

— What happened? What happened?

She must wash and perfume more than she paints or even makes love: There is no odour of cats.

He tells her that the last time he was back in Ireland he met the man who had played the saxophone in that same pit. And asked him how was Big Joe. And heard: Poor Joe, he went to London and dropped one day running along Shaftesbury Avenue.

— He took on too much territory. Alexander knew when and where to stop. Rationalize, Filomena, rationalize.

But no use in talking to her. She is surrounded, possessed, coiled around by pythons, and perhaps the only man who could be all the world to her would be that odd Egyptian officer mentioned by Thomas Mann whom she read so carefully in college: Weser-ke-bastet, what a bloody name, on imperial duty in the city of Shechem. But known to the Shechemites, wise guys, simply as Beset.

He mentions to her the name of that gentleman. But if in the course of her college reading she had ever noticed the fellow she has long forgotten him.

— What was about him?

— His two passions in life were flowers and cats. The local divinity of his home-town was guess what?

— A cat.

— Bright girl.

— Scarcely a flower.

— A cat-headed goddess called Bastet.

— What a fun idea. I'll paint her.

— Everywhere he went, and morning noon and night, he was surrounded by cats. All colours. All ages. All breeds and sexes. Not only living ones. But mummies. Before whom he placed offerings of mice and milk. And wept as he did so.

— Another fun idea. Could I decorate my studio like that?

He does not remind her that Beset was what used to be called a pansy: and Filomena's nature, it might seem, cries out for more than cats.

* * *

— Tarry with me.

She has actually used that word. Tarry.

Perhaps it is that old usages, old words survive in the south. Or is it just remembered from her reading?

— Tarry with me, she says, until they come.

— Tarry with us, he says, for already it is late and a perverted world seeks to blot Thee out of sight by the darkness of its denials.

— What is the man saying?

— That's part of a prayer my mother used to read out loud. At night prayers. With the Rosary. On the first of every month. Consecrating the household once again to the Sacred Heart of Jesus. The reference is to the disciples on the road to Emmaus.

— Wow!

No, it was not Judith here beside him and waiting for her men, it was Fiammetta, Marion, who did most of her study in the reading-room attached to the chapel because the crucifix was on the wall and she could look at it when she was depressed. Judith who was plump and into pragmatism, and who said there was always hope, and that fat girls always knew, is now beautiful and the desired of all or, at any rate, of four men. Correction: three. Four, only for a very brief moment.

— Tarry with us for the drink and the discussion.

— Would I not be, to coin a phrase, *de trop*? Four's company, five's a . . .

— Quorum. Be our chairperson. My master.

— And they knew him in the breaking of the bread.

— Be then my saviour. Marion used to say: Cannot we know God.

— The chaplain used to say.

Her nervous laughter. Three men arrive. All together. He feels that it would be apt if they paralleled the cats: one Manxman, one Persian, one Siamese. But that would be too much to hope for. They are as he heard they would be: two of them married although that doesn't show, one of them Irish

which is obvious, one of them quite as obviously English, one
of them an American academic: and how would you guess?
Not one of them is of any particular interest. That is not
just because they have come between himself and Filomena:
Judith. No, the cats have already done that, those three cats,
that invisible tomcat, that humid heat. Jean-Paul Sartre's
octopus, that python.

If there was to have been a discussion my presence has put
an end to that. Nothing above or beyond uneasy badinage.

What a word. What does it mean? Nothing to do with
badminton? Or shuttlecock?

— Hope, she had once said, there is always hope. Fat girls
always know.

Fat girls hope that some day they may be slim. For what?

She leaves us for a while to go to the loo. It is the Irishman
who says: Gentlemen, let us settle this. Once and for all.

No pistols, no swords are to be seen.

Carefully he takes from his wallet a small airmail envelope
with green, white and gold trimmings. The Irish Republic.
He shakes it. It rattles. He says: This envelope that you see
in my hand contains three quarters. One of them is marked
with a cross.

To me he says: Sir, as an impartial member of the audience
inspect this envelope and the coins therein to see that there
is no deception. It contains three quarters, coins peculiar to
the United States of America, one of them marked with a
cross clearly cut. When you have made your inspection and
assured yourself of my veracity and bona fides, kindly pass
the bag along, keep it moving, look, inspect, satisfy yourselves
that all is fair and square, ladies and gentlemen; in for a
penny in for a pound, come in your bare feet, go home in a
Studebaker . . .

All is fair and square. The coins are restored, the envelope
rattled, and he who finds the cross takes the woman. The
Englishman finds the cross. They shake hands all round. And

also with me. Fair field and no favour. The Englishman buys a round of drinks. All smiling, yet perhaps nervous, she returns from the loo. My advice or chairmanship is never needed. Later on the Englishman takes her by the elbow and gently leads her away. Quite uncomplainingly she goes: insofar as I can tell. Snarling cats stand there to prevent me from doing anything about it. A drink with the losers, perhaps myself a loser. A friendly goodnight.

That was all yesterday and late last night and now it is four in the morning, and the phone rings and rings, and the daft dark woman with the glistening teeth will be waiting, air-conditioner working: no cats.

I come, I come my heart's delight.

What do I mourn for? Lost innocence? Lost opportunity? The crowded condition of the world? The fury and the mire of human veins?

In the penthouse the python sleeps and the piranha stare into the darkness.

# A letter to Peachtree

Always I prefer not to begin a sentence with an I, so I'm beginning this sentence and letter with the word Always. Which can be a beautiful or a terrible word, all depending on where you are, how you feel, who you are with, what you are doing, or what is being done to you. Days may not be bright always and I'll be loving you always. That last bit I really do mean, you, over there, soaking in the Atlantan sun on Peachtree.

Do you know that there was an Irish poet and novelist, a decent man who, as they would say over here, never laid his hand on a woman, and who tore up his mss. and died a Christian Brother, and who wrote a lovesong to say that he loved his love in the morning, he loved his love at noon, he loved his love in the morning for she like the morn was fair. He loved his love in the morning, he loved his love at noon, for She was bright as the Lord of Light yet mild as Autumn's moon. He loved his love in the morning, he loved his love at Even. Her smile's soft play was like the ray that lights the western heaven. He loved her when the Sun was high. He loved her when He rose. But best of all when evening's sigh was murmuring at its close.

Clear, godamned clear that he knew nothing about it. How could he keep it up, always?

Howandever, as Patrick Lagan says, here we are on this crowded train, the cameraman called Conall, and Patrick and Brendan and Niall and myself, and this plump girl in jodhpurs, well, and a red sweater as well, and good horsey boots to walk about in. And a mob of people, a jampacked train, dozens standing in the corridors, and going towards the wide open spaces of the Curragh of Kildare where the great horses run. There's a man with a melodeon sitting on the seat in the john, merely because he has nowhere else to sit, his big, squaretoed boots nonchalantly over the threshold, the melodeon tacit, the man sucking an orange. Jodhpurs leans her right shoulder, her round cheeks flushed, against my necktie spreading like the Shannon between Limerick and the sea, the tie you gave me when I took off for Ireland, a tie wide, I say, as the Shannon, a basic blue and green and, floating on that, slices of orange, a bloodred cherry and a branch of blossoming dogwood. Some tie. The tie that binds us.

This all about Jodhpurs I tell you not to make you jealous but to explain to you how crowded the train is and to give you a general idea of the style and spirit of the journey. Conall the cameraman has asked Jodhpurs to pose against my tie, your tie. She has been on the train with some friends on the way to the races. But when she sees Conall she drops out and joins us. She has the hots for Conall. He is quite a guy. Italianate handsome, dark wavy hair, quick gestures, good tweeds, and style, and as tough as a hawser and, to add the little dusting of pimento, a slight stutter, only noticeable when he's sober. But good-humoured and talking all the time.

Now let me tell you something. My grandmother came from Ballintubber in the county of Mayo. She had the old belief about how it was ill-luck to meet a redheaded woman on the way to market. Jodhpurs is sure as hell redheaded. But howabout, for added value, a redheaded man, big as Carnera, dressed in rustcoloured chain mail tweed, whose too-tight trousers betray him and burst wide-open between the legs when he is straphanging in this crowded train? What would you do on an occasion like that? Walk the other way? Look the other way? As any lady would or should.

One little railway-station, two, three, four little railway-stations whip by, then wide-rolling, green spaces with racing-stables, a silhouetted water-tower, a line of exercising horses. Conall says that over there in the national stud by Kildare town he once did a set of pictures of a famous stallion, and he, the stallion, was the smallest thing you ever saw, every where and every way no bigger than a pony, Conall says, and says that he, Conall, was himself better hung and I'm prepared to take his word for it. But he is clearly meditating on the goodness of God to the big man who burst. Who has had to borrow a mac from somebody to cover his glory, or his shame. Which it just about does. He is a very big man. Seems to me that that earthquake or revelation, or whatever, just about sets the tone for all that is to follow. Conall puts his curse on crowded trains and on the sharp corners of the leather case he carries his camera in, and says that if there isn't a fight at the play tonight his time will have gone astray. Because of the crowd on the train he missed a proper, or improper, shot of the red man who burst: at the actual instant of bursting, that is. But he knows the red man and the red man's two comrades. Three army officers, out of uniform for a day at the races. The big red man has not, say the other two, been out of uniform, except when in bed, for years. So they have almost forcibly fitted him, or stuffed him into that tweed which, under strain, has not proved a perfect fit from Brooks Brothers.

Then the crowd leaves us at the railway halt, one platform and a tin hut, out on the great plain of Kildare: and off with them all to the races. Conall, who already has had some drink taken, must have sucked it out of the air, no jug visible at any time since Dublin, sings after the racegoers that the cheeks of his Nelly are jolting like jelly as she joggles along up to Bellewstown hill. Which Lagan assures me is a bit of a ballad about another race-meeting somewhere to the north. He promises Jodhpurs, whose cheeks, fore and aft, are firm and by no means jolting like jelly, that he will sing it for her later on. He's a good man to sing a ballad or quote a poem. She latches on to us, and to hell with the races, and we are else where bound, and not to any market.

But how did we all come to be on that there train when the red man was unseamed from the nave to chaps? Listen!

The previous evening, a lovely May evening, Dublin looking almost like one of those elegant eighteenth-century prints, I walked over the Liffey at O'Connell Bridge, then along Eden Quay and for once, the name seemed apt: and into the Abbey bar to meet Patrick Lagan, a man I've mentioned in previous letters. Like, when I went to Brinsley MacNamara to talk to him about his novels and my dissertation, he passed me on to Patrick Lagan. He said that Lagan had more of his books than he had himself, all autographed by me, I mean all autographed by Brinsley. He said that Lagan knew more about his books than he himself did. Curious thing, he said. Brinsley begins many statements with those two words: Curious thing.

Life seems to him almost always absurd and he may well be right about that. He even made a collection of some of his short stories and called it: *Some Curious People*.

Along Eden Quay, then, and left round the corner at the Sailors' Home, and past the burned-out shell of the old Abbey Theatre. Which has recently gone up in smoke taking all sorts of legends and memories with it. With Brinsley I walked through the rubble, a big man, Brinsley, once a great walker by the river Boyne, but now moving slowly, arthritic feet, and leaning on a stick, and remembering and remembering many curious people.

But the Abbey Bar, round yet another corner, still survives, and Lagan was there in all his glory and a few of his friends with him. There was a lawyer and a professor of history, and a bank-manager, who is also a music critic and who plays the organ in a church, and two actors from the Abbey Theatre, and two reporters from the paper Lagan works on, and one cameraman from same: a mixed and merry throng. And Brinsley, dominating all in physical size and mental dignity, and being treated by all with respect which is only his due.

Curious thing, he says, how landscape, buildings, environment, physical surroundings can affect the character of people. Take, for instance, your average Dublin workingman. A rough type. A man with a young family, he goes out to the pub in the evening. He drinks a pint, two pints, three, four, five, six, perhaps ten pints. He's a noisy fellow. He sings. He talks loud. He argues. He may even quarrel. He staggers, singing, home to the bosom of his family, in tenement apartment or corporation house, goes to bed quietly and, soundly, sleeps it off. But down in the so soft midlands of Meath and Westmeath, where I come from, things are different. The heavy heifers graze quietly, and the bullocks, all beef to the ankles. The deep rivers flow quietly. Your average working man there is a bachelor. Living most likely with his maiden aunt, and in a labourer's cottage. In the quiet, green evening he cycles six or so miles into the village of Delvin for a drink. He drinks quietly. One pint, two, three, anything up to ten or more. In the dusk he cycles quietly home and murders his maiden aunt with a hatchet.

Curious thing, environment. Curious thing.

The name of Conall, the cameraman, is also Lagan, but no relation to Patrick. Patrick says that Patrick was a saint but that Conall Cearnach was a murderous bloody buff out of the mythologies before Christ. There's a poem about the fellow, Lagan says, you'll hear it from me sometime, as I feel we will, he's a helluva man to quote poetry. In a booming bass barreltone that would put Ariel to sleep.

Then, when I tell Conall that I am over here from Harvard to write about Brinsley's novel, *The Valley of the Squinting Windows*, about village and small town hatreds, and in relation to Sinclair Lewis and the main street of Gopher Prairie . . .

How are you over there on Peachtree Street in sunny Atlanta? Think of me in the Margaret Mitchell museum.

And in relation to Edgar Lee Masters and all the tombstones on the Spoon River, and Sherwood Anderson away out there in Winesburg, Ohio, and a Scotsman called George Douglas Brown and his House with the Green Shutters, about whom and which Brinsley has put me wise, and about all the dead life of small places . . .

Well, then, Conall Cearnach he says to me, but, man, you

have to come with us to where we are going. You'll be missing copy if you don't. This is going to be it.

At this stage Brinsley leaves us but only briefly and only to travel as far as the john and back again. We are sitting in a nook or corner of the bar. The door of the john is right in there. For the reason that his feet give him some discomfort Brinsley doesn't stand up rightaway but slithers, sitting, right up to the door of the locus. Niall of the Nine Hostages, ancient Irish King, and Brendan the Navigator, ancient Irish saint, who sailed an open boat all the way almost to Peachtree, who are sitting between Brinsley and the holy door, stand respectfully out of his way. Then he stands up finally to his most majestic height.

Curious thing, he says. This reminds me of the only good parody I ever heard on the style of John Millington Synge. It was the work of that great player, J. M. Kerrigan, and it began like this. Was it on your feet you came this way, man of the roads? No, 'twas not, but on my arse surely, woman of the house. As in the Shadow of the Glen.

Then with an amazing agility for a man so big, he dives into the john and we laugh at the joke and respectfully hold our conversation until he returns. When Conall tells me that there is this company of travelling players and that, in this country town, they are planning to put on in the parochial hall this play, says Conall, by a French jailbird about a Roman Catholic cardinal taking off his clothes in a kip. Or worse still, says Conall, about two women, a madame and a hoor, (anglice: whore), disrobing or disvesting or devestmentizing a peacock of a cardinal, and think of that, for fun, in an Irish country town. So the parish priest naturally, or supernaturally, prohibits the use of the parochial hall and, having done so, takes off for the Eucharistic Congress in Antananarivo, or somewheres east of Suez. He didn't have to read that play to know it was no go, and the players have booked another, non-sectarian hall and are going ahead and, Conall says, the man who owns that hall must fear not God nor regard the parish priest, and must be so rich and powerful that he needn't give a fuck about King, Kaiser or cardinal.

But there is this organization called Maria Duce, like the Mother of God up there with Mussolini, which will picket the hall to keep the clothes on the cardinal, and a riot is confidently expected, says Conall, and if you want to see what life is like in an Irish countrytown, man, you gotta be there.

Conall lowers his voice.

Even Brinsley himself at his worst and wildest, he says, never thought of that one. A cardinal in a kip. In the buff.

For kip, here read brothel. Not kip as in England where it may mean merely a place to sleep in.

So here we are on the train, Patrick and Conall and his camera, and myself, and Brendan and Niall and Jodhpurs: and the world and his mother are off to the races: and, somewhere ahead, a red cardinal is roosting and waiting to be depilated: and the priest of the parish is awa, like the deil with the tailor in Robert Burns, to Antananarivo: and Patrick is singing that on the broad road we dash on, rank, beauty and fashion, it Banagher bangs by the table of war. From the couch of the quality down to the jollity, bouncing along on an old low-backed car. Though straw cushions are placed, two foot thick at the laste, its concussive motion to mollify, still, the cheeks of my Nelly are jolting like jelly as she joggles along up to Bellewstown hill.

Onwards and upwards. The play's the thing.

Eighty miles from Dublin town.

The poet Cowper points out, as I would have you know, that not rural sights alone but rural sounds exhilarate the spirit and restore the tone of languid nature, that ten thousand warblers cheer the day and one the livelong night.

He means the nightingale. I reckon.

What lies ahead of us is not going to be exactly like that.

* * *

The gallant lady who leads the strolling players holds back the raising of the curtain for our arrival. But with the best or the worst intentions in the world, or with no godamned niggering intentions whatsoever, we succeed in being late and the play is well advanced when we get there. We have been delayed in the bar of one of the town's two hotels. Not drinking has detained us but a sudden attack of love, or something, not on me, already, as you know, wounded and possessed, but on Conall the fickle, the flaky, the volatile, the twotimer of all time, who wouldn't even curb his bronc until Jodhpurs had gone for a moment and what else to the powder-room. No, just one look over the bar-rail at the barmaid and he was hogtied, and said so out loud, very very loud. Like I love my love in the ginmill, I love her in the lounge. A mighty handsome brunette she is.

Jodhpurs, though, takes it all mighty cool. She is by no means in love with Conall, just lust, and she tells me that he does this everywhere and all the time, and Lagan intones like a monk of Solesmes: O'er Slieve Few with noiseless trampling through the heavy, drifted snow, Bealcú, Connachia's champion, in his chariot tracks the foe: and, anon, far-off discerneth in the mountain hollow white, Slinger Keth and Conall Cearnach mingling hand-to-hand in fight.

Prophetic?

Wait and see.

That's the beginning of the poem about the ancient hero or whatever.

Lagan explains in considerable detail that Slieve Few is a mountain in the heroic north, and in the mythologies. A few notes I make. Research? You never can tell.

For Connachia read Connacht.

Conall is now behind the bar. He went over it, not through it. He's a pretty agile guy. His arm is around the barmaid's waist. She is laughing most merrily. Nobody by now in the place except the four of us. For Brendan and Niall have really gone ahead to the theatre. But when Conall had first attempted to go over the top, Lagan and myself decided it might be wiser to stick around and keep a snaffle, Lagan said spancell, on him. That may be not all that easy.

Jodhpurs, I may tell you, has the same surname as myself. Except that she spells it differently. Carney, not Karney. So much I found out by standing beside her when she was filling in the hotel register. Waiting my turn I was. With the register.

We are now at last in the theatre. Or in the substitute hall. Which is by no means in the most elegant part of the town. There are no praying pickets. Conall is outraged. No pickets, no picture.

Perhaps they have prayed and picketed and departed before we got there. But no. Later we are to hear that they were never there. Also flown to Antananarivo?

To get to the hall we go through a dark entryway. Seventeenth century at the least. Footpads? Stilettos? Christopher Marlowe? No. Bludgeons? Newgate calendar? No. Nothing but bad lighting and potholed ground underfoot. Easy here to sprain an ankle. We are in an ancient market-place, long ago forsaken by markets and by everything and everybody else. A hideyhole for Art? A last refuge for strolling players? Then up a covered and creaking wooden stairway that climbs the wall, then down four shaky wooden steps and here we are, and where is the kip and where is the cardinal?

But there is no kip. There is no cardinal at the moment to be seen.

Conall, as is his custom, has got it wrong. Or so Lagan later booms.

What we are looking at is a weeping broad in a long, black dress, kneeling down before a roaring Franciscan friar. Or a fellow roaring, and wearing what might be a Franciscan habit except that it's so badly battered from strolling with the players that it's hard to tell. He could be Guy Fawkes or Johnny Appleseed or Planters' Peanuts or the man who broke the bank at Monte Carlo. But whoever or whatever he is, he sure as hell is giving that broad hell. Boy, is he giving her hell. What I mean is, he is telling her in considerable detail where she will find herself if she doesn't mend her ways and get smart, and get real smart and give up that old wop trick of screwing her brother. If you can tell by a slight protuberance she seems to be in the family way by her brother.

Curious thing, Brinsley is later to say, but there was always a soupçon of that in the midlands where I come from. John Ford, not the man who makes the cowboys, seems to have been much possessed by the idea. As T. S. Eliot said Webster was by death. Curious fellow, Ford. And Webster. And Eliot.

Brinsley met Eliot when Eliot was round the corner from the Abbey Bar to give a lecture in the Abbey Theatre that was. My research proceeds. Curious thing.

But listen to the friar as the broad is listening or pretending to listen.

He is telling her about a black and hollow vault where day is never seen, where shines no sun but flaming horror of consuming fires, a lightless sulphur choked with smoky fogs in an infected darkness: and in that place dwell many thousand thousand sundry sorts of never-dying deaths, and damned souls roar without pity, gluttons are fed with toads and adders, and burning oil poured down the drunkard's throat, and the usurer is forced to sip whole draughts of molten gold, and the murderer is forever stabbed yet never can he die, and the wanton lies on racks of burning steel.

Watch it, chick, watch it.

The friar also wises her up about lawless sheets and secret incests. About which, we may reckon, she knows more than he does. And tells her that when she parks her ass in that black and gloomy vault she will wish that each kiss her brother gave her had been a dagger's point.

Jasus Christ, says Conall, this is worse than any sermon I ever heard at any mission. What was the parish priest beefing about? He couldn't do better himself.

He says all that out quite aloud and several people hush him up, and the friar thinks they mean him and gets rattled, and, to my high delight, the incestuous broad giggles. For her it is mighty obvious that hell hath no furies.

To you, down there on Peachtree, a mission would be a sort of a tent-meeting, hellfire a-plenty, the Baptist tabernacle in Marietta, yeah Lord Amen, and washed, when the time is ripe, in the blood of the Lamb or the Chattahoochee river. What has the Good Lawd done for you, as the preacher roared and pointed by mistake at the harelipped, hunchbacked cripple, and the harelipped, hunchbacked cripple, in so far as his cleft palate would allow him to articulate, whistled back that the Good Lawd damn near roont me.

Then when the curtain creaks down to separate the scenes, something has to separate them, and the lights come up in the body of the house, Conall stands up to take pictures and to make a speech.

Jesus and Amen!

We are, *in tempore opportuno*, to find out that the valiant woman, far and from the furthest coasts, who leads the strolling players was so annoyed with the parish-priest that she cancelled the kip and the cardinal for something in which, when most of the cast has been massacred, another cardinal and the Pope get any loot that's left.

For we're off to Anarivo in the morning.

Then and thereafter Conall has bad luck with his photographs. For why? He keeps dropping the camera. The audience love it. Light relief. Charlie Chaplin. The audience need it. Some of them know Conall very well. He has been around. They cheer when he drops the camera. But in a mild, friendly, appreciative sort of way and not so as to disturb the players. Overmuch.

Conall's speech begins by thanking the audience on behalf of the valiant woman and the strolling players. Then he thanks the players and the woman on behalf of the audience. Then he sits down where his seat is not, or a place to put it. He has a standing ovation for that one. Then Brendan and Niall

and Jodhpurs persuade him into a corner at the back of the
hall and hold him there, good old Jodhpurs, and the curtain
creaks up again, it sure as God creaks, and here we are back
in Renaissance Parma and nothing worse going on than incest
and multiple murder.

Not one picture all night long did Conall capture.

Up on the stage, Grimaldi, a Roman gentleman, has just
knocked somebody off, the wrong person, as it so happens, or,
at any rate, not the person he means to knock off. The cardinal,
when the matter is drawn to his attention by the citizens of
Parma, is inclined to take a lenient view. For why? See text. The
cardinal, in brief, argues that Grimaldi is no common man even
if he is somewhat inclined to first-degree homicide. Grimaldi is
nobly born and of the blood of princes and he, the cardinal, has
received Grimaldi into the protection of the Holy Father.

Hip, hip hurrah, cries Conall, for the Holy Father. Send
Grimaldi to the Eucharistic Congress.

There are some murmurs but more laughs among the
audience. Stands to reason they're the laughing rather than
the murmuring sort of audience. Otherwise they wouldn't
be here.

Then Soranzo who is a nobleman, who wishes to marry
Annabella and who thinks he has all the boys in line, is raising
his glass which he has filled from the weighty bowl (see text),
to Giovanni who is screwing Annabella, but not just then and
there, who is, as I may have already explained, Giovanni's
sister, and Soranzo, in all innocence or something, is saying:
Here, Brother Grimaldi, here's to you, your turn comes next
though now a bachelor.

Then to Annabella Soranzo says: Cheer up, my love.

Conall repeats that, and shouts something that sounds like:
Tighten up there, M'Chesney.

Lagan basebarrelltones: Gag him, for God's sake.

And the house is hilarious.

Then enter Hippolita, masked, followed by several ladies in
white robes, also masked and bearing garlands of willow. Music

offstage. They do a dance. Not the Charleston, you may safely speculate. Soranzo says: Thanks, lovely virgins.

Conall says: How do you know.

The house rocks.

You see the joke, such as it may be, is that Soranzo has been having it off with Hippolita and now wishes to jettison cargo, and she, knowing this, is out to waste him but, before she can do so, Vasquez, a low type and no nobleman, slips her the old trick of the poisoned cup, and the friar, wise guy, says, fairly enough, that he fears the event, that a marriage is seldom good when the bride banquet so begins in blood.

He sure is the greatest living authority on hell and matrimony.

Curious thing.

Read the rest of it for yourself.

Enter Soranzo, unbraced, and dragging in Annabella, and calling out: Come strumpet, famous whore.

Conall: Give the girl a break. She'll come on her own.

Soranzo: Wilt thou confess and I will spare thy life?

Annabella: My life. I will not buy my life so dear.

Soranzo: I will not slack my vengeance.

Conall: They're not getting on. There's a rift in the flute.

Soranzo: Had'st thou been virtuous, fair, wicked woman.

Conall: Thou can'st not have everything.

Soranzo: My reason tells me now that 'tis as common to err in frailty as to be a woman. Go to your chamber.

Conall: Politeness is all. Carry the chamber to her, sir.

Conall seems to know his Shakespeare.

Curious thing.

Three pictures are taken.

Not by Conall Cearnach of whom, the original warrior I mean, more hereafter. But by Brendan the Navigator who proves to be a good man in a crisis. He is a blond block of a man in a brown, serge suit. He is a Fingallian. That means that he comes from the north of the County Dublin, or Fingal, the land of the fairhaired foreigners where, Lagan assures me, some of the old farmhouses still preserve the high, pointed, Scandinavian gables, à style brought in there a thousand or so years ago by sea-rovers who settled.

One picture Brendan takes of Giovanni entering from left with his sister's heart impaled on a dagger, and dripping. A red sponge, I'd say, soaked, for additional effect, in some reasonably inexpensive red wine.

All hearts that love should be like that. Mayhap, they are.

One picture he takes when the banditti rush in and the stage is strewn with corpses, and Vasquez, I told you he was a low type, tells the banditti that the way to deal with an old dame called Putana, whose name's a clue to character, is to carry her closely into the coalhouse and, instantly, put out her eyes and, if she should be so unappreciative as to scream, to slit her nose for laughs.

Exeunt banditti with Putana.

And that's about the next best thing to the riot that didn't arise.

The survivors are the cardinal, and Richardetto, a supposed physician, and Donado, a citizen of Parma, and Vasquez, the villain, who rejoices that a Spaniard can, in vengeance, outgo an Italian. Giovanni has just cashed in his chips. So the cardinal wisely advises those who are still able to stand up, that they should take up those slaughtered bodies and see them buried: and as for the gold and jewels, or whatsoever, since they are confiscate to the canons of the church, he, the cardinal, or we, as he calls himself, will seize them all for the Pope's proper use.

Conall: To pay for the . . .

But Jodhpurs has put her strong hand over his mouth.

Hautboys.

Sennet sounded.

Curtain.

The third picture Brendan takes is of the valiant lady making her curtain speech, and all the players, to the relief and felicity of all of us, resurrected and reunited. She thanks the audience. She thanks the gentlemen of the press. She thanks Conall personally and as Conall Lagan and not, as Patrick says she should have done, as Conall Carnage. To loud applause. Even I am astounded. Ireland is a more wonderful place than I ever thought it could be. Later I find out that Conall and the valiant woman are firm friends, that she even loves Conall as a mother might love a wayward son. Also I find out that to make absolutely certain of a good house, she took no money at the door: and that the picketers did not bother their ass picketing because the priest was far awa, far awa, and the weather was raining.

Up to that moment none of us have noticed or mentioned the weather.

And the next act opens back in the bar in the hotel.

The night is in full swing.

We return to our festivity and do our best to put the corpses of Parma out of our thoughts. We manage to do so.

To tell you the whole truth as I have promised always to do, well to tell as much of the whole truth as a lady should hear or wish to hear, we sit drinking, slowly, sipping, no gulping, spilling or slobbering, and the talk is good. We sit for several hours after official closing time and in the learned company of two uniformed police-officers and two detectives in plain clothes. One of the detectives has been among the audience and thinks the play the funniest thing he ever laid eyes or ears on since he saw Jimmy O'Dea, a famous comedian, in the Olympia theatre in Dublin when he, the detective, was in training in the Phoenix Park.

Jasus, the detective keeps saying, I tought dey'd never stop. And de lad coming in wit her heart on a breadknife. I could have taken me oat 'twas a pig's kidney. And Himself dere was de best part of de play.

The detective comes from a fairly widespread part of Ireland where they have problems with a certain dipthong.

By Himself he means Conall whose constancy and endurance is astounding, for talking and dancing and singing and telling the women he loves them: Jodhpurs in one breath, the barmaid in the next, with a few words to spare for any woman in the place, under or over sixty. He sits with us for a space. Then he is up at the bar or behind the bar and occasionally kissing the barmaid who objects, but mildly. To much general laughter. He is, believe it or not, most courteous. He knows *tout le monde* and it knows and likes him, and I do notice that he seldom renews his drink, and I wonder is it booze that sets him going or is he just that way by nature. Outgoing. Extrovert. You could say all that again. He can dance. He can sing. He does both at intervals. He even wears a wedding ring. He uses all his talents to the full.

We may be forced, Lagan says, to hogtie Conall as his namesake, Conall Cearnach, was hogtied by Bealcú, or Hound-mouth, from Ballina, the champion of Connacht before Christ was in it. Not that Christ ever had much influence in certain parts of Connacht.

Nothing I know can stop Lagan. He will boom and drone on now until the sergeant and the guard and the two men in plain clothes, and anybody else who cares to listen, will know all about the wounding and healing of the ancient hero. But, hell, what am I here for? Research is research. And where is my notebook?

Lagan explains to the plain-clothes men and the guard that when Bealcú urges his charger and, ergo, his chariot across the snow to the place where he has seen the two warriors in combat, Slinger Keth lies dead and Conall Cearnach, wounded, lies at point to die. The guard and the plain-clothes men show every evidence of interest. The sergeant is up to something else. He has the ear of Brendan, the Viking sea-rover or the sanctified navigator, what you will. He, the sergeant, is saying slowly, spacing out the words carefully: Soap . . . necktie . . . chocolates . . . cigarettes . . . pipe and tobacco-pouch . . . book or book token . . . shaving-cream or aftershave . . . socks . . . record or record-player . . . pen . . . handkerchiefs . . .

Or rather he is reading those mystic words out of the newspaper that employs Lagan, Conall, Brendan and Niall. He asks Brendan what he thinks of all that. Brendan says: Aunt Miriam is a very good friend of mine. And a most considerate and efficient colleague.

This is extremely curious. Niall is, for the moment, at the far end of the bar, engaged at conversation with some friends he has encountered.

Lagan says: Put jockstrap on the list. For Conall over there.

Seems Lagan can narrate to four men and simultaneously listen to a fifth. There is much general laughter at mention of the jockstrap. Over at the bar, but on this side of it, Conall has one arm around the barmaid and the other around Jodhpurs. All seem happy. Am I losing contact? Events mingle and move too fast for me. It is a long way from here to Spoon River.

But aside from all that: When Houndmouth sees Cearnach flat on his ass on the snow he proceeds to badmouth him. Calling him a ravening wolf of Ulster which is where Conall, hereinafter to be known as Cearnach, comes from. Who answers: Taunts are for reviling women.

That's pretty good.

— Hush up, he says, to Bealcú, and finish me off.

But no, Bealcú will not have it noised abroad that it took two Connachtmen to knock off one Ulsterman. His game is to bring Cearnach home with him to Ballina or wherever, to have him patched up by the Connacht medicos and then, for the glory of Bealcú, and whatever gods may be in Connacht, to kill him in single combat. So Bealcú binds Cearnach in fivefold fetters, which is what Lagan thinks we should do with our Conall, then heaves him up or has him heaved up on the chariot, to be somewhat cheesed when he tries to lift the Ulsterman's war-mace.

What a weight it was to raise!

Brendan interrupts, reading out aloud from the newspaper. This is what he reads: The girl in the picture is playing with her white mice. Do you have a pet mouse? If so what colour is

it. Do you like mice? If not, write and say why. Could you write
a poem about a mouse? Try.

— Christ of Almighty, says Lagan. What are you all up to?

And the sergeant says that his sixteen-year-old daughter is
a magician all-out at the painting and drawing, and can turn
out a poem that should be printed.

Brendan explains. Mostly or totally for my benefit. The
others know all about Aunt Miriam. Which is the name of the
mythical lady who edits the page from which the sergeant and
Brendan have been reading: Aunt Miriam's Campfire Club.

The sergeant's daughter and a slew (sluagh, in the Irish)
of her schoolfriends wish to join. Brendan says that he will
look after all that. He reads further to explain to me about
that odd list of objects: Choosing birthday presents for fathers,
uncles or older brothers can sometimes be quite difficult. So
what about carrying out a birthday survey? Ask your father,
brother, uncle, teacher or any man over twenty-fiveish to put
the birthday presents on this list in order of their choice. Bring
your completed list into class next week. Check the answers and
count up in class how many men put socks or soap . . .

Or de jockstraps, says one of de plain-clothes men.

Let joy be unconfined.

It is early in de morning. Am I losing my diptongs?

Brendan later admits, blushingly, that Aunt Miriam is his
beloved wife. That is not true. Aunt Miriam, in fact, is a
somewhat eccentric and retired clergyman. That is supposed to
be a wellkept secret. But Brendan writes down the names and
addresses of the sergeant's daughter and all her friends. He says
that he will see to it that Aunt Miriam's secretary, who doesn't
exist, will send to each and every one of those young enthusiasts
the Campfire Crest, a sort of badge. He promises that the letters
they write to Aunt Miriam will be printed in the paper. And
the poetical works of the sergeant's daughter. All this, for sure,
he looks after when back in Dublin. But the entente he sets up
between us and the sergeant is to prove real precious some hours
later when Brendan and Niall are on the road, by automobile,

to Limerick city where they have something else to report. Or on which to report. Even in Ireland, English is English.

Action stations!

The clock strikes three.

Jodhpurs says she will hit the hay. A challenging thought. The barmaid has vanished. Brendan and Niall have taken the road for Limerick city. Conall and Lagan and myself would seem to be the only living people left. One of those corrugated things has been pulled down and the bar is closed. Lagan and myself set sail for the bottom of the main stairway. But is that good enough for Conall? No, no, by no means no. He says that he wants one more drink. But he is a lot more sober than he pretends to be and he has something else, as you may imagine, in his calculating mind. We try to reason with him. To talk him into calling it a night, or a day. No use, no use. Down a long corridor that leads towards the back of the building he sees, and so do we, a light burning. That, it may appear, is where the barmaid has found covert. So hitching his wagon to that star, Conall Carnage steams (block that metaphor), down the corridor and through the heavy-drifted snow, and thunders on the door of the room of the light as if he owned the world, and barges in, and finds . . .

Two young clergymen drinking-up. The curates, or assistants, or lootenants of the parish. The mice relaxing while the tomcat is farawa; farawa in Antananarivo. One of them turns angry-nasty. Through embarrassment, it may be, at being found out. Tells Conall, and in a clear shrill voice, that this is a private room. The barmaid is nowhere to be seen. So Conall demands to know what in heaven, or hell, two clerics are doing drinking-up and being merry in a private room in a public house at three o'clock in the morning. And why are they not at home writing sermons and banning plays as any zealous sacerdotes should be. Cleric Number Two asks him, politely enough, to leave. Then Lagan grabs Conall and begins to urge him out and Lagan, although an anti-clerical of the old style, apologizes to the polite priest, explaining that Conall has a drop too many taken. Out of nowhere the proprietress appears, a tough sort of a lady in late middle-age. She exhorts Conall to have some respect for the cloth. From halfways up the stairs Conall intones: Bless me, fathers; for I have sinned.

Lagan chants, but only so as to be heard by Conall and myself: *Dies irae, dies illa, solvet saeclum in favilla* . . .

We propel Conall as far as and into his room. That day, we reckon, has been called a day.

So Bealcú urges charger and chariot westward through the borders of Breffny. Bearing with him the corpse of Keth the Slinger and the wounded and captive Cearnach. They come to a place called Moy Slaught where the ancient Irish used to worship a pretty formidable idol called Crom Cruach. He was a hunk of stone or something and his twelve apostles, twelve lesser hunks, sat round him in a ring. Along came Jones, meaning St. Patrick, and thumps old Crom with his Bachall Iosa, or the staff of Christ, and Crom bears forever the mark of the bachall, and the earth swallows the twelve lesser idols: and, just at that moment in Lagan's narration, all hell breaks loose in the street outside the hotel.

Lagan and myself are sharing a room. Where Jodhpurs has vanished to, we do not know. Jealousy, at last, may have driven that tolerant girl to roost in some faraway place. The hotel is a corner house. Our room is right on the corner and right above the main door. On which door Crom Cruach and his sub-gods twelve seem at this moment to be beating. Where, cries Lagan, is the staff of Jesus.

He looks out one of our two windows but the angle is awkward and he can see nothing. The beating at the door lessens. Then ceases. But there is a frenzy and a babel of voices. Then the door of our room opens and the sergeant steps in. And says most modestly: Mr. Lagan, as the eldest member here present of the press-party, could you please come down and put a tether on this young fellow before he wrecks the town.

For Carnage is off on the warpath again, with or without benefit of chariot. Meantime, back at the ranch, Cearnach has been unceremoniously dumped on the fairgreen of Moy Slaught where he is getting a poor press from all the widows he, in happier times, has made in the West of Ireland.

And Bealcú says: Let Lee, the leech, be brought.

And Lee, the gentlefaced, is brought from his plot of healing herbs. Like Lagan walking down the stairs to see what healing he can bring to Conall Carnage in the hall below. Followed, at a safe distance, by myself and the sergeant who gives me a brief breakdown on what has caused the brouhaha. Seems Conall made down again to the door of the lighted room. To find it locked and bolted. To Carnage that presented no problem. He bangs on the door and roars out that he wants somebody to hear his confession. Lest he die in sin. Then comes arunning the lady of the house and with her a big guy she has somewhere drafted so as to throw Conall out. This big guy is a mighty-big big guy. So he pushes our Conall back as far as the main hall where Conall, who is nifty, steps backwards up two rungs of the stairs, so as to gain purchase, and throws a hard, roundhouse swing at the big guy, who is also nifty. And ducks. And Conall knocks down the lady, and the lady screams bloody murder, and the big guy and the clerics just about manage to heave Conall out the front door and lock it, and Conall goes to work with fists and feet, raising holy hell on the oak, three inches thick, and ringing the bell, and roaring Bless me, fathers, for I have sinned, and lights going on and children crying all over the town as if, says the sergeant, Jesus had come again, and the lady phones the fuzz, and here we are again, happy as can be, and Jodhpurs, neat girl, and one of the plain-clothes men are holding Conall, and Lagan is saying that Conall is a good kid, and the lady is shouting that he's a pup, a pup, a pup.

Lagan shows himself to be some diplomat. M. de Norpois. Hit the Guermantes trail. The matronly presence of Aunt Miriam is still there to aid him. He and the sergeant mutter together in one corner. Conall calms down. Jodhpurs is good for him. Like Hector in Homer she is well known as a tamer of horses. Then Lagan and the sergeant come to this arrangement. That Conall will go for the night to the calaboose with the lawmen. For no way in hell will the lady have him for the night in her hotel. What, she says, will my husband say when he comes home and hears that I was assaulted under my own roof. What, says Lagan, will the parish priest say when he comes home from wherever in heaven he is and I tell him that his two curates were drinking in your office at three o'clock in the morning.

Détente.

The lady screams that rightaway she wants to prefer charges. The Sergeant, gently but firmly, says that she must wait until the next day or, to be exact, daylight of the same day. She screams again that Conall's swipe has smashed her spectacles. For corroboration, the big guy has already gathered up the fragments, *colligite fragmenta ne pereant*, into a brown paperbag. Evidence? Or second-class relics? Jodhpurs, gallant girl, offers to go with Conall. To burn on his pyre. But Conall, like a hero going into transportation, kisses her farewell, several times, advises her to catch a few hours sleep, she may need them: that the night to come, and still so far ahead, is yet another night. The lady of the house is about to have a fit. So the big guy leads her away. The clerics have vanished. Up the chimney? Then Conall marches off, taking the lead with the sergeant, the plain-clothes man bringing up the rear. But halfways across the street, the plain-clothes man stops, shakes hands with Conall and goes off another way. Home to his bed and his wife, if he has one. Conall marches on, under escort, to his lonely prison cell. Or so I sadly and foolishly think.

Carnage now lies in the hoosegow. Cearnach lies under the care of Lee the Leech. Who, gentlefaced as he is, still strikes a hard bargain with the victorious and vengeful Bealcú. Has Lee, like the sergeant, a soft, melancholy voice and a moustache that droops as if the humid heat had gotten to it?

— Do you know what he said to me, Lagan says.

Not Lee the Leech, but the sergeant.

When the two of them, Lagan and the sergeant, were muttering in the corner.

— He said to me, Lagan says, that if the lad never did worse than knock that damsel down, he won't do much wrong in the world. She would skin a flea. (For the price of its hide: a native colloquialism.) 'Tis well known, says the Sergeant, that she adulterates the whiskey. Anyway, the lad never hit her.

No direct hit. The wind of his passing, like that of a godamned archangel, simply flattened her.

— Anyway, the Sergeant said. The lad struck out in self-defence. And missed. The only bruise would be on her backside where she sat down with a thump. He that cares to feel that way may find it.

— But keeps an eye on things here, the Sergeant said. You and the Yank. And I'll watch the young fellow. We want no trouble. Nor capers in the courtroom. We're overworked as it is. And that's the true.

Then Jodhpurs kisses us goodnight.

And that's the true, as the Sergeant says.

And we rest our weary heads. And somewhere in gardens, and on the fringe of the town, and all over Ireland, the birds are beginning to sing.


— Curious thing, Brinsley says to me through my tumbling halfsleep.

— Curious thing. Georgia is famous for peaches. Or that's what the Irish Christian Brothers told me.

Once I had told him that there was a dame on Peachtree Street, Atlanta, Georgia. Meaning you. Well aware I am that there are many and various dames on Peachtree.

He capped my statement by telling me that there was once, he had heard or read, a dame in Belmont, richly left, and she was fair . . .

Then he went on about the peaches.

Seems there is or was a geography compiled by an Irish Christian Brother for use in schools run by the Irish Christian Brothers. It lists or listed the chief products of various places. Inchicore, a portion of Dublin, has rolling-stock. Georgia has peaches.

It is the dawn. The summer dark, the poet said, is but the dawn of day. That's Lagan quoting. He is up and shaving at the handbasin. No rooms with bath here. Rise up, he says, and do begin the day's adorning. He is a healthy man. He needs no cure. He tells me that Lee the Leech says that healing is with God's permission, health for life's enjoyment made. My American head is a purple glow and my belly full of the linnet's wings: and Lee the Leech agrees to heal Cearnach but insists that when the healing is perfected there shall be a fair fight and no favour, and that if Conall is triumphant he is to have safe conduct back to the Fews, his native part of Ulster. Also: that while the healing is in process no man shall steal through fences to work the patient mischief or surprise. He demands an oath on the matter: to Crom the God, to the sun, to the wind.

Lagan pulls open the heavy window-curtains and the sun comes through with a scream.

All quiet on the street outside. The good folk here do not arise betimes.

What healing is there for my hapless head?

My eyes I close and see viscous, bubbling peaches.

What healing for Carnage in his dungeon drear?

Lee the Leech has unlocked Cearnach's fetters.

Valiantly I face the razor.

— Curious thing, Brinsley says, Plato never bothered his barney about anachronisms. Curious thing.

But I swear by God and Abraham Lincoln, and by the body of Pocahontas, lovely as a poppy, sweet as a pawpaw in May,

he is there in the diningroom and leathering-in (as Jodhpurs
says), to his breakfast when she, me and Lagan get downstairs
to the diningroom. He? Who? Brinsley? Plato? Bealcú? Lee the
Leech? Conall Cearnach? Crom the God? No, but our own
dear Conall Carnage for it is he. Eating egg and bacon and
sausage and black pudding and drinking black coffee by the
bucket. And eating butter, putting it into his mouth in great
globs. Lubrication, he tells me. Oil the wheels. And the big
end. Never did I see the like. Almost threw up to watch him.
The lady of the house hovers in the background. Out of arm's
reach and the swing of the sea. Amazed me that they served
him anything. But he's a hell of a hard man to resist. Jodhpurs
is all joy. Growing boys need food, she says. She glows. She
is, I blush to say it, looking ahead to the night ahead.

Then while Carnage roisters and we nibble he tells us about
the night or the remnants of a night just passed. Seems he
never had it so good. Here is what happened. Conall and the
sergeant walked back to the barracks. Who should be there
but the second plain-clothes man (as in Shakespeare), and
the garda or guard who had been drinking with us earlier in
the night. Conall asked if they were going to lock him up and
they said no way. Then another garda appeared with a tray
and teapot and bread and jam. Everybody was, as Conall put
it, fierce polite. Then the lot went home except Conall and
one man or guard or garda, or what-in-the-hell, who was on
night-duty. Who placed six chairs in strategic positions. Then
produced a spring and a mattress which he balanced on the
chairs. Then the all-night man said hop in and the two of
them, and the town and the cattle in the fields and the birds
in the bushes, slept until the sergeant came in at dawn, and
with a bottle of wine from faraway Oporto. There were drinks
and handshaking all round and that was that. Curious thing.
Curious country, Ireland.

The healing of Conall Cearnach is, by now, well under way.
He is still on his bed or on the scratcher (a Dublin usage),

and he heaves thereon, Lagan quotes, as on reef of rock the ocean wildly tosses. Don't quite get that. The bed, the ocean, should be tossing, not Cearnach, the Rock. And the sons of Bealcú are worried. What is Lee the Leech up to? How fares the Ulsterman, the man from the Fews? So from a distance the sons of Bealcú spy, as best as they can, on the medical treatment. The patient no longer tosses on the bed nor does the bed toss under him. Now he is up and about even if he is pallid as a winding-sheet. Swear I do to Edgar Allan Poe that I do not know, nor could wildly guess at the pallidity of a winding-sheet.

Now Cearnach is out of his chamber. This isle is full of chambers.

Cearnach is walking on his feet. What else?

We have paid our bill to the barmaid who is doubling in reception and who has the giggles. She giggles beautifully. All over. She kisses Carnage a fond farewell. The lady of the house is not there to be seen. Nor to see. We walk on our feet, all four of us, on eight feet, through the town to the other of the two hotels. It is an ancient and historic town. And looks the part. But I have a hunch that we have become part of the history. For the people on the pleasant side-walks are peeping at us and trying to pretend that they are not peeping. As are the sons of Bealcú peeping away out west, not in Kansas, but on the fair green of Moy Slaught. To see Cearnach, a ghastly figure, on his javelin propped he goes. But day follows day and Cearnach convalesces and convalesces, and with herbs and healing balsams he burgeons like a sere oak under summer showers and dew, and the sons of Bealcú are fearful for the future of their father.

Or the Dazee, as Carnage puts it.

Another Dublin usage.

Carnage is beginning to show some interest in the story of the healing of his namesake.

We have reached the other hotel. A mighty handsome place. But it is now bright morning and, after last night and all that happened where we were, even a roominghouse on Ponce de Leon, which flows into and out of the street of the Peachtrees, as you know, could be a mighty handsome place.

The valiant woman is here, having her morning gin, and some of her players around her. She is a widow. Her husband, who was a playwright, had a long enmity with Brinsley who is, also, a playwright. But valiantly she did her best to keep the peace between them. She tells me a lot. Research, research, research. The hardships of strolling players in rural Ireland. The money she is losing. Sean O'Casey, she tells me, is a cantankerous bastard when it comes to giving permission to anyone to put on his plays in Ireland. He wants money, for God's sake, money. Ah well. To make him madder still the Maria Mussolini Duce people picketed a play of his in the Gaiety in Dublin, and the Sinn Féiners, long ago, nearly wrecked the old Abbey over *The Plough and the Stars*, and one old nut of a theatregoer roared at O'Casey that there were no prostitutes in Dublin, and O'Casey said, mildly, in return, that he had been accosted three times on his way to the theatre and the old nut cracked back that if there were prostitutes in Dublin it was the British army put them there.

— Good on the army, Carnage says.

Lagan hushes him up.

But all that about O'Casey is history. Away back in the 1920s. Return to the here and now.

We have one hell of a lunch. The valiant lady pays.

Then honking in the street and shouting at the door come Niall and Brendan, all bright and glittering in the lunchtime air, and all the way from Limerick city, and all ready to drive you all back to Dublin town.

They have had their own adventures.

For on the way to Limerick city they rested for a while in a roadside tavern. Not a roadhouse. Just an Irish pub, open day and night and to hell with the law. Niall had driven that far. And in the tavern they got to talking with this elderly

farmer who lived back in the boondocks in mountains called
the Silvermines. He sang songs. He hobbled on a stick. So
kindhearted Brendan reckoned that the old-timer was too old
and too hirpled (an Ulster usage) to walk home. Off with the
three of them, and a bottle of whiskey, through a network of
mountain roads to a shack where Senex lived alone. Brendan
uncorked the whiskey. Senex produced three cracked and
yellowing mugs. Out with Niall to the henhouse to rob the
nests. Shall it be my lot, he thought, in the screeching and
fluttering dark, to be beaten to death by the wings of hens in
a cró, or hutment, on the slopes of the Silvermine mountains.
Then out of all the eggs he could find he made, he says, the
world's biggest-ever bloody omelette, chopped it into three
fair halves, and they ate the lot and drank the whiskey,
and Senex staggered safely to bed and, with Brendan the
Navigator at the wheel, the pair of them set out to try to
escape from the mountains. Which does not prove to be all
that easy. For the dustroads go round and round about to
find the town of Roundabout that makes the world go round.
Nor is an overdose of whiskey the best navigational aid. In
the chill dawn, with Brendan asleep and Niall at the wheel,
they stumble on Limerick city which is beautiful, as everybody
knows, the river Shannon, full of fish, beside that city flows:
and Niall, shaking Brendan awake, says where is Hanratty's
hotel, and Brendan sings out: You find Hanratty's. I discovered
Limerick.

Then they find the hotel and are no sooner asleep than the
phone rings from the Dublin office to say that it has heard
that a pressman has assaulted a woman during or after the
performance of the banned play, and would somebody please
tell the other end of the phone what in hell is going on down
there.

Enter now the garda of the previous night.

Not into Limerick city but into that handsome hotel in
which we are washing down our lunch. Seems the lady of
the other hotel has called the Dublin office to report the

disorderly behaviour of two cameramen, Patrick Lagan and John Karney, meaning me. Now I have become a cameraman and a knockerdown of ladies. She has threatened legal action. The old blackmail – settle-out-of-court trick. The office disowns both of us. Lagan is on holidays and I was never there, and even Conall Carnage is under semi-suspension for some previous misdemeanour and, anyway, he hasn't been mentioned. So Lagan calls the lady and says that if she wants legal action or counteraction she is more than welcome any time, and that those two young clergymen would sure smile to be subpoenaed, and about the hell there would be to pay when the boss gets back from Antananarivo.

Enter the sergeant.

To approve of Lagan's diplomacy, or whatever. To bid us godspeed and a safe journey, and to say that things will surely settle if we see Carnage safely back to Dublin.

*Exeunt omnes.*

One little town. Two little towns. Three little towns.

No stops, Niall says, until we're safe in Dublin. Or, at any rate, as far as Roche's of Rathcoole.

Meaning a famous singing public-house about twenty-five miles from the city centre. The public-house does not sing. Only the people in it. Well, they try. A master of ceremonies at the piano. Ladies and gentlemen, one voice only, please. And the saddest man in the house stands up and wails: Caan, I forget you, when every night reminds me . . .

Well you know that I cannot forget you. Accept this letter in lieu of vows.

Anyway, Lagan is quoting: Forbaid was a master-slinger. Maev, when in her bath she sank, felt the presence of his finger from the further Shannon bank . . .

— That guy, says Carnage, had a mighty long finger.

Jodhpurs smacks him. But gently. She is sitting on his knee. It is a small auto. We are six people. We are counted, Brendan says, like the elephants, after they are washed, at bedtime in Duffy's circus.

Lagan annotates his quotation. Research.

Conall Cearnach, do you follow me, had killed Aleel, the last husband of Maev, queen of Connacht. Aleel and Maev started a war when they quarrelled in their bed because he had a bull and she hadn't.

— So, Carnage says, that we don't have to be professors or literary editors to know what that was about.

Again Jodhpurs smacks him. Then they kiss. Niall who is at the wheel says that somebody or something is rocking the boat.

Then, after the killing of Aleel, Maev retires to an island on Lough Ree in the river Shannon. Once a day and at dawn she takes her bath in a springwell on that island. Vain woman, she thinks there isn't a peeper in Ireland dare peep on a queen. But Forbaid of Ulster has long sight as well as a long finger, and spots her from afar, and comes in the dusk secretly to the well and, with a linen thread, measures the distance back to the far shore. Then he stretches the thread on the ground, in a safe and secret place, plants a wooden fence-pole at each end of it, puts an apple atop of one pole, stands at the other, practises with his sling or handbow until he can take the apple ten times out of ten. Then one fine morning he stands where the river Shannon's flowing and the three-leaved shamrock grows and, across the wide water, where my heart is I am going to my native Irish rose, he clobbers the queen between the eyes with a two-pound rock, and she falls into the well, and that is the end of a queen who was longer in the bidnis than Queen Victoria: and the moment that I meet her with a hug an' kiss I'll greet her, for there's not a colleen (cáilín), sweeter where the river Shannon flows.

— Smart guy, Carnage says. But he hadn't much to peep at. She must have been a hundred if she was a day.

More smacks and kisses. Niall heaves to. Threatens irons for mutiny. Jodhpurs kisses back of Niall's neck. On we go.

Then more kisses, did I stop them when a million seemed so few?

That was Lagan. Courtesy of Mr. Browning.

Wait for it, Carnage says.

Then we get the entire spiel about Oh, Galuppi, Baldassaro, this is very hard to find, I can scarcely misconceive you it would prove me deaf and blind, but although I take your meaning 'tis with such a heavy mind . . .

And much more of the same.

That's Lagan's party piece. Or one of them.

We know now, Carnage says, who broke up the party in Fitzwilliam Square.

Much laughter. For the benefit of the visitor Lagan explains: It is, John, one of the many afflictions of my life to have the same surname as our dear friend, Carnage. Here and now happily restored to us, through my, shall we say, diplomacy, and the friendship of the sergeant. Although, if the case had gone to court, even the most humane District Justice would have felt compelled to give him six months without the option. For last night's performance and, furthermore, for his previous record. That gold ring he so proudly wears. Consider it.

Carnage raises and swivels an elegant right hand. The ring glows.

That ring is by no means his ring, Lagan informs me. He is not married. Do not think it. Not a woman in Ireland would have him. In wedded bliss, that is. No, that ring belongs to a lady with whom he is, shall we say, familiar. Who received it from her husband. From whom she is now sundered.

Life, life, says Carnage.

And twists the ring on his finger.

Who to support herself, Lagan says, ventures out occasionally on the scented and sacred sidewalks of Dublin.

We all, says Jodhpurs, have to do our best. Poor Maryanne.

Jodhpurs has a lot of heart.

So Carnage has a friend, Lagan explains. Odd as it may seem, he still has friends. This friend lives in an apartment in

Fitzwilliam Square. A select area. And invites Carnage and
Maryanne to a party. Invitation instantly accepted. Conall
Carnage is hell for parties. And two or three or four, accounts
and authorities differ as in Edward Scribble Gibbon, two or
three or four cabloads arrive somewhat noisily in the elegant
Square, Carnage and Maryanne, and some of Maryanne's
business colleagues, and some of their friends, and create such
immortal havoc that the gardai or the guards or the guards
or the police or the coppers or the bobbies or the peelers or
the fuzz or the pigs or the gendarmes or the effing Royal
Irish Constabulary or whatever in hell you visiting American
scholar, or embryo scholar, may care so to describe them,
are called by the startled and highly respectable neighbours,
and the unfortunate man is evicted from his apartment in
Fitzwilliam Square . . .

With more kisses, who could stop them, Jodhpurs is keeping
Carnage quiet.

Does that sentence, or does it not, need a question mark.
This one does????

Niall is singing about the sash his father wore.

Brendan, his voyaging o'er, is asleep.

The green countryside flows past.

And the great and much-appreciated joke, Lagan says,
was that the news went round the town that I was the Lagan
responsible.

More green countryside. Beautifully sunlit. One more small
town.

How lucky, Lagan says, was Conall Cearnach to live so
long ago.

But the sons of Bealcú are on the warpath and one of
them reminds the other of the method by which Forbaid, the
master-slinger, had fingered Maev, the Queen. Every morning
from afar they watch Cearnach grow stronger and they fear
for their father, and watch Cearnach coming at dawn to the
fountain or well-margin to drink: while Cearnach is thinking,
in the words of the poet, how a noble virgin, by a like green

fountain's brink, heard his own pure vows one morning, faraway and long ago, all his heart to home was turning and the tears began to flow . . .

Jodhpurs likes that bit.

Not many pure vows, she says, do I hear. Nor Maryanne, in the course of her career.

So Lagan explains that Cearnach is thinking, while he weeps, of the wife and the weans (children, to you), back home in Ulster in Dunseverick's windy tower. Then up he leaps in a fit, runs round like a whirlwind, swings the war-mace, hurls the spear, and Bealcú, also peeping, but from another point of vantage and unseen by his sons, has the crap frightened out of him.

Cearnach, Carnage opines, has had his morning gin-and-tonic. There must be good stuff in that there fountain. Mayo poteen? Mountain dew? Georgia Moon Cawn whiskey?

Which may be more-or-less what Bealcú thinks. Not in relation to booze but about a god who, Bealcú thinks, may be in the fountain and to whom Cearnach prays, and Bealcú reckons he might just sneak in and, himself, mention the matter to the god.

But what about his vow, cries Jodhpurs. His vow to Crom Cruach and the sun and the wind.

She seems to know more about the story than a man might imagine.

She and Carnage are cheek-to-cheek.

Even if not dancing.

Has she tamed him?

Briefly we pause at Roche's of Rathcoole. Just long enough to hear six times on the jukebox one of Niall's favourite songs. Idaho, Idaho, I lost her and I found her at the Idaho State Fair, he broke twenty broncos and one grizzly bear, but she broke one cowpoke at the Idaho State Fair, Idaho, Idaho . . .

Once in my life I passed, by Greyhound, through Boise, Idaho.

No singing customers are present in Roche's of Rathcoole.
It is too early in the evening.

Caan I forget you . . .

No questionmark here needed.


But this is not Dunseverick's windy tower. No, we are back
somewhere in the environs of Dublin and we are in a tower,
one of four, and one of them at each corner of an ancient castle.
For Lagan, Patrick, has been invited to a party in this tower.
A friend of his rents it. Just the one tower. He is a prominent
painter, this friend. We get there about midnight. There is a
tree in the courtyard that was planted there more than five
hundred years ago. At Lagan's suggestion Carnage tears off
a bit of the bark and some leaves to send to you. They are
safely in a small box and I will bear them with me across
the broad Atlantic. There is a tradition that Edmund Spenser
ate his first meal in Ireland in this castle. As for myself I ate
there what, but for the grace of God, might have been my last
meal on earth: the ghost of the poet, perhaps, looking over my
shoulder and babbling of a goodly bosom like a strawberry
bed, a breast like lilies e'er their leaves be shed, and all her
body rising like a stayre, and you know the rest of it, and I
love my love in the morning, I love my love at noon . . .

Poor fellow. No wonder he entered the Christian Brothers.
Not Spenser. But that other gentle poet.

But speaking of ghosts, this castle is haunted by a peculiar
shade. Or by peculiar footsteps that are heard going up the
winding stairs. But never coming down. Steps only. No person.
No wraith.

Carnage says: Don't blame me.

The Castle has other associations which I will enumerate
when I see you. And a pleasant seat which I was unable to
see. For it is now past midnight. We enter the great hall. Not
of the castle. But we enter a pretty commodious room halfways
up the tower. To see a fine throng, glasses in hands. And
to be welcomed. And to see a distinguished-looking, elderly,

moustachioed gentleman trying to climb the wall. Uttering
foul oaths the while. Seems that he has been attempting to
climb the wall for several hours. Nor is he alone at that caper.
Several of the guests are having a go. A hop, step and jump
across the room. Then a roar and a run and a leap at the
wall. Does not make sense at first. Then it dawns on me. The
aim of the game is to leap higher than the door, turn round in
mid-air and end up seated on the wide lintel shelf. Solid oak.
Only one guest succeeds. A small man with a Chaplinesque
moustache. A painter. Or, also, a circus acrobat. He is rewarded
by a bottle of champagne. Which he drinks while sitting on
the shelf.

Lacking the long finger of Forbaid, the master-slinger I
stay safely on the carpet. For the wear and tear of the journey
to renaissance Parma and back is beginning to tell, and all I
want to do is to lie down. So up with me, up the haunted,
twisting stairway, up two more floors, the furore dying away
below me. No rough men-at-arms do I meet, cross-gartered to
the knees or shod in iron. No footfalls do I hear but mine own.
A small room I find and, joy of joys, a bed. On which, fully
clothed, I collapse with a crash. Then down below in the Hall
of Pandemonium, Carnage becomes aware of my absence and
is worried. Believe it or not, but Carnage is a real human being.
He begins searching all over for me. He runs downstairs and
looks all around. All around the grounds and in the pouring
rain. Checking all the cars. Climbing the ancient tree. Then,
systematically, he begins to search the tower from the ground
up. Where, at the end of an hour, he, inevitably, finds me.
Shakes me awake to find out if I am still alive. Puts a pillow
under my head. Tucks blankets around me. All the while
assuring me that I should come downstairs and have another
drink to help me to sleep. He is very concerned about me.
He says that he mainly worries because I seem so tall, blond,
thin and innocent, and mild-mannered, that I can only come
to harm among the rougher Irish. Even the women are hard,
he assures me, and you have got to be tough to stand up to

them. He is taking care of me all the time, talking to me like a worried father to a not-too-bright, not-too-strong son. He is twenty-one. As you know I am twenty-five and have survived even the army.

At four in the morning I arise to begin the day's adorning. Still slightly stupefied. Go down the haunted stairway. My host gives me coffee and sandwiches and tells me that I should write not about Brinsley but about Joyce. He is actually a relation. Not of Brinsley. But of Joyce.

So in honour of James Joyce we go for a morning swim off the Bull Wall where Stephen Dedalus walked and saw the wading girl and cried out heavenly god and all the rest of it. Research, research! Oh, the delights of a dawn plunge in the nude in the dirty water of Dublin Bay. Jodhpurs and all, or Jodhpurs without her jodhpurs. My eyes I modestly avert. Credit that if you can. She swims well. Not Dedalus himself, when he walked into that epiphany, ever saw the like. So strip I do and clamber down the rocks. Brendan, who has more sense, stays clothed and warm and holds my spectacles for me. The water is colder than ice and about as comfortable as broken glass. But it almost restores us to sobriety. We splash around there for thirty minutes or so and nobody, praise the Lord and hand me down my bible, is cramped or drowned. Then we sit on the rocks and watch the day coming up over Dublin city, and over the bay, and over Clontarf where Brian Boru bate the Danes, the dacent people, Lagan had said, without whom there never would have been a Dublin. For Brian, Lagan had argued, was a wild man from Limerick or thereabouts, as bad as or worse than Carnage or Bealcú . . .

Now Lagan has gone. For unlike the rest of us he has a home and a family to attend to, and Jodhpurs tells to the end the tale of the killing of Bealcú, another sore case of mistaken identity. She has read the poem, or has had it read to her, at school. Seems hard to believe that a strong broad like Jodhpurs ever went to school or to anywhere except the racing-stables. But Carnage says she was very bright at school, prizes and scholarships, and still is, and in all sort of places and ways, and can hold her own in talk on such topics even with the learned Lagan himself who is, says Carnage, as you have noticed, a sound man, and he will have my suspension lifted, he has the decency, he has the influence and he doesn't really mind being mistaken for me, it gives him stories to tell, and you may have noticed that he has a weakness for telling stories.

It is now the intention of Carnage to finally (Lagan would violently object to the split infinitive but since he's not here to hear me I'll split it wider still), get in the sack with Jodhpurs, when she will be once again divested of her jodhpurs, and Jodhpurs is raising no objection. As for me, I walk alone because to tell you the truth I am lonely, I don't mind being lonely when my heart tells me you're lonely too . . .

Then Karnage who is Kind, forgive that one, says come home with him to his apartment, he has a spare room and Maryanne is not, at the moment, in it, and he wants me to sleep for eight hours while he and Jodhpurs do what they have to do, and he loves his love in the morning and all the way to noon. So he hits the gas and speeds back towards Dublin city. Only the three of us left. The roads are wet and slippery. They almost always are in Ireland. We turn a corner. We approach a bridge. We go into a spin, an all-out spin. To you I pray. We ram the brick wall of the bridge. It rams us. Karnage is thrown out of the Kar. The front windshield kisses me, my only kiss since I left Atlanta. But it holds up under the strain and Jodhpurs gets the reins, the wheel, and tames the horse and all is almost well. What I sustain, you may be glad to hear, is, merely a stunned elbow, a bruised black-and-white forearm and a cut finger. They will be perfect again when I get to Peachtree.

We are now somewhere on the outskirts of Dublin city. It is very early on a Sunday morning and nobody to be seen and, to top it all, it begins once again to pour rain. We try to push the car over off the road into a vacant lot. But the front right fender is crushed into the tyre and will not allow the wheel to move. We pull, we push, we grunt, we strain. No deal. Well, we make twenty-five yards but that gets us nowhere except into the middle of the road. But, God a mercy, along comes a big milk-truck, ties a rope to the battered bumper or fender, drags the wreck into the vacant lot. The rain continues. We start to walk downtown. The truck is going the other way. Another truck. Going my way. Offers us a ride. Do we accept? You're goddamn right we do. And gratefully settle back. To travel half a block when Truck Number Two cranks out. Oh Gawd! We walk on. The rain continues.

In the north of Dublin city there stands a small hotel. More than one, but one will do. It's not the Ritz nor the Savoy but the door is open and the coffee hot and strong. Karnage has left his Kamera in the Kastle. Now we krack. Karnage and I. Not Jodhpurs. She pours the koffee. We sit in the lounge. Just the three of us. But when Karnage talks to me I hear instead the booming voice of Lagan. Not imagination. Really, the booming voice of Lagan. He sings about the sash my father wore. He sings in Irish about a maiden in Donegal whose cheeks were like the roses and her little mouth like brown sugar. Honey with the mouth like brown sugar. A good beat for a black combo. He recites about dear Pádraic of the wise and seacold eyes, so loveable, so courteous and so noble, the very West was in his soft replies. But Lagan is nowhere to be seen. He says that free speech shivered on the pikes of Macedonia and later on the swords of Rome. He says Love that had robbed us of immortal things, and I rise to protest, but he is not there.

This is ghastly and I tell Karnage who says that, Good God, he hears him too.

We search the lounge. But he is nowhere to be found. Nobody anywhere to be seen except an unconcerned and bored female clerk. We pay for our coffee. We depart.

In the spare room of Karnage I lie down and try to sleep,

remembering Thee, oh Peachtree. But rightaway the room is full of voices and above them all the voice of Lagan intoning that by Douglas Bridge he met a man who lived adjacent to Strabane before the English hung him high for riding with O'Hanlon.

Then up I leap up and dress, and tiptoe, almost running, out of the house to walk, in a daze, the awakening streets and find a restaurant, and eggs and coffee. Then I go to my lodgings.

I might not have bothered to tiptoe. Karnage later tells me that when he has done the gentleman by Jodhpurs they sleep, off and on, for thirty-six hours. You may have noticed that I have just broken one of my rules.

Stretched out again on a bed and sleeping, I suppose, I have this strange dream. This poem I have written and I am reciting it to a group of Roman citizens. It ends like this: A wooden sagging is in my shoulders and wood is dogma to an infidel.

Those words I take from my dream exactly as dreamt. No meaning. No connection with anything. But in my dream they made sense. Houseman said that each man travails with a skeleton. Lagan had been booming about Wenlock Edge and the wood in trouble and then 'twas the Roman now 'tis I. Perhaps I was trying to say that each man carries within himself a cross, the shoulders the crossbar, the spine the upright.

Damned if I know. Or care.

Time passes.

We are back in the Abbey, the bar not the theatre. A lawyer, a professor of history, a bank-manager who is also a music-critic and who plays the organ in a church, two actors from the theatre, and Niall and Brendan and Karnage and Lagan. No Jodhpurs. No Maryanne. Maryanne I am never to meet. But Brinsley honours us by his entrance.

Huge, stately, brown overcoat, wide-brimmed hat. Leaning on stick.

Karnage has confiscated your, or my, necktie of many colours which he is wearing with wild ostentation. Cleverly he conceals the coloured body or expanse of it under a modest pullover, then whips it out like a lightning flash to startle and dazzle each and every newcomer. Lagan says that he and Karnage will wear your necktie, week about, so that they will never forget me nor the voyage to Parma. I am touched. (For a second time I have broken one of my rules.) Leaving that resplendent necktie with them I know that as long as it lasts, and the material is strong and well-chosen, I will be remembered and spoken of in the land of my forefathers.

And Lagan has used his influence and Karnage is no longer suspended.

They go off to work together.

Time passes.

Curious thing, Brinsley says to me, but there are young fellows who say about me that I belong to a past time. I don't mean a pastime. But a previous period in history. But there is no time that is absolutely past, and little time in the present, it passes so quickly and, for all you or I or anybody knows, there may be no time in the future. Only eternity, we have been told. A most dismal idea. Imagine listening to (he mentions a well-known name), and God help and preserve him and lead him to a better and happier way of life, but imagine listening to him forever. So here's to the young fellows who think they know more than their elders. The total sum or aggregate or whatever you call it of knowledge, or whatever, in the human brain is always about the same. You might as well listen to your elders. You'll end up like them and nothing much accomplished. Lagan, though, is different. He raises his cap, mentally, to men older than himself. He admits that we

have been here first and he knows that he is on the way to
join us. Curious thing.

Time passes.

But whatever exactly did happen to Bealcú who broke his vows
to the god, to the sun, to the wind. The poem I will read to
you when I meet you, as arranged, in Washington D.C. My
vows I have kept and will keep. All of the forty-one verses of
four lines each I will read to you when you have the leisure
to listen.

Conall Cearnach is safely back in Ulster.

Time passes.

If anybody in time to come ever reads this letter, found in
a tin box in a hole in the ground on Kennesaw mountain, it
may be said that it is merely a zany folktale from an island
that once was, way out in the eastern sea. All parish priests
and all that. And drink. Well, there are a lot of parish priests
in Ireland and there is an amount of drink consumed. Apart
from a curious crowd called the Pioneers. Not a damn thing
to do with Dan'l Boone and the New River that runs west
where so many rivers run east.

Here I give you a genuine slice, or bottle, of old Ireland,
as I ate, or drank, it.

There may yet be worse things than parish priests in store
for the new Ireland.

Time passes.

My money from home has arrived.

To Lagan I owe ten pounds. Not that he would remind me.
In an envelope I fold the notes, and leave them, no message
enclosed, at the counter in the front-office of his office. Way back
behind, the machines are rattling for the morning paper.

Farewells I abhor.

So from the far shore of the Liffey I salute his lighted window and walk home to pack.

Peachtree, here I come.

By way of Cork city and Cobh and a liner over the wide Atlantic.

Look for my ghost on Eden Quay. Round the corner from the Sailors' home . . . . . . . . . . . . .

# A Selected List of Titles Available from Minerva

While every effort is made to keep prices low, it is sometimes necessary to increase prices at short notice. Mandarin Paperbacks reserves the right to show new retail prices on covers which may differ from those previously advertised in the text or elsewhere.

The prices shown below were correct at the time of going to press.